Stumbling and Raging:
More Politically Inspired Fiction

Edited by Stephen Elliott

With Associate Editors
Greg Larson, Anthony Ha, Karan Mahajan,
and Ashni Devendra Mohnot

Stumbling and Raging:
More Politically Inspired Fiction

Edited by Stephen Elliott

With Associate Editors
Greg Larson, Anthony Ha, Karan Mahajan,
and Ashni Devendra Mohnot

MacAdam/Cage

MacAdam/Cage Publishing
155 Sansome Street, Suite 550
San Francisco, CA 94104
www.macadamcage.com

Library of Congress Cataloging-in-Publication Data

Stumbling and raging : more politically inspired fiction / editor, Stephen
Elliott ; associate editors, Greg Larson ... [et al.].

    p. cm.

 ISBN 1-59692-158-7 (pbk. : alk. paper)

 1. Political fiction, American. 2. United States—Politics and government—
Fiction. 3. Current events—Fiction. I. Elliott, Stephen, 1971-
II. Larson, Greg, 1982-
 PS648.P6S78 2006
 813.008'0358—dc22

                                                    2005024832

"Your Mother and I," by Dave Eggers, was first published as a chapbook for Democracy
for America. "John Ashcroft: More Important Things Than Me," by Jim Shepard, was
originally published in the story collection *Love and Hydrogen* (Vintage Press). "An
Open Letter to William Kristol, Richard Perle, et al." by John Warner, and "To the
Director of Air Defense Marketing" and "Letter to Florida State Department of
Corrections," by Adam Johnson, were originally published on McSweeneys.net. The
rest of the work in this collection is originally published in print here, with the exception of work published as a preview.

Manufactured in the United States of America
10 9 8 7 6 5 4 3 2 1

Book design by Dorothy Carico Smith.

OHIO
RECOUNT?
BUSH
MICHIGAN
EXHAUSTED
O'BAMA
RECOUNT?
BUSH
CONSERVATIVES
BUSH
VOTES
PENNSYLVANIA
OHIO
LAWYERS
KERRY
RECOUNT
DEMOCRATS
CONCESSION?
FLORIDA
RECOUNT?
OHIO
LAWYERS
ISSUES
BUSH
RECOUNT?
VOTE FRAUD
OHIO
CONCESSION
MORAL
REPUBLICAN
PARTY
BUSH
On Election Night 2004 I went to bed with the radio on. All night long I dozed and woke, while politicians spoke of concession and victory, while votes were counted in Ohio. Of course, nothing was decided, and when I woke up the next morning there was speculation and confusion coming out of the radio. But not for long. Pretty soon it was all business as usual. Now I can't sleep.
A. NIFFENEGGER © 2005

Table of Contents

Introduction

November 2, 2004, Broward County, the most Democratic county in Florida, the only major county to finish their recount in 2000. Volusia finished their recount as well, but nobody cares about Volusia, too small. All week I stood with lines of voters waiting up to six hours to cast their ballots. All those John Kerry voters lined up around schools and cultural centers and shopping malls. I thought there were so many of them.

I was in the voting equipment center, watching the election board fight over various ballots, while the tabulations flashed on a black and green screen. Kerry was supposed to win Broward by 225,000 votes, but he fell 15,000 votes short. There were thirty-five members of the media in that small room and the election officials sat behind a giant oak table. The lawyer for the Republicans, a stalk of a woman with sharp elbows and translucent skin, whispered to an associate producer from 60 Minutes, "I have some good news for you."

By three PM the next day I was deathly ill, lying on a bathroom floor with a wet towel over my face. I couldn't keep down food or water. I slept for twenty-four hours, and when I woke up George Bush was still president.

I remember the poll closing at the American Legion Hall, November 2nd, at seven PM. The Kerry people packed their signs in their trucks and cars and drove off to grab a nap, a shower, have sex, before going to the party at the County Convention Center. The Bush supporters laid their signs in the grass and gathered in a prayer circle, arms linked across each other's shoulders, whispering against one another's cheeks.

"Look at them," I said to my friend Josh Bearman, from the LA Weekly. "They're going to be so disappointed when this is over." I couldn't wait.

I had access to the Democrats' internal polling data as well as the latest exit polls from CNN. All the early polls were showing John Kerry crushing George Bush. I called my friends in California and Nevada to tell them that Kerry had won. But my insider information turned out to be wrong. To add insult to injury, I lost $100 to my girl-friend; we had a bet on this thing. She's from Texas.

On Friday, when my illness passed, I sat in the backyard with Larry Davis, the Democratic attorney for the county. I told him I had been dehydrated or hungover or something and he laughed. He said he must have been dehydrated as well. It was eighty degrees and there was a slow wind off the ocean. You could say it was perfect outside. For the first time in my life I understood why someone might want to live in Florida.

I had presumed after the election—as I had presumed after finish-ing the first Politically Inspired anthology—that as soon as it was over I would go back to my comfortable teaching job and my comfortable apartment. But three days after Americans chose war as peace, deficits as prosperity, and anti-gay legislation as social values, I didn't feel like that at all. I didn't feel anything like I thought I would feel.

It's not that I don't want to give up, but in democracy one doesn't have the option of not being involved. The entire system is built upon participation. It would be nice to think that we could leave it alone, let it run by itself, spend our time on other things. I've come to understand that's not possible. We are the government; we are responsible for its actions, its makeup, and for protesting the things we disagree with.

And that's why I decided to put together another book of original political fiction, this time to raise money for progressive candidates running in 2006. I'm not feeling like giving up on democracy; I'm feel-ing like winning back the House. And I still believe in fiction in a post-9/11 world, because fiction can help us see things that nonfiction can't. Fiction can get closer to the truth because it can follow events to their natural conclusions and exhibit case histories in a unique way with access to the participants' inner voice. And I believe that writers are the voice and thoughts of their time and they always have been.

So here is a second anthology of wonderful fiction inspired by current political events and written by some of the very best writers working today. I'm already looking forward to the third.

—*Stephen Elliott, August 2005*

POLITICALLY INSPIRED

Tom Ridge
Submissions Editor
Stumbling and Raging: More Politically Inspired Fiction
MacAdam/Cage Publishing
San Francisco, California 94104

Dear Writer:

As you know, the tragic events of September 11, 2001, touched us all.
That morning we woke up to a different world, one that demands our
constant vigilance and awareness that it is the strongest wish of our
enemies to destroy us.

As Director of Homeland Security I made vigilance and fear my top
priorities. I don't think it's a coincidence that during my watch we
saw a 100% reduction in terrorist attacks. I like to think I had some
influence on that statistic, although I suppose posterity will render
its verdict.

But with the beginning of a second term it was time to move on, and to
think of new ways to serve this great nation. As I'm sure you can
imagine, I had a number of options open to me. And I won't assume a
tone of false modesty -- it was not easy to choose from among them.

In the end, I took on the role of Assistant Short Story Editor because
I saw that we must fight the war on terror on all fronts. Not just the
military, political, diplomatic, economic, and social fronts, but the
cultural front as well. It is critical, I believe, in a post-September
11 world, that even the smallest literary anthology join in lockstep
with our cause.

It was in that spirit I took up the responsibility of selecting the
works to be included in this volume.

I saw immediately that we would need to make changes. I
understand anthologies typically showcase what is called "literary
fiction," which I take to mean stories about a character who undergoes
a crisis and achieves, by passage through some internal psychological
conflict, a brief enlightenment that assists the reader in understanding
what it means to be human.

Put another way, the signature quality of these kinds of stories, in
my understanding, is that they don't really matter to anyone.

While this is all well and good, there seemed to be a number of publications already doing this very thing, and doing it quite well, and for -- if I can be frank -- a fairly small target audience.

My hope was to mold this collection to a new way of thinking, and to a broader agenda, one that serves our President and our country as it serves the cause of literature.

As a step in that direction, we have adopted a new policy with regard to the feedback we provide to our writers. For this project, we are responding to submissions according to a strict color-coded format. Therefore, instead of actual feedback on your story, we are enclosing a colored slip of paper. The reviewer of your story may have written additional comments if he or she wished, but the idea is that the color of the sheet will tell you all you need to know.

The color codes are organized into two categories of rejection: ideological and artistic. On the ideological side, black means you didn't adhere to our prescribed political message and should have familiarized yourself with my thinking before submitting your work. Grey means you advocated a proper view but were too timid about it.

We also have color categories for artistic feedback. Blue means your story had strong characters but lacked narrative energy. Red means the narrative moved like a locomotive but your characters were flat. Yellow means the conceit of the piece felt strained, for reasons we could not articulate. Forgive me if I am misusing some of these terms. They are new to me. Consult your code sheet for a complete explanation.

Our color-coded responses represent more than just a canny way to reduce my workload. They also impose obligations on you, the writer. So please, no follow-up queries about why we didn't like your submission. You have our color-coded response sheet. That ought to be enough.

Let me close by noting that if we were, for ideological reasons, ultimately unable to accept your work, we took the liberty of forwarding a note to that effect, along with the original of your submission, to the Domestic Surveillance Branch of the Homeland Security Department. A representative from their offices will be in touch to discuss your views as expressed in your story. We trust you'll cooperate and answer their questions to the best of your ability.

Thank you, and God bless America.

Sincerely,

Tom Ridge

Tom Ridge

The Politics of Children

The Soldier as a Boy

by Otis Haschemeyer

WHEN MY FATHER FIRST TAUGHT ME TO SHOOT, HE SAID, "DON'T PULL the trigger, don't squeeze it." He sat smoking a cigarette, with his back resting against a tree. We were out in the woods at a special place my father liked to go, and I had my first rifle, a .22 Henry repeater. I inhaled crisp air through my teeth. The breath calmed me. I was eight years old, and it was my birthday.

My father said, "Imagine an invisible string, and imagine that the invisible string is attached right there on your finger." He got up and stepped over to me. He took my hand, opened the palm, and pressed down in the center of my index finger. He coaxed, "Go on, try it." I shouldered the rifle and made an even spacing in the iron sights. I could smell the cold scent of tobacco on his hunting jacket, as he leaned in close. "Imagine the string. It's real straight, right?"

"Yes, sir."

"And imagine that it gets pulled more slowly than you can feel."

Pressing my cheek against the polished wood stock, I imagined the string attached to my finger and it being pulled. Keeping steady, I asked, "What's pulling it?"

He coughed and dragged on his cigarette and exhaled. "Well, I guess I don't know."

So, I aimed down the barrel at a soup can hung from a tree—my father and I had punched holes and fed string through the holes in the can earlier that morning—and thought of the imagined string, not the real string that the can hung on, I imagined the string in my finger being pulled by something that even my father didn't know what was pulling it, though he seemed to know just about everything, and so I didn't know either and didn't think about it. And the rifle fired and the bullet was away and the soup can didn't twitch though it had been hit clean through.

Toward evening when we got home, my mother, having heard the car pull up, poked her head to the window and then opened the door for us.

"Well, how'd he do?" she asked.

My father put his thick cold hand on the back of my neck, just resting it there. "He's a real straight shooter," he said. I stood there and felt that I was supporting him in some way, like a crutch might. I didn't yet know what pride was, what it was to have it or lose it, that pride could provide necessary service or destroy, but I think that the feeling I had then was derived from pride—that I had newly become of service to my father and that our relationship had changed.

My dad worked at auto part distribution, and his territory was the border areas of Oklahoma, Arkansas, and Missouri. He was on the road a lot, so when he was home, I knew he wouldn't want to waste a lot of time teaching me how to shoot. He'd want to get out in the woods. So in the days and months and years that followed my eighth birthday, I practiced with advice my father gave me: that an engine doesn't work unless each part does its job. I broke down shooting into its component parts and removed variables, which sounds sophisticated for a boy, but that's basically what I did. I discovered many interesting things that I would relate to my mother, like that a bullet shoots flat over water or that up hill or down, a bullet strikes low. She'd always say about the same thing: "Hmm" and "What do you know?" and "I wonder if your father knows that?"

One day I found a box of toothpicks in the catchall hutch by the front door. After I'd done my homework—I'd only really been thinking of the toothpicks because they'd be a good way to work on my aim—I took my rifle and the box outside along with a roll of Scotch tape. I pulled a garbage can from the side of the house and dragged it up to the metal shed at the edge of our property where my dad had a pile of gravel that he used for various things. I put the garbage can in front of the gravel pile and then taped a toothpick to the top of the garbage can.

I backed up until I couldn't see the toothpick anymore and then took one step forward. I could just make it out. I levered a .22 into the chamber. I aimed and fired. I went through half the box like that even though my back got sore and my arms ached from steadying the rifle, a hundred-something toothpicks. I put one or two holes in that garbage can.

My mother was in the house, doing something in the kitchen. I heard the plastic rollers on the glass door, and when I looked over my shoulder, I saw her step out onto the back deck. I turned and watched her as she closed the door and the screen—she didn't like to have any bugs in the house—and stepped off the deck. She walked toward me, growing larger and larger as she closed the distance. She wore a white and pink flowered dress that day and had her brown hair pinned back, but for all the niceties, she walked barefoot and with the light stride and confident step of a country girl who knew where she was going.

My mother's people were real hill folk who lived in the Ozark Mountains, sixteen miles from a little town called Mountain View, and my mother always had some of the old hills in her, even though my father made fun of her for it and looked down on her people. At a party or such, one of the stories he liked to tell, though my mother would blush with embarrassment, was how when my maternal grandfather died, my grandmother brought his casket through town and into the churchyard on a horse-drawn cart. He'd slap both hands down on the table and say, "No kidding." He'd laugh and everyone would laugh and my mother would giggle, though there was a slight but firm cast to her mouth, not unlike the expression set on the face of my grandmother, a big round woman, that day she drove her clap-trap sixteen miles and through town, a pipe clamped in her teeth and the reins folded into a hand on her hip, the mare that led, swollen bellied and frothing. I was there and remembered it. It was true that that area had some backwardness—it had pride and the people there were strong, but there was backwardness too. I remember another time on a visit, we passed the McTargett place and the biggest McTargett boy was chained to a tree in front of his house. I asked why that was, and my mother explained to me that this was so he'd do none of the Devil's business—a phrase that encompassed many unmentionables. My father was driving his silver blue Buick, sweeping the steering wheel into turns with two fingers clasped with his thumb, a casual disregard he must have picked up from the movies of his day. He said, this time vexed, "There's no Devil, Catherine." In the stale smoke-filled car, those words hung for a moment. I watched the countryside sweep by and then I moved to open my window a crack. My father must have been watching me in the rearview mirror. "You leave that be," he said.

My mother smoothed her hands over her knees. "I know that, Bill. You explained that to me already." Her tone was defeated, but in a moment she looked into the backseat at me, and I wasn't nearly quite so sure. We were in her hills now, and here superstition and Bible religion mixed so that God and Devil waged constant war and spoke in a thousand signs, and I thought that in the case of some mild possession—I didn't yet know what it was I might do—chains could be brought out for me as well. "You open that window if you want to," she said to me.

For all my father's mockery and disdain, my mother never did give up those superstitious roots completely. At our home, I'd see my mama stop what she was doing, place cans back in their sacks, take the sacks up in her arms, and walk backward out of the house. That was one of her superstitions—to undo omens by reversing them. And she saw a lot of omens, small things like a can turned upside down, or a broken branch pointed in two cardinal directions at once; it was only the Devil who would try to misdirect us by making a right angle in nature. And God forbid a hen should try to crow in front of your door—that meant death, and according to my mother, a person could die within minutes of such an occurrence. But what I learned from observing my mom—and contrary to her wishes—was that omens didn't seem to have any logical connection to what they foretold. So I decided early on that I'd just move straight ahead, which is what I saw my dad doing. Though I believe now that this disposition allowed that I could be absolutely broadsided, finding myself in the middle of something that I couldn't get out of and couldn't stop.

As my mama approached up by the shed, I levered the arm under the breach of the rifle and ejected the little brass shell. I left the rifle that way, open. I wanted my mother to see that the rifle wasn't loaded and that it was made safe. My father taught me that this was the most considerate thing to do when handling a firearm around other people. When that breech was open, there was no possible way for that weapon to fire.

"I think that's enough of that now," my mama said. "You're gonna make yourself deaf and dumb by all that." I told her, all right, and laid the rifle on the ground and ran up to the garbage can. On my way back with the toothpicks and tape I saw the furrows between my mother's eyebrows deepen and her face set in a look, like the one I'd seen in the car that day, as if she'd dropped down into herself and found a very sturdy rock to stand on. "Are those my fancy toothpicks?" she said.

She waited for me to answer. I cocked a foot. I didn't know if they were fancy or not or if she had other toothpicks. Toothpicks were toothpicks, I thought. I kept my mouth shut. She pinched my shirt and swung my shoulder around to face her. Leaning down, she said, "Who told you to shoot my fancy toothpicks, mister?"

The bright sun narrowed her pupils to pinpricks in the center of sparkling shafts of aqua and emerald greens. My fear of the chains made me repress the only answer that occurred to me. "Nobody told me, ma'am," I said.

"Nobody?" she said. And by "nobody" I could tell that she could only mean my father.

"No, ma'am," I said.

She thought about that for a second. "All right then," she said and smoothed my shirt. I picked up the rifle. She turned toward the house, and I trotted up beside her. Pulling me into her hip and catching me up in the folds of her flowered dress, she said, "But still, those don't grow on trees, you know." I put one arm around her waist and still held the toothpick box and the tape. In the other hand I held the rifle— I'd collect up my ammunition and brass later. It was difficult to walk with the sway of her hip into my side, but I didn't want to let go of her, so I walked along awkwardly, one foot sort of skipping out to the side.

"Well, they do, mama," I said.

"Do what?" she said, pulling me closer.

"They grow on trees. Toothpicks do," I said.

She ran her fingers over my ear and then tugged it lightly, a threat of things to come. "Don't you smart-aleck, me."

"I'm not smart-alecking, mama. I'm just saying the truth. Because toothpicks come from wood and everything wood comes from trees— even paper, because paper's really wood."

"Then I suppose you're not likely to care whether you roll out the dinning room table and shoot that?"

"No, ma'am."

We stepped up on the porch, and she took her arm from my shoulder. Then she held out her hand for the box of toothpicks. "Well, that's what it sounds like you're saying, mister," she said. "And if you were to do something like that, you'd get a whipping you wouldn't likely forget."

I slunk my head, feigning a fear I only partially felt. A whipping from my mama wasn't nearly as bad as a sit-down with my dad. As he talked, you could see the tendons striate in his neck. He didn't like to explain something you should have understood already, what he called common sense. But still, the whipping was very hard on my mother, and I never wanted to make my mother have to whip me, even if I knew I was right. So on the subject of the toothpicks and the dining room table I was agreeable. "Yes, ma'am," I said.

She brushed the hair out of my face and then leaned down. She pinched my cheek just a touch and looked into my eyes. "Still," she said, "It's nice to have a man around the house." Then she pulled my ear and said, "Come along." When she pulled me into the kitchen, it smelled of spearmint and pig fat.

My mother wanted me to deliver a salve, which was the real reason she'd come up to get me. Now that it was mostly cooled in a pan, she scooped it up with a spatula and spread it into a mason jar. Then she wiped down the jar with a paper towel and handed it to me. The salve looked like gray lard, and the jar was warm in my hands.

I walked down a trail in the woods with the salve in a greasy brown paper bag in one hand and the Henry in the other. I thought I might shoot a squirrel on the way home, as it would be close to dusk and they'd be out and active. I didn't shoot animals larger than squirrels because, for one reason, it would be cruel with a .22, and for another, my father didn't esteem it, which he told me one weekend he was home, when we were walking along south of the Sebastian County line.

My father had his shotgun, choked down to .410. I had my Henry. I'd hunt squirrels along the way to the fields where we'd flush birds. He'd had dogs before—my mama and I had heard plenty of stories about what those dogs were capable of—but we didn't have dogs at this time, because, for my father, dogs worked and they didn't work so well with a boy in the house to mistrain them. As we walked along, my father put up his hand for me to stop. I did and then followed his hand in the direction it pointed. In the bush, not forty yards away, was a beautiful buck, so close I could see the dirt and twigs and burrs marring his slick brown coat, maybe twelve points. When they're that big, you know a few things about them—he was smart and he was proud. The buck looked at us for a moment and then bolted off into the underbrush.

We were quiet then and walked along. When we got to the edge of the woods and the field, my father stopped me and asked if I understood why he didn't hunt deer.

I didn't, so I said no. I was hoping to bring it up with him before the season began. I already knew boys who'd taken their firsts.

He asked me if I could have hit that deer when we saw it.

I said, "Sure, Dad. It was as big as a barn."

He said, "There you go, Son. That's the reason. I'll shoot a deer the minute I can't go to the grocery and buy a steak and I'll stop the moment I've got two dollars in my pocket."

For some people in Arkansas, Oklahoma still represented Indian Territory, and folks from there, like my father, were viewed with suspicion. My father was 1/16 Choctaw, though you wouldn't know it to look at him. He had a thin, slightly hooked nose and very pale white skin. But I don't think it was my father's Indian blood that made his points of view unpopular with the locals. I think it was because my father had been in the Navy, and he had more experiences than most. He didn't live his life like it was a popularity contest. Because of what he said that day, I never hunted a big animal, regardless of what other boys said of the virtues of taking a stag. I knew it would have been barbaric to kill that animal.

But I did shoot a lot of squirrels—there's sport in that. They're small and difficult to hit and you have to start thinking like a squirrel, which was what I was doing more or less as I walked to Mrs. Whitknot's house with the salve, looking into the trees and wondering where I might hide if an unknown animal came down the trail.

At the far side of a bare dirt patch where trucks would drive in, I walked along the edge of an old foundation that was said to be full of snakes. The woods were deserted and quiet, but when I turned up a dirt road before climbing up onto the paved road, I heard a rustling of leaves in the bushes to my left. I stopped and listened. I could hear the sound of shallow breaths—not human, but from an animal close to the ground in the tangle of weeds. I knelt down to take a look, but once I'd done so, I imagined something coming out of the bushes at me, and in my childish imagination, there was a perfect sense in turning from hunter into hunted.

At first the running felt like a release and then like an exhilaration. The salve swung in the paper bag and the rifle hung heavily in my hand and tugged at my shoulder, and I ran farther just because it felt good. As I rounded a curve in the road, I slowed down and saw Mrs. Whitknot's old farmhouse set back from the road—farther back than most of the new, modern-style houses. Mrs. Whitknot was what used to be called a granny woman, which meant she was a midwife. She would have most likely delivered me, except my father insisted on a hospital. Mrs. Whitknot seemed to give me a crinkle-eyed sort of look because of that, even though a lot of folks used the hospital for births. Her family had lived in the area before everything got broken up into small parcels. Now, her family had all gone off and she was alone—which was common for granny women. They were said not to suffer men lightly, and as they had a way with herbs and roots, malingering, unfaithful, or otherwise undesirable men seemed to disappear in their care.

She opened the door for me and stood broad and stooped for a moment to get a look at me, and then she glanced at the rifle. "You here to put me out of my misery?" she said.

She bade me lean the rifle up on the inside of the door, then I followed her in. The house smelled of cool mold, and I remembered the few times she'd babysat me, lecturing me on the evils of running barefoot—she told me I'd have to eat mud if I got the ringworm—and the one time scrubbing under my fingernails with a dish brush. I said, "If I'm gonna eat mud, what's the difference if my fingernails are dirty?" She then cuffed me for sass.

"I've just got something for your mother," she said as we passed into her kitchen.

I answered her politely and looked around. The kitchen, painted in light blue and at the back side of the house, caught all the afternoon light. The chrome toaster and the white enamel range gleamed. She looked back at me then as she had her hand in a jar. "Expecting a cookie?" she said. She pulled out a handful of one-dollar bills, counted out a number, and handed it to me. "That's ten dollars for your mother. Put it deep in your pocket and don't lose it."

I held the bills for a second and then handed them back. "I may not take it," I said.

"Yes, you will," she said.

"No, ma'am. We're not to take money for a favor." I put my hands on the back of a chair but then took them down and folded them behind my back. If she were to slap my face, it wouldn't be polite to restrain her swing anyway.

"Take the money for your mother," she said. "A woman needs a few dollars of her own."

"Ma'am, she wouldn't want me to take money, and it would just mean that I would get a whipping and then she'd drive me back here and have me hand it back to you."

She seemed to consider that for a moment. I set my firmest expression on my face, because I knew what I'd said to be true.

"Well, at least take these. Fresh today." She took the paper bag from me and gave me a paper bag in return. "Eggs for your father. He loves fresh eggs. How's he keeping?"

"Good, ma'am," I said. I looked at the bag of eggs, heavy in a potent way in my hand.

"That's a favor in return," she said.

She looked off. "Though, I could use a little help applying this potion. I don't suppose you much take to helping people? Your father doesn't talk to you much about Christian charity?"

"Ma'am, I'm going to have to hurry home," I said, though it was the idea of rubbing any part of her old body with the salve that really had me in a hurry.

"All right," she said. "Off you go."

I was glad to escape and walked with a long fast stride from her house and down the road.

Once I reached the trail that cut into the woods, I remembered the fear I'd felt when I stared into the dark bush. I wasn't afraid of anything in the woods, but then again why go down there purposely to test that theory? I decided to continue along the paved road. About twenty yards farther down, I saw dark brown and black smears on the roadside. I'd seen dried blood before and knew that's what it was. The streaks of blood led to the edge of the road and down the embankment. I stepped over to the edge and peered down, my rifle held in front of me. The brush formed a thick dark skirt, and as I inched closer to improve my view, the loose gravel at the edge of the road gave way and my feet came out from under me. The rifle seemed to jerk up in the air of its own accord as I fell on my butt and slid down the hill, feet-first through the brush to the bottom.

My mind raced through several worries. First, did I scuff my rifle? I was pretty sure that I'd held it up the whole way down the slope. Second, how to get the hell out of there? But I couldn't leap to my feet because my hands were full of my rifle and a bag of eggs and my feet weren't connecting to anything firm; my right leg pushed into tangled brush and my left into something soft that gave with each extension of the leg. Third, was I bleeding? My pant leg was wet. And lastly—I got through the first three very quickly—what the hell was I stepping on?

The dog was practically in my lap, its back end smashed and hobbled. As I pushed away from it, I felt its mangy fur spiky with blood. I scurried backward, fearing attack or something, but once I felt safe, I then inched closer, leaving the rifle behind but for no good reason continuing to hold the sack of smashed eggs. I moved forward on my hands and knees. Its head was cocked up and twisted over its back, as it seemed to have somersaulted down the embankment, and its long tongue rolled out and faded to a blue gray. And there was something to see in the flickering look of one yellow eye, something like fear and disdain that told me that this wasn't some mangy brown mongrel. It wasn't a dog at all, but a coyote, though I didn't think we had any in our area.

I should have jumped back again, but I didn't. An injured animal is a dangerous animal—I knew that all right, but I knew too that the animal had no capacity to fight me. Her back end was completely crushed and I figured her spinal cord had been snapped. It must have taken a super effort for her to drag herself off the road. But the reason

I wasn't afraid was that her nostrils twitched and she stretched her long tongue to the side to lap the egg leaking through the sack. Her attempt was feeble and she couldn't bring her tongue into her mouth. It just lay there touching the wet paper. I sat back and thought about that for a moment, me sitting here with this animal down the side of the road. I felt very alone and it occurred to me that no one knew I was here in all the world.

I reached into the sack and pulled out a whole egg. Most of them hadn't smashed when I came down the hill. I pulled my rifle over, broke the egg on the barrel, and separated the shell over the animal's mouth. When the egg slid down on her, she jerked her muzzle. I pulled back, but just as quickly she lay her muzzle back down. The egg hung over her lips and the yolk broke on the ground between her teeth. Her tongue swelled deep in her mouth, but she could do no more with it. I took another egg and broke that, and tried to open it closer to her throat. I poured the egg over her lips and teeth and the egg slid over her tongue and onto the ground, her tongue swelling and her lips pulling back. I thought she appreciated me. I took another egg from the sack. And with each egg I broke and tried to feed her, I felt a greater sense of isolation and loneliness with this animal. And I felt a sense of dread too. There was only the happiness of acting, of taking each egg and breaking it and pouring it on her mouth. I twisted a small stick from a bush and pushed the egg white and yolks toward her. She could still do nothing with them. And I took more eggs and broke those. If I'd had a thousand eggs, I would have fed them to her all night or until she died. I didn't have a thousand. I had one dozen, and in a few minutes I'd broken them all and poured the remnants of the smashed ones and looked at her and then I stood up. I knew even then that this was an intimacy with a wild animal and that I would never ever forget it. I took my rifle, chambered a round and pressed the muzzle to her head below her ear. Her eye looked at me still, but as the light was fading, I could barely make it out. I didn't feel what I'd felt before, that she feared me or held me in disdain. I didn't feel anything from her. I felt nothing from her at all. I felt my father to be there with me. Put her out of her misery, he would say, just as the granny woman said earlier. That's the humane thing to do.

But then I felt so alone again. I pressed the rifle against her head, and I touched the trigger of the rifle, and I felt the trigger's resistance to my touch. It would take the smallest pressure to make that weapon fire. The bullet would enter her brain and she'd be gone, dead. The smallest pressure and I couldn't do it. I could not do it.

I put my rifle aside. I covered her face with the paper sack. And then I climbed up the embankment. When I got home, my mother's worry shifted on her face from relief to anger—everything I'd been doing seemed to confirm the worst for her—willfulness. I would not tell her what happened to my clothes or the eggs she'd found out about from calling Mrs. Whitknot. "Worried sick," she kept saying as she beat me with one of my father's black leather belts that night, her face contorted and mine braced with pain. But I couldn't tell her. She beat me and beat me, trying to get the Devil out of me, beat out the willfulness. But it was no use and finally we adopted an unspoken truce. She had to believe—though she knew it wasn't true—that she'd succeeded in something. And I didn't tell her that she'd succeeded only in illuminating me as to the gray nature of the world, that I could keep my shame inside as a secret from her and everyone.

Requiem for Sammy the Magic Cat
by Andrew Foster Altschul

HIS NAME WAS NORMAN KLAIMAN. HE WAS EIGHT YEARS OLD AND normal in every way, if what you mean by "normal" is that he was rambunctious and didn't give a lot of thought to the consequences of his behavior, he did passably well in school, loved Coca-Cola, Pokémon, and Shaquille O'Neal, pouted when angry, wondered about things like space travel and women's breasts, and watched 3.2 hours of television each day.

His mother, a harried paralegal for a Sarasota firm, frequently told Norman to get his head out of the clouds, though secretly she hoped he would never change, that the real world, with its hidden edges and failures, would never catch him. She envied her youngest child's innocence, his detachment from what went on around him. Lying alone in bed, worrying about her husband, a Naval air traffic controller who'd spent much of their marriage deployed in places like the Philippines and Diego Garcia, she tried to imagine her own childhood, a time when she was as carefree as Norman. What she saw instead was a pile of legal briefs, an unused treadmill, the latest run in her nylons.

Their two oldest children—Stanley, seventeen and hot to follow his father into the service; Janelle, sixteen and hot for Eddie Vedder—amazed her with their adult sensibilities, the wry bitterness with which they threw off their own disappointments. They seemed to her so worldly, perched to join the great march into a life of compromise. But not Norman. Norman was a pretty soap bubble, floating untouched through the branches.

Really, though, Norman Klaiman was unremarkable. You wouldn't recall him, if I didn't remind you that it was his face you saw—beaming and gap-toothed above a plaid bow tie, his hair carefully combed and parted—sitting in the first row directly in front of President George W. Bush at Emma E. Booker Elementary School in Sarasota,

Florida, on the morning of September 11, 2001.

It was into the eyes of Norman Klaiman that the president looked as Miss Daniels began the reading exercise, tapping out sentences with her pointer. Norman spoke loudly, like his mother had told him to, smiling and occasionally losing his place in his enthusiasm. It was at Norman that the president winked when he picked up the reading book and opened to "The Pet Goat," a wink that made Norman want to laugh, as if he'd been tickled. He decided it meant that the president thought "The Pet Goat" was a dumb story, just like Norman did. And it was into the eyes of Norman Klaiman that the president stared when an aide entered the room and strode toward him. The president saw the look on the aide's face, a look that pierced him somewhere below the navel and shot coldly through his groin, and he already knew: this would be the worst news he'd ever heard. The aide whispered something and waited, the president's mouth opened slightly but made no sound. To the other children in the front row—Trina McKee, whose tight new cornrows were stinging her scalp; Jamila Reese, following so carefully as the teacher tapped the words; Michael Pepper, making a list in his head of potential birthday presents—it seemed as though the president wanted to ask Norman a question. Norman began to fidget. The president's eyes narrowed and his lips pursed with an avuncular sadness that Norman had seen only once before, years ago, when his father told him that Sammy the Cat had died.

But no one had died today, and Norman's mother had warned him to stay still in class. "Make your father and me proud, Norman," she said, squeezing his arm and straightening his tie. "You'll remember this morning for the rest of your life." She kissed him on the forehead, and he bounded out of the car to catch up with Michael Pepper, his best friend.

Miss Daniels was looking at him now, tilting her head the way she always did when he wasn't paying attention. The tip of the pointer tapped on her desk. "The goat did some things that made the girl's dad mad," said the president, and Norman struggled to catch up, but something about the way the aide had backed out of the room, how the grown-ups were all whispering by the door, made it hard to follow the story. The president looked at him one more time, put down the book, and smiled.

It got very loud after that. The president was hurried from the room in a riot of black suits, the principal shouting to be heard, the scrape of chairs and doors banging and somewhere a bell ringing. Michael Pepper said it was a fire drill, but when they got out into the hallway, no one seemed to be moving toward the front door. A hand grabbed Norman's elbow, and Miss Daniels led the class down to the basement, feet clanking on metal stairs, led them past giant pipes and mop buckets and shadows and left them to stand nervously in the rumbling semi-dark. Quiet now, they could see all the teachers down the corridor, hissing at each other and hugging or just leaning against the wall. Many of them were crying. Their whispers rasped thinly over metal pipes. The teachers did not know what to tell the children. They did not, themselves, understand. They looked at the children, lined up against the cinder blocks, quieter than they'd ever been in the classroom, and they knew that the suspicions of their own inadequacy that had haunted them throughout their careers had been correct.

By the time the parents began to arrive, they were back in the classroom. The kids had seen the footage on television, heard the principal struggle to explain it over the intercom: "Sometimes people get angry…" he'd begun, then cleared his throat several times. "Some people don't like freedom." There was a longer pause. "God bless America," he said. Now the mothers streamed through the doorway like marauders, mascara streaked and shoes in hand. Norman's mother knelt at his desk and buried his head in her shoulder, and when the television flickered again, she covered his eyes. In the car, she stabbed at her cell phone, trying to locate Stanley and Janelle, trying to find someone who could contact her husband, smacking the rim of the steering wheel and muttering, "I can't believe this." Norman watched the streets of his neighborhood blurring past. He was pleased, but then scared, to realize that soccer practice—for the first time ever—would be canceled.

"Your dad's gonna call later," she said, flipping the phone shut. "He'll know what to tell you, Norman. He'll explain it to you." But what Norman really wanted to know was about the president, and what that sad smile had meant, that little twist of his lips.

His mother said she needed cigarettes and veered into the parking lot of the convenience store near their house. Norman had never seen his mother smoke. As she was getting out of the car, she stopped, frozen in a half stance. Through the glass he could see the funny man behind the counter who always wore the red cloth on his head. Whenever they stopped there, the man gave Norman a tiny Tootsie Roll and bowed to him very seriously and made him laugh.

Behind them, cars were honking on the boulevard, an angry chorus of horns. His mother's hand rose to her mouth as she stared at the door. A minute later she said, "I can't," under her breath. She got back in and sat without starting the car. "I just can't," she said to her hands. "I'm sorry."

They watched the TV all day, until it started to get dark outside. Stanley and Janelle came home and joined them on the couch. His sister took calls on her cell phone, wept loudly, and pulled Norman close to her body, the same way his mother had done. His brother sat, arms folded, and snorted a lot. He shared cigarettes with their mother. Everyone kept asking Norman if he knew what certain words meant, if he knew where Arabs were from. His brother pointed to the screen, the skyscrapers falling, and said, "You know that's *real*, right? It's not a movie. Those dirtbags really did it."

Janelle cradled Norman's head. "Jesus, Stanley, he's not a baby," she said.

Later, their mother put a platter of hot dogs on the living room table, but only Norman ate. She was pale and shaky, her voice raw from smoking. The phone rang, and she talked to their father in the other room. Norman could not hear everything she said, only his father's name, repeated over and over again.

When she put Norman on, his father sounded hurried, as if someone were pulling him away from the phone. "You know I love you, right buddy?" he said. "No one's going to hurt you, Norman," he said, and Norman heard him take a deep breath. "I promise. Your dad promises."

Norman had always been told that his father was far away. His mother had showed him the map, had put postcards on the refrigerator. But it was tonight that he really understood what far away meant. "I'll be home as soon as I can," his father said. But Norman knew that he might not be home for a long time. No one had to explain that to him.

Back in the living room, the TV showed pictures of men with long beards and black robes, shooting guns and smiling. The pictures were all in slow motion. The president came on and said they would find whoever blew up those buildings. Norman remembered the way the president had winked at him. He watched the president's face on the TV, the way his eyes did not blink and his lips pressed together— angry now, not sad. Norman tried to move his mouth that way but it made him want to sneeze.

His brother thumped down the stairs with a packet of papers in his hand and started filling them out on the coffee table. "Enlistment papers," he told Norman. His mother put down her drink. "Please don't start that again," she said, lighting another cigarette. "Stanley? Please. Not now."

His brother did not look up. He shook his head and pointed to the TV and said all of his friends were going to join. They all agreed it was their duty, he said, someone had to go out and stop the sand niggers.

His sister stood and backed away, pointing a finger at Stanley. "That's disgusting," she said. She stomped her bare foot on the carpet and said, "That's so disgusting, you asshole." Her eyes got really small and she looked at Norman and then sat down in the middle of the room. Their mother put her face into her hands and cried, the cigarette held between her fingers, smoke drifting through the light of the

television, the big white cloud filling the screen. Nobody said anything when Norman got up and left the room.

He went to the backyard and sat on the swing, watching the blue light
of the TV and the backs of their heads through the window. It was still
warm out, and the hazy sky looked like a silk sheet pulled over their
town, like last year in PE when they'd held the edge of a parachute
and billowed it in the air and sat inside the bubble it made. He
thought about the sound of his father's voice on the telephone, how
heavy and distracted, many other voices rumbling in the background.
He tried to picture where his father was, tried to fly in his mind over
the mountains and the oceans, tried to see the distance.

"We have to look out for each other now," his father had said on
a long-ago Sunday, when they'd gathered as a family to bury Sammy
the Cat. He had been home for almost a year, the longest Norman
could remember, but he was about to go away again. "That's what families do," his father said. "They stick together."

At the back of the yard, where the overgrowth began, he spied the
little wood cross they'd erected. It was leaning to one side, covered
with dirt and fallen branches from the last big rainstorm. Behind it the
dark woods sizzled with summer insects. He thought again about how
the president looked that morning, like he was disappointed in something, how angry he looked later on TV. He remembered his father's
face at Sammy's funeral, how his hand on Norman's shoulder felt sad
and strong. Norman had known then that there were things in this
world that nobody really wanted to happen but they happened anyway. You could pretend that wasn't true, but you'd just be pretending.
He understood that. No one had to explain it to him.

But he stood before the wood cross, under a stretched silk sky, and
he could feel it: the invisible crowding of everything outside that bubble, everything he couldn't know. I know some of those things now,
but there's no way for me to explain it to him—the wars that will be
started, the crimes that will be committed, the deaths that will occur,

all in his name. Norman, eight, didn't know what death was—not really—only that it had something to do with why his mother stayed awake at night, sipping wine and staring out the kitchen window. Only that the emptiness that lurked in the house when his father was away could one day grow bold and swallow him up forever, that from inside of it everything might look the same, but no one would hear you, or even know you were there.

That was why they'd needed Sammy the Cat. But if Sammy the Cat could die, then anyone could. Because Sammy wasn't just any cat, he was a *magic* cat, a cat without body or mew, a giant cat who could fly great distances and rescue drowning babies and who'd laid his powerful paws over their roof each night to protect Norman from the monsters who might otherwise sneak out of his closet and kill him in his sleep. Sammy had watched out for all three Klaiman children—through night terrors and hurricanes, through months of fatherlessness and the deaths of grandparents. He'd sent presents on Christmas and a dollar for each lost tooth, signed with a paw print. When Norman got a good report card, Sammy bought him candy, and when they went on vacation, they made sure to leave plenty of food, so that Sammy would guard the house. Having Sammy felt like being wrapped in a warm blanket all the time. And despite the fact that he was invisible—or maybe because of it—they'd known that he was everywhere, at all times, that nothing happened that Sammy wasn't ready for.

But the tallest buildings can fall down, and even magic cats die. Norman was older now, old enough to know that Sammy wasn't real. Maybe he'd known it even then, even when they buried him and said prayers, and what he wondered now, in his eight-year-old's vernacular, was how you can grieve over something that never existed. And whether those weren't the things that hurt the most.

He heard the phone ringing again inside and he picked up a rock and threw it at the cross. It made a sharp, plunking sound and almost hit him in the knee as it bounced back. For a moment, the woods were silent. Norman knelt to wipe the dirt and grass from the grave. He righted the cross and gathered rocks around its base. With both hands he pulled up weeds and tossed twigs aside, until the bed of purple flowers his mother had planted looked like someone was taking care of it. He did not cry. He stood and walked back to the house with excellent posture. He hoped his mother would not want to talk anymore. He didn't want anything else explained. He already understood the important things—that nobody really knew what was going to happen; that this scared everyone, even the president, as much as those buildings did. And that for many nights to come, he would lie in bed and think about Sammy the Magic Cat, flying happily through the starriest skies, doing the heroic things that magic cats do, in a galaxy far, far away, the place where all make-believe things eventually have to go.

El Fin del Mundo
by Michelle Herman

ELECTION DAY.

Now, May woke up thinking. *Now is when everything changes.*
She was so excited she couldn't even eat. She just stirred her bowl of cream of wheat between sips of Raspberry Zinger, bringing the spoon to her mouth periodically to blow on it. "May," her mother said. "Please." But she said it distractedly, and she wasn't even sitting at the table, so it was easy for May to say "Sorry" and then just keep on stirring and blowing, putting on a show of eating without actually taking a single bite.

Her mother was jumpy this morning, standing right by the coffeemaker and not eating any breakfast either, just drinking coffee, refilling her mug after every couple of sips. May thought about saying, "Why don't *you* eat something?" but she knew better. When her mother was in a good mood, she could get away with that—it would make her laugh, in fact, and if May's father said, "Don't take that tone with your mother, please," her mother would say, "No, no, I *like* her sass. It'll come in handy for her later." But when she was angry or anxious or sad or *wound up*—that was May's father's phrase for when she was like this—it could send her over the edge and she would snap at May in a way that made her stomach hurt.

May was jumpy too this morning, but not *bad* jumpy like her mother ("Watch your mama the tiger," her dad would say. "Take cover—she's about to spring"). *Today's the day*, she kept thinking. She'd woken up twice before dawn thinking it. And when she woke for good just before seven, she'd wanted to say it to her parents—she'd come running downstairs before she'd even washed her face or brushed her teeth, still in her pajamas—but she saw right away that they were in no mood, and then she remembered that she'd heard them last night. Not arguing, exactly. You couldn't really call it that when there was nothing the people doing it actually disagreed about, could you? This was something she'd been wanting to ask them lately, but she didn't know how. She wasn't even supposed to be listening when they were arguing—or doing whatever it was they were doing. They were so careful to do it when she wasn't around. But she could always tell, even when she hadn't heard them. Even if she'd been at school or over at her friend Willa's house. It was as if they had leftover bad feelings and they had to carry them around for a while, like when you took food home from a restaurant but you had stops to make first, and you were just carrying around this paper bag and you sort of wanted to throw it away but you couldn't bring yourself to do it, because maybe you would want it later, and besides, it was wrong to waste perfectly good food.

May left her spoon sticking up out of the bowl of congealing cereal and started arranging and rearranging the slices of green apple and orange sections her mother had put on a little plate beside her bowl. "School should be closed today," she said, not saying it particularly to either one of them, just saying it. "It should be a holiday."

Her mother didn't even look at her. Her father, who was sitting at the table, glanced at her, then glanced over at her mother, but he didn't say anything either. He just kept eating his breakfast.

"I shouldn't even have to go to school today," May tried again—bravely, she thought, but really her parents deserved to be excited today, like her. Still, her mother, who at just about any other time would have taken the bait, would have started in on how *completely screwed up this country is*, how *we don't even know how to do goddamn Election Day right*—and then she'd be off and running, about how "in Canada, for instance, just for instance, they don't wait for people to go register to vote, they come right to your door and register you"—kept silent, tapping her fingernails against her mug. Her father stopped eating just long enough to say, "Well, you do," and then, "Eat some fruit, at least, May."

It wasn't until an hour and a half later, sitting bored to death in her language arts class, that she realized she had taken the wrong tack entirely this morning. Instead of trying to get them as excited as she was—as excited as they'd been in the weeks, the months, leading up to this day—she should have made them mad. At *her*. Because they never stayed mad at her for very long. And if she'd gotten them mad at her, it would have taken their minds off being mad at each other. And then maybe they would have remembered how excited they were and what could—what *would*, May told herself fiercely—happen today.

* * *

After language arts, with Sra. Quehl—May went to a Spanish-immersion school, where the teachers called her Maya and she was required to call them all *señora*—came social studies. Sra. Nelson was a better teacher than Sra. Quehl, and May usually didn't mind her class, but today she was having a hard time concentrating. You'd think in social studies, at least, they would be talking about the election. Even if they had to do it in Spanish—May wouldn't have minded that. But they were just continuing what they'd been doing yesterday.

"*En el año 570 nació en la ciudad de la Meca una persona muy importante…*" Sra. Nelson paused, looking around the room in that way she had—head tilted, one eyebrow up, waiting for someone to volunteer to finish her sentence.

May knew the answer to today's opening non-question—anyone who had done the homework knew that the *persona muy importante* who was born in Mecca was Muhammad—but she didn't feel like supplying it. Her mind kept skittering back and forth between the election and her parents being mad at each other.

They had been planning to vote this morning before school—before her mother went down to campus, to her job at the contemporary arts museum, and her father went into his room at the back of the house to start *his* workday—but her mother drove her to school without her father coming with them, just as if it were any other day. Her father had gone off into his room before they even left the house, and May knew better than to say anything about this, or to say anything other than "Okay" when her mother suggested they drive by their polling place on the way to May's school, "just to see." What they saw amazed them both: the line snaked out the door and around the playground equipment in the yard of the school May would have gone to if they hadn't entered the lottery for an alternative school.

"Will you look at that," her mother said, and whistled. "We wouldn't have made it anyway. Good thing we decided to vote later, huh?" And then, without waiting for May to answer, "It's a good sign, I think." May wanted to say, "Yes, definitely!" but she could tell her mother wasn't talking to her. She hated it when her mother talked to herself—it made her feel invisible.

JP had his hand up. Sra. Nelson nodded at him. "*Sí, José Patricio?*"

"Muhammad."

"*Mahoma.*"

"Sorry. I forgot."

May knew he hadn't forgotten. Saying that he *had* was just his way of making up for always knowing the answer. Or what passed for an answer, in Sra. Nelson's no-question world. May didn't bother trying to make up for knowing things. Not anymore. She used to, though. When she was younger, she tried to fit in all the time, pretending to be stupider than she was, or that she cared about some idiotic movie the girls in her class were all talking about, or that she hated math, or liked the Backstreet Boys, or didn't like her parents—but she had quit all that just this fall. It wasn't working anyway: they didn't like her no matter what she did. But that was fine, she'd understood suddenly, the first day of school this year, because she didn't like them. She'd watched the girls in the sixth grade greeting each other like long-lost sisters—even the ones who'd played together all summer long, like Madeline Westheimer and Sarah Marshall, or gone to Girl Scout horseback riding camp together, or just hung out at the same pool every day—and she realized that she was never, ever going to fit in with them, that she had almost nothing in common with them and never would. And why should she care? She had a friend, a *best* friend—Willa Perelman Durnford, who lived six blocks away (and finally, this past summer, she'd been given permission to walk there on her own) and went to the arts alternative public school, which she assured May was just as bad as the Spanish-immersion school (and which May's parents assured her was in fact even worse). She and Willa understood each other perfectly, had everything in common, didn't have to pretend *anything* with each other.

"*Mahoma era camellero y comerciante y…*"

Sra. Nelson was the only teacher in the whole middle school who took the Spanish-immersion program seriously. Even their Spanish teacher would switch to English when she wasn't getting anywhere in Spanish, and Sra. Quehl didn't even pretend to teach language arts in Spanish—although sometimes, if someone was talking in class, she'd clear her throat and say, mock-sweetly, "*Perdone usted. Es usted maestro?*" in a way that was more sarcastic sounding than "Excuse me, are you the teacher?" would have been in English, as if the sarcasm weren't just in the question, but in the fact that she'd asked it in Spanish.

May knew the answer to Sra. Nelson's last "question" too, but she was in no mood to jump through hoops today, so she sat back in her chair and waited for JP—it was always one or the other of them, pretty much—to raise his hand. Which finally he did.

May almost laughed. JP was so predictable. It was sort of what she liked about him—or, really, what she both liked and disliked about him at the same time. Then there were the things she *just* liked (that he was smart, for example, and that he played tenor saxophone in the school band and was really, really good at it—maybe better than anyone else in the band on *any* instrument—and that he wrote funny stories and poems and wasn't ashamed to read them aloud) and things she *just* hated (mainly the fact that he was a Republican, that his whole family, *both* his families—his father and stepmother, his mother and stepfather, his half-brothers and half-sister and stepbrother and step-sisters, all of whom went to this school—were Republican. They all wore Bush-Cheney buttons to school every day, and last Thursday May had had a fight at recess with JP and his twin half-brothers in the fourth grade when May called them fascists, although to tell the truth she wasn't even sure what that was, exactly. But her mother was always referring to the neighbors two houses down, the ones with their garden of American flags and their huge SUPPORT THE PRESIDENT yard sign, as "a couple of fascists").

"*Y considerado un profeta por su pueblo*," JP said.

Sra. Nelson beamed at him. "*Sí*," she said, "*al tomar contacto con los judíos y cristianos comenzó a predicar basado en sus principios propagando un nuevo culto…*" She paused again.

May sighed. Even Sra. Nelson's *tests* were fill-in-the-blanks and essay questions that weren't questions at all but statements followed by the one-word command: *discute*.

And the tests weren't even supposed to be *in* Spanish. By sixth grade, May knew perfectly well, only 50 percent of their schoolwork was supposed to be in Spanish. The total-immersion part of the Spanish Immersion Alternative Academy for Elementary and Middle School Children was just for kindergarten and first grade. Every year a little more English was added—15 percent of the work was in English in second grade, 25 percent in third grade—but the truth was that by middle school most of the teachers had pretty much given up on Spanish, using it a lot less than they were supposed to. May guessed that it was just too much trouble: the teachers would ask questions in Spanish and get answers in English, or the kids wouldn't answer at all, because they had no idea what the questions had *been*.

But Sra. Nelson was determined to teach in Spanish, and it didn't matter to her what she was *supposed* to do: she taught middle school social studies not 50 percent but entirely in Spanish—and as a result, May figured, 50 percent of the kids understood no more than 50 per-cent of what she was talking about—and she never spoke a word of

English until the bell rang at the end of the day. And then it was kind of shocking, when you saw her in the hall as you raced to your locker, and she said, cheerfully, "So long—have a good evening!" She'd even use your real name then. You wanted to just stop and stare at her.

But then most of the kids were just staring at her now. It didn't matter that for homework they'd read a whole chapter last night (in English; the textbook, like all their textbooks this year, except for their Spanish book, was all in English) on ancient religions, part of the unit on ancient culture and civilizations they'd started last week, and there was a whole section of the chapter on Muhammad and "the birth of Islam." Her mother had glanced at that as she walked past where May sat doing her homework last night at the kitchen table before dinner. She snorted. "Islam was not *born* when Muhammad was. I can't believe they're telling you that. Muslims believe that Islam was created by Allah at the beginning of time. Did you know that Muslims regard *Adam* as the first Muslim?"

But how could she have known that? How did her *mother* know that? She wondered sometimes how parents knew the things they knew. Not from school, she was pretty sure.

Her mother sat down at the kitchen table with her and drank a glass of wine while the pot roast simmered on the stove. "You know, Muslims believe that Muhammad wasn't the first messenger through whom Allah revealed the true faith to the world, but only the final one, the best one. The earlier messengers, now, they were just—"

"Wait. Like who?"

"You know who. Moses. Jesus."

This shook May up. The whole chapter, actually, had shaken her up. The whole idea that there were all these religions, all these different stories people believed to be the "real truth" of how things were, made her uneasy. How were you supposed to know which one was true? And now this—the idea that Muslims thought Judaism and Christianity were just, like, early *guesses*—like the theories you'd test and would be proved wrong, one after another, in a science fair project—well, this really disturbed her. She didn't tell her mother that, though. She just nodded and listened and finally she said she thought she'd better finish up her homework, she had math problems too. Because her mother got upset when she knew *she* was upset, and just the other day when she'd told her mother that lately it had been worrying her—in a way it never had before—that her father was Jewish and her mother was Christian, her mother had started to cry. Which shocked May. Her mother *never* cried. All May had said was, "Sometimes it's hard to figure out which thing I'm supposed to believe, and what I *am*," and her mother started answering in that reasonable way she always answered everything, about how it took a while to sort things out when you were growing up, and everything was changing now for May, and this was a time for "questions about identity," and blah blah blah, but then all of a sudden she started to cry. So May decided to shut up about it for a while.

But just because she'd stopped talking about it didn't mean she'd stopped thinking about it. Because which *was* she supposed to believe? Not that either of her parents made a big deal about either being Jewish or being Christian. "God is love," they'd been telling her since she was a baby. But she'd known all her life, since she was, like, two years old, that Christians believed that Jesus was God's son, and Jews didn't—and she knew that her mother, even though she was quiet about it, didn't make a fuss over it, believed that Jesus *was* God's son. She knew because she'd asked, a long time ago, and her mother had told her. "But Daddy doesn't believe this," she'd said, as casually as if she were saying, "My favorite color is green, but that's not Daddy's favorite color—Daddy likes yellow." May had been very little then. She remembered the conversation, though. She remembered that the three of them had been in the car, her parents in the front—her mother was driving, as usual; her father hated to drive—and her in the back, in the middle seat, on her booster, and that she had said, "What do *you* believe, Daddy?" and her father had said, "About Jesus? I believe that he was a kind man, a teacher, a good man." And *she* had said, "Well, I believe both things. I believe he was God's son *and* that he was just a good man and a teacher." Her father had laughed. He'd reached into the back seat and taken her hand in his and said, "Well, honey, if you can keep both those thoughts in your mind at the same time, more power to you."

And she *had* been able to. Until recently. When suddenly she couldn't anymore. When suddenly a lot of things had started changing, all at once.

Except right here in the classroom, where everything stayed exactly the same, day after day—where right now everybody was just sitting there daydreaming or passing notes or whispering, acting as if this were any other normal day, as if their whole lives didn't depend on the outcome of it. May couldn't stand it anymore. Without raising her hand, she finished Sra. Nelson's sentence:

"*El Islam.*"

"*Excelente! El Islam, que profesaba la existencia de un Dios único. Esto provocó que algunas tribus se le enfrentaran pero en el año 632 sus seguidores se apoderaron de la Meca y en poco tiempo Mahoma logró unir a todos los árabes en un Estado organizado y religiosamente unido.*"

Bailey Morgan, sitting directly behind May, poked her, hard, between her shoulders. "What is she *talking* about?" she hissed.

"You know. Like, he was considered to be a prophet, and he united the Arab world," May whispered without turning to face her.

"Who?"

"Muhammad."

"What's a prophet?"

Was she kidding? May turned around to look at her. Bailey's face was blank. "You know, someone who's…um, divinely inspired." Bailey frowned. "Someone who can see the future," May told her. She didn't even whisper it; she just said it out loud. It didn't matter. Sra. Nelson never noticed when anyone talked in class. That was what everyone said, anyway: that she didn't *notice*. Lately May had been thinking that she noticed, all right, but just chose not to say anything.

"Oh, yeah," Bailey said. "I'm a prophet too. I prophet that this class is going to continue to be extremely boring."

"Prophesy," May said. "Or just predict."

A bunch of people laughed—at Bailey's prophecy or at May's correction of her grammar, May couldn't tell. Probably the former. But Sra. Nelson just kept on about her business. "*Las enseñanzas de Mahoma fueron reunidas en un libro…*"

May glanced at JP, who shrugged. *It's your turn,* she mouthed. He grinned at her then. He was the closest thing she had to a friend in class, which was pretty weird, considering.

"The Koran," JP said. He didn't raise his hand either.

May wondered what he knew about the Koran besides what their social studies book said. Her parents had talked about the Koran last night too. As they ate their pot roast and her parents drank red wine (May was allowed two sips, a quarter of a shotglassful—"like in Italy, or France," her mother always said when she poured it), her mother told her father what she and May had talked about earlier, while dinner was cooking, and her father was interested. "Did you know, May, that there are passages in the Koran that preach religious tolerance? The thing is, Muslims are like Christians in that they believe in a single judgment and eternal life either in heaven or hell. That's a theology that can lead to some serious intolerance. And for plenty of Muslims— like plenty of Christians—it has. But there are also moderate Muslims who don't read the Koran that way. They look at the passages that say, essentially, 'To each his own—you to your religion and to me to mine,' and that's the aspect of Islam they emphasize."

"Of course," May's mother said, "it's the extremists who dominate the religious dialogue—all those people who read the Koran as declaring all other religions false."

"It's fascinating, really," said her father, and May got that tennis match feeling, looking back and forth, one to the other, worrying a little if one was going to smash the ball too hard for the other to smack back, "how similar Christian theology is to Islamic theology.

Christianity also posits the doctrine of a single God, and of 'the only begotten son'—and the history of Christianity is riddled with periods of persecution of non-Christians."

"But things have changed," her mother said. "Although one of the things Bush is trying to do, one of the reasons he can't win tomorrow—the thing I just can't imagine the country falling for—is turn back the clock of religious tolerance. There's a *reason* the church and the state are separate in this country. There's always been religious fundamentalism in the West, but there's a history of religious tolerance, too, that goes back to the Age of Rationalism. Churches and synagogues exist side by side."

"And Jews and Christians marry each other," May put in.

Her mother blinked at her, and May could tell that she'd forgotten that she was even part of this conversation, forgotten that the whole purpose of it was to teach May something.

"You know," her father said, "one interesting thing about the Western world *is* its tolerance—sometimes condescending tolerance, but tolerance nevertheless—toward religion. There are all those New Age religions that are relatively well-tolerated here, religions that borrow heavily from Eastern theology, especially Hinduism and Buddhism. And unlike medieval Christianity and radical Islam, Hinduism and Buddhism are very tolerant of religious diversity. In fact, just about all the ancient religions were tolerant of other religions. Taoism, Platonism—they considered lots of prophets and teachers as authentic. The ideas was, 'Hell, there are lots of different paths to spiritual salvation—'"

"Except they wouldn't say 'hell,' no matter how tolerant, right?" May said. She was determined to keep them from forgetting she was there. "You want to hear something stupid? In school, kids don't say 'hell'; they say 'double hockey sticks.'"

Both her parents looked at her strangely, and she blushed. Okay, so maybe it was a dumb thing to say. But they'd gotten carried away, and she hated when they forgot to include her in their conversation over dinner. If there was one thing they weren't ever supposed to forget, not for a second, it was that they were *her parents*, not just two people in the world.

It wasn't even so bad to say something dumb to them once in a while—just to remind them that she was still a *kid*.

* * *

The whole drive to school this morning, she had wanted to ask her mother about last night, about the way she'd heard them talking when she was supposed to be asleep. They were talking about the election, but they weren't *fighting* about the election—not about who to vote for, or about Iraq, or about the defense-of-marriage amendment to the state constitution, or even about the local issues on the ballot this year, like the smoking ban or increased funding for public schools. They agreed about all that. They agreed about *everything*. So what was there to argue about?

"You'd never even *voted* in a national election until you started going out with me," her mother had said at one point, and her father had said, "If you're going to malign me, Jesse, do it right. I didn't vote in *any* election until I met you. But that doesn't make me any less committed now than you are. That was thirteen years ago. I was a different person."

"You *were*," her mother said. "It's true. A completely different person."

"So were you, Jesse."

What was wrong with them? You'd think they didn't even like each other. If you didn't know them, if you didn't know they were married to each other, and you were listening in the way May was, and you weren't even listening to the words, just to the sound of their voices, their *tone*—a tone that would have gotten *her* sent to her room "until you can maintain civility," her father would say, "until you can be respectful to the people who love you," and if she ever went this far, way beyond "sass," even her mother wouldn't defend her—you'd think they were two people who hated each other.

But you wouldn't know why, any more than May did.

* * *

Sra. Nelson was still at it.

"*Algunas de las enseñanzas del Corán son...*"

Since the first day of sixth grade, May had been trying to make up her mind whether she loved or hated the way Sra. Nelson taught—the way she insisted on Spanish whether or not anyone in the class understood her; the way she never asked a question outright. She sometimes wished she knew something about Sra. Nelson *other* than the way she taught social studies. She didn't know anything about any of her other teachers either, but it only bothered her when it came to Sra. Nelson. Like, she didn't know if she had children. Or even if she had a husband. All the teachers were called *señora*, married or not (which drove May's mother crazy, but which *she* thought was just sort of funny. As if the school were afraid that there was something...well, May wasn't sure what—*subversive*, her mother suggested, but maybe just weird— about not being married). All the mothers were called Mrs., too, even the ones, like her own mother, who had their own last names and went by Ms. Even the mothers in two-mother families were Mrs.— Danielle Lincoln-Lumerry's mothers were called "Mrs. Lincoln" and "Mrs. Lumerry," which was just...well, just *stupid*.

Overall, she thought her school was stupid.

But most things weren't that clear. When she thought about the way Sra. Nelson taught her class, it was more like she both liked it *and* it drove her crazy. There were things about her parents that had this effect on her too. With her father, it was the way he took everything so seriously, even little things, and got so worked up over them. She loved him for this—loved that he had started a boycott of the local paper after it endorsed Bush, and that he'd gone door to door this election trying to convince people in their neighborhood (even people who had Bush signs in their yards!) to vote for Kerry. But she hated that he wouldn't ever lighten up, the way her mother was always telling him to, that for him everything was life-and-death, like her mother said. Even when he tried to make jokes, they came out sounding serious.

And her mother—well, she loved that she would crank the stereo up and dance like a teenager, and that she'd get so passionate about things she'd thump her fist on the table or use swear words without even stopping to think that there was a kid around…but she also kind of hated that her mother didn't act like a mother. That she hardly ever stopped to think that there *was* a kid around…

It was something she hadn't puzzled out yet—how it was possible to be so pained and irritated by something that also delighted you, that made you love the person.

And it was funny that she couldn't explain, not even to herself, what it was that she liked, exactly, about Sra. Nelson, a teacher the other kids were always complaining about (partly because of the Spanish, but also because they thought social studies was boring, and especially the history and geography parts of it—"Like, who *cares* about what happened a billion years ago, a gazillion miles away?"). But May did like it—like *her*—even when Sra. Nelson's class made her impatient, like today.

It seemed ridiculous to be in school at all when there was so much going on out in the real world. On the way up High Street this morning, she and her mother had seen college boys with Kerry-Edwards signs on nearly every corner, and her mother had honked the horn and waved at them, every one of them, block after block. "Fucking miracle," she said under her breath as they passed North Broadway, and even though May didn't like it when her mother said "fucking"—just the sound of the word made her feel a little sick—she was happy too. "Four years ago, you couldn't get the kids on campus to the polls if you beat them with a stick," her mother had told her. This time around, everyone was going to pull together; this time they would win. "A miracle," May repeated.

And here was another miracle. Heather Brennan raised her hand and filled in Sra. Nelson's blank. "*No existe…um, más que…un Dios?*" she said. Slowly. Then she added, "Um…Allah, right?"

Sra. Nelson clapped her hands as if Heather had just pulled a rabbit out of her binder. "*Sí!*" She held up one finger. "*Sí! Primero: no existe más que un Dios, Alá. Y*"—she held up two fingers—"*el segundo: el alma es inmortal y a la muerte de la persona va al paraíso o al infierno según se haya portado en vida.*" She held up three fingers. "*El tercero: Alá dispone que un ser humano sea—*"

May didn't even wait for her to stop, and for the second time today she didn't bother to raise her hand. "*Bueno o malo desde su nacimiento.*"

This was another thing that had troubled her last night when she'd read it in the textbook, and as Sra. Nelson went on to item four—praying four times a day facing Mecca—May kept thinking about number three. *Allah would decide from the moment of a human being's birth if he were going to be good or bad.* It was the opposite of what her parents had taught her: that people *became* what they were, slowly, making choices one by one, responding to what was around them all their lives. That they could choose to do right or do wrong, to be good or to be bad.

JP raised his hand to ask Sra. Nelson a question. If her parents were right, May thought, maybe there was still hope for him. She wanted there to be. Because she liked him—she really did, she liked him a lot—and that didn't even feel like something she'd made a *choice* about.

She hoped he'd ask his question in Spanish. That would make Sra. Nelson so happy.

* * *

After social studies, Spanish. Then came science. After science, there would still be lunch to get through, and then the whole afternoon ahead before she could go with her parents to vote.

When her mother had dropped her off this morning, she'd promised to pick her up after school and take the rest of the afternoon off. "That way, even if there's still a long line, it won't matter. We'll wait it out." It was a family tradition for the three of them to go together to the polls, and for May to push the buttons for one of her parents, so that she could feel like she had voted, too (and she kept track; she knew which parent she had gone into the booth with at the last election, even if they couldn't remember, and it amused them that she insisted on taking turns. Last time—the midterm elections—she'd pushed the buttons for her mother; now it was her father's turn).

"I'll pick you up and then we'll swing by the house and get your dad," her mother said.

"Will you call him from work and let him know you're coming?" May wanted to make sure they were talking to each other *before* she and her mother picked him up, but also she knew her father needed a half hour's notice, at least, before he could get up from the piano and get ready to go out. Her mother didn't seem to understand that (she didn't understand why May and Willa needed advance notice, too, to tie up the loose ends of whatever game they were playing—why they couldn't just stop right in the middle of things and be ready to say good-bye, why they required periodic warnings about how much time they had left). "Will you? Just give him the thirty-minute warning," she told her mother, as if it were a joke. Her mother smiled but didn't answer her.

"And then we'll go 'throw the rascals out,'" May said. "Like Daddy always says. Right?"

"Right," her mother said.

But the other night, when May had used that phrase, her father had said, "It may not be that simple after all."

"Why not?" May had asked him, at the same time that her mother said, "Well, things will be a damn sight better. They can't get much worse, can they?"

"I didn't say they wouldn't be better," her father said. And then to May he said, "Because *nothing* is that simple," and to her mother he said, "Look, I am just pointing out to our daughter that things are more complex than they appear to be on the surface, that the world isn't black and white, good and bad—"

"Why would you think that I think it is?" her mother said.

"This has nothing to do with you, Jesse." Her father sounded tired. "I'm afraid we've given May the idea that things are less complicated than they really are."

"I think May knows very well how *complicated* things are."

This was about as close as they ever came to arguing in front of her, and they had stopped right there, both of them looking at her, then going silent. But now, as she sat in science, turning a rock over in her hand and trying to decide if the mineral was calcite or fluorite, she remembered something that she guessed she had made herself forget: that she had heard them *that* night too—had woken up in the middle of the night to her mother's voice. "You know how much I hate it when you talk to her that way," she was saying. And her father said, "What way is that?" but the way he said it was a way May hated to hear him talking to her mother. "Nothing is black and white," her mother said, and she was mimicking him, and May wanted to get out of bed and go into their room and tell them both to stop it, stop being so mean to each other. Her father said, "Oh, right. Fine, Jesse. All I want to do is teach our daughter that we live in the real world and have to abide by real-world facts. Isn't that what you want?"

"Our *daughter* has no problem living in the real world. Why don't you save the lecture for yourself, David?"

May had put her pillow over her head then, so she wouldn't have to hear any more. And then she must have fallen asleep, because she couldn't remember what came next.

* * *

At lunch she sat with Megan and Lucy, who weren't quite as bad as the other girls in her class—at least they actually liked to read, and they were also the only other girls in the class who didn't play sports, not softball or basketball or soccer or "team cheerleading," which gave May *something* in common with them—and she just ate her cream cheese and olive sandwich without saying a word while the two of them talked about some TV show she'd never heard of. She was absolutely sure she was the only kid in the whole school who didn't have a TV at home. It was one of the things—one of the *many* things, she reminded herself—that her parents were in complete agreement about. She liked to tick these things off on her fingers, reassured by how long the list was. They were both Democrats, of course, and they both had no use for TV; they both loved art and music, especially Jackson Pollock and Willem de Kooning, and jazz and old blues and Bach and Beethoven and "contemporary classical" like the music her father wrote, *and* punk rock. They both liked to cook—they took turns cooking dinner. They both read history for fun (her mother had started out in college as a history major before she found out that she liked art history even better; her father had been a music major in college, and he'd hardly paid attention to anything else then, he said, but "your mother turned me into a history buff"). Her father never read novels, like her mother did, but he read poetry, which she didn't. Anyway, they both loved books: there were rows and stacks of books all over the house—history and novels and poetry and biographies and gigantic art books that May had loved looking at her whole life.

Neither one of them had brothers or sisters—they were both only children, like May. They both loved mountains and didn't care for the beach. They were both allergic to cats.

The one big difference between them—that one of them was Jewish and one was Christian—didn't seem to bother either of them. *She* was the only one who worried about that, and even then, what worried her had nothing to do with them, was all about her—about how she was supposed to be both Jewish and Christian, the way they'd always said she was. The way she'd thought she was, until recently, when she'd started thinking that just wasn't *possible*, that it didn't make sense.

It seemed to her that the more she knew, the older she got, the less things seemed to make sense. Which was the opposite of how you'd think it would go.

Well, some things she did understand better now. Politics, for example. When she was younger, she'd been pretty simpleminded about it. Not that she hadn't *cared*—she had always cared; she'd been taught to care about politics just as she'd been taught to care about art and music. But thinking about the way the world worked was different from looking at paintings or listening to music. She remembered how, during the last presidential election, she'd made a poster, drawing Bush the worst way her seven-year-old self could imagine: naked, with very messy hair, driving a big car without wearing a seatbelt. She had drawn wavy lines all around him to indicate that he smelled bad. Her mother had studied the poster and asked: "Do these lines mean he's…shivering? Hmm, he's driving, right, so he can't be *running*…" May had been outraged. "No! Stinking!" she said, and her mother had laughed and hugged her and taped the poster up on their front door, where everyone who passed by their house could see it.

She remembered the aftermath of the election too—all that time when it hadn't been clear who had won. She remembered it as a period of terror. Her parents were distraught too, but May was beside herself. Even her parents were alarmed by how upset she was. She couldn't make them understand that it was a disaster—a disaster that everything was so muddled, that no one was in charge. They ended up canceling the trip they'd been planning, to visit her mother's family for an early Christmas celebration, because May made herself sick, she was so upset: she couldn't sleep, and for several days she threw up everything she ate. "She's too sensitive to live," she heard her mother tell her grandma on the phone, and she said it as if it were a joke, but May was afraid, then, that it might be literally true. That she was so sensitive she might die.

She understood now that things would muddle on, that a few days or a few weeks, and maybe even longer, might not be enough for a disaster to occur. That the country would keep going, somehow.

But she also knew some other things she hadn't known four years ago—that a bad president could take the country into a war, for example; that he could tell gay people, like her mother's assistant, Stephen, and his partner, Kristoff, that they didn't have any rights; that a bad president could destroy the whole environment, so that someday there wouldn't even *be* a world.

When she allowed herself to start thinking about all these things, her stomach started to hurt and her breath started coming too fast, so she had to stop. That was one disadvantage of getting older and understanding *some* things better—there were even more things to feel bad about.

In art, the last period of the day, someone—Sra. Gerber, the art teacher—finally said something about the election. "Let's work with red, white, and blue today, shall we?" Like Sra. Quehl, Sra. Gerber never bothered with Spanish. They probably figured Sra. Nelson made up for it, so they could each forget their own 50 percent.

May could just imagine what her parents would say if she told them they'd made red, white, and blue paintings today. Usually she didn't even tell her parents this kind of thing anymore. When they asked how her day had gone, she just said fine. It only started trouble if she came home complaining, like when she was in third grade and she'd tell them how they'd sometimes spend the whole morning filling in blanks on mimeographed sheets, or at indoor recess they'd watch game shows on TV—or how, in fourth grade, Sra. Malori would say sarcastically, every time May used a word in English that was longer than two syllables, "Ooh, a fifty-dollar word!" Now she only told them the good things, when there were any to tell (usually that meant something from social studies, or once in a while science). Even so, at least once a week, her father would say, "Tell me again why we're sending her to that school?" May knew her mother's answer by heart: "Do you have any better ideas?" They'd picked Spanish Immersion as the "least of all the evils." May believed Willa when she said her school was no better. "What passes for 'art' in that 'arts alternative' school would curl your hair," her father had said when May had asked him once why she couldn't go there. "My hair is already curly," she pointed out, but it didn't make him laugh. "I could go to private school," May had said once, but both her parents had been horrified, and that was the last time she'd ever mentioned *that*.

When her mother said there *was* no alternative to the Spanish Immersion Academy, that they were stuck, her father would say, "Tell me again why we live here, then," although he knew perfectly well why—May's mother had a job here, a good job that she loved. When May overheard them arguing at night, when she was supposed to be sleeping, this was one of the things they'd talk about. But they didn't *argue* about it. Like when they talked about the election, it wasn't even so much what they said as how they said it. And the fact that they were talking about it at all, when they should have been sleeping. It wasn't as if May's father wanted her mother to quit her job. He was happy that she liked it, and when she'd gotten promoted to head curator he had gone out and bought her flowers and a bottle of champagne. And they didn't argue about the city they lived in, because *neither* of them liked it. They'd moved here—for May's mother's job at the museum—before May was born. Before her mother was even pregnant with her. But May's mother was resigned to living here; she'd gotten used to it. And it wasn't as if she could just pick up and get a job she liked as much as this one just anywhere. Her father knew that. But he, on the other hand, could have lived anywhere. All *he* needed was a piano and a little peace and quiet—May knew this by heart too.

* * *

When she got outside at the end of the day, her mother was leaning against the car, her arms folded, looking pretty in the short green jacket May's father had bought her last Christmas and blue jeans and the red cowboy boots she'd had since graduate school. She was wearing May's old stocking cap—May felt childish in it, but her mother didn't mind looking childish—and a pair of red-and-black-striped mittens May had never seen before. Her mother noticed her noticing. "I went shopping. Isn't that dumb? I left early. I was feeling anxious"—May nodded; she wished *she* could have left early and gone shopping, gone anywhere—"and then there was nowhere to go so I went over to T.J. Maxx." She looked embarrassed. It wasn't like her mother to go shopping for no reason. She was a shopping's-not-something-you-do-for-fun kind of mother. Unlike Willa's mother, who loved to go shopping and was always "just stopping in" at places like T.J. Maxx and Marshall's, digging through the racks of discount clothes and bins of jewelry, but would cheerfully declare that it was terribly frivolous of her, that she was ashamed of herself. May's mother would set her jaw and go shopping every Christmas, buying all the presents in one trip to the mall, and the week before school started every year, she'd take May to Kohl's and buy her everything the two of them could imagine she would need for the whole year, but that was it. "Oh," she said now, as she unlocked the car and opened the back door for May. "I bought you something too."

"You're kidding," May said. She lowered her backpack onto the seat and shoved it over, then slid in beside it. She still didn't weigh enough to sit in the front with her mother. Sometimes she worried that she never would.

Her mother handed her a small plastic bag and sat watching, not starting the car, as May took out the little white box and opened it. On a bed of cotton was a tiny gold half-moon on a chain. "Mom? It's beautiful, but what—?"

"The moon, Maybud," her mother said. "It's what we'd give you if we could." Was she crying? Her mother couldn't be crying. "Are you buckled up? We've got to get moving."

"The election isn't over yet, is it?" May asked, suddenly frightened. If her mother was crying, it could only mean that Bush was winning.

"No, it isn't over. It's too soon to tell what's happening. We're running neck and neck, it looks like."

So what was wrong? she wondered as she put the necklace on. She fingered the little half-moon. Could it be "running neck and neck" that was making her mother cry?

It wasn't until they turned into the parking lot of the school where they voted that May understood that they weren't stopping at home first. "Where's Daddy?"

"He went ahead and voted on his own, earlier," her mother said. May watched the back of her head and her shoulders—she didn't turn around when she said it. But she couldn't read her mother's back, or her voice. And then May was thinking again about the last election, when she hadn't been able to eat or sleep—when for days, weeks, it seemed to her, she hadn't slept at all, or only fitfully, so that when she did sleep, she'd wake up in the middle of the night crying because there was no president. "What if someone did something to the United States?" she asked her father. *Then* what would happen to them, with no one in charge? "Did what?" her father asked her gently. "What are you afraid is going to happen?"

But how could he ask that? she'd wondered. She heard her parents talking, she heard them reading bits of the newspaper out loud to each other every morning—her father reading the *Washington Post*, her mother the *New York Times*. Even then, four years before the boycott her father had started, before they'd put the homemade bumper sticker that said BOYCOTT THE H-T MESS on their car, they couldn't bear to take the local paper, the *Herald-Tidings-Messenger*, because it was so conservative. Terrible things happened every day, everywhere. May knew it. Anything could happen. Anything could happen at any time.

And then in the middle of December, when Bush was declared the winner, it felt like the end of the world. Her father had been saying all summer and fall that if Bush were to win, the world would "go to hell in a handbasket," and even though the phrase didn't make any sense to her (no matter how she tried to put the two ideas together—a basket like the Easter basket her mother still fixed for her every year, which was embarrassing because she was probably getting too old for it; and hell, which she wasn't even sure she believed in—she couldn't figure it out), it terrified her.

As if her mother knew she was being watched, she said, still without turning around, "He didn't want to wait. He said the lines would just get longer as the day wore on. He went on over around one o'clock, he said when I called home. He only had to wait half an hour."

This wasn't right—this was definitely not right—and May felt scared, but her mother was getting out of the car now, slamming the door behind her, starting toward the school building. She had to hurry to catch up, and then they were in the building and it was crowded and noisy, there were hundreds of people, and at the door there were questions about district, and instructions about which side of the auditorium to sit on, and she would have had to shout to be heard, so she gave up. They pushed their way past people standing every which way and found seats in the back, way over on the left side of the auditorium, where they'd been told to go.

Once they were sitting down, they were able to talk, but May's mother started talking before May had a chance to. "Did I ever tell you the story of the presidential election of 1992? When Bill Clinton won his first term, took it away from Bush the first?"

May shook her head. "I wasn't even born yet," she told her mother.

"I know that, silly. That's the point."

"What is?"

"Listen. I'm trying to tell you." Her mother took her hand—jewelry, hand-holding: what was going on? She thought of saying, jokingly, *Who are you and what have you done with my mother?* but she was afraid to. Because really she wanted to ask, *What have you done with my* father? The three of them had gone to vote together in every single election—not just presidential elections, but all of them—all of May's life.

"Was Daddy with you?" she asked.

"In 1992? Of course he was. That's what I'm trying to tell you. On November 3, 1992—that was Election Day that year—"

"But how can you re—"

"Shh. I'm trying to tell you. I had an appointment that afternoon with the obstetrician. My first OB appointment. For a sonogram. I was about ten weeks pregnant. Daddy went with me. He was really nervous. He was afraid he was going to faint. You know how he is about anything medical."

Despite herself, May smiled. Once her father had fainted when she fell off her swing and cut her head. She was okay, but there was a lot of blood. He ran out from his room—one wall of it, facing the yard, was all glass, so he'd seen her fall—and picked her up, but then he started swaying and he just managed to put her down on the grass before he fell down himself. It had scared the wits out of her and it was only then that she started screaming. Then her mother, who'd been upstairs reading, came running. She didn't know which one of them to attend to first.

"But he didn't faint," her mother said. "He was too amazed and happy to faint. Because there you were—little arm and leg buds wiggling. It was incredible, May. We got the *doctor* started crying, because the thing was, she was pregnant too, but I didn't know it then, she hadn't told any of her patients—she was about two weeks behind me. So there we were, all three of us crying, and there you were, gorgeous and mysterious—just your beginnings, you know? And then we went straight from there to"—she swept her hand in the air—"*here*. We came to vote. We were—oh, you know, we were full of hope, we were so excited and so emotional. We were both feeling a little shaky, still. And then we voted, and we went home and climbed into bed and took a nap together. We slept till way past dinnertime, and then we got up and Daddy made dinner—I even remember what he made: spaghetti with chopped tomatoes he got out of the freezer, tomatoes

we'd frozen from our own garden that summer, and rosemary and bal-
samic vinegar. And then we went back to bed, and in the morning we
woke up early to the news that Clinton had won. And we just started
to dance around the room, and we were crying again, and I remember
Daddy saying, 'We threw the rascals out! We did it!' and we just felt
so perfect, so completely hopeful. Everything was going to be new and
good, a good man of our own generation was going to take us to a new
place—we were at a turning point"—but now she was crying, not just
a little, either, like before, but crying hard, and May felt the way she'd
felt when her father had fallen to a heap beside her in the backyard
when she was six years old, helpless and frightened and responsible,
knowing she had done it, it was all her fault, but she hadn't meant to.

"—and it didn't work out that way after all, did it?" her mother
said, but then after that May could hardly understand anything else
she said, because she was crying and talking at the same time. May put
her arms around her mother and patted her and said, "It's okay," and
"Don't worry," but she didn't know what she was telling her not to
worry about, or *what* was going to be okay.

"Move up," someone said, and May looked up and saw that half a
dozen rows ahead of them were empty, that they had to move forward.
"The line's moving faster now," someone said.

"Come on, Mama," May whispered. "Come on. We need to get
ready."

Her mother shook her head—not saying no, but only shaking herself like a dog coming in out of the rain. Shaking it off. "All right. I'm
all right." She stood up. She waved May upward too and then she led
her down to the first row of empty seats. "You're going into the booth
with me, right? And"—she lowered her voice—"pushing the buttons,
like always?"

"Like always," May said. "Of course!" But for the first time in her
life, she didn't feel grown up and excited about this. She felt...she
wasn't sure. Sad about it, sort of. Like...she was too old for this, to
push the buttons for her mother. But too young to be allowed to vote

herself. She wouldn't be able to vote for president until *two* elections from now. That seemed forever away. And who knew what would be happening then? She knew what *should* happen: President John Kerry should be at the end of his term, and she would be voting for...who? Hillary Clinton? She wanted to say this to her mother, but when she looked over, her mother was crying again. "Don't cry, Mama," she whispered. "We're going to win. We're going to *throw the rascals out.*"

Her mother smiled faintly. "Yes we are. Now or never."

"No," May said. "Not now or never."

"No?" Her mother was looking at her as if *she* might have an answer—as if she might have all the answers.

"No," May said. She touched the gold half-moon on its chain around her neck. "If not now, then later. I promise."

"You promise?" Even though there were still tears rolling down her face, her mother started to laugh. "Okay, I accept your promise." She took May's hand again, the hand that had been touching the moon, and closed May's fingers into a fist, then kissed the fist. "If not now, later. I'll hold you to that. I'm counting on it."

For some reason, then, May felt as if she had voted—or anyway as if she had done *something*—something that had kept the end of the world from coming.

The Politics of Culture

Your Mother and I
by Dave Eggers

I TOLD YOU ABOUT THAT, DIDN'T I? ABOUT WHEN YOUR MOTHER AND I moved the world to solar energy and windpower, to hydro, all that? I never told you that? Can you hand me that cheese? No, the other one, the cheddar, right. I really thought I told you about that. What is happening to my head?

Well, we have to take the credit, your mother and I, for reducing our dependence on oil and for beginning the Age of Wind and Sun. That was pretty awesome. That name wasn't ours, though. Your uncle Frank came up with that. He always wanted to be in a band and call it that, the Age of Wind and Sun, but he never learned guitar and couldn't sing. When he sang he enunciated too much, you know? He sang like he was trying to teach English to Turkish children. Turkish children with learning disabilities. It was really odd, his singing.

You're already done? Okay, here's the Monterey Jack. Just dump it in the bowl. All of it, right. It was all pretty simple, converting most of the nation's electricity. At a certain point everyone knew that we had to just suck it up and pay the money—because holy crap, it really was expensive at first!—to set up the cities to make their own power. All those solar panels and windmills on the city buildings? They weren't always there, you know. No, they weren't. Look at some pictures, honey. They just weren't. The roofs of these millions of buildings weren't being used in any real way, so I said, Hey, let's have the buildings themselves generate some or all of the power they use, and it might look pretty good, to boot—everyone loves windmills, right? Windmills are awesome. So we started in Salt Lake City and went from there.

Oh hey, can you grate that one? Just take half of that block of Muenster. Here's a bowl. Thanks. Then we do the cheddar. Cheddar has to be next. After the cheddar, pecorino. Never the other way

around. Stay with me, hon. Jack, Muenster, cheddar, pecorino. It is.
The only way.

Right after that was a period of much activity. Your mother and I
tended to do a big project like the power conversion, and then follow
it with a bunch of smaller, quicker things. So we made all the roads
red. You wouldn't remember this—you weren't even born. We were all
into roads then, so we had most of them painted red, most of them,
especially the highways—a leathery red that looked good with just
about everything, with green things and blue skies and woods of cedar
and golden swamps and sugar-colored beaches. I think we were right.
You like them, right? They used to be grey, the roads. Insane, right?
Your mom thinks yellow would have been good, too, an ochre but
sweeter. Anyway, in the same week, we got rid of school funding tied
to local property taxes—can you believe they used to pull that crap?—
banned bicycle shorts for everyone but professionals, and made everyone's hair shinier. That was us. Your mother and I.

That was right after our work with the lobbyists—I never told you
that, either? I must be losing my mind. I never mentioned the lobbyists, about when we had them all deported? That part of it, the depor-
tation, was your mother's idea. All I'd said was, Hey, why not ban all
lobbying? Or at least ban all donations from lobbyists, and make them
wear cowbells so everyone would know they were coming? And then
your dear mom, who was, I think, a little tipsy at the time—we were
at a bar where they had a Zima special, and you know how your mom
loves her Zima—she said, How about, to make sure those bastards
don't come back to Washington, have them all sent to Greenland?
And wow, the idea just took off. People loved it, and Greenland wel-
comed them warmly; they'd apparently been looking for ways to boost
their tourism. They set up some cages and a viewing area and it was a
big hit.

So then we were all pumped up, to be honest. Wow, this kind of
thing, the lobbyists thing especially, boy, it really made your mother
horny. Matter of fact, I think you were conceived around that time.

She was like some kind of tsunam—

Oh don't give me that face. What? Did I cross some line? Don't you want to know when your seed was planted? I would think you'd want to know that kind of thing. Well then.

I stand corrected.

Anyway, we were on a roll, so we got rid of genocide. The main idea was to create and maintain a military force of about 20,000 troops, under the auspices of the U.N., which could be deployed quickly to any part of the world within about thirty-six hours. This wouldn't be the usual blue helmets, watching the slaughter. These guys would be badass. We were sick of the civilized world sort of twiddling their thumbs while hundreds of thousands of people killed each other in Rwanda, Bosnia, way back in Armenia, on and on. Then the U.N. would send twelve Belgian soldiers. Nice guys, but really, you have a genocide raging in Rwanda, 800,000 dead in a month and you send twelve Belgians?

So we made this proposal, the U.N. went for it, and within a year the force was up and running. And man oh man, your mother was randy again. That's when your fecundation happened, and why we called you Johnna. I remember it now—I was wrong before. Your mother and I were actually caught in the U.N. bathroom, after the vote went our way. The place, all marble and brass, was full of people, and at the worst possible moment, Kofi himself walked in. He sure was surprised to see us in there, on the sink, but I have to say, he was pretty cool about it. He actually seemed to enjoy it, even watched for a minute, because there was no way we were gonna stop in the middle—

Fine. I won't do that again. It's just that it's part of the story, honey. Everything we did started with love, and ended with lust—

But you're right. That was inappropriate.

We went on a tear right after genocide, very busy. I attribute it partly to the vitamins we were on—very intense program of herbs and vitamins and protein shakes. We'd shoot out of bed and bounce around like bunnies. So that's when we covered Cleveland in ivy.

You've seen pictures. We did that. Just said, Hey Cleveland, what if you were covered in ivy, all the buildings? Wouldn't that look cool, and be a big tourist attraction? And they said, "Sure." Not right away, though. You know who helped with that? Dennis Kucinich. I used to call him "Sparky," because he was such a feisty fella. Your mom, she called him "The Kooch."

We're gonna need all three kinds of salsa, hon. Yeah, use the small bowls. Just pour it right up to the edge. Right. Your brother likes to mix it up. Me, I'm a fan of the mild.

Right after Cleveland and the ivy we made all the kids memorize poetry again. We hadn't memorized any growing up—this was the seventies and eighties, and people hadn't taught that for years—and we really found we missed it. The girls were fine with the idea, and the boys caught on when they realized it would help them get older women into bed. Around that time we banned wearing fur outside of arctic regions, flooded the market with diamonds and gold and silver to the point where none had any value, fixed the ozone hole—I could show you that; we've got it on video—and then we did the thing with the llamas. What are you doing? Sour cream in the salsa? No, no. That's just wrong, sweetie. My god.

So yeah, we put llamas everywhere. That was us. We just liked looking at them, so we bred about six million and spread them around. They weren't there before, honey. No, they weren't. Oh man, there's one now, in the backyard. Isn't it a handsome thing? Now they're as common as squirrels or deer, and you have your mom and pop to thank for that.

It's jalapeño time. Use the smaller knife. You're gonna cut the crap out of your hand. You don't want one of these. You see this scar on my thumb? Looks like a scythe, right? I got that when we were negotiating the removal of the nation's billboards. I was climbing one of them, in Kentucky actually, to start a hunger strike kind of thing, sort of silly I guess, and cut the shipdoodle out of that left thumb.

Why the billboards? Have you even see one? In books? Well, I guess I just never really liked the look of them—they just seemed so ugly and such an intrusion on the collective involuntary consciousness, a blight on the land. Vermont had outlawed them and boy, what a difference that made. So your mother and I revived Lady Bird Johnson's campaign against them, and of course 98 percent of the public was with us, so the whole thing happened pretty quickly. We had most of the billboards down within a year. Right after that, your brother Sid was conceived, and it was about time I had my tubes tied.

Give me some of that cobbler, hon. We're gonna have the peach cobbler after the main event. I just wanna get the Cool Whip on it, then stick it in the freezer for a minute. That's Frank's trick. Frank's come up with a lot of good ideas for improving frozen and refrigerated desserts. No, that's not his job, honey. Frank doesn't have a job, per se.

I guess a lot of what we did—what made so much of this possible—was eliminate the bipolar nature of so much of what passed for debate in those days. So often the media would take even the most logical idea, like private funding for all sports stadiums or having all colleges require forty hours of community service to graduate, and make it seem like there were two equally powerful sides to the argument, which was so rarely the case. A logical fallacy, is what that is. So we just got them to keep things in perspective a bit, not make everyone so crazy, polarizing every last debate. I mean, there was a time when you couldn't get a lightbulb replaced because the press would find a way to quote the sole lunatic in the world who didn't want that lightbulb replaced. So we sat them all down, all the members of the media, and we said, "Listen, we all want to have progress, we all want a world for the grandkids and all. We know we're gonna need better gas mileage on the cars, and that all the toddlers are gonna need Head Start, and we're gonna need weekly parades through every town and city to keep morale up, and we'll have to get rid of Three Strikes and mandatory minimums and the execution of retarded prisoners—and that it all has to happen sooner or later, so don't go blowing opposition to any of it out of proportion. Don't go getting everyone inflamed." Honestly, when lynchings were originally outlawed, you can bet the newspapers made it seem like there was some real validity to the pro-lynching side of things. You can be sure that the third paragraph of any article would have said "Not everyone is happy about the anti-lynching legislation. We spoke to a local resident who is not at all happy about it..." Anyway, we sat everyone down, served some carrots and onion dip and in a couple hours your mother and I straightened all that out.

About then we had a real productive period. In about six months, we established a global minimum wage, we made it so smoke detectors could be turned off without having to rip them from the ceiling, and we got Soros to buy the Amazon, to preserve it. That was fun—he took us on his jet, beautiful thing, appointed in the smoothest cherry and teak, and they had the soda where you add the colored syrup your-self. You ever have that kind? So good, but you can't overdo it—too much syrup and you feel bloated for a week. Well, then we came home, rested up for a few days, and then we found a cure for Parkinson's. We did so, honey. Yes that was us. Don't you ever look through the nice scrapbook we made? You should. It's in the garage with your Uncle Frank. Are you sure he's asleep? No, don't wake him up. Hell, I guess you have to wake him up anyway, because he won't want to miss the comida grande.

After Parkinson's, we fixed AIDS pretty well. We didn't cure it, but we made the inhibiting drugs available worldwide, for free, as a condition of the drug companies being allowed to operate in the U.S. Their profit margins were insane at the time, so they relented, made amends, and it worked out fine. That was about when we made all buildings curvier, and all cars boxier.

After AIDS and the curves, we did some work on elections. First we made them no more than two months long, publicly funded, and forced the networks to give two hours a night to the campaigns. Around when you were born, the candidates were spending about $200 million each on TV ads, because the news wasn't covering the elections for more than 90 seconds a day. It was nuts! So we fixed that, and then we perfected online and phone voting. Man, participation went through the roof. Everyone thought there was just all this apathy, when the main problem was finding your damned polling place! And all the red tape—register now, vote then, come to this elementary school—but skip work to do it—on and on. Voting on a Tuesday? Good lord. But the online voting, the voting over the phone—man that was great, suddenly participation exploded, from about, what, 40 percent, to 88. We did that over Columbus Day weekend, I think. I remember I'd just had my hair cut very short. Yeah, like in the picture in the hallway. We called that style the Timberlake.

And that's about when your mom got all kinky again. She went out, bought this one device, it was kind of like a swing, where there was this harness and—

Fine. You don't need to know that. But the harness figures in, because that's when your mother had the idea—some of her best ideas happened when she was lying down—to make it illegal to have more than one president from the same immediate family. That was just a personal gripe she had. We'd had the Adamses and Bushes and we were about to have the Clintons and your mother just got pissed. What the fuck? she said. Are we gonna have a monarchy here or what? Are we that stupid, that we have to go to the same well every time? This isn't an Aaron Spelling casting call, this is the damned presidency! I said What about the Kennedys? And she said Screw 'em! Or maybe she didn't say that, but that was the spirit of it. She's a fiery one, your mom, a fiery furnace of—

Ahem. So yeah, she pushed that through, a constitutional amendment.

That led to another busy period. One week, we made all the cars electric and put waterslides in every elementary school. We increased average life expectancy to 164, made it illegal to manufacture or wear Cosby sweaters, and made penises better looking—more streamlined, better coloring, less hair. People, you know, were real appreciative about that. And the last thing we did, which I know I've told you about, was the program where everyone can redo one year of their childhood. For $580, you could go back to the year of your choice, and do that one again. You're not allowed to change anything, do anything differently, but you get to be there again, live the whole year, with what you know now. Oh man, that was a good idea. Everyone loved it, and it made up for all the people who were pissed when we painted Kansas purple, every last inch of it. I did the period between ten-and-a-half and eleven-and-a-half. Fifth grade. Wow, that was sweet.

Speaking of ten-year-olds, here comes your brother. And Uncle Frank! We didn't have to wake you up! Hola hermano, tios! Esta la noche de los nachos! Sí, sí. And here's your mother, descending the stairs. With her hair up. This I was particularly proud of, when I convinced your mother to wear her hair up more often. When she first did it, a week before our wedding, I was breathless, I was lifted, I felt as if I'd met her twin, and oh how I was confused. Was I cheating on my beloved with this version of her, with that long neck exposed, the hair falling in helixes, kissing her clavicles? She assured me that I was not, and that's how we got married, with her hair up—that's how we did the walk with the music and the fanfare, everything yellow and white, side by side, long even strides, she and me, your mother and I.

How Little We Know About Cast Polymers, and About Life
by Ben Greenman

ON THE DAY THAT THE HOSPICE PATHETIC DIED, I WAS READING ABOUT genetically modified linseed plants. Created by scientists in a laboratory environment, the plants accumulated high levels of very long chain polyunsaturated fatty acids in seed. This was good news, you see, because prior to the appearance of these engineered oils, the most reliable source for very long chain polyunsaturated fats was fish, and wild and farmed fisheries were straining at the seams to meet increased global demand. Now, with the help of science, we could get the oils from linseed plants. It was a miracle, or so the scientists in the article said. To be honest, I didn't really care. I was reading about the oils only because it was the lead article in the in-flight magazine. I would have rather read about the Hospice Pathetic. Matters of life and death interested me greatly. Still, I made do with what was available to me; I returned to the article and learned several additional interesting facts about very long chain polyunsaturated fatty acids.

I was traveling from New York City to Boston, where I had a four-hour layover, and then I was going on to Mexico City, then to Stockholm, then to Tallinn. If this seems roundabout, it was. I was a spy. I can't tell you what government agency I was working for, or whether or not my mission involved assassinating a foreign dignitary in the Boston airport, or whether I was traveling under the name "Rodolfo Pilas" and affecting a slight Spanish accent, or even if anything in this paragraph is true, except for the thing about the linseed plants, and even that might, in theory, be a code that I'm using to send a message to certain people who would, let's say, need to know how to assemble a certain piece of equipment, like some fancy gyroscopic circuit that's being used in a cutting-edge missile-location system that would, if it fell into the wrong hands, wreak havoc on what little bit of peace we have left in the modern world.

In theory.

So, there I was, reading about linseed oil, wondering how the Hospice Pathetic felt—if she felt anything at all—hovering in the space between existence and nonexistence. Before I go any further, let me make sure that we are talking about the same Hospice Pathetic. She was a Florida woman who collapsed in her mid-twenties after years battling eating disorders, suffered severe brain damage as a result of that collapse, went along in that brain-damaged state for more than fifteen years, and then became the center of a national controversy when her husband, who was also her court-appointed guardian, argued for her feeding tube to be removed, insisting that he was acting in accordance with her previously articulated wishes. Though her parents immediately objected to the decision, their appeal was rejected, and as the Hospice Pathetic neared death, her case was taken up by all manner of politicians and activists. The governor of Florida and even the United States Congress tried to intervene. They believed they had a right to promote life, and that those who supported her husband's attempt to remove the tube were promoting death. The Hospice Pathetic was, for the last weeks of her life, the center of intense media scrutiny as she lay largely immobile in her bed. She had a name, of course, but I called her the Hospice Pathetic, both to protect her privacy and to illustrate the way in which her personal identity became secondary to her use as a political symbol.

In theory.

I can't say any more, to be perfectly honest. I may have information about the case, or a person or persons involved in the case, that would reflect badly on other people—people in power—and that's why I'm relieved that I have at least something to report from that long day of traveling. It is a distraction, a story about traveling, but it can be a compelling distraction, especially when it could possibly involve a man clasping his hands together, saying "Madre de Dios," humming a snatch of *Carmina Burana*, and then moving his hands to the back of his head, where instinct led him to believe that he might catch whatever blew out.

But I am getting ahead of myself.

A slight cold was beginning to fog my head as I read the linseed article. This was a shame, because I had many miles and many hours still to travel on what I should probably describe as "a little trip taken by a Spanish-American cast polymer manufacturer seeking new business partners in Estonia." I had never been to Estonia, or at least there was no record of my ever having been. I was looking forward to drinking some local vodka and maybe making the acquaintance of a young lady, ideally paid, in the moody, somewhat threadbare hotel where I would be staying courtesy of the United States government—or, to be more circumspect, courtesy of Mar-Corp, a leader in supplying synthetic marble surfaces to Southern California contractors since 1989.

The idea of watching a long, young Estonian girl slip out of bed as I hovered on the border between sleep and waking both aroused and saddened me. I had done too much thinking about the link between youth, beauty, and death. I sighed as I screwed the silencer onto my gas blowback Maruzen Walther P99. I was in the bathroom stall, which never quite felt dignified, but it's one of the only places in an airport where you can have your gun out. I glanced at the tiles and wondered if they might not look better in synthetic marble.

From the bathroom, I went to the newsstand. "Excuse me," I said to an attractive young redhead standing by the financial magazines. "Did you by any chance grow up in San Diego?"

She looked up at me, took a beat, and beamed. "Mr. Pilas," she said. "Hello. Yes. I'm Jennifer Lee. I was friends with your son David."

"I thought so," I said. "How are you?"

"Good," she said. "And David?"

"Good," I said. "He's married. Just had his first child."

"I had heard that there was a baby on the way. So you're a grandfather? Congratulations."

"Thank you," I said.

"Say hi to David," she said. "I actually have to go. My plane's boarding in a minute."

"Nice to see you." It was nice to see her. A certain quantity of necessary information had been conveyed to me in an efficient, clandestine manner.

I went to the gate. If I had a target, I was expecting to see him pass through the lobby in exactly twelve minutes, wearing a brown leather jacket, which isn't to say that I had a target at all. I opened up my laptop computer to a rather anonymous-looking spreadsheet. If I had been asked, I would have said that I was figuring out wholesale prices for adhesive-backed waterproof tiling. I would have said it apologetically, as if I could not help but furnish excessive specifics in the vain hope of making a boring subject at least ironically interesting. "You know how things are with adhesive-backed waterproof tiling," I would have said. "No one likes to think about it, but people depend upon it every day."

Next to me two men were talking. The one closer to me was short and bald; the one farther away was taller and wore a knit cap. They were in their early thirties and they were clearly close friends.

"I read an article that bothered me," the first one said.

"Yeah?" said the other.

"It's just those liberal magazines," the first one said. "I know you probably agree with everything they say, but they make me mad."

"Tell me why," the second one said. I searched his face for sarcasm. I am practiced at detecting any kind of disjunction between what is said and what is felt. Sometimes it means the difference between life and death. In this case, the man seemed to have a genuine interest in what his friend was saying.

"Well, you know, even knowing about the bias ahead of time, I was quite disappointed with how they covered the case." They were talking about the Hospice Pathetic. Everybody was.

"'Bias' in what sense? You're not one of those people who secretly thinks that liberals wanted her to die, are you?"

"I don't secretly think anything. Look, as far as I'm concerned, there are only two real issues in the case: what she wanted to happen to her if she was ever brain-dead, and whether or not she was really brain-dead at the time the decisions were being made." He put his hands out on his lap and folded them formally. "Let's start with the first. I believe that there is strong reason to doubt what she actually wanted. I find it difficult, though not impossible, to believe that she told her husband at the age of twenty-three, or twenty-five, that she would rather die than be in a persistent vegetative state. So her wishes are in question, right?"

"But wait," the second man said.

"Let me finish," the first man said. "Please let me finish. I have heard you go on defending your candidates, attacking the president. Can I finish?"

"Sure," the second man said. "Finish."

"The second issue, of course, is whether or not she is in a persistent vegetative state. Again, I don't know. It is well-known that the diagnosis is very difficult. Since the advent of new brain-scanning techniques, many patients previously diagnosed as vegetative were shown to have brain life, and some even went on to have substantial recoveries. If the diagnosis is so certain, then why not allow another neurologist to examine her? Some things don't add up. For example, a major criterion of the persistent vegetative state is the complete lack of awareness of pain. If she is in that state, then why has her physician been giving her morphine? I think we need more certainty. I think that without it, these activist courts are possibly sanctioning, if not committing, murder."

I glanced at my watch. I had eight minutes left until my target was scheduled to approach. His movements would seem to him to be an exercise of his free will, but they were in fact choreographed by an organization much larger than he could imagine. The taxicab that picked him up from his hotel, for example, was outfitted with tiny, nearly undetectable heaters that would subtly dehydrate him on his way to the airport. Once inside the airport, he would proceed to the first kiosk, where he would purchase a bottle of water. You could say that there was a good chance of this occurring, but the fact is that there was a certainty of this occurring. Habits had been studied, special signage created, and so forth. The probability was so high that it was almost godly. Thanks to a miniature delivery system mounted on the engagement ring of the cashier at the snack kiosk, the water he was sold would have been dosed with a powerful time-release diuretic. This additive would take effect exactly three hundred seconds later, when—if his foot speed held—he would be twenty yards away from the entrance to a bathroom. I would follow him into the bathroom, at which time janitorial personnel would instantly block off the entrance. Inside, at the urinals, I would come up behind the man, ask him to kneel, and then discuss manufacturing advances in synthetic marble tile. I can say no more.

The gate area was strangely silent, despite the announcements overhead, and after a few seconds, I realized why: I no longer heard the two men next to me talking. I turned to look at them. The second man was staring at me. My blood chilled around my bones. I had been lost in thoughts of my plan, and I had violated the first rule of my profession, which was to remain vigilant. Was the man another spy? I tightened my hand around my Walther.

"You know," the second man said to his friend. "I can't say you're wrong, though I know you're not right. I've been ignoring the issue as best as possible for a number of reasons, chief among them the fact that there's no way to really know anything in this case. At this point, the situation has been so politicized that it's become more about grandstanding than about anything else. I'm sure her husband doesn't remember exactly what she said. Who would? But a better question is this: who else would? For that matter, what difference does it really make? This is a private dispute that the courts helped to settle. The rest of this is toxic, as far as I'm concerned. I don't like seeing her case, in life or death, be used for further divisiveness. It's just not a clear enough example, with enough legitimate facts, for there to be anything smart said about it."

My grip on the gun relaxed. The two men sat facing one another wordlessly for a moment. Their disagreement, civil as it was, had put something between them. When they got up to leave, I checked my watch again. Four minutes to target. Time sped up. Two minutes. One minute. And then he was there, younger than I had expected, his walk full of a life that he would not have for long. I followed him into the bathroom; I introduced myself; he exchanged what he thought was the proper set of code words; he accepted the appearance of the Walther with equanimity at first, convinced that it was merely a pre-caution; he even knelt without much resistance; at the click of the hammer his hands flew up to cover the back of his head; I ended the sentence with indisputable punctuation.

Coming out of the bathroom, I went down the concourse to a bar to have a beer—I always liked to have a beer before I left America. The news was about the Hospice Pathetic. She had died. Her fate was inevitable and yet it affected me profoundly. I dabbed at my eyes with a napkin and I was not the only one there who did so. Some of the others were men too. The nearest one to me said that he was a grand-father from Kansas. "I didn't know exactly how to feel about this," he said. "It was bad on every side." I nodded. "What's the world coming to?" he said. I told him about linseed oil and that improved his mood. "Sounds great for a landlocked state like Kansas," he said. "When I get home tonight I'm going to tell my grandkids that they're going to live forever."

I had another beer and headed back toward the plane. On my way I saw the two men from the gate, walking toward me. They had evi-dently not yet made their peace. They stood apart from each other, and as they came closer to me, I saw that their expressions were less friendly than before. They got closer. The short man was on my left. The tall man was on my right. They were still angry enough with one another to let a stranger walk through the middle of them. I pulled nearly even with them. The short man grabbed my left arm. I went for the Walther, but the tall man had already put a needle in my right shoulder. I could not move, but the tall man was strong enough to keep me upright, at least long enough until we had gone through a door and were in a large, bare room. The tall man did not say anything. The short man reached inside his jacket while he whistled *Carmina Burana*.

Even Steven

by Aimee Bender

IN THE COUNTRY IN QUESTION, EVERYTHING IS MATCHED. IF YOU ROB A box, somebody will rob your box. If you shout Fuck You, everyone will shout back Fuck You. If you make love to a magazine, the magazine will be placed in your bed in the morning with a yearning look.

One day I was curious and stole a lipstick, and the next morning a lipstick was gone from my makeup drawer. A different one. I heard of a man who beat up on a man and the next day he was beat up too. A woman cheated on her tax return and the next time she put money in her bank, they cheated and she lost a thousand bucks, just like that. A kid lies and then his parents lie to him. We don't love you, they say. You are really a girl, they tell him. He cries in his room for a long time, and he checks his pants over and over.

In the country in question lived a perfect citizen, named Steven.

Somebody hurt Steve. So he went and broke their heart back. Even Steven. He broke her heart by making her fall in love with a man he was paying to be charming, and then stopping paying the man. Steven, in his apartment, danced a little jig. The woman in question moved out of town, to the country next door.

Someone cut Steve off in traffic. He cut off someone else in traffic. Someone gave Steve a smile. Steve smiled back. They call me Even Steven, he said to the mirror, but the mirror, being mute, couldn't respond.

A murderer came into town and killed Steven's brother. The quick background on this murderer is that he, too, was born into murder, the murder of his own father, and he never got to kill the murderer of his father, but Steve's brother slightly resembled his father's murderer, so to him it made some sense. This tangled up the high courts for a while but finally they decided that too much time had passed, and after all, Steven's *brother* hadn't killed anyone. Looking alike didn't count. But now he was dead anyway. The rules were such that now Steve, acting as the brother, got to kill the murderer in the same way. He shot him in a grocery store, in the same aisle. The murderer fell into a pool of blood. The store owner asked Steve to help clean up. Steve said that the murderer should help clean up, but the store owner pointed out that the murderer was now dead and would no longer clean anything. Steve helped clean up and then asked if the store owner might come by and help clean up his apartment. No? said the store owner.

But who will help clean MY apartment then? asked Steve.

In ran the murderer's mother, sobbing. Steven left the store, uninterested, and that is not the point anyway. The murderer's mother would've liked now to kill Steve, but she was sobbing and didn't see where he went. Where he went was he stole a glass jar of juice and broke it into pieces on the sidewalk; when he got home, his own jar of juice had been broken all over the floor of his kitchen. Grape.

Steven's brother, meanwhile, was still dead. Steven kept calling him up. Hello, Buddy? he'd say into the message machine until he remembered, and then he kicked the wall. He missed his brother; they got along good. Where's Buddy? he'd say to the wall. He'd already murdered the killer. He felt ready to murder more killers. But his brother had only died once. But it's like he's died over and over and over! Steve said to his bartender at his bar. The bartender nodded. So who else can I kill for it? asked Steve. The bartender shrugged. You can kill another drink, he said.

Steve drank too much and puked all over the bartender. The bartender, who was bulimic—which is the only way a person could hold that job in that country—puked all over Steve right back.

We cannot tolerate a lack of balance, stated the president in his weekly news address. Symmetry is our God-given right!

In the country in question, plastic surgeons' biggest money came from making the face as symmetrical as possible. Lyle Lovett had to pack up and move away.

In the country in question, if you said Thank you, usually someone just said Thank you back. Nobody said You're welcome. If you said I'm sorry, they said I'm sorry back. No, I'm really sorry. I'm really sorry too. But I'm trying to apologize because I was the asshole. No, I was the asshole. No you were not, you were nice. I'm SORRY. I'm sorry too, I'm sorry too.

Somebody has to respond. Reflection does not equal response.

Steve hurt his sister's feelings. She hurt his feelings back. He called her ugly. She called him ugly. He hit her. She hit him. If not for the passing police, it could've been the end of their sibling line right there.

Steve could not sleep. Where was Buddy? Where was Mommy? Kill everybody! yelled Steve up to the ceiling. His neighbors yelled back.

See, if I can FIND the SOURCE, yelled Steve, to the government headquarters, if I can DO THAT, then it will be solved!

But sir, you already killed the man who killed your brother, said the government bean-counter with his clipboard. He checked several papers and nodded his head to confirm.

But there must be MORE! said Steve. People have been robbed from me!

But sir, you already robbed the people who robbed your people, said the clipboarder.

MORE! said Steve. MORE MORE MORE!

No, said the clipboarder. There are no more. It is all even, Steven.

It is all even, Steven, he said again, just because he liked saying it.

If it were EVEN, yelled Steven, then I would feel SMOOTH AS A BOARD!

But he did not. He felt bumpy and rough as water in wind.

He called his sister but she was still mad at him. She called him back because that was the law.

I miss Buddy, she said. I miss Buddy so much.

Oh shut UP, Steve said.

You shut up, she said, I'm moving.

Where will you move? he said. Huh? Where do you plan on moving? To that stupid crying country where they just cry all the time? Are you as stupid as that? and she hung up.

Steven killed himself, and solved the final dilemma beautifully. After all, it was the perfect action. It collapsed all the actions into one action. His sister was left with nothing to complete. Who do I kill? she cried to her government representative. Huh? The representative gave her a small stipend, which she had to give back once she was feeling better. She tore months from her calendar, months that she would now not even feel. I'm moving, she told her silent mirror.

She applied for the visa even though every day she got mail from the government telling her to beware. You will not be safe there, they said, in big red font on glossy postcards. All will be ruined.

Next door, in the uneven country, everybody mourns all the time. All the buildings are not symmetric. There are crying stations next to gas stations. You fill up your car; you empty your eyes. There are men and women whose only job is to pet down the hair of those who have lost people, and they walk the streets, searching for faces to comfort. You are supposed to talk to strangers. You are supposed to visit grave-yards once a week.

The government writes her back. We would love to have you, they write, but we are full to brimming. We are creating lakes. Please try again soon. As you know, we do not have much land. There is no evenness here.

MORNING

Martyrs

by eric orner

JUST 3 YEARS AGO, ON NOVEMBER 15 2012, SERVANTS OF GOD ACROSS OUR CONTINENT SEIZED HUNDREDS OF BABY MURDERING MILLS SIMULTANEOUSLY. FINALLY, HALLELUIAH, THE STATE SANCTIONED KILLING WAS DONE.

FROM THE CLINICS THESE HEROES FANNED OUT QUICKLY TAKING THE COURTS, SCHOOLS AND SEATS OF LOCAL GOVERNMENT. ON NOV 20TH, THE GODLESS U.S.A. FELL.

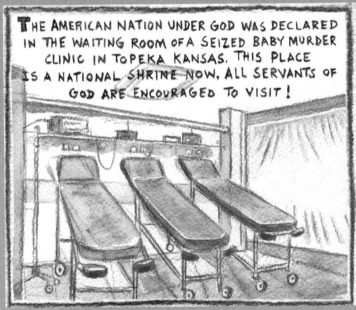

THE AMERICAN NATION UNDER GOD WAS DECLARED IN THE WAITING ROOM OF A SEIZED BABY MURDER CLINIC IN TOPEKA KANSAS. THIS PLACE IS A NATIONAL SHRINE NOW, ALL SERVANTS OF GOD ARE ENCOURAGED TO VISIT!

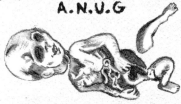

HEROICALLY,
JAEL PHILLIPS RECOGNIZED
THAT WHEN ENDEAVORING TO BUILD
A CULTURE OF LIFE,
IT'S SOMETIMES
NECESSARY TO UTILIZE
THE MACHINERY OF DEATH.

Jewy Jew
by Neal Pollack

Avi Sherman played basketball at the Belmont JCC on Wednesdays. It was the only place in Chicago where the other players gave him respect, because sometimes he could take control of the game. To succeed at Jew Ball (which is what Avi called it, after the other players rejected Hoopin' with the Jews), you had to pass with precision and hit a twelve-foot jumper with regularity, both of which he did. Plus, at the J, Avi could wear his blue and white headband, his oversize goggles, and his T-shirt that read *Mah Nistanah, Baby!* without having to explain anything to the other players.

Another reason Avi dominated Jew Ball: the court was about three-quarters the size of a regulation one. It had been reduced a few years before so the J could expand its kindergarten art room. So Jew Ball fudged the game a little bit. So you could only go out of bounds if you smacked against the padding that lined the walls and you could always get back on defense no matter how lazy your attitude. So what? The results were still the same. You still got to go home with a soaked T-shirt, accelerated heartbeat, and tales of hardwood dominance.

Try playing at Foster Beach, Avi said. See if they let you touch the ball twice in an hour. There, at best, you're Dolph Schayes. In this gym, it's 1937, and you're Inky Lautman of the South Philadelphia Hebrew Association. You're a sure-shot superstar on the shtetl precursor to the NBA's first great team. Avi, who spent too much time reading the Internet, had found a Depression-era quote from the *New York Daily News*: "The reason, I suspect, that basketball appeals to the Hebrew with his Oriental background, is that the game places a premium on an alert, scheming mind, flashy trickiness, artful dodging and general smart aleckness." Damn right. Basketball had once belonged to the Jews.

Avi nailed a free throw, completing a three-point play, guaranteeing a double-digit scoring total for the seventh consecutive week. I look badass in my Jew-fro, he thought. He jogged backward across mid-court to the top of the opposing team's key, and right away had his hands up in that jagoff patent lawyer's face. Don't bring your junior-high bounce pass shit into my house, he said to himself, feinting with his right, slapping away the ball with his left, swooping the ball ahead to some teenager for an easy layup. Ernie Grunfeld to Larry Brown for two.

I love this game, Avi thought. Jew gotta love it too.

Schweet.

Midway through the third quarter, Avi went up for a rebound. Some sweaty Jewbacca named Shostack had decided to come out competitive after the half. As they fought it out two feet below the rim, Shostack's elbows loomed. Avi's left hand shot straight up and met the ball halfway. The ball glanced to a teammate, whose outlet pass had the rest of the players zipping across the room. Avi stayed under the basket, holding his hand still. The second the ball hit, he'd felt a familiar *thwop*. Pain shot up his arm and into his eyes. That index finger wasn't moving. The Jew Ballers were coming back now, charging toward him as one.

"Time out!" he said.

Avi had broken two fingers in three years of Jew Ball. This didn't feel like a break, but it was starting to get puffy and purple. Just a bad throbbing jam, NBA Jam, Avi thought. *Ahhhh! Boom Shacka-Lacka! He's Heating Up! Oh! He's on Fire!* He'd been playing video games all his life.

"I'm done for today, you *machers*," he said in the huddle. "Win it for your fallen comrade."

Avi had a bottle of Vicodin in his bag, useful under any circumstance, but this moment represented the drug's shining hour. As he filled a hand towel at the ice machine, the buzz had already started to set in. His high was pretty much full-bore by the time he headed for the exit. That, combined with the makeshift ice pack, made his finger feel less than sore, almost pleasant. If he stopped off for a Scotch on the way to the El, he wouldn't even remember the ride home.

A man wearing a yarmulke and tallis and tefillin was blocking the exit doors. He kind of looked like Eli Wallach, post–spaghetti western period.

"We've been waiting for you," he said.

"Me?" Avi said.

"Someone like you, anyway," said the man.

"Why?"

"We usually have twelve people in our group," he said. "But three of them didn't show."

"So?" Avi said.

"You can't discuss Talmud without a minyan," said the man.

"Of course not," Avi said. "But my finger hurts."

The man walked past Avi, down the hall.

"Go ahead," Avi said, sort of to himself. "Make my minyan."

The man turned around. He wagged his right hand a little.

"Let us pray," he said. He gave a little chuckle, and Avi was seduced.

"All right," Avi said. "But only for half an hour."

The man clapped his hands together happily.

"Of course!" he said. "Thirty minutes is all we need!"

Avi followed, thinking, now I'm gonna get all Jewy Jew and shit. Maybe I could turn this into something. Plus I'm so high right now. Hilarious.

* * *

Avi made his money as a DJ, specializing in mash-ups, and also as a freelance graphic designer. Sometimes he wrote copy for corporate brochures. But his life's work so far (he was twenty-six) had been the creation and upkeep of *Kike: The Magazine for Today's Modern Jew with Attitude*. The idea for *Kike* first seeded in college because the rabbi at Hillel was a real schmo. Avi'd had enough of that *Tu Tu Tu Tu B'Shvat* song; he'd gotten sick of his boyhood rabbi with the acoustic guitar and temple in the round long before bar mitzvah time, so he wasn't about to spend Friday night celebrating a tree-planting festival in a run-down office building on the far edge of South Campus. Instead, he'd persuaded the guys who lived in Monster Haus, that legendary party pad passed down from generation to generation of the coolest juniors, to throw the first Hebrew Harvest Festival.

There was only one crop to celebrate that Tu B'Shvat. Avi and his band, which he'd decided to call Moil and the Foreskins, made their debut that night, playing mostly covers. They adjusted the lyrics of one Hebrew-school classic to sanctify the sweet smoke that filled the basement:

> It is the tree of life to those that put spark to it
> And all of its consumers are
> (clap clap)
> Happy.

Being a Jew was funny and cool.

For the first couple of years, Avi did *Kike* on QuarkXPress, a couple of pages a quarter, copied and stapled together at Kinko's, and distributed it around campus. He wisely kept his name off the sheet; the rabbi at Hillel wrote an editorial in the campus daily denouncing the lack of seriousness in today's generation of Jews, who didn't appreciate the sacrifices their grandparents had made for them. You've got that right, Avi thought.

Come graduation, Avi didn't have anything much to do, so he decided to take *Kike* glossy. That first issue, he scored interviews with Jonathan Richman and Sarah Silverman, wrote a guide to making gefilte fish at home using illustrations that looked like 1950's clip art, and put together a center spread on "Semitic Pimpin'," which featured pictures of himself as the World's Baddest Jew, getting whipped cream licked off his nipples by a couple of hot black chicks. He scored a distribution deal with Last Gasp, no problem.

Just before issue three appeared, *Kike* got written up by the *Tribune* as part of the "explosion of independent-minded magazines that's happening right here in Chicago, using modern technology and fresh ideas." A denunciation from the ADL of B'nai Brith followed shortly, with the attendant publicity and circulation spike. Salon did a piece on the "New Ethnic Irreverence," which, in addition to *Kike,* included a Chinese-American comedy troupe in New York that put on a show called General Tso's Chicken Choke, and Puta, an all-Mexican girl punk band from Long Beach. "It's about taking old epithets and turning them to our advantage," Avi said in the article. "When someone called my father a kike, it was an insult. If they call me one, it's a compliment."

This, then, was the tenth man for a Wednesday night Talmud study group at the Belmont JCC on Chicago's North Side. Avi walked into the study room with the man who looked like Eli Wallach. There sat eight other men, none of whom were younger than forty-five, all of whom were decked out in full prayer regalia. Why all the duds, Avi thought. Do you really think God cares what you wear?

"S'up?" Avi said. "I'm Reb Tevye."

"He is who you found for us, Eli?" said one of the men. He looked like he hadn't done anything fun since the Kennedy administration. Eli pointed at Avi like a blond would indicate a showcase prize on *The Price Is Right.*

"Can you deny that this young man is a Jew?" he said.

They looked Avi up and down, and shook their heads.

"No," he said. "You cannot." Then, to Avi, he said, "Please have a seat."

Avi looked around the room. It actually appeared to be a synagogue in miniature. He guessed that made sense. This was the *Jewish* Community Center, after all.

"I like your ark," he said. "It looks pretty old."

"Thank you," said Eli. "We rescued it from a warehouse in the Ukraine."

"Awesome!" Avi said.

One of the men said, "Now we can resume the discussion from last time. We were talking about what one can or cannot do during a period of Jewish mourning. It's known to everyone that you can't take a haircut on the Sabbath."

Take a haircut, Avi thought. No one says *take* a haircut!

"Is it also true," said another of the men, "that you're not permitted to take a haircut during a thirty-day mourning period?"

"It is," Eli Wallach said.

"What if the final day of mourning falls on the Sabbath?"

"Then," said Eli, "one must wait an extra day to take a haircut. Possibly two or even three because many barbers are closed on Sundays and Mondays. However..."

Here we go, Avi thought.

"The Talmud makes an exception for bathing. It is acceptable to clean yourself on the Sabbath if you've been mourning for thirty days."

"I have a question," said another of the men.

"Yes," Eli said.

"What if one is mourning a parent? Is the forbidden-haircut period longer then?"

"You may go as long as you want without taking a haircut if you are mourning your parent," Eli said. "When my mother died, I didn't take a haircut for nearly three months. But when people begin to criticize you and tell you that you need to take a haircut, then you must."

Avi found himself sliding down in his chair. This was exactly why Jews needed a kick in the ass. He never got a haircut just because someone told him to. He got a haircut because he wanted to *look good*. And he always looked good.

"What if," said another of the men, "you go traveling on the road or on a ship during your period of mourning, and there is no one to tell you that you need a haircut?"

"Then," Eli said, "you'd better hope your dog recognizes you when you come home."

The men all roared with laughter. Avi didn't get the joke. He looked at his hands, which were feeling all floaty from the Vicodin. Then came another question from the minyan:

"What if a close relative dies in the middle of a haircut?" he said. "May the haircut be completed?"

No way, Avi thought.

"Yes," said Eli. "And, in fact, if a barber learns of a dead relative while he is conducting a haircut, the barber may complete that haircut, because the law does not require one to be subject to humiliation."

"I have a question," Avi said.

The men turned to him, surprised.

"Our superstar of the NBA has something to add," Eli said.

"I do," Avi said. "Are you permitted to shave your pubic hair while you're in mourning? What if you shave Hebrew letters *into* your pubic hair? What if you develop pubic lice? What does the Talmud say about pubic lice?"

"That is an interesting question," said Eli.

"No," Avi said. "It's not."

He stood up, though the Vicodin made this a little difficult. "Everything you talk about makes you sound retarded," he said. "Do you really need ten people to talk about whether or not to *take* a haircut after someone dies? *Of course* you get your hair cut! Who wants to go to a funeral looking like a slob?"

The men all looked a little stunned.

"There's no need to be rude," Eli said.

"Why do you feel the need to insult?" said another man.

"Show some respect," said another.

Avi picked up his gym bag, slung it over his shoulder, and walked out of the room, singing, *If I were a rich man, idle deedle didle didle didle deedle deedle dum...*

* * *

Kike threw its first Jewgy in February 2003. Avi borrowed a loft at 16th and Halsted from one of his clients, in exchange for rather amorphous services. He charged $10 a head, which included a drink ticket and a complimentary copy of the magazine, and divided the party into three separate areas. In "Meat," you got to see a local performance artist who called herself Blaze Starrstein do a striptease while she sang Lotte Lenya songs. There was also a wig-making demonstration early in the evening and later, a "Make Out with Bubbe" booth. For $2, you and a friend got to put on various costume items from the old country, and, as Avi said, "reclaim your identity in private, with a dub soundtrack." The next room, "Milk," was devoted largely to the consumption of alcohol, and also had a dance floor. Since this party, unlike subsequent ones, got advertised through an exclusive online mailing list and flyers, Avi also provided a tray of joints and little smiley-face button pills, served up by a gum-smacking waitress of the old school in a low-cut blouse. The final room, "Trayf," was all about private couches and curtains, though after midnight, a "klezmer lounge" band played a few sets.

The party proved such an incredible success that Avi threw another one two months later. That summer he spent in New York, with a small coalition of like-minded people of means. By the second New York Jewgy, which happened on the Lower East Side, the blogs were already calling *Kike* "over," but Avi knew better, because that's when the reporters from the *Observer*, the *Press*, and the *Sun* showed up. Nothing was ever really over until *Time Out* did a feature. Avi offered up a choice quote to the *Observer*. "We just wanted to show that we've got a different aesthetic from our grandparents' generation," he said. "But we're still proud to be Jewish, so you'd better not f*** with us." A party in Los Angeles loomed. *Kike* didn't make any money, but Avi Sherman was the Boss with the Hot Sauce, the Alan Freed of Cool Jews. His touch was golden, and such a deal!

Avi had left the JCC and was halfway down the block, still humming, *and one more leading nowhere just for show.* From behind him, he heard, "Hey, Jewy Jew!"

He turned. A baseball bat hit his chin. Inside his head, he heard something like glass breaking, but it felt like a million tiny knives were slicing apart his jaw. He fell on his back, instinctively raising his arms to cover his head. The next strike shattered his right forearm. With his left, he somehow managed to flip over onto his stomach; he was suddenly using raw instinct, just like, he somehow managed to think, when your basketball game *really* gets into a groove. But this wasn't basketball, and he felt pain far beyond a broken finger. For no good reason, he'd been thrown into the fifth circle of hell, had gone from being captain of his destiny to a dish of offal on the low end of the human food chain. Life was harsh, and also unfair. A dry choke stopped in the middle of his throat, and blood dribbled into his eyes. He never saw the faces, or even the torsos, of the men (or at least he assumed they were men), who kicked and pounded him. He never knew who, after he blacked out, rolled him into the gutter and spray-painted a yellow star on his forehead. Avi's anonymous torturers took his gym bag and his *Mah Nistanah, Baby!* T-shirt, leaving him there bare-chested, smeared with the sticky-wet leaves of early autumn.

* * *

Avi got a nice room in a nice hospital because he was still covered by his parents' health insurance. For three days he slept a lot but didn't lose consciousness in the coma sense. There'd been one moment in the ambulance when the world reduced to a smear of blurry red light, but then Avi snapped back. An efficient black guy, about Avi's age, was checking the fluid level in Avi's IV.

"Tell me it's all good," Avi had said.

"Excuse me?" said the paramedic.

"I want to hear that it's all good."

"Try not to talk."

Black people are so cool, Avi thought.

He'd had visitors. His mother spent the whole first day with him, skipped the second day because she had to run an event at the Cultural Center, but had been in and out since then. His sister, who lived out in Northbrook, brought his little niece, Shira, in. Everyone laughed when Shira said, "Look mommy! Uncle Avi's a skeleton!" Avi didn't think that was funny.

Laura Brinkman and Alexis Markoff had stopped by separately with pills and herbs, which, combined with what the hospital was already giving Avi, were certain to have trippy effects. They both asked Avi if they could give him a hand job. Alexis had great technique and was real gentle with the balls, so Avi lifted the sheets for her. Laura was hot, but had average skills; he told her he just hurt too much.

Mostly, that was true. Avi had a splendid amount of pain. It felt like little shards of bone were rattling around his chest. Both his shoulders, as far as he knew, had completely disconnected from his torso. He'd never been in a knife fight, but he imagined that if he had, his face would have been about this sore. He was preoccupied with the pain, but pain also has a way of distracting focus. On his third night in the hospital, when he was alone except for a DVD of *I Heart Huckabees*, his brain wandered.

"Someone beat me up because I'm Jewish," he said, or at least he thought he said. "It's kind of freaking me out."

"You will know the one true God," a voice said back to him.

The movie was paused. Avi hadn't heard anyone come in. Enough light was filtering in between the blinds so that he could see he was alone.

"Hello?" he said.

He heard a little squeak, like someone was cracking a window. A little wave of cool air, a directed breeze, really, shot up the length of his body from his toes, so quickly that Avi immediately only felt it in his memory. He heard a great sound, a flapping, a WHOOOOOSH!, and in his mind, he saw a giant bird diving off a mountain. Suddenly, desperately, he wanted to *know*, though about what he had no idea.

Why was he choking back tears? These drugs were good!

The room filled with a great flash. Avi didn't know that white could be so...*white*. Before him stood a column, or a totem pole, or something along those lines, but regardless, it seemed to be larger than the room itself. From the top of the pole, all the way down, giant flaming Hebrew letters loomed—no, screamed!—down at him.

"I am the Aleph and the Daled," the voice said.

"What?" said Avi.

"Avi Sherman," said the voice.

It knows my name, Avi thought.

"The ladder," said the voice, "leads to me."

The next moment Avi knew, the nurse was opening his blinds and the candy striper had brought his breakfast. But it hadn't been a dream. He knew that.

"I saw God," he said.

The nurse examined his drip.

"Maybe we should lower your dose," she said.

Avi slept again. When he woke, his minyan from the JCC was in his room. A couple of them stood by his bed. One guy was reading a magazine by the windowsill. The rest of them were watching the Cubs game.

"I saw God," he said.

"That is not surprising," said Eli Wallach.

Avi hadn't gone into that room by coincidence, or so Eli said. It was planned for him to jam his finger, and to storm out of the study group at a particular moment. This was his trial. The group would guide him, teach him, and help him shrug off the superficial banalities of Jewish identity. They were mystics, kabbalists, ascetics, followers of the true path. Avi could be as well.

"So I, like, have to take it to the next level or something," Avi said.

"Exactly," said the old man. "We foresaw it all along."

"You *knew* I was gonna get the shit kicked out of me?"

"Honestly, we didn't think it would be that night."

"I don't understand."

"It will take some time."

"I love being Jewish," Avi said.

"It doesn't matter whether you love it or not," said Eli Wallach, "because it's who you are."

Avi looked at the minyan. They were a bunch of old dudes, but they were *cool* old dudes. Totally ancient Jews like from an Isaac Bashevis Singer story or something. How rockin' that guys like this were still around. When I heal up, he said to himself, I'm going to their study group again. Unless my team makes the playoffs.

A Conversation Over Tea

by Chris Abani

"REALLY?" HE ASKED. "AFRICANS HAVE A GAY PARROT?"

"No," she replied, muttering "*stupido*" under her breath. "Gray Parrot. Gray. The African gray parrot."

"Oh," he said. "Still, they could be gay for all those colors."

"Gray parrot," she repeated.

"And the Africans too," he said. "Come to think of it, I mean they could be gay because they are so colorful. All those clothes, you know the ones, you've seen them. Even Americans like Stevie Wonder have taken to wearing them, not that I blame him, of course. I mean if I could get away with it I would wear bright oranges and reds and purples, but it's my skin, you know. Too pale for anything but grays and blacks."

"Colorful?" she asked, sounding half distracted as she stirred the cinnamon into the chai brewing on the range. "I would have thought monochromatic, no? I mean they are black so how colorful can they be?"

"You've seen them, come on, you've seen them. Those Tuaregs with their blue robes. Aren't they called the blue people?"

"Tuaregs aren't African."

"Don't be silly."

"They aren't."

"Anyway, I think the Africans are a colorful lot, and not just with clothes, I mean there are those South African whites. I don't know how come they have white Africans. I guess it must have to do with South Africa not getting as much sun."

"Isn't the lack of sun a northern thing?"

"But this is Africa, you know. Everything is different there. They are the opposite of us. Like Bizzaro world."

"So they don't have Superman but weakling woman and she can't fly, so instead she crawls?" she asked, thinking how stupid men were.

"No, she probably bounces. You know on those bootylicious backsides that they have."

"Oh, like the Venus Hottentot?"

"No, I was thinking more of Beyoncé."

"Aren't *you* hip?"

He smiled, picked up a cookie from the plate and took a bite.

"I try. You know me, I'm down with OPP."

"Don't push it, buster," she said. Just like that: "buster."

He shrugged.

"I wonder if the Africans are gay, being so colorful and all. Maybe we shouldn't be worried about them raping all you white women. Maybe that whole thing is just a ruse to direct attention away from their real target…"

"White men?"

"Well, you have to admit it is perfect. No white man is going to report being raped by a black man."

"Is that all men ever do? Think with their dicks about their dicks?"

There was an uncomfortable silence. He ate another cookie. She poured the sweetened milky tea into a pot. Set it on a tray with two cups and the plate of cookies and looked pointedly from him to the screen door. He held it open. Sitting at the table on the patio overlooking the back garden, she poured him a cup, stirring the tea before passing it. He sipped.

"You make good tea," he said.

"Why, thank you," she said.

He smiled, wondering why she became so English every time they had tea. It wouldn't be so bad if she weren't from Brooklyn.

"You could almost be Indian."

"I do have a sari."

"Saris are colorful," he said.

"Beautiful," she said.

They were silent. They drank tea. The sun slowly set.

Bill Thurber,   24 September
Deputy Secretary
Florida Dept. of Corrections
2601 Blairstone Rd.
Tallahassee, FL 32399-2500

Mr. Thurber,

I am writing to you as a concerned citizen, but one with an action
plan. As you know, our prison system is in a wanton state and in
dire need of remediation. It will require a long and wincing state
of strict discipline on all our parts.

Yet I have a plan which could possibly alleviate this stress on the
prison system, and consequently, on all the good citizens of
Florida. Citizens play an active role in the prosecution and
sentencing of criminals via the jury system, but why does our
prudence and participation end there? Why don't we, as people, do
our civic duty when it comes to incarceration? I propose we do just
that.

I suggest that dutiful citizens of our fair state take turns housing
and remediating prisoners from our overburdened system. In
particular, I make a personal offer to house such a deviant from
society; she would get attention and tenderness, yet I am not afraid
to correct, correct, correct. I have had experience in this area as
a sponser for a young refugee. She has since moved on, poor thing,
but her room is now available to do more good. I also volunteer at a
local teen center as well.

You have my word all the prisoner's needs would be met. She would
get ample food, frequent showers, and lots of exercise and
discipline. Certainly hygiene would be an issue. I have studied some
pamphlets on the matter, so these women could expect monthly
checkups and regular exams. Of course you would want some type of
monitoring system, but I am one step ahead of you on that one, too.
As I'm pretty handy with a Sony-cam, I could send in regular tapes
of the prisoner's re-domestication: cleaning, calisthenics and
training in social intercourse. I understand restraint and
confinement will be a concern, but I insist that I have all the gear
to both ensure the prisoner will not be at large, yet still
guarantee her full range of motion.

In Phase II, the vision is much grander. All the punishment and
discipline would end. Phase II leaves the carrot and the stick
behind. Improper behavior and willfulness would be met only with
positive praise and constant rewards. I see atime when the insolent
and fallacious criminal bites her lip in shame as I stroke her
swelling self-image as if she were my own daughter. I'm sure it's
obvious I've had some psychological training, if only informally. I
understand all too well the concept of the inner-child.

I have some gentlemen friends I am in daily contact with on an internet chatroom who I'm sure would volunteer to do their civic duty as well by housing hardened men and even troubled juveniles.

Enclosed is a check for 3 dollars and a request that you send me some studies done on the minimum needs for the incarcerated woman. Also, could you include perhaps a list of mugshots from the candidates for our little program?

I look forward to hearing from you, Mr. Thurber. Until then, as the good book says, "toward the bosom must the slapped hand go."

A fellow concerned citizen,

611 Sunshine Dr.
Tallahassee, FL 32301

The Politics of Desire

Social Contract
by F. S. Yu

"YOU HAVE THE RIGHT TO BEAR ARMS," SHE SAYS, SLIPPING THE ROPES through my fingers, and then around my elbows, pinning them painfully together and cinching them through the window handle above my head. "Just not these arms."

Her skin is the color of pasta. She has large cheeks, a careful mouth. "Harry Truman invented the national security state," she says, my right leg pulled at the ankle by a long cord that finally connects at the base of a radiator. My other leg spread, the rope looped around the refrigerator. My legs spread, my body vulnerable. "'The people have to be afraid,' Truman said. That was the way Harry Truman thought. We have to fear the communists. Franklin Roosevelt was dead. Long live Franklin Roosevelt."

The nipple clamps hurt. The ball gag she has stuffed into my mouth makes it impossible for me to answer her, if there was an answer to be given. She didn't ask me if I wanted this. She's stronger than me, especially since my accident. I never fight her anymore. She does what she wants.

"The Geneva Convention holds that you can't torture prisoners. America is a signatory to the Geneva Convention. Are you a prisoner?" I nod my head. She closes my nose shut with two fingers. I can't breath through the gag she has forced into my mouth. There is a moment of peace. This is it, I think. I am going to die. And then my body starts to flop, the panic coming through me involuntarily, and she's laughing, and she lets go of my nose, and the air rushes into my body in deep, sweeping breaths, and her laughter fills the room with its cruelty.

"We don't care about treaties," she says. "Hitler didn't care about Versailles and they gave him Czechoslovakia, the Rhineland, and Austria. Anschluss. That's what they call it. But Hitler had his problems.

Repressed homosexual." Her hand runs along my stomach and the top of my leg and then down beneath me, her finger touching my anus. "Are you a repressed homosexual? You don't seem to like sex very much. I think you are." I feel her finger slip slightly into my anus and then out. "So he died in a bombed-out bunker in Berlin in 1945, with his new wife. What the hell for?" I watch as she stands and walks to the closet and dips through the door, rummaging through the sound of paper bags. She has such long legs. She's a cyclist. Her long, thin body is knotty with strips of muscles. Then she's in front of me, between my legs, looking gleefully into my eyes, forcing something large into my ass. I scream into the gag, a muffled gasp, a blunt, dulled shriek. Whatever it is goes in and it burns and it stays there, throbbing slowly. The pain begins to subside. But she still has something in her hand and she squeezes it and an electric shock shoots through my bowels, my eyes bulging in my face, my body pouring sweat onto the sheets.

"I was wondering if that would work."

She smiles warmly, happy and content. It's been twelve years now since the first day we met. A couple of waiters in a young restaurant on the edge of the city, working to make ends meet. We didn't know what we had.

"We don't care about treaties," she continues. "In 1954 Eisenhower signed a treaty that provided for free elections in Vietnam in two years' time. But when it came due he changed his mind. He said if Vietnam had free elections, Ho Chi Minh would receive 80 percent of the vote. And that wouldn't be good for America. So much for democracy. Do you feel cheated? Look at the Iranians. The shah served us well for twenty-five years. Then they took hostages." She steps forward, her naked foot on my stomach, she walks over me, and then places her foot on my face. She rubs her foot over my face, back and forth, across my nose. She steps on the clamp on my nipple and I let out another involuntary dull scream. "Cheated by our vows, to have and to hold, to love and to cherish, to protect, till death do us part. Do you think we've parted too early? Did you think things would be different when you pledged your allegiance in school and at the baseball games? That your country would protect you while the bombs fell and U.S.-installed dictators sent death squads into the villages of South and Central America to kill the women and children first? Here is your democracy." Her foot presses hard on my face, and my nose hurts, I think it's going to break. With the heel of her foot she pushes the gag farther toward the back of my throat. Tears spring from my eyes, soaking the fabric around my ears. "You should be able to answer some of my questions. You should.

"I'm not blaming America," she says, sitting heavily on my chest, and then turning around, facing away from me. Her long back, straight and proud, the bulb of spine and her dark hair, which she's taken to wearing short. She's wrapped a chain around my penis and balls and she's slowly making it tighter. "I was born here, same as you. I'm not blaming anybody. It's just that you have the right to remain silent, and maybe the Republicans really did win the election, and maybe they didn't. It's too close to call. Both sides believed in 'three strikes you're out.' Life sentence, no parole. How many strikes do you have?" she asks, turning her head to me briefly and then going back to her task. "There's no welfare here. You'll have to work for what you get."

I've surrendered myself to the continuous pain. I've allowed the pain running through my body to numb my mind. This is my wife. This is what we have. Who would have thought we would have lived in this apartment all this time.

"And then the wars came." Another shock rings through the electric plug in my ass, pain striking through me, her hand in my hair pulling hard, her other along my ribs, buckling forward as if she were riding a horse, her feet sliding back toward my cheeks. And then stopping. She's loosening the chains. Gently wrapping her thumb and forefinger around my penis and balls. "And they flew planes into our buildings and our buildings crumpled and fell to the ground. We have to defend ourselves. They would have done it anyway, whether we deserved it or not. That's the way people are. And the president didn't want to consult Congress anymore. He asked them to dissolve themselves, to remove themselves from the conflict. And of course they did. Self-preservation in the face of terror."

She slides her body back, so her ass is just in front of my nose, the smell of her and her flesh totaling my vision.

"Do you remember Bukharin?" she asks. "It was 1936, and he confessed in a public address to the people. He turned on his fellow Bolsheviks, Kamenev, Trostsky, Zinoviev, all Jews. He wanted to save himself. But Stalin placed him under house arrest anyway. *Koba, why do you need me to die?* he asked in his unanswered letter to Stalin. But who was he to ask for forgiveness? All of the original Bolsheviks subscribed to a doctrine of terror, of starving their own people. It was merely the rooster coming home to roost." Her hand is in my mouth, fishing out the gag, plucking it from between my cheeks. She rubs her fingers inside my lips, massaging my gums. And she's right, I breathe so much easier now. She undoes the rope at my ankles and my knees slide together, my legs bending on their own will. She undoes my hands from the window and releases my elbows but keeps my hands tied together. My hands tied, I curl into a ball, pulling the tear-soaked sheet with me. And she curls behind me, her body circling my body, her knees forcing between my knees, one hand underneath my head and across my chest, the other between my legs, gripping my penis. I can feel her body, her strength, which seems to increase every day even as mine declines. Her body is so firm, intent, and purposeful.

"My darling," she says, a whisper, her voice like the cars on the street, penetrating into the darkness. Thank God for the evenings, when the sun is down. "I'll protect you." Her breath swimming across my ear, searching through my hair. "You don't have to worry. Never worry. Never ever worry again. I am here. I will keep you safe."

Questions of War
by Ellen Rossiter

WE ARE AT WAR. ELEVEN DAYS AGO, THE UNITED STATES GOVERNMENT deployed troops to the Yucatán, just miles from what used to be Mexico but is now contested jungle tenuously controlled by the Cielo Blanco guerrillas, a leftist insurgency group that has vowed to respond to last December's assassination of Fidel Castro with a mass extermination of North American public officials. The Cielo Blanco began its campaign in Honduras, and the *New York Times* has reported at least twelve deaths caused by everything from poisoned water to sabotaged scaffolding in provincial courthouses. Our involvement results from the murder of a senator's teenage son, who was run off the road by another car. There has not yet been a single shot fired or a single bomb exploded.

Because of the insidious, almost abstract nature of the violence in this war, the press is having great difficulty treating it with the formal gravity typically reserved for such circumstances. Newspapers and television programs alike are filled with public opinion polls, most of which take the form of complex ethical dilemmas compressed into questions that demand simple affirmation or negation. "Would you support the United States if it retaliated against the Cielo Blanco with similar terrorist tactics?" "Would the armed protection of our borders send the wrong message?" Perhaps unsurprisingly, results are inconclusive. About 66 percent of adult men seem to support the war, as opposed to only 38 percent of adult women. One cable TV psychologist proposed that the low support among women is proof of the age-old adage that women are the gentler gender, unwilling to endorse violence even when national security is at stake. This is ample indication of how these polls fog the truth, or how respondents fog the pollsters: to suggest that a majority of women oppose the troop deployment is, quite simply, laughable.

My husband, Robert, a bright blond boy who worked as an army engineer before the war, is now off knee-deep in peninsular swampland. Perhaps they will seek my reaction to his absence in a poll. "Do you love your soldier husband?" I cannot answer, because my mouth is stretched wide between my lover's legs.

She rubs my head, says my name hard once, then softer. "Do you love your soldier husband?" she says. She is not being cruel, at least not intentionally. She's merely repeating the poll. Her voice is dreamy.

If I chose to respond to such a question, I could answer only with another question: what do we want with these men? They use their fists. They drive too fast. They mistreat at will and have no talent for sensing their own cruelty. With Robert home, I frequently find myself shaking with wordless rage. With my lover, I can be at rest, and I can begin to understand that rest is not a state of weakness. We eat breakfast together each morning before work, and Sunday morning we buy bagels and wedges of cheese. It's hard to believe we are at war, which I account for by the fact that we are not. They are.

My lover and I watch the news, and we stare with dull disregard at the war's progress. The outcome of the conflict is meaningless; all that is important is its duration, the length of peace it grants us. What kind of war is this, I often ask my lover, that can fail only in its completion?

My lover works in public relations, assisting in the promotion of concerts and festivals. Writing runs in her family. Her mother was a columnist for *Oz*, as well as the author of a published pamphlet titled "From 'My Time of the Month' to the Time of Your Life: Five Ways to Help Jane Dodge Dick." Three years ago, when I was a senior in college, my lover's mother died of cancer. We were just friends then, connected through men. Robert, the boy who became my husband, was friends with her brother Alan. At the funeral, she wore a black jacket and a thin canary-colored scarf, and she stood over her mother's closed coffin with an expression like savage weather. I fixed my attention on the features of her face: her rigid mouth, her thick, proud nose, her unyielding and unblinking eyes. She met my gaze and I was taken at once, so strong was her passion for another woman. That the woman was her mother hardly matters. It was love at first sight. It happens.

At breakfast we sit opposite one another, cross-legged on my lumpy couch. "We can keep some men for our entertainment, if they understand their place," I tell her while I skim the hairs on her arm.

"Their place?" She is on to me at once.

"Away from us, except in cases of biological need."

"No such thing as biological need. Don't you know that yet? Anyway, we'll have facilities for things like that."

"Why don't we just say that men have to be issued a visa to enter our country?"

"Why don't we just say this?" She reaches between her own legs and it is as if she is reaching between mine. The image of her smooth coffee flesh floods me. This is the aspect of a woman that men cannot understand, the benefits of a body that is both subtly familiar and sublimely foreign. I cannot find myself at all in Robert. He prefers instead to push on my clit too hard or force his cock into my mouth as if I do not understand the fundamental principles of fit.

When I first kissed my lover, just three months ago, I felt as if scales had dropped from my eyes. We were at a small birthday party for her brother Alan, and the boys sat in a solemn crescent in the backyard and spoke fearfully about Central America as I cleaned up the cake plates. My lover was leaning into her kitchen counter writing a press release, some blues concert on the bay front, and she asked me if I knew anything about the band. To me that was an invitation. I'm not sure that I can explain exactly why. I bent down toward her with a cake plate still in hand and tipped my head and kissed her.

My lover explains it this way: everyone is attracted to women. Men are and women are. To ensure their own desirability, men acquire status, power, money. Women may acquire these things, but they do not need them: no matter how scarce their worldly resources, women are capable of a wrenching beauty that eludes all men. As my lover asked me the first night of the war, when she came over to keep me company and we got drunk in my queen-size bed, "Who wants to be taken by beings who refuse to understand you?"

I grew up in suburban Atlanta with a mother who said "nigger" but called sexual organs "tinkertoys." I accept my sister as my sister no matter what her tan and call a cunt a cunt. As I have learned from my lover, cunt is not only the grip of inner fist. Cunt is the woman herself, the woman and Nothing Else, the woman who, being Nothing Else, could never be other than cunt.

"If my mother were still alive," my lover says, "she would write an article on the role of cunt in war. She used to talk about Pat Nixon's cunt, and how it could have stopped Vietnam if she'd wanted it to."

As I make waffles for the two of us, my lover imagines the pillow talk in the White House eight weeks ago, in the days before the president responded to the Cielo Blanco threat.

First the executive tones, half-muffled by his pillow: "I'm not sure what to do. I can send in advisors, and maybe a few troops, but starting a war is a massive responsibility."

Then the wife responding: "Can you afford to back down?"

"Would preserving peace through prudence be considered backing down?"

"These are terrorists. You preserve nothing through prudence except their sense of security and boldness."

"You're right, of course. I must force them back. I must display our nation's power. It's settled, then."

"And you must go visit the troops to bolster their morale."

"Yep. 'Prez Dons Fatigues near Front Lines.'" Hip-shifting toward her, lowering his own zipper. "Honey, could you?" The childlike uncertainty with which the First Hand withdraws the First Member. "Aah, ohh. That feels wonderful. Could you use a little bit more tongue across the top? Just sort of skim quickly, like you're speaking Spanish.

Uhhh...Do you think this war really is the right thing to do?"

"Mmm-hmmm."

The inarticulate assent, rendered in a pair of muted syllables, is the most potent politics imaginable, says my lover. Their dicks are in our mouths. We've got them where we want them.

As if to offset the repressed presence of my mother, I had a bright and forward-thinking aunt who used to tell me about life during World War II. The bliss of wartime society, she said, is that there's work for every woman, as well as the freedom to love who you wish, how you wish. There's time for self-examination.

And then in peacetime, she said, the men return, and with them the terrible scrutiny. They take away the jobs, they force the women back into the home. Rosie the Riveter gladly surrenders her gloves, boots, and visor for a cake pan and a sharp order to have dinner on the table by six thirty. Thousands of women comply less willingly. Wives once again begin to lie still and suffer, to despise the weakness of their husbands, and to covet in their hearts the invincible masonry of women's bonds. The masonry metaphor came to me from my aunt. I have since learned it was George Eliot's.

My husband, Robert, who majored in history, told me on our wedding night that women have a finer insight into human nature than men but a relatively poor grasp of ideas and authority. "Do you honestly think a woman could have given Churchill's Iron Curtain speech?" he asked, and took my silence for concession, barking a harsh, triumphant laugh. Later, as we made love in the hotel sauna, he apologized, and took my silence for forgiveness. In remembering that night, I am bothered by one thing. How can I condemn his essentialism when I have used the same argument elsewhere in insisting on the superior spiritual and emotional character of women? The answer: I cannot. Women, you see, are irrational as well.

In bed, my lover and I are reading *Heart of Darkness* to one another. A few pages each night recited twice, first in her clear voice, then in my rougher, cigarette-scarred tones. "'I went on along Fleet Street,'" she says, "'but could not shake off the idea. You understand it was a Continental concern.'" In light of the Cielo Blanco, it is rather morbid material, and it has inspired my lover to ask another of those infernal poll questions: "Can you defend the morality of women who use the horror of war for bedtime entertainment?" Once again, I must answer with a question: Have I murdered if I have schemed to promote conflicts that must end in death? If yes—very well, then, I have murdered. It is in every sense a crime of passion.

On TV they are reading correspondence from the front. The letters are voiced by the sleek brunette anchorwoman, and it is jarring to hear her mouth repeat the platitudes of men. "'Dear Suzy, I love you. I cannot stop thinking about you. I am praying that we will see each other soon. My heart is home with you.'"

Can they possibly mean these things? Do they believe that they mean them? Robert writes the same and yet I know he's one of those men you hear about on public radio, one of those soldiers raping fourteen-year-old Mexican girls with rifle butts. He has always reacted to his own terror with monstrous cruelty.

I pity the Mexican girls. What woman wouldn't? Ideally, we could protect them. But in an imperfect universe, where suffering and pain are everywhere, the best that you can do is to save yourself. To set our world right, we have exported our plague. This is what war is.

The Cremation Ground
by Karan Mahajan

THE INDIANOIL PETROL STATION IS BLUE, RED. THE LAST CUSTOMER WAS a young woman in a sari. She leaned out of her Ambassador car and gave Pratap a tip. He smelled her perfume, warmed the vehicle with eleven liters of premium-brand unleaded. Perfume mingled with petrol is the only smell that can make him laugh—and he did, the car throbbing away on the horizon's punch line.

The same cars always: Esteems, Zens, Ambassadors, Fiats on their creaky axles.

Now, Pratap watches as his reflection ripples on a succession of tinted windows by the storefront. His scraggly white beard is dyed with henna, his kurta is Islamic-green, and another car is peeling off the tangent of the road, swerving toward the station. It's a Maruti Gemini. Pratap notes this in his diary, scrawling deliberately. The sun is rubbing its greasy palms on the heads of the two red pumps, each one rising out of concrete like a plastic gravestone.

He takes position by pump number one and waits for the car to stop. He's used to waiting, likes to think of it as a petroleum-addled game: can he accurately predict what type of oil will be purchased? Can he preempt the driver's command with a firm swoosh of the hose? Will there be applause? No, he can obsess over his tiny flourishes as much as he did when he was a stage magician twenty-one years ago, but the only ovation he ever hears is the inertial revving of a car before it speeds away. Part of the reason for the drivers' indifference, Pratap surmises, is that he's given up on patter—the magician's call-and-response—completely. He rarely feels the urge to speak. Instead, he fills his diary with dramatic descriptions of the most mundane events (*Today is my fifty-first birthday: a cow ambled into the station. We had to ask a man driving a Fiat. Help us, we said. He applied his horn several times. To no avail. Whatsoever.*)—a cheap substitute for the grand verbiage of his stage routine.

The Maruti Gemini cuts a firm arc across the tarmac, halting inches from Pratap. He tucks his diary under his armpit and steps back. From the condition of the car—which is blue and battered like an overcast sky—the wheezing exhaust, the choice of bronze hubcaps, the dirt-obscured license plate, he guesses that this is a rolling midlife crisis.

Or: five hundred rupees of Vikas-brand Unleaded.

It is a wonder, truly. He knows everything even before the window rolls down, he can release the hose from its aluminum clasp and key it right in if he so wishes. Yet, he won't be confident till he sees the driver's face. These are the perils of being out of practice. One loses the nimbleness that marries instinct to action and forces the audience's hand. If he were younger he would trust the cars, their oracular metallic bodies, the evidence they carry about Aurangapur, its people, associated fashions, hairstyles, radio tastes—the city of Aurangapur that used to be his home before he escaped in the orange blush of communal riots twenty years ago. But he cannot trust the cars because they tell him almost nothing about himself, and how can they? He hasn't left the station's neighborhood for ages. He's exiled himself from the city. He feels safer here. The sun sparkles overhead. The reflection on the tinted window of the Gemini says: *With your beard and kurta, you look more Muslim than Hindu.*

He couldn't always pass for a Muslim. When Mr. Virmani, the station's owner, hired Pratap three days after the riots subsided, Pratap had still looked as Hindu as the day of his mundan. Seeing him huddled and shivering next to a pump overlooking the ruined city, Mr. Virmani said, "You look troubled," and Pratap, having just lost his entire family, his fiancé, and his job as a stage magician, said, "I am troubled. I suppose." That was how their friendship began. Mr. Virmani, a young man at the time (his hair slick from inheritance) said, "You can live here in the storeroom in the back and you won't have to pay the rent as long as you work the pumps." It was difficult to get people to work with flammables in those days, but Pratap had agreed, and stayed.

The Maruti Gemini's engine hasn't died; its tinted windows aren't sliding down. Are the people inside going to develop pre-pumping paranoia, drive away? Are they overturning mounds of shabby uphol-stery in search of a single wallet? Pratap waits a few seconds and then knocks on the reflection of his fist on the driver's window. He wants to see a human form stir inside the car—any longer and he'll have to lust it into existence through a play of light: the tiny blue Viagra pill he swallowed twenty minutes ago is taking effect. This is his one and only indulgence.

He likes the feeling of blood rushing to the greatest point of contention in his life.

And still he's not prepared when it happens, the whole event taking only a few seconds—the Gemini's back door clicking open, the sudden whoosh of a body pulsing past metal. He hears it, turns too slowly, and before he can react, there is a hand at his kurta collar. The glint of a young man's stubble blinds him—he shouts but the petrol station is empty. His heels dig into the tarmac, clothes stretching to tearing, head jerking. He lets out a low shout as he is grabbed by the neck and shoved against the damp upholstery of the back seat. A hand clamps his mouth.

A voice says, "Fuck yaar, fuck. We *should* have got the petrol first." A woman screams from the front seat—too much noise for too little space. He passes out, the sound etched in his ears like fresh skid marks.

Minutes pass. He wakes in mild shock as the car enters Aurangapur. He opens his eyes and sees that there are three people in the car. The young man seated next to him is puffing a cigarette. Between the par-allel blurs of the city showing in the car window, Pratap is a flash of lucidity. He notices the shawl over the boy's shoulder, the way he con-stantly pushes his digital wristwatch up his thin arm. He must be full of complexes, Pratap thinks; he can always feel time slipping.

The young man—seated behind the driver—suddenly turns to face him, grinning. "Hi," he says, fiddling with his watch before extending his hand. "I'm Ravi," and then bursts into laughter. Pratap lies back, the light reflecting off the knife by Ravi's feet.

Ravi asks in a careful, nervous drawl: "Do you speak English?"

The city is abrupt and packed with life. The cars are an unflattering soundtrack. The buildings are hideously modern, Soviet-era skyscrapers coated with dust and flanked by colorful hoardings advertising Hindi movies. The islands harbor wild shrubs. Pratap pulses in and out of shock.

"No, it doesn't look like it, yaar," Ravi informs the driver.

The girl in the front turns in her seat—wrapping her arm around the leather headrest—and peers at Pratap. She is ugly in a conventional way—a stub nose, disproportionate eyes—and it is obvious that she has been crying. She leans toward the driver, saying, "Varun, he's so old." Her voice is soothing like a slab of cold marble and Pratap thinks, *maybe she likes older men,* but then clenches his diary tight in his right hand, covering it with the folds of his kurta.

Varun growls, "He *is* a fucking mullah, right? Look at him: he's *got to be* a fucking mullah." He repeats it in Hindi, "Are you a Muslim?" but receives no response.

Ravi says, "The beard, yes, maybe. What does the beard mean?"

Varun turns around and says, "Take his fucking pants off, yaar. He'll be circumcised if he's a mullah."

"Fuck man, why don't you do it?" Ravi responds.

"Because I'm driving. You can't undress men and drive at the same time…unless you want to, like, crash naked at my apaaaart-ment," says Varun, breaking into song. The girl laughs timidly.

"Okay, old man," says Ravi. He flicks the cigarette butt away. Pratap closes his eyes because he is now trembling with fear; his penis has not seen anyone in years. The cigarette smoke creeps beneath his eyelids and he blinks furiously to stay conscious. Ravi lifts the loose cloth of Pratap's kurta, his hands trembling toward the pajama's draw-strings. He starts back in shock.

"Shit man," he says, his voice low. "He's got a boner."

The boner changes everything, as it should. Everyone looks away from the tent of Pratap's pajamas. The men in the car are sullen.

Ravi blurts, "Listen, man. Are you sure you want to do this? I think he's frightened enough. And where are we going?"

The girl asks, "Yes. Where are we going?" Ravi is sitting diagonally across from the girl, and stares into the light pooling on her cheek.

Varun adjusts the collar of his red shirt but doesn't speak. From the crack between the seats in front, Pratap sees his ringed fingers grip the steering wheel. The city of Aurangapur shoots out like a flame from the hood, and the speedometer needle on the teak-finished dash-board trembles. The old landmarks riot into Pratap's mind; they seem smaller than he remembers. The car slides past the Kailash district where he used to perform onstage. The brick buildings are the same but the hoardings are not. The Paramount Theater—a stupa-like structure with a pink façade—now shows movies.

Varun doesn't speak. The girl pulls her blue skirt over her knees and turns toward the driver. She says slowly, "Do you love me, Varun?"

Pratap wants to say, *ask me, ask me, because yes, yes, yes, yes, I want to love you, I was once loved, I was once the most famous magician in India. Maybe.*

Only, it's not the magic he remembers, but a faceless woman's naked thigh pressed against his crotch backstage after a long night of lying, her breathy whispers of "Show me your wand" tickling him into panic, into rage, the climax of condescension that follows the utter-ance of cliché: *My penis is not white at the ends,* he wanted to say; *and please! No more jokes about close-up magic!* But he was too weak to protest and he learned to make love despite his apprehensions. He was too young to know better. But he doesn't remember protesting against Zaib, his fiancée. No, she was the only one he didn't regret.

Varun says, "Yes, of course I love you." The car speeds up with every word. "You don't understand. Just trust me. I've always trusted you, Afsheen. I'm doing this for you, you know that."

Afsheen, a Muslim name.

"You're cruel," she says, placing her palm on Varun's thigh.

"Don't," he says. "He's got an erection. Two erections in one car is a bad thing."

The car stops at a red light. Pratap notices that the Paramount—which used to be the site of his act—is advertising a movie called *Raat ka jaadu: An Erotic Tale of Longing.* Young men in dhotis are streaming out of the hall. He clears his throat.

He says, "Shit."

Ravi turns to him in surprise.

"What did he say?" he asks.

"Is that a Muslim word, Afsheen?" says Varun, stroking his stubble.

"No. Didn't he say 'shit'?" Afsheen says.

Pratap doesn't answer. He looks ahead. He is back in the riots, the eager bodies of men and women scattered about him, the squat apartments curiously serene as they open into blazing streets. Where are they going? he wonders.

It is the first time he has thought of the future in years.

The diary is discovered. The diary is read.

Ravi flips through it and says, "This is some weird nonsense or what, yaar? He writes well for a mute."

He reads, "'I had a dream yesterday in which Zaib and I were at the cinema. The screen was black and white, as if backlit by dawn. It was Mother and Father on-screen. Chatting...'"

Varun says, "What the...?"

Afsheen has calmed a little, and she hushes him, "Let him read, okay?"

Ravi continues, "'I think it was Mother and Father on the cinema screen. Maybe it wasn't. I am beginning to forget their bodies. It is comforting.'

"'The screen paused. Mother and Father just held each other there. We sat awkwardly. Zaib and I held each other. We still had time for the movie to end. We were not leaving. Then, a cell phone rang, and the audience, all couples, continued watching. The screen flickered and the cell phone rang again. The characters on-screen did nothing. The hall was vibrating with the same beep now, every chair creaking in one frequency. Everyone reached for their phones.'"

Varun's mouth twists in the rearview mirror and the girl says, "That's sweet." She flashes a private, ugly smile at Pratap. Pratap feels violated; the patter has been read.

"Yes. But what does it mean?" asks Ravi.

"That he can speak English. The fucker can speak English. You can speak English, you sister-fucker. Do you even know that?" answers Varun.

Ravi raises his hand to Pratap's face, suddenly energized. "Don't play with us, all right? You goddam...mullah." He slaps him across his sagging cheeks and holds his hand there, letting it sink into skin. Pratap's face burns and he wants to say, "I am not a Muslim," but whimpers instead.

Pratap expects the questions to come fast now. But they don't. The kidnappers do not know what to ask of an old, bearded, turned-on man.

Varun tries. "You're a sick old man, do you know that?" and "Are you afraid?" coupled with "Do you prefer light rock or alternative bhangra?" and "Fan or A/C?"

Then they are all the same mood, four people pressed against one-way windows, eased into thoughtlessness because the world slips by without effort. The car cruises on the road, a series of taut silences.

Sliding his hand off the steering wheel, calmed as the car enters a quiet, decrepit area, Varun says, "Ask us something."

In the dying afternoon light, the world has soft edges. Varun gets out of the car and Ravi clenches his fists, shifting a little toward Pratap. This is a narrow alley with brick-faced buildings pressed close together. Varun heads to a short gray wall that borders the road and stands there for a minute, silent, his back turned toward the car. Then he unzips his fly and pisses.

In the car, Ravi unclenches his fist and reclines. He says, "Afsheen, you okay?"

Afsheen turns on the radio. The static resolves into music. Ravi jerks in his seat, "I love that song!"

Afsheen turns around in her seat and her gaze is soft, loving. "Yes, I remember singing it in the school bus every day in class nine, I think. My parents didn't let me listen to it at first."

Then she turns to Pratap, suddenly, and says, "Did you always work at a petrol pump? What did you do when you were young?"

He realizes that this is her charm: the way each word she speaks seems carefully chosen and slowly articulated, as if the sentence itself is a series of questions, so that to not give an answer would be to ignore not one, but many, pleas.

He says, "I was a magician."

Afsheen pauses for a second, as if unable to believe that Pratap has finally spoken. She says, "You were a magician?"

"Yes."

Her eyes light up. "Can you tell us how some tricks are done?"

Pratap says, "Maybe." The blood rushes to his penis.

"How do you make an elephant disappear?" Ravi asks.

"That's easy," says Afsheen. "It's just mirrors, isn't it?"

"Okay, but how do you saw a woman in half?" asks Ravi.

The question is so poignant and perfect that Pratap almost cries. Sawing a woman in half is easy. Two compliant women settle in one divided box, each one contorted fantastically in her hidden compartment. You see one woman's head and the other woman's feet. You see pretty heads and pretty feet and you think they belong to the same pretty woman. Then the magician takes the saw and places it above the marking, the slot that divides all that is already divided, the woman's head screaming on cue, softly at first, a moan, then a scream, the hall dizzied by animal rhetoric—sex, only with the bodies separating. Sex undone—faked.

Pratap knows. Pratap was a savage lover. Like Varun, maybe. He was confident enough to take the stage under the influence, even. And why not? He had the best act of his time. Unlike his contemporaries' cheap sliding-knife mechanism, his buzzing electric saw actually ripped through the wood, spewing the fake coffin's shaved guts onto the stage. They needed a new box for every show, Monday, Wednesday, and Friday. The used boxes were tossed backstage and removed once a month. *"The Ratnam Act: India's Greatest Magician saws Muslim woman in half—An act of communal healing and heartache,"* that's what the posters said. In a tense political situation, that was controversy. That was romance. To saw one's lover in half and to tell everyone, *only I have the power to put her back together.* To tell everyone: that is why Zaib of the dew-dripping eyes is mine. Because I will let her be *the* head of this act, I will unmake her in this public ritual of faith.

And that night, before the riots began, standing on the stage in his designer robes, the saw bearing down on wood, he was sure of everything, he knew that this was adulation, that the woman beneath him in the box was his lover, their trust beyond testing. His patter was perfect: "Watch the box, how it holds her body. This is the same coffin that was used originally by the Mughals, a design from that era of monarchs." *Pause.* "Look at her face, on the brink of this decisive moment. The body is only waiting for separation, for proof that it can exist without organs but not without the soul. Watch the coffin because I will now prove it to you." He did. Her screams were violent, a thrashing he thought he recognized. He cut through with a vicious velocity.

When Zaib's screams stopped, and the head jerked on its neck and the legs continued to thrash, that was when the audience hushed and

Pratap broke down on the stage, puking air. It was a packed hall one minute and a constellation of empty chairs the next. He had cut into her compartment. Someone had sabotaged the markings. He had sawed through her abdomen, missed the divider—killed her. There were people milling onstage, blood clotting on the pitch-black floor, a red cross rippling in the backdrop and a pair of live legs (the other contortionist's screeching live legs!) being wheeled off to a corner of the stage in their half-sawed coffin. The legs twitched as if they were dancing a smothered tango, and he had never seen so much sadness in legs, those slender branches that one pulls tenderly in bed and tickles to the top. Legs! Legs! Legs! Let us have more of them! In the riots it was only the legs that mattered, the legs that carried you to the corner of the stage where you broke down and cried. And you—your love died contorted! And for this, the woman who is all legs twitches in her box! For you!

Pratap shakes. Sometimes, the day dulled by the whirr of traffic, he wonders if Zaib was buried. Or was everyone cremated?

He knows he will never find the person who sabotaged his props and shifted the marking; he knows there is no graveyard for the riot victims.

The riots began because he had killed her, because he was Hindu and she was Muslim.

It has been ten minutes.

Ravi asks again, "How do you saw a woman in half?" and soon it is a chorus, Varun, Afsheen, and Ravi all asking, over and over again.

"With a saw," says Pratap. He has never told anyone how an illusion works. He will not now.

"How?" shouts Varun.

"With a saw."

"Are you sure?" he says, hissing into the dashboard, the car swinging in the dusk like a lantern.

"No."

The car slams to a stop. Ravi pulls his wristwatch up his arm, where it bites into flesh. "We're here," says Varun and opens the door into the wide expanse of an empty parking lot.

They take Pratap out of the car and smash his face with a hockey stick.

Holding the old man from behind, Ravi feels the impact break against his chest like a low tide. Even secondhand, it is too much: he leans over and tries to vomit. He staggers to the car and holds a trembling Afsheen by the shoulders.

Varun slaps Pratap across the face, blood oozing between his fingers. He turns and shouts, "I love you, Afsheen, do you see? Do you believe me now? Goddam Muslim. Faggot mullah."

Pratap screams and drops onto the concrete. "I'm not, no—please," he whimpers. His eyes search for a car to attach themselves to—something familiar in this parking lot, but there is only the crooked chain-link fence and the continuous blue spasm of sky. He feels his face resolve into a network of aching veins, each one draining the other of life. The riots have hunted him down. And is this how it happens? He imagined it would be a deadly warmth—the blood boiling before it erupts from you—but no, it is freezing.

It is freezing like the cold he had when the riots began. He remembers his mother holding his head in a cradle of steam as a child, his sinuses throbbing to dryness.

A fist of hot air against the cartilage of his nose.

"Varun, *that's enough, man*. Let's go."

"Goddam mullahs, think they can get erections for our women. Does this kill your boner?"

He remembers the people collapsing on a city-size strip of Kleenex.

"Varun, don't kill him. Fuck, man."

He is pushed against the fence. Varun's large hands on his beard. He tries to shield himself, he begs, "No, I'm not," don't let me die here, don't let me die, because then I will be the tragedy I created—watch: the world is imploding and I am running to the one place that refuses to burn, the petrol station, because that is safety, it is the edge of the town. It is night and the station is dormant now because all the fuel has been stolen. The city is rolling up into fire like a carpet of gasoline. Everything but this source is on fire and I am huddling against this pump, this long arm smashing into me, and I am never asking for my family again, only life, only life.

Varun breaks Pratap's ribs. They leave him to die.

Pratap lies by the side of the road and the diary lands by his head with a thud as the car revs away.

He lies there dying, a big puddle of blood seeping under him. He is the center of a dilating, bloodshot eye. He thinks of love.

He tries to remember Zaib, her long eyelashes, her chronic arguments, the moments backstage. He hears screams. Are they Zaib's or Afsheen's?

The erection is gone. His periscope into the past is gone. It is like the years of his life between Zaib and Viagra—those were the worst. To forget a face, and then to lose the abstraction of lust that held you to that face, that was the worst. The face would come back sometimes, but mostly it was a feeling attached to a voice, the features of a lover one remembered from another's compliments, not intimacies.

And what was one face in a riot? Blood gurgles in his throat.

He remembers Zaib saying, "I think you bore your audience sometimes. You're too much like a preacher when you get onto the stage." He remembers her turning on her side, her beautiful face chiseled by shadows. Just shadows. Her saying, "I love you because you're quiet now. You aren't telling me what to expect. I don't know what to expect. Why should I?"

And she was right—he had always been more interested in the patter than the trick, in the speaking, in the writing, both acts a deliberate movement, the buildup of momentum imploding in the freeze-frame of the flourish.

"Do you ever worry about what our children will think when they see Papa sawing through Mama's coffin?"

"No. Because I won't let them watch," he had said, laughing.

He has been lying there for five minutes when a car pulls up.

A man lifts him into the car. It is Ravi. Ravi of the shawl. Ravi of the long fingers. Ravi says, "Oh my god. Oh my god. Don't be dead. Don't be dead."

He hauls him on his shoulder, and when they are near the car, he adds, in a steady voice, "We're almost out of petrol, so we were heading back there anyway." He makes sure Varun can hear him.

There is nothing to report. The diary is gone, but it is only one of many; it is only the parts that happened this year; it is only short-term memory. He does not begin a new day without reading the events of the last one, without seeking comfort in the near past. But he will have to now.

He breathes softly in Ravi's lap, the sensation of other lives spreading around him like a steady swirl of traffic, the sudden jerks of the car mapping out the position of each body in each car in each lane, the whole organism now a collection of ball bearings sliding off the other, the space between each life created only to be filled, only to be gripped by the grooves of a tire and emptied again.

Being below window-level in the car reminds Pratap of being backstage. The magician listens while the audience moves, while their distant bodies perform. Then the magician chooses which coffin will be rolled onto the stage for the grand trick. The audience hushes.

"You missed the turn for the hospital," grunts Ravi, holding Pratap's head as it twitches in his lap.

"Yes. I know," says Varun slowly. Afsheen sobs and Varun lowers his head into the steering wheel. There is a scratching sound as his chin meets the plastic. He says, "I need to shave," and bites his lip.

Pratap is thinking: Why are these people saving me? Will I have to work tomorrow?

Varun pulls up at the empty lot by the petrol station. Aurangapur recedes in the distance.

Varun says, "Afsheen, don't cry, please don't cry. He's fine, can't you see, he's fine? We'll make Ravi get off with him. Ravi will make it alright. And if Ravi's with him when the ambulance comes, they won't buy the old man's story. Why would the attacker lead his victim into an ambulance? Yes, it'll be better if one of us is with him."

She is shivering and he places his arm around her. "Look, the hospital wouldn't have worked. We couldn't have made it on the petrol we had." His voice is frantic with excuses as she cries. "Afsheen, we'd have stopped on the road. He'd have died. He'll be fine. He's breathing. He's alive. He's breathing, just like you are. Slow your breathing." She says, sniffling, "Yes, Ravi will make it alright." Ravi watches her along the diagonal of his vision and Pratap notices his lips trembling. Then she breathes deeply, places her hand on the gearshift and leans into Varun. She kisses him on the ear. Ravi holds Pratap's aching head down. In the darkness, the indistinct landscape of Afsheen's homely face seems perfect and welcoming to them both.

Pratap cannot flex the fingers of his right hand, his chest is badly bruised, but he has now regained consciousness. Ravi settles him in front of the shop behind the pumps and calls from his cell phone. Varun and Afsheen have left. Pratap can feel the twenty-one lost years nipping at every inch of his body. He looks at Ravi for an explanation.

Ravi splashes water on Pratap's beard from a bottle of water and stares out at the highway. He says, "It's actually Afsheen's fault. Afsheen's weird at times. She never believes that Varun loves her, so he has to keep proving it to her. How can I possibly explain something this bizarre to you? He wanted to beat up a Muslim to show her that he didn't love her because she was a Muslim, but despite the fact that she's a Muslim. Do you see?"

Ravi's breath is a hot flash as he hurries through his words.

"I don't understand," Pratap says.

"Varun's father is a Hindu swami. Swamiji Vivek. Varun doesn't like his father."

"Haven't heard of him," says Pratap, slowly. His teeth are jagged and broken.

Ravi shrugs his shoulder, trying to be nonchalant. "God, I'm sorry. I didn't want to be mixed up with this. I never thought this would happen. I'm just their friend."

"I'm sorry I'm not a Muslim."

"You're not?"

"No."

"Oh." He reaches into his pocket. "I won't tell Varun that."

He offers Pratap a cigarette, saying, "You like Four Square?" Pratap nods, places it between his lips, and waits for it to be lit. His bruises ignite into pain.

A Honda Accord draws into the petrol station. It stops by the pump, finds no attendant and drives away. Pratap hates the Honda Accord. His cigarette is lit.

Suddenly, he wants to burn this place down. He wants to ask for another cigarette, smoke it down to size and then toss it against the pump, the base where the plastic is most vulnerable, most susceptible to the temptation of sparks. He wants to watch the station explode into a cuboid of fire. He wants the cars to press against the heat and swerve away into the city, all of them watching from a distance, watching this giant cremation ground, unconcerned.

Ravi says, "Hold on. Don't fall asleep. The ambulance is almost here." Pratap is dozing off.

Ravi says, "Tell me something about your life. Talk to me. About working here. About being a magician. About anything."

Pratap thinks now of the car, the way the bodies in it will raise smoothly, like airbags against unbroken glass, Varun and Afsheen making love in a closed space.

He thinks of Zaib.

"That sawing trick—you have two women in there. Each curled up. You cut through the middle."

Ravi says, "It's that easy?"

"It's as easy as burning down a petrol station."

"Only everyone knows how to do that."

Yes, he thinks. That's the problem. Everyone knows how to do that. There is no magic in death.

Then he looks at Ravi's face and remembers being young. His chest throbs. He's delirious. He thinks: our bodies will soon be gone. What is the point of the body? I've never understood it. No one does. No one even notices the splinters flying as the saw buzzes through the wood of the container, no one ever asks—why are you putting the body back together, but leaving this fake container splintered and discarded? Why?

He shifts on his shoulder. He remembers turning away from the scene of Zaib's death and walking through the curtains. He remembers stopping. There was no explosion of applause here. Only silence. He bowed his head down. He looked.

Backstage was like a pillaged graveyard, so many used coffins lying broken and empty.

Machu Picchu

by Sandra Cisneros

UNDER THE SKY AND ON THE EARTH LIVED A WOMAN AND A MAN. THE woman's name was Nada, which meant *hope* in her language and in his language meant *nothing*. Literally. It was hard for the man to get used to calling her "Nothing! Nothing!" At first he'd wanted to laugh, and he did, often and without guilt since they did not speak the same language.

The man did not know what his name translated to in her language, Serbo-Croatian. His name was Serafín Jaramillo. Serafín Gustavo Jaramillo Beltrán to be exact. Only now he simply went by Serafín Jaramillo because Serafín Jaramillo Gustavo Beltrán was too long a name to sign on paintings.

Serafín Jaramillo. It was a name good enough for Nada Maloviç of Zagreb, *city NW Yugoslavia of Croatia pop. 565,000,* a city Serafín had only recently positioned in his mind with the help of a Rand McNally atlas in the Austin Public Library, because this Serafín Jaramillo intended to take this Nada Maloviç as his lawful wife.

Serafín had discovered, finally, the formula for a happy relationship—*Make sure you don't speak the same language, man,* he had scribbled on a postcard to his cousin Mando in Mexico City.

Poor Serafín! He did not know what went on in the head of his future bride, Nada Maloviç, girl from Zagreb. He could only guess. But how was that any different than the women who spoke the same language as he. As far as he was concerned, his spouse-to-be might as well be mute. They made themselves understood mainly by laughing, because laughing, after all, is universal. Laughing and sex.

This Nada, with skin as white as a Bernini and a face like a Botticelli, was the type of woman who laughed when she was nervous. As a consequence she laughed often. Even if the situation was inappropriate.

As for sex, she was Catholic, yes, but she was not Mexican

Catholic, which is not the same, you know. Mexican Catholic girls did not allow sex until after the marriage vows. Or if they did, they went so far as to permit everything but sex in the one place where sex counted for a man. Anything but *that* until after the priest's blessing. That is how Mexican Catholic girls are. Due to Mexican men.

Poor Nada! If she could, she would've liked nothing better than to explain herself to Serafín in tedious detail. How a course in Latin American archaeology at the university in Zagreb had introduced her to her husband's face via Tlaloc the rain god. How a certain art professor had planted the seed of a love affair with Texas by way of Janis Joplin. Unfortunately, this was not the only seed planted. One abortion too late, she abandoned said art professor and accepted a position in Stillwater, Oklahoma, as au pair to a professor of Slavic languages, eventually hitching a ride south to Austin and her destiny with the windshield wipers slapping time because freedom is just another word for nothing left to lose.

Serafín Jaramillo was the weekend janitor for Club Mambo, a salsa club on South Congress, and the weekday dishwasher at the Dos Hermanos, a restaurant owned by two liberal brothers from Berkeley who believed in human rights for the oppressed in Latin America, but did not believe in the same for their Latino employees. As a result, Serafín Jaramillo was paid minimum wage and worked maximum hours. Since he did not have his green card, he knew better than to complain.

However, Serafín was neither dishwasher nor janitor! He was an artist from Mexico City who spoke a straight Spanish and a crooked English. He had come to the United States not wading across the Rio Bravo, but riding the current of an art scholarship from the Instituto de Bellas Artes. The Mexican oil boom and a *politico* who owed Serafín's father a favor had intervened on Serafín's behalf. Thus, it had been possible for Serafín to complete his bachelor of arts at the famed Art Institute of Chicago.

Serafín Jaramillo planned to continue his studies in Los Angeles, but Mexico's destiny was inextricably bound with his. First the Mexican oil bust of '82 made the chance of another scholarship slippery, and finally the '85 earthquake sealed his financial fate and legal status.

Before the quake the Jaramillo home had been a four-room apartment in a hastily constructed high-rise built with government funds. The contractors had cut corners on the materials, and the building had collapsed like the Mexican economy. Serafín's family had survived only because they had been visiting relatives in Jalisco that week. Their past buried behind them, they moved to a one-story in Guadalajara and began their life anew.

The world and Mexico continued. The *politico* who had pulled strings for the art scholarship was now dead. There was, besides, a new president in office, the old one gone with the treasury in his pockets. There was no going back for either Mexico or Serafín Jaramillo. Forward, forward!—Serafín Jarmillo charged like a Quixote on the Rocinante of his dreams. Thus spurred, he had gotten as far as Austin and the janitor/dishwasher jobs. Until enough money could be saved for the trek west and enrollment into CalArts, Serafín Jaramillo was reduced to the status of illegal alien.

The proprietors of the Club Mambo on South Congress took a liking to Serafín Jaramillo, perhaps because they too had been poor, and remembered what it was to be desperate. When they discovered Serafín was sleeping in the University of Texas library and washing his socks in the men's room sink, they donated a dirty futon with a menstruation stain shaped like the outline of Texas and gave him use of an upstairs storage space, which he converted to atelier/apartment despite the building code violation. Why not? It had all the charm of a French garret. Dust, exposed brick, thirteen-foot ceilings, and tall windows that offered a postcard view of the capitol building, provided one straddled the ledge and leaned out a little. It even had history— Janis Joplin had slept there. But that was a claim every Austinite made about the building they lived in.

Despite its romantic advantages, the atelier/apartment had neither shower nor air conditioner. However, this did not dampen Serafín's spirit. Until the mean season began. Three times a day he took a sponge bath in the Club Mambo's bathroom downstairs, or, if he was in love, more often.

It was not an easy life. Nor had it ever been. Serafín Jaramillo did not have to pretend to be a starving artist. He had inherited nothing from his mother's family of garbanzo farmers except a legacy of arrogance, which, as a painter, suited him very well. He liked the idea of living la vie bohème, imagined himself a cross between Diego Rivera and Pablo Picasso, painter in exile, and this role pleased him. While wrestling with Nada on the dirty futon, he liked to shout at the moment of ecstasy, "I am monster, monster!" and growl. It was lucky Nada had no words to confess he made love not like the minotaur he aspired to be, but more like a barnyard animal. Perhaps a duck.

On the other hand, there was something of the ferret or the weasel in the way Nada Maloviç loved. It was dark and amphibious and had sharp teeth. It frightened Serafín Jaramillo a little, but in a way that was a pleasant frightening, like when one has been drinking for a while and suddenly stands up and discovers one's feet have grown fat.

But I haven't told how this Serafín met his Nada, which is worth telling. Nada of the Tina Modotti body and Modigliani face worked at a women's lingerie shop on the drag, directly across from the university. Maybe you know it? HEROTICA, Unusual Lingerie, Silks & Cottons, Corsets-Garter Belts, Fishnets & Seamed Hose, Love Oil & Candy Pants, Baby Dolls & Teddys, Bikini Pieces Sold Separately, Free Parking in Rear. Nada was assigned the Sinful Pleasures counter, where her exotic accent and fleshy lower lip could be exploited to their best advantage. She was busy unpacking the Kama Sutra Oil of Love and Honey Dust display when Serafín walked in intent on buying a pair of edible underwear for an angry girlfriend.

"Can I be helpful for you?" Nada bubbled.

Serafín was so taken aback by both the question and the questioner, he forgot what he had come in to buy.

"Yes," Serafín said, only he pronounced it with a "j."

"This," he said pointing to the nearest item at hand, a velvet box with two brass balls the size of large marbles.

"Ben Wa Balls?"

"I buy it," he said even though he didn't know what they were for.

The following day he returned to purchase an ostrich feather. And the day after, two fur mitts, long and short. And the next day, the Kama Sutra Enchanted Weekend Kit. Then the Prisoner of Love Package (two pairs of fabric restraints and one blindfold). And finally the Mmmm Mmmm Good Massage Oils in Kahlua, lemon sorbet, French vanilla, and root beer.

By the end of the week Serafín Jaramillo had spent his entire pay-check without the benefit of enjoying his purchases. He had been especially unnerved the day he bought the flavored massage oils and Nada had lisped, "My flavor is mango delight. How is yours?"

He did not know why this Nada Malović had such a terrifying effect on him. He was not usually afraid of white women, but this woman was not only alarmingly beautiful but alarmingly forward. He could not know Nada Malović's country had a long-standing love affair with Mexico and anything Mexican. This included a national crush on the golden age of Mexican cinema as well as a passion for Mexican folk music that bordered on religious fanaticism. Unlike her American counterpart, Nada Malović did not see a wetback when she saw Serafín Jaramillo. She saw an ancient Olmec stonehead more exquisite than the carved jade and turquoise masks she had viewed in her pre-Columbian art books.

Serafín, in turn, envisioned Nada Malović as a smoky-limbed mirage resurrected from a mahogany blackness like an El Greco sav-ior. Or perhaps faithful as a Duchess of Alba. Yes, a Duchess of Alba pointing downward to his signature at the bottom of the frame: *Solo Jaramillo*. Only Jaramillo. Jaramillo only!

He would devote himself to this woman, he decided. Paint a series

of Nada Malović. Nada howling and protesting like a Guernica. Nada
as courtesan from Ingres reclining on his dirty futon upstairs from
Club Mambo. Nada of the Nike of Samothrace grace. Nada with her
La Gioconda grin. Nada with furious Renoir-blue eyes. Nada lean-
boned as a Giacometti. Or all in a play of summery patterns à la
Matisse. Or with only that wonderfully symmetrical face of hers balanced perfectly on the pillow like a sweet Brancusi.

Poor Serafín! Poor Nada! They had no common language
between them at which they were fluent. Nada's Spanish consisted of
a few words she remembered from Mexican songs she'd heard on Yugo
radio. *Bésame mucho*, for example. But since Serafín had a mouth like
an Olmec jaguar, it was enough.

Thus, they communicated in a mock Esperanto invented by
necessity, a hodgepodge of Me-Tarzan-You-Jane dialogue that no one
but they understood.

"Nada, how is you *no estudiare español en* Zagreb *universitat und*
now is *problema.*"

"No problem, no problem, *mi cielito lindo. Je suis feliz navidad*,
baby."

Ay, ay, ay, ay. The matter of Serafín's legal status still hovered like
a bee. "Get married," Serafín's painter buddy Octavio had advised years
ago when Serafín was living in Chicago. "Then you won't have to worry
about *la migra*, man." Octavio had been married four times, twice in
Mexico and twice in the United States. He had a wife in Tampico, and
perhaps he still had her. Serafín was not sure. On this side of the border
Serafín knew Octavio was married to a Molly Somethingorother, a
once-sculptress who brought home a steady paycheck through an
administrative job with the Illinois Arts Council. His legal status
resolved, Octavio came and went, sometimes living in Mexico months
at a time, because art, after all, is an artist's true mistress.

Serafín reasoned he too would be able to end his legal exile once
he married. U.S. citizenship meant financial aid and graduate school.
It meant minimum wage and overtime. It meant anytime he washed a

red sock with his clothes and turned all the wash pink, he didn't have to go around dressed in pink T-shirts and pink corduroys that were way too short even in flash-flood weather. He felt especially happy about being able to make money to send home. When the earthquake had hit, Serafín was helpless to do anything but read the newspapers and bury his face in his arms. If he were a citizen, he could at last help his family out financially. They didn't complain because they wanted their son to continue working toward graduate school, but he knew too well they were hurting.

"Nada, *le marriage ist muy importante* for my *cultura*. Live like this no good *el* Papa John Paul say no, no, *capich?* How is if you my wife? You like?" Serafín asked.

"Serafín, *mi cucurucucú, sí, sí, sí.*"

Thus through many nods, overabundant laughter, combined efforts at English, and a few words of Serbo-Croatian that sounded to Serafín's ears like wheat fields being threshed, this Nada agreed to become Serafín's wife.

And so Serafín Jaramillo and Nada Maloviç were wed on the following Monday, because that was Serafín's day off. To save money they would move into the Janis Joplin flophouse; that is, the atelier/apartment above Club Mambo. For her wedding Nada wore a Mexican blouse and a black velvet vintage skirt with the pyramids of Tenochtitlán sewn in sequins. Serafín splurged and wore a new pair of Levis, a hand-painted T-shirt with Pancho Villa's rough riders galloping across his chest, and a BOYCOTT GRAPES pin.

Nada's girlfriends from the Herotica shop did not even have time to organize a bridal shower, but they attended the reception after the ceremony with their Herotica gift boxes in hand. The Dos Hermanos furnished tacos, the Club Mambo supplied the alcohol and use of their club, and a band called Los Tejanotes donated their services for the evening.

Well, it was a fun wedding, as *bien* fun as could be expected on a night in which everyone had to go to work the next day. Anyone who was a Latino artist in Austin was there, even those who just pretend-ed to be. After everyone had danced *el* Ho-kee Po-kee, and sashayed to conjunto, and shimmied *nalga* to salsa and merengue all night, it was time to send everyone home. Serafín made sure they picked up after themselves, because he would have to clean up the next morn-ing.

Serafín insisted on carrying Nada upstairs to the Janis Joplin-flop-house-honeymoon-night retreat because he was hopelessly romantic as well as hopelessly drunk. But love conquers all obstacles, and he managed to get Nada to the dirty futon without dropping her. Before he could unhook Nada's vintage Mexican skirt with the sequined Aztec pyramids, Nada struggled free and took his face in her hands.

"Serafín, my hot stuff, thank you, *mi amor*. Now I *ist* American woman. I *ist* USA citizen today. I *ist* your wife. You *ist* my man. And I *ist muy* pregnant with our love baby. *Tutto bene. Comprende?*"

"Nada, what you say?"

"Today *ist* my first day USA citizen. Thank you, my love. Now I can go to Zagreb to visit my *pobrecita* mama *und* show her our beauti-ful American baby with no problem, no problem *inmigración* because *mi bellissimo* husband *ist* USA citizen."

"Nada! *¡Ay caray!* I no *ist* USA citizen."

"*Kako* you *no ist?* Don't be playing brain games with me, man."

"No, Nada, *por favor*. I no have U.S. green card. I *ist* citizen United States of Mexico."

"Mexico?"

"And you? You have green card, *no?*"

Nada shook her head.

"MAchu PICchu!" Serafín howled trying to pronounce and only approximating a terrible Yugoslav obscenity that has to do with one's mother.

Enraged to tears, Nada spat the first words that fluttered to con-sciousness, "Popol VUH!" It wasn't quite a profanity in any language, but it had the desired effect.

There was a skinny silence for what seemed an uncomfortably long length of time. Nada sucked the hem of her skirt, and Serafín stared at the Texas-shaped menstruation stain on the futon.

"Nada?" Serafín said finally.

"Serafín?" Nada sniffled.

Serafín looked at his Nada in her crumpled Mexican skirt. Nada looked at her Serafín.

They burst out laughing. They laughed and laughed.

Until their eyes were filled with tears beyond translation.

The End/*El Fin*/*Konac*

Camp Whitehorse

by Alicia Erian

ERROL TOOK A HIATUS FROM HIS GIRLFRIEND, LOUISE, THINKING THAT he might want to be with Audrey instead. Then it turned out that he didn't want to be with Audrey, he wanted Louise again, except that Audrey was clinging to him. Errol had an idea to pass Audrey off to his friend Marcus, a Marine who had just come back from Iraq. Marcus had killed a kid on accident. He was taking antidepressants for it and seeing a therapist, but neither were really helping. Errol thought that maybe Audrey could help Marcus. Mostly, though, he was hoping to get her to stop clinging.

By way of introduction, Errol showed Marcus a video of Audrey masturbating with her vibrator. She'd made the video for her ex-boyfriend, who was also a Marine, and when she came, she said his name: *Hutch.* Errol didn't know much about the guy, except that Audrey had come to Connecticut to try to forget him. She said that he was always vanishing, and that it was time for her to move on.

When she first gave Errol the tape, Audrey instructed him to watch it with the sound down. He said fine, then left the sound up. It turned out that hearing Audrey say another man's name when she came was the least of Errol's worries. What really got him was Audrey herself. The way she writhed and moaned and whimpered and cooed. The confidence with which she held her pussy open. He'd never really known the woman on the tape, but she was the one he wanted.

He had, however, caught a glimpse of her when they'd first met. She'd come into his western-wear store to order a pair of boots and had treated him with indifference. She was slightly taller than Errol, which contributed to the effect. He started chasing her immediately. He was still with Louise, but he didn't really think about that. This was something separate. He wanted to know if he could get Audrey to like him.

It turned out that he could. At first, this was gratifying. Audrey was pretty and smart. She taught video production at the local college. Anyone would've wanted her. Then Errol told her about Louise, and everything changed. Audrey grew anxious. Even with the hiatus, she couldn't seem to relax. She panicked constantly that Errol wouldn't pick her. He tried to tell her that it was a self-fulfilling prophecy, but that only made her panic even more. And her panic sent her into action. His dick was sore from the constant blow jobs. He was getting fat from the cookies she was always bringing over.

Then she gave him the video. For a while, it made things better. He would watch it, and he would see who she was supposed to be, and he would want very much to fuck her. Then, afterward, she would ask hopefully if he was going to pick her, and things would go back to the way they really were.

Finally, he put the video away. He was beginning to hate himself. He had ruined her, and the tape was the evidence, and he couldn't stand to look at it anymore. Meanwhile, he'd started to miss Louise. Maybe she was a little distant and cold, but here was someone he could never ruin. Here was someone who would never let him get that close.

Errol let Marcus keep the video overnight, then called the next day to see what he thought. Marcus said that he'd enjoyed it and agreed to a meeting. Errol had Marcus come to his store, then he invited Audrey on the pretense of showing her some new boots. When she arrived, he introduced her to Marcus, saying that Marcus had just happened to drop by. She seemed irritated by this, like she had thought it was just going to be her and Errol. Then Marcus started talking about being a Marine, and that calmed her down. She said that her ex-boyfriend had been stationed in Nasiriyah. She said that apparently she attracted Marines like flies. Marcus laughed. He asked her if that was such a bad thing, and she said that maybe it wasn't. Errol excused himself then to go and get the boots. He hoped that this was actual flirting, and not just Audrey trying to get to him through his friends.

A couple of days later, Errol called her. He made small talk, then told her that his friend Marcus had really liked her and was bugging him for her phone number. Immediately, she started to cry. "You're passing me off to your friend?" she yelled. "You're passing me off to your friend?"

Errol was taken aback. He hadn't expected Audrey to notice, and now he realized that this had been stupid. He said, "He just came back from Iraq."

"You're pimping me out?" Audrey wailed.

Errol thought that pimping was a strong word. "No," he said. "Of course not."

Audrey kept crying.

"Maybe I made a mistake here," Errol said.

"I guess so," Audrey sniveled.

"I'm sorry," he said.

"I demand to know your feelings for me," she said.

Errol thought for a moment, then told her the truth: that the hiatus was over, that he was getting back together with Louise.

Audrey hung up on him. He sat there for a while, holding the phone, then called Marcus and gave him her number.

At first, Marcus reported, Audrey was furious. She said that she'd never given Errol permission to hand out her number, and that Marcus had no right to be using it. Marcus told her that he understood, but that he'd like to check back with her one more time, just in case she changed her mind. When he called again in a week, she'd softened a little. She said that even if she was interested in seeing him, she couldn't, because she'd promised Hutch that she would never fuck another Marine. "Who said I wanted to fuck you?" Marcus asked, which she had apparently found funny. By the third week, she'd decided that Hutch had no right to tell her who to fuck since he was probably fucking God knew who as she spoke, and so she agreed to a date.

Marcus told Errol that he'd taken her to dinner and a movie, then tried to have sex with her afterward but couldn't because of the anti-depressants. Audrey took it personally, like she thought he didn't find her attractive. She started crying and curled up into a ball. Marcus didn't know what to do. He wanted to hit her for not knowing what a real problem was, and then he did. On the ass. He couldn't believe he'd done it. He thought she would kick him out, but she didn't. She uncurled herself and began to suck his dick. Finally, he got a little hard.

Errol didn't know what to say to this. He and Marcus were sitting in a bar, drinking.

"Was she like that with you?" Marcus asked.

"Like what?" Errol said.

"You know," Marcus said. "Submissive."

"Yes," Errol said.

"And you didn't like that?"

"I did like it," Errol admitted.

"But you passed on it."

"I passed on it, but I liked it."

Marcus said, "It's making me feel a little bit better."

"About what?" Errol asked.

Marcus shrugged. "Everything."

"Don't hit her," Errol said.

"She likes it," Marcus said.

"Just don't," Errol told him.

Errol was having a hard time readjusting to Louise. She was depressed a lot and always talking about her painful childhood. Errol appreciated how this kept her distracted, but at the same time, he missed having a woman pine for him. He tried calling Audrey a couple of times to see if he could get a dose of it, but she wouldn't answer.

He still had the video she'd given him, so he watched that instead. Lately, though, he'd begun to turn the sound down. He was starting to get a little jealous of Hutch.

Now that Louise was coming over again, she stumbled across the video. "What the hell is this?" she asked Errol one night. He had just come home from the store.

He looked at the tape in her hand. Errol had never told Louise about Audrey. When he'd suggested that they take a hiatus, his reasoning had been that he was overwhelmed. "Overwhelmed by what?" Louise had asked him, and he'd said just "overwhelmed."

"Who is this woman?" she demanded now, shaking the tape. "Who's Hutch?"

Errol took his cowboy hat off and hung it on the post at the end of the banister. He tried to explain to Louise about the video. When he was finished, she said, "You're watching a tape of a woman masturbating for another man?"

"Yes," Errol admitted.

Louise sat down on the couch. She was still holding the tape. Errol was desperate to get it back from her, but he knew that now wasn't the time. He knew that any sudden movements could result in its breakage.

"I don't know what to say to this," Louise told him.

Errol tried to be quiet and leave her to her rage.

"Is this why you wanted a hiatus?" she asked.

He nodded, then said, "But I don't want it anymore. I pick you."

"Gee," Louise said. "Thanks."

Errol didn't say anything.

"Is this the kind of thing you like in a woman?"

"No," Errol said, even though it was.

"Because I can't make you any videos. That's just not me."

"I wouldn't want you to," Errol lied.

Louise started to cry then. She said that the last thing she needed was some woman making her feel insufficient in the bedroom. Errol sat down beside her. He gently took the tape out of her hands, set it to one side, and explained about how sufficient he found her. He accidentally used the word "sufficient," and that made her cry even harder. She got her coat and went home.

* * *

Errol hoped that Louise would leave him because of the tape. He hoped that she would make some kind of final decision, since he felt unable to. The next day, though, she called to say that she was staying. She said that she was hardly going to be threatened by someone who hadn't even managed to steal her boyfriend. She added, however, that he had better get rid of that fucking tape.

Errol knew that Audrey wouldn't pick up if he called, so he drove over to her place. When she answered the door, he saw that she had a black eye. "Jesus," he said.

"What?" she said.

"Your eye."

"Oh," she said, touching it.

"Did Marcus do that?" he asked.

She nodded.

"I don't want you to see him anymore," Errol said, hoping to sound like Hutch.

"Are you going to see me?" she asked.

He paused for a moment, then said, "No."

"Why not?"

"Because I'm seeing Louise," he said.

"Why?"

He was starting to get agitated. "Because," he said, "she's my girlfriend. You know that."

Audrey didn't say anything.

"Here's your tape back," he said.

"You don't want it?" she asked, hurt.

"It's not that," he said.

"How come you don't want it?"

"I do want it," he said. "It's just not a good idea."

She took the tape.

Errol didn't know what to do then. He thought he should probably call the police about her eye. He took out his cell phone.

"What are you doing?" Audrey asked.

"I don't know," he said, putting the phone away.

"I can't believe you passed me off to your friend," she said.

"It was wrong," he agreed, and then he left.

Errol went over to Marcus's house to tell him to stop hitting Audrey. "Why?" Marcus said. "She likes it."

"What are you talking about?" Errol said, even though he kind of knew. Still, he thought that there was a difference between letting someone suck your dick endlessly and hitting them.

"Look," Marcus said, "this is mutual consent. I'm not hurting anyone who doesn't want to get hurt."

"How's she supposed to teach her classes if she has a black eye?"

"It's spring break," Marcus said.

Errol didn't know what to say to this.

"Lighten up," Marcus told him, and he closed the door.

Errol knew that "Hutch" was short for "Hutchinson," and that night he called every Hutchinson in Manhattan until he found the right one. "Who is this?" Hutch asked.

Errol said that he was a friend of Audrey's, and that Audrey was having a problem. "What problem?" Hutch said.

"Some guy is roughing her up."

"She likes that."

"Yeah, but it's too much," Errol said. "He gave her a black eye."

"Can't you take care of it?" Hutch asked. "What kind of man are you?"

"I don't think I can take care of it," Errol said.

"Well," Hutch said, "that's her business."

"He's a Marine," Errol said.

"What?" Hutch said.

"The guy who's roughing her up."

Hutch was quiet for a moment. Then he said, "I told her not to do that. I don't care if she fucks you, or anyone else. But I told her not to fuck another Marine."

"I don't think she's actually fucking him," Errol said.

"Why not?"

"He's on antidepressants. They mess up his sex life."

"He's beating her without even fucking her?"

"I think so," Errol said.

"That's fucked up," Hutch said.

"He killed a kid in Iraq," Errol said. "On accident."

"Oh Jesus," Hutch said.

"He's got problems," Errol said.

"How do I find this guy?" Hutch said, and Errol told him.

A couple of days later, a man roughly Errol's height came into the store. What Errol noticed about him was that he was very broad. There was his head, then the extension of his shoulders out from his neck. To Errol, they seemed never-ending.

The man was wearing sunglasses, and he took them off, exchanging them for a pair of regular glasses. They looked like the kind you would find in a magazine. The latest style.

Once the man could see, he said, "Are you Errol?"

Errol said yes, and the man came behind the counter and hit him in the face. Errol fell back against the wall a little.

"You fucking set her up with that guy," Hutch said. "You left that part out, asshole."

Errol took a moment to right himself, then said, "Yes. I did."

There was one other customer in the store, a man, and he asked then if he should call the police. "No," Errol said. "It's all right."

The man walked out, and Errol felt relieved. He was pretty sure he was bleeding, and he didn't think that was good for business.

Hutch paced the store a little before returning to the sales counter. This time he stayed on the right side of it. "Have you seen her face?" he said. "She looks terrible."

"Yes," Errol said.

"How's she supposed to teach like that?"

"I don't know," Errol said.

"You're the one responsible, do you understand? You passed her off to your friend. She's not a whore to be passed off to your friend."

"I didn't mean it that way," Errol said.

"She thinks you did," Hutch said. "She thinks that's exactly how you meant it."

Errol didn't say anything.

"Jesus Christ," Hutch said, and he started walking around the store again.

Errol couldn't tell if Hutch's pacing was a way for him to calm down or a way for him to get more excited. In general, he didn't seem that excited. Even when he had hit Errol, he'd seemed vaguely fatigued.

Now he stopped in front of a hat rack. He reached over and took down a beige Stetson. "This would look good on her," he said.

Errol nodded.

Hutch put the hat on, dipping it down a little in front so that it cast a shadow across his eyes. "She could maybe teach wearing this."

"Yes," Errol agreed.

Hutch took the hat off. He examined the inside of it. "Would this fit her?"

"What size is it?" Errol asked.

"Seven and a half."

"She's a seven and an eighth," Errol said. "Let me see if I have any more in back." He went in the back room and found the hat, then brought out the box. "Here you go," he told Hutch.

Hutch came up to the counter. He took out his wallet and gave Errol a credit card.

"It's on the house," Errol said.

"Nope," Hutch said flatly. "We don't want anything from you."

Errol paused, then took Hutch's credit card. He rang up the hat for him, then tied string around the big box, so that he'd have an easy time carrying it out of the store. He took a while doing this because he didn't want Hutch to go. He wished that he could spend the rest of the afternoon with him. He wished he had something that Hutch wanted.

Later, Marcus called Errol to tell him that Hutch had come to see him, and that it had been helpful. He said, "That guy was at Whitehorse. The fucking detention center. He didn't kill anyone, but he did stuff on purpose. I only did stuff on accident."

"Did he hit you?" Errol asked, and Marcus said, "Why would he do that?"

Errol had a split lip. When Louise asked him where he'd gotten it, he told her the truth, and she cried. She said that he'd been the real man in all of this. That hitting wasn't the answer.

Privately, Errol disagreed. He liked his split lip. He liked the way it implied that he had hit someone too, instead of just standing there. When it healed, he grew miserable again. He waited for Audrey to come back into his store, but she never did.

Islanders

by Stefan Kiesbye

DEATH WAS EVERYWHERE, THOUGH NOT YET WHERE THEY SLEPT IN THE cold of their tents. Moritz had arrived alone, but after two days of fighting they were a good dozen at the foot of the Emperor William Memorial Church. The war was far away and not of their making. It was Saddam Hussein's war, George Bush's war. Yet on Radio 100 they had heard how the burning oil would change the global climate, and they suspected nuclear weapons in Saddam's hands and knew what he was capable of doing. They also knew that America's pride would top any of Iraq's sins. With the oil fields burning, it had become everyone's war. Moritz wanted his share.

On the day the U.S. ultimatum expired, he called the post office and quit his part-time job. He grabbed the lightweight tent and locked his apartment. It took Moritz ten minutes on the subway to get from the district of Wedding to Zoo Station, and once he reached the top of the stairs, he stood in front of the Memorial Church. That morning, Radio 100 had announced that protesters would set up camp in the city, but no matter where he looked for other tents, there weren't any. He had to decide on his own where to stay.

The Memorial Church, bombed during World War II and never restored, stood sandwiched between a new church and a bell tower— Lipstick and Powder Box as they were called—both made of concrete and stained glass windows. At night they were lit from within, the windows glowing red and blue. To the east, at the far end of the square, stood the tall Europe Center, a mixture of office complex and mall. A large fountain in the shape of a globe had been built in front of it. To the west stood office buildings, two multiplexes, the CityMusic record store, and a small coffee shop where a cup was only one mark and you had to drink it standing at tiny tables.

He wanted to demonstrate against the war, so the tent had to be clearly visible to the thousands of tourists promenading Kurfürstendamm south of the square and the businesspeople hurrying along Hardenbergstrasse north of it. Yet he also wanted to be safe against attacks by loitering teenagers and drunks, who regularly crowded the skateboardable spaces, benches, and steps leading to the churches.

Finally, Moritz decided on the passageway between the new and old churches. It was less windy there, and despite the fact that he called himself an atheist, he loved the thought that if not God, at least the Lutheran church might offer some protection from thieves and intruders.

Within minutes, his tent went up in the middle of what had until recently been West Berlin. Moritz wasn't sure how long he would stay, but had come prepared. He unpacked a small, blue cooker, a "mummy" sleeping bag, and a compass—there was no need for it, but he had never camped without one. In his backpack, he carried warm socks, underwear, and shirts for a week.

He had hoped to have company, to find at least a handful of other protesters who would make him feel like part of a base camp in the Himalayas. Instead, he pinned a poster—"*Kein Krieg Nirgends* - No War Nowhere"—to his tent and sat on his sleeping bag by himself, watching the afternoon traffic on the boulevard.

After two hours of protest, he had to pee. This wasn't a problem in itself, Wertheim's department store being only a few hundred yards away, but who would look after his belongings? He held out another half hour, then zipped up the tent and left.

His backpack was gone when he returned, leaving him without the canned food and socks. But two more protesters had arrived. One was a guy in his fifties, Holger, with a slight stutter and an army-surplus tent. He had round spectacles and wore a brown poncho and brown woolen hat. He greeted Moritz cheerfully, as if he had entered a bar and come across an old friend, and Moritz helped him secure the lines of his tent with bricks Holger had carried in two plastic bags.

The other newcomer was a woman named Bettina, who was small with long, strawberry-blond hair, freckles, and a tiny nose. She didn't look as if she had planned on coming—she had neither sleeping bag nor food, and curiously looked on as Holger and Moritz worked on the tent. Neither she nor Holger had seen Moritz's backpack or the person taking it.

Bettina wore only a white cardigan over a button-down shirt that closed beneath the shadowy spot where her breasts met. She had a squeaky but pleasant voice that seemed to tell you a secret even when she asked you for a light.

"We've met before," she said after staring at Moritz for a minute with her head tilted to one side. He stared back. She seemed familiar, the way she looked up at him, her eyes twinkling, a smile forming on her lips, as if he were a not-yet-understood punch line.

"Were you at the Ratibor?" she asked. "I played there two months ago."

"No," he said.

"Maybe the Modernes Theater? When I saw you, I thought I must have met you with lots of other people around."

"The Schiller Theater?"

"I never go there. Are you an actor?"

"Sort of. Maybe the Schaubühne?"

"No. I'm an actress, but I just left an engagement. The director— she had so no clue of what she was doing. I guess she hates me now. It was only our fourth night. The reviews were terrible. Where are you playing?"

"Right now? Nowhere."

She looked at Moritz for a while, then smiled. "We've met, though. I know you."

"Are you here for the protest?" he asked.

"Yes," she said, her smile widening, her lips opening like a blossom to reveal the most beautiful teeth he had ever seen. "Now I am. Will you keep me company on a short shopping tour to Wertheim's?"

He agreed. The thought of replacing what had been stolen by
going home never entered his mind. Instead, Moritz spent half of the
money he had brought for a week on new things, while Bettina bought
a green sleeping bag with little cacti printed on it.

"Do you think I'll need a tent?" she asked.

He kept his eyes on the iso-mat he had picked up from a shelf. "If
you don't want to spend the money, you could sleep in mine," he said,
running his hands over the mat's aluminum surface.

"That'd be fine. If you don't mind."

"No," he said.

Neither Holger nor Bettina had brought any protest signs, and when
they got empty coffee boxes from the small café, the three discovered
that they hadn't thought of pens to write catchy lines on them.
Bettina offered to buy markers, but Moritz stopped her. "We might
need money for emergencies," he told her. Instead, they decided to ask
tourists to borrow their pens. The passersby, of course, didn't always
take the time for them to invent and outline and color their slogans,
so that they could only write one or two words at a time.

Toward the end of the afternoon, the space between Bettina's
breasts turned red and blue. And even when she later wore Moritz's
yellow down vest, that spot remained visible. The slogans, such as THE
GULF WAR IS A WAR AGAINST THE WORLD and NO OIL FOR
WARMONGERS, NO OIL FOR BUSH AND SADDAM, were hardly legible
and reminded Moritz of the signs the bums in front of Zoo Station put
behind their hats. I HAD A HOME AND FAMILY JUST LIKE YOURS, or
WHY SHOULD I LIE—I NEED A BEER.

In fact, the bums warmed themselves in the same café on
Joachimstaler Strasse that the three started to frequent when it got too
cold to sit in front of the tents. But there were all the other types too.
Managers on their breaks, secretaries in suits and sneakers, lawyers
and middle-aged ladies screeching with friends. And Holger, Bettina,

and Moritz felt they didn't belong to any of them. On their first evening, right after the stores had closed at six o'clock, they sat together and listened to the noise around them, feeling as if they had been trapped in a cage full of parrots. And they knew more than any of the other patrons. Doom would come within days or weeks at best, and the chatter around them was nothing but a farce. They saw the world as it really was: a place over which black clouds would soon appear, more dangerous than the fallout after Chernobyl, but this time—and all of them took a strange solace in this—it would be visible. Never had they felt so solemn.

"It's cold," Bettina said in the middle of the first night. Holger had wished her and Moritz sweet dreams around ten, looking quizzically at them as the two retreated into their tent. But Moritz hadn't been able to find any sleep. The outer skin of the tent didn't shut out enough light from all the streetlights and neon signs around the square for it to get dark, and the traffic, which even at one in the morning still seemed to go right through the tent, wouldn't let him close his eyes.

"Yes," he answered Bettina.

"Wouldn't you like to be at home?" she asked.

"No."

"You must be single," she said.

"Well."

"Are you with someone?"

"Not really." He hadn't heard from his girlfriend in a week. She lived in Tempelhof, near the old airport, and in the mornings they were awakened by the planes. She had a five-year-old son, and more often than not, he would arrive before the airplanes and jump on them in the half-dark of the bedroom.

Moritz had meant to leave her, but never found the right time to say so, and there had been no one else to take her place. It wasn't all convenience, though. It was a tender relationship, he told himself, and Moritz truly adored the boy.

"Are you?" he asked after a while.

"Am I what?"

"Are you single? I mean..."

"I know what you mean," she said, when he wasn't sure what he'd meant. "Yes, now I am."

"You broke up?"

"I guess," she answered. "It was on-again, off-again, and now it's very off." Then she turned to face him, and in the light filtering through the tent, he could see her smile. "But tonight I'm sleeping in a tent with a sweet and sad man."

Moritz smiled back at her, grunting because he couldn't imagine an answer to what she had said.

"Are you still in love with her?" she asked.

"I don't know." He didn't want to sound heartless.

"Then you are."

"How about yourself?"

"I'm not in love with her," she laughed. "Kidding. No, I think I fell out of love with him."

He stared at the roof of the tent, looking for some appropriate phrases.

"I'm cold." Bettina said instead. "I know it's sort of funny, but since we've met before—I hope you don't mind. This is really not the warmest of sleeping bags. Can I come into yours—if there's any space in your mummy? Do you mind?"

She was still fully clothed but slid off her jeans before trying to find space next to him. Her legs were cold, her breath smelling faintly of basil, as she wriggled into place. But when she had finally settled in, they couldn't zip up the sleeping bag anymore. Instead they wrapped hers around the cleft.

"Better?" Moritz asked, not knowing where to put his hands.

"Hug me," she said. "You smell good," she added shortly after. "Are you good?"

"I'm fine," he lied. It felt too good to hold her to complain about his arm growing numb and his shoulder getting sore. Pressed tightly against him, she slept, seeming to feel entirely safe with him. Though he wasn't sure what to make of that, Moritz was pleased with the situation. She'd come like a present for a birthday you have forgotten about, and his disbelief slowly turned into excitement and kept him awake. But he lay as still as any mummy and held her wrapped in his arms, and after a while she started to snore softly.

The next morning Holger, Bettina, and Moritz knew they'd been right to come and protest. Newspapers declared "It Is War." Over the loudspeakers of the coffee shop they heard a reporter in Baghdad exclaiming, "The sky is burning. I don't know if you can hear me. We're under attack. One thing—the boys are aiming well, they've already hit that oil refinery over there four times." Then they listened to the sound of bombs exploding. The radio host asked if the reporter was still there, if he was hurt. "Well," they could hear him answer in his staticky voice. "We're a little excited. There's another explosion," and the line went dead.

The start of the war brought six new protesters to the camp. But in the afternoon the police showed up. They wore tough-looking, green winter coats and hats that looked like green milkman caps. Their pants were ill-fitting, and their shoes black and heavy. Without warning, they searched the tents for weapons and drugs. Two dogs sniffed backpacks and sleeping bags.

Moritz and the others were unprepared for the cops' visit. They had no leader or spokesperson, and spent the first moments looking helplessly from one to another. Then, because he had been the first camper, Moritz approached the police.

"Stop that," he said. "You have no right to do that."

Instead of an answer, the officer without a dog stared at him, letting his gaze wander over the polar-fit clothing. Looking over to the globe fountain, he said, "You have to clear this space."

"We won't," Moritz said, looking around and finding that the others had started to surround the cops. "We have the right to protest," he continued. "If we have to die in this war, we will die here."

The mentioning of the war provoked the dogless cop to inspect the black and green and blue posters, stooping to be able to read the words.

"They're clean," one of his colleagues told him after dragging his dog out of Holger's tent.

"We can evict you," the first cop said. "In a minute."

"Try," Holger said, his reply earning agreeing grunts from the circle of protesters. Their faces were gloomy but full of resolve. The cops had to be resisted.

Moritz had once watched two cops getting beaten up by a young man they had tried to search. This had happened in front of a subway entrance, and none of the passersby had stopped to help the police. He knew they'd be hesitant about messing with more than one or two offenders. "Try," he echoed Holger and sat down, the others slowly following his example.

The first cop looked at his two colleagues, then looked down at his boots. "Look," he said. "We don't need any trouble. Just move your tents out of the way so that parishioners don't fall over your stuff on their way to church." He was still talking to his boots when he added, "We could call for assistance at any time." Then he looked over to the Europe Center and, after a second, motioned his colleagues to follow him. They left the circle, got into their green and white van, and slowly drove off.

"They'll come again," Holger said, his voice somber and prophetic.

The first encounter with the police, which the camp celebrated as a victory, also gave Moritz a valuable idea. Despite the early success, the protesters were too vulnerable, he felt, and they needed to voice their protest more effectively to avoid being silenced.

In order not to be taken for bums, and to affect the public, which surrounded them every day until long after midnight, they symbolically founded the Free Kurfürsten Island, a new state.

From Wertheim's they bought yellow stationery, and Bettina stole a pocket-size stamp set. With the help of an old Polaroid camera, a passport office was established, and everyone who donated at least five deutsche marks was given a yellow document with his or her photo and the stamp of the state's name. After two slow days, their business took off, bringing in enough money to buy bread and lunch meat for their now twenty-three-people-strong republic.

"We should have guards for the night," a young guy in a red down coat with a goatee suggested one evening.

"Yes," his friend, in ski pants and snow boots chimed in. "We should start at ten and take turns every two hours."

"I have a can of tear gas," the first guy added.

"How about a campfire and beans and coffee?" Holger snorted. "We don't need guards; we need a government." In the end everyone agreed to meet every other evening. Together they would decide how to spend money, how to ensure safety, what to do in case of a confrontation with the cops. Only people who had spent at least three nights on the island were allowed to vote. Every new camper received a yellow passport with the entry date stamped into it.

"Can you promise me that you don't have AIDS?" Bettina asked, taking off her pants before coming under the covers.

"No," he answered. "I mean, I don't think I have it."

"When was your last test?"

"A year ago." The turn of the conversation made Moritz fear she would slip away from him. All day they had been together, and at dinner—potato chips and Coke in front of the tents—she had taken his hand and held it all evening. With a kiss, she had announced that it was time to go to sleep.

"And you had unprotected sex?" she now asked.

"Um...we can buy condoms."

"They give me rashes," she said and lay silent for a while.

Moritz cursed himself for not having used condoms with his girl-friend. Bettina was trying to make love to him, and through his past adventures he might have made it impossible. And to make matters worse, Bettina's silence got him all the more excited.

"Oh God," she finally said, and sighed and kissed Moritz, her hair falling on his face and tickling him. "You have such pretty hands," she whispered when he stroked her cheek. "They're twice as large as mine." Then she lay down and directed him to lie on top of her. "Oh God," she sighed again, as if Moritz were a punishment she had to accept, making love a sacrifice she was willing to endure to make up for whatever had gone wrong.

"You're a healthy young man," she later said, laughing silently, only her breath making slight staccato noises. "Now we've done *that* and don't have to do it again."

Moritz grunted, not understanding what she meant.

"Now we can go back to being friends," she explained, as if it were self-evident.

Still too satisfied, he nodded.

But whatever she had meant, she never brought it up again. Bettina stayed in Moritz's tent every night, and every night they "made heat," as she called it. Often they did it fully clothed, with only her pants down as much as needed so he could enter her.

Holger had been right about the police. Yet when they returned, they didn't come after the protesters. They patrolled the square and stayed away from the camp. As time went by, though, they stopped at the tents to talk, even offered coffee from their thermoses. Dieter, the cop they had talked to on the first day, told Moritz, "You are lucky. None of you ever got a permit to camp here, but the administrators can't decide which office is responsible for you guys, the district's or the city's. So right now, they don't know what to do." He often came by to discuss soccer and tennis with Moritz. They also talked about the war, but dropped the subject when it led to tensions.

"Bomb that Saddam to Hell" was his opinion, and Moritz's concerns over burning oil wells and eco-disasters, he shrugged off. "Better dark clouds than being ruled by a terrorist," he said.

On January 22, the day Iraq torched Kuwaiti oil wells and turned their fears into reality, the campers stripped down to their underwear and stood out in the cold, their legs turning bright red. Moritz and the others lined up around the globe fountain, and though they didn't have enough people to build a complete chain around it, their nakedness made them visible. Tourists dressed in woolen coats or down jackets, and a reporter from one of the local newspapers, stopped and took pictures.

The chain started at noon, and even though their bodies grew numb within minutes, they continued the protest until dusk. By then, Moritz's feet and hands looked like claws, and Bettina stood in front of the fountain crying, because she had lost all feeling in her limbs. She fell and couldn't get up. Weakened by the cold, it took four of them to carry her back to the tent.

The next day, after the first week of their protest, Holger and Moritz took the subway to Potsdamer Strasse and went up to the offices of Radio 100. They introduced themselves to the host of the "Big-City-Fever" show, and after looking at their rumpled clothes with something between awe and amusement, he ushered the two into a studio.

"You guys came just on cue," he said. "The Russian National Circus blew us off today."

Instead of lion tamers or clowns, Moritz and Holger were interviewed. "You guys out there should...follow our courageous...example," Holger trumpeted into the microphone, his sentences interrupted by awkward pauses during which the words seemed to get stuck in his mouth. "We're going to show the politicians that...people are concerned. When we're going to choke on the air we're breathing...when the sun won't warm us anymore because the rays won't get...through the black clouds, then everyone will suffer, not only a few. So...come out now and stop…this war. Join the Naked Chain." He went on for a few more minutes. In his excitement, the interruptions became more frequent, and he already seemed to choke on the blackened air he prophesied. But despite his red head, and despite words that he seemed to throw at listeners from a pulpit, Moritz was touched. The show's host, like a child listening to his grandfather with wide eyes, never interrupted him, and after the interview, he shook hands with Holger.

As agreed upon, they gave free passports to the first five callers, to be picked up at the camp. Only three callers showed up, but starting with that interview, the protesters from the Free Kurfürsten Island became local celebrities. After a few more days, people stopped by to just hang out at the camp, donate what money they had, or bring coffee and cookies. People with six-packs came too, but after a Free K-Island government council—all twenty-three members attending— they banned alcohol from the premises of their country. "We have started a wave of protest," Holger said firmly. "And not a holiday resort. Alcohol would only give the cops ammunition to evict us."

"What does your apartment look like?" Bettina asked Moritz one night. They were lying side by side, their sweaty skin growing uncomfortably cold.

"An efficiency. Coal stove and a boiler instead of running hot water. And a piano."

"Do you play?"

"Not yet," he answered. Six months ago Moritz had bought a huge upright piano by Schimmel. He had paid half price because of minor damages to the finish, and even then it was so expensive that after he had put down everything he could squeeze from his credit card, the payments were still going to run through the next three years. The piano had the potential of making him homeless. He didn't even know how to make the next payment.

Whenever he walked through his apartment, the wood panels

swung and the piano gave off small, hollow, yet melodious sounds, like a person humming.

When he had bought the instrument, he had also spent the money that would have financed the lessons. Not that this kept him from playing. During the first months Moritz played every day for at least an hour, improvising with stiff fingers. When he came home from acting lessons or from the post office, he sat down and played. It was soothing and exciting, his fingers exploring and touching sounds. He liked to release the mute and fill the room with echoes of every note he played. Moritz loved the sheer volume and scope of sound. Recently, though, his fingers had quieted down, embarrassed by the lack of direction. It was time for lessons, but the monthly payments ate all the money he could afford to spend. Moritz left the piano humming to itself, and put a blanket over it; it had looked at him with reproach.

"Will you ever invite me when this is over?"

"Sure," Moritz said. "If this comes to a good end."

"You don't think so?" She turned her face toward him. Though it was light enough to see the contours of her face and the dark spots where her eyes were, he couldn't detect if she was smiling, laughing at him.

"Do you ever miss him?" he asked instead of answering her.

"Who?"

"Your boyfriend."

"Ex-boyfriend."

"Ex-boyfriend."

"I'm with you now," she said.

Moritz wondered if she was avoiding his question. "Now. Yes," he said. They'd had sex, but even though they were living in the same tent, they'd never talked about "them." In that instant it occurred to Moritz that there is a love in necessity that doesn't need to be talked about. You don't care about long noses, bank accounts, or whether or not the left breast is bigger than the right one or if legs are too spindly or hips too wide. You care because you made a choice, and that's all there is to it. Moritz wanted to keep it that way.

"What do you think will happen?" Bettina asked.

"I'm not sure." Moritz knew she was changing subjects but let it go. "The Americans won't go home without winning the war, and Saddam—he will do anything to keep them from winning."

"How long are you going to stay here then?"

"However long it takes to stop them," Moritz answered, hoping he would hear her agree. But she just sighed. "What about you?" he asked. Her head sank back into the folds of the sleeping bag's hood, and he couldn't make out her eyes anymore.

"I'll stay," she said.

The islanders never elected a president, but Holger became spokesperson. He handled interviews with newspapers and local television, and more often than not it was he who sat in the "office," stamping the passports. Many people came to visit now every day—friends, lovers, bums, tourists. Dieter, the cop, became a regular on the island. He shared the contents of his lunch boxes, talked sports, and left them his paper after his visits. Being an inner-city cop, he came almost daily, and Moritz would ask, "How's Boris?" and he would report who Becker had beaten down under. Dieter was fond of Michael Stich, but Boris, being only a year younger than him at age twenty-three, was Moritz's hero. He was hoping he would go on to win the Open.

As busy as their days became, at night the protesters were left with their eleven tents and about twenty-five people. One of the newcomers was Petra, a literature student Moritz had worked with at the post office. She still went to some of her classes at university, but slept every night on the island. There were couples who had taken time off from work to join the ranks of the protesters, a carpenter without a job, and a fifty-year-old retired judge.

Every day a woman in her sixties sat with them in front of the church, posters in ten languages around her, all saying, "Fucking for

Peace." She was always smiling a beautiful, friendly smile and explained to whoever stopped by that people who had good sex would not engage in abuse, violence, and war. She never stayed overnight, though. Her protest belonged only to herself.

A construction co-op from the district of Kreuzberg decided to support the islanders' fight, and built a six-foot cubic bunker on their premises. Then they hoisted a flag on top of it, an idea Bettina had come up with. The flag showed the contours of Berlin, with a green, raised island in the middle of it, yellow stars encircling it.

Dieter and his cops supervised construction of the bunker and made sure it complied with the permit the co-op had obtained from the city. When they finished the bunker, Dieter nodded appreciatively.

"That won't help you if a bomb falls on your heads," he said. "But good work it is anyway." He wrote down the co-op's number; he needed work done on his small house in an allotment in Rudow.

The Free Kurfürsten Island repeated the Naked Chain on January 28, after the Allies had bombed Iraqi-held oil facilities, officially to stop Saddam from pouring more oil into the gulf. Two oil slicks were already moving south of Kuwait. No one knew if Iraq dumped oil into the sea or if American bombs were to blame. Both were probably true, everyone agreed.

The chain attracted a large audience, and by noon a throng of tourists surrounded the protesters, so when Dieter came for one of his visits, he had a hard time working his way through to Moritz. The cop leafed through the sports pages, then grunted. "Look at that," he said without showing Moritz what he was reading. "They played the Super Bowl yesterday."

"There's a war," Moritz said.

"It's show business," Dieter replied as if he were King Solomon himself.

"Who won?"

"The New York Giants."

"Uh-huh."

"Your teeth chatter," Dieter said. "How long are you guys going to do this? You'll end up in the hospital if you continue, that's all."

"Who lost?" Moritz asked.

"The Buffalo Bills."

"Never heard of them."

"Well, they lost." After a moment he added, "Oh, and Whitney Houston sang the National Anthem."

"They're at war," Moritz gasped.

"Not in Tampa, they're not. Not in their own country."

There are photos of the growing chain in *Chronik,* one of the books reviewing 1991. At the time the pictures were taken, there were more than a hundred naked people protesting. They didn't camp around the Memorial Church, but they came to strip and stand with Moritz and the islanders for a few hours. People came and told the protesters they'd been on national television.

Moritz's skin was broken by then. He had bloody sores on his feet and legs and things were not much better for Bettina. They could have bought lotion, gone to a spa for relief, but whenever they went back to the tents and crawled into their sleeping bags after another day of protest, they needed and greeted the pain that came with what little warmth they could give each other. The danger, the war, and the protests were for real, and any soothing lotion Moritz could have bought for a few marks would have robbed him of his hard-earned pride.

Even with two sleeping bags around them, the nights were often so cold that Moritz awoke in the early morning hours and jogged outside the tent to get some of the feeling back in his limbs.

On these occasions, he often strolled with Bettina along Joachimstaler Strasse, where loud music came from basement discos, and where flower vendors offered their roses to lovers, or husbands in need of a gift for their wives arriving on the night express at Zoo

Station.

They walked outside the Beate Uhse sex shop and marveled at the videos and sex toys displayed in the windows, giggled at pink "screamers," and stared impressed at the variety of condoms and vibrators.

On Hardenbergstrasse, across from the train station and the Zoo-Palast, a multiplex, stood a twenty-four-hour porn theater. And one night in early February, Bettina and Moritz could no longer resist the temptation. They paid for tickets, took off their coats, their bodies absorbing the warmth like Oil of Olay. For seven straight hours they sat through *Six Swedish Blondes in Bavaria, Orgy in White,* and *Four Pricks for a Halleluja.*

Bettina fell asleep almost immediately on Moritz's shoulder, straggly hair falling over her face. She smelled of smoke and peppermint, and he longed for sleep, but the sour odor of the theater kept him awake. Only toward morning did he doze off, people moaning in his dreams, bodies being ripped open, blood spilled, and breasts swinging above Moritz's head like pendulums before sinking down to slowly choke him.

The next day, February 3, the Allied air campaign passed the 40,000 sortie mark—10,000 more missions than had been flown against Japan in the final fourteen months of World War II. Six days later, Mikhail Gorbachev warned the United States that their operations were exceeding the U.N. mandate and talked about his plan of sending an envoy to Baghdad for talks with Saddam Hussein. The news scared Moritz. The Cold War's constant threat had seemed to be over, now battles between the superpowers were again a possibility.

The camp, after more than three weeks, was still growing. The protesters woke up to the ascending frenzy of the early-morning traffic, bought coffee and sandwiches, then sat wrapped in blankets in front of their tents, watching the salespeople and office clerks hurry to work.

"You smell," Bettina said one morning.

"You too," Moritz quickly replied, and she laughed.

They knew plenty of bathrooms, and once a week, a few of the group went to a laundromat to supply everyone with fresh clothes, but nobody was able to take showers.

"I need a bath," Bettina announced.

"That's against...I mean, I need one too," he said. "But if I go..."

"You're not betraying anyone," she said. "Not by taking a bath. Look at Petra. She is taking classes, and you don't feel betrayed. I can take a bath whenever I want." Her voice grew higher.

"We can't." He felt uncomfortable at the thought of leaving the church. Once he broke the routine of living in the camp, Moritz feared, he would sell out.

"There are enough people to protest, to watch our things, to carry the torch two hours without us. But if we stay only one day longer, we will have turned into bums, just like those over there"—she pointed at Zoo Station.

"You want to leave?"

"No," she said, but Moritz could hear that she had thought about it. People left every day now. Holger was still there, Petra returned every night, but most of the other campers were newcomers. The old ones had gone back to jobs, careers, or only their beds.

Moritz figured he would lose Bettina if he kept refusing to take a break. Yet he also felt that he would certainly lose her should they ever leave the camp for good.

"You can show me your piano," she said.

Finally he agreed, and together they went to his apartment. He had a hard time finding the keys, and for a few anxious and hopeful moments, he was convinced that they had been stolen on that first day of his protest. But no, he still had them, and with dirty and cold fingers, Moritz opened the door.

Mail was piling in the hallway, having been thrown every day through a slit in the door. With a pang Moritz realized that he had forgotten about telephone and electric bills. He had even forgotten to pay the rent.

The rooms had not been heated, and the apartment was cold, yet to Bettina and Moritz, it seemed cozy. Above all, it seemed incredibly silent. No car noises, no tumultuous voices from hundreds of curious passersby. All sounds seemed to have been sucked out of their ears.

The power had not been switched off yet. Moritz turned on the thirty-liter boiler in the bathroom, then carried the space heater he kept in the kitchen into the bedroom.

Bettina stood in front of the piano, lifting the pink sheet. "You really don't play?"

He shook his head.

"You have a piano and don't play," she said, more to herself than to him, then sat down on the stool, opened the lid and moved her fingers over the keyboard without touching it. Then she exhaled and started to play.

The space heater roared, and over its noise she played Fauré. She seemed to be alone in the room, alone with the piano, and Moritz sat down and felt lonelier than he ever had.

Two of the letters were from his girlfriend, and he opened them only to decide not to read them.

When the boiler was ready, he touched Bettina's shoulder, not wanting to interrupt her play, but she stopped. She undressed, and as she did, she became a woman Moritz had never seen. She stood in front of him, her feet slightly dirty, her breasts heavy and quivering ever so lightly when she spoke.

"What are you looking at?" she asked, her words followed by a squeaky laugh. "You've seen me before."

Yet it seemed that he hadn't. He'd watched her standing in black underwear and bra at the fountain; they had made love in his tent, but here she looked naked for the first time.

"Are you going to wash me?" she asked.

In the shower, Moritz grew embarrassed, as if all the awkwardness of new lovers that he and Bettina had skipped, finally insisted on being lived. He ran his hands over her shoulders, soaped her body,

washed her long, strawberry-blond hair, rinsed it. He felt sluggish—
the feelings of intimacy he'd had seemed presumptuous now.

They showered until the water turned cold again, then sat
wrapped in towels in front of the space heater.

"I'll have a hard time going back to our island," Moritz joked.
Bettina didn't answer. He stroked the rough skin of her hands, pushed
his nose gently against her neck. "We should take everyone to the
movies tonight," he said, but again she just stared ahead of her, at the
shiny black piano.

"Were you living with someone?" she suddenly asked.

"No."

"I was," she stated, matter-of-factly, her eyes still on the instrument.

"So..." In his mind he was going over the possible meanings of her
words.

"That's why I came with you. To your apartment."

"But what is it you're saying?"

"That you are a very sweet boy who has a piano he keeps hidden
under a pink sheet, and whose apartment looks like...as empty as...a
tomb."

"But..."

"I didn't even intend to stay in the camp in the first place."

"But you did," his voice drowning in the noise of the heater.

"That was a mistake," Bettina said in a grave voice.

"A mistake?" He stood up, the towels falling to the floor. Moritz
stood naked in the room, but here he didn't feel like a human shield.
He wasn't part of a chain. His nakedness only felt uncomfortable, a
joke.

"*You* are not a mistake," she said in the same grave voice, now
looking up at him. "But I made one." She paused, averting her eyes.
"I've been calling him."

Moritz looked at her, the meaning of her words sinking in quickly,
with sudden absoluteness.

"He threw me out that day," she said, talking to the wooden panels.

"He doesn't mind what...happened. But he wants me back."

"And you are going?"

"What do you think?"

"You should stay," he said feebly.

"But I don't know you."

"So what?"

She didn't answer, but he knew that there was no sense in arguing. She had given him what she wanted him to have, and now she wanted to go.

On Valentine's Day, the Pentagon announced it had destroyed at least 1,300 of Iraq's 4,280 tanks, 800 of 2,870 armored vehicles, and 1,100 of 3,110 artillery pieces. Moritz sat on the roof of the bunker, listening to the radio someone had donated. He bought fresh batteries every day and kept it going at all times, except between midnight and six. He had been waiting for the big bang every day.

Dieter stopped by to tell him they were discussing the end of the war.

"It will go on," Moritz said. "Saddam is not going to give in."

"He will," Dieter replied. "The *Amis* are too stupid to catch him, but he's too smart to continue. If he stops now, nothing will happen to him. He's like Castro. He'll be the leader for the rest of a long life."

"Saddam has a nuke, I'm sure," Holger interrupted. He still wore the same brown poncho, but the weather had gotten warmer, and he wasn't wearing his hat.

"He's not going to fire it," Dieter replied. "Believe me. You guys should go home," he added sternly.

Thirteen days later, the war ended. How much damage was done remained unclear, but independent experts said that fighting the effects of oil slicks lapping at Saudi Arabia's coast would be a billion dollars over the next six months. The oil wells would go on burning for years.

On the last day of February, the police raided Free Kurfürsten

Island, arresting five, among them Holger and Moritz. They said they had been tipped off that the protesters were selling drugs to tourists, but everyone knew that was an excuse. Dieter headed the police, and he avoided talking to anyone, addressed Moritz not once.

"Traitor," Holger shouted. "You screwed us." Dieter didn't reply.

Nothing was found in the tents, but they were taken down anyway. Forty-eight hours after the raid, Holger and Moritz were released. They went straight to the church square. Only the bunker was still standing, but their flag was gone.

"I wonder who took it," Moritz said, suspecting Dieter to have taken it, as a souvenir for his allotment house. After all, he had shared in something important.

A week later Moritz started to work at the post office again, each morning crossing the territory of the defunct republic on his way to Rankestrasse.

Sometimes he woke up at night, suddenly hearing the inner-city traffic noise and seeing the lights shining through the tent. Bettina wasn't listed in the phone book, and though he'd been to many theaters since, as an actor and as spectator, he hadn't seen her again.

Soon the cops also took down the bunker, and nothing obstructed the passage between the two churches anymore. Bush gained in stature, then lost the elections. Saddam still ruled Iraq. Moritz could not be consoled.

The Politics of Fear

Level Orange
by Doug Dorst

SLIGHT CHANCE OF SHOWERS HERE IN THE VALLEY—JUST ENOUGH TO make the roads slick, so drive with extra caution. Slight chance of hail. Slight chance of seismic activity along the fault line. Slight chance of lightning and lake-effect snow. Slight chance of partial cloudiness. Slight chance of darkness at the end of day. Slight chance The Maker disapproves of you and your lifestyle. Slight chance of mild discomfort. Slight chance of flurries at high elevations and monsters under your floorboards. Slight chance of a loved one surrendering the will to live. Slight chance they know. Slight chance your children will end up ash in the forest hag's oven. Slight chance that you are alone. Slight chance you will be forced into a long black car with matte-black windows. Slight chance of voices that are not to be trusted. Slight chance of bloodcurdling screams. Slight chance of plummeting black boxes. Slight chance of fear and funnel clouds and early-morning frost. Slight chance of widespread butchery and low-lying fog. Slight chance they've known for longer than you think. Slight chance of the great and final Deluge. Slight chance also of a gorgeous shiny summer day. Be sure to pack a hat and sunblock and dark, dark glasses. Leave nothing exposed.

False Cognate

by Jeff Parker

WHEN I FIRST ARRIVED HERE, I HAD A SIMPLE REQUEST OF OUR LIAISON, a handsome, tall woman with steel blue eyes and a pancake face. I wasn't yet confident in my Russian and needed a haircut. I asked her, in English, "Do you know, Tanya, where I can get a barber? I heard they go for about thirty rubles here."

She looked at me with a rather sharp glance and said, "Thirty rubles is one dollar."

"About what my last one was worth," I said, mussing up my hair.

"That's not for me to judge," she said. "The best thing to do is wait at the bus stops. They'll come up to you."

"Come up to me?" I said.

"Eventually," she said.

"That's how people go about it?"

"I think so," she said, then clip-clopped away.

I spent the better part of a week hanging out at the bus stops trying to look like I wanted a haircut. The only people who ever approached me were thin-lipped prostitutes.

Tanya avoided me after that. The whole cohort avoided me. At first I thought they were just an unsociable bunch, but sometimes, walking home at night, I'd see them all at the beer garden near my flat, laughing and having a good time. I'd pull up a chair and they'd suddenly evacuate. Later on, I convinced this Spanish guy who considered himself a Defender of Women to tell me why everyone hated me, and he said word got around that I had showed up the first day and asked the program liaison where I could find a whore. He added that I was what was wrong with Americans and didn't I have a sister and—poking me in the chest with his finger—how would I feel if his Spanish ass came over to America expressly to fuck her?

I couldn't figure out what he was talking about, but he looked like he was going to hit me. I left.

I gave it some thought, and the only explanation was that she'd mistaken the English word "barber" for the Russian word "baba"—a funny thing because I had a history with the word "baba." I had written a prize-winning essay for my upper-level Russian Composition class in which I'd identified a flaw in a notorious Babel translation. Babel had a situation in which a simple young peasant girl, referred to as a "baba," strolls into a bar drawing all the men's attention. The word "baba" has three meanings: plumpish old woman, simple young peasant girl, and, in slang, whore. The translator had rendered it as an old haggard babushka, which didn't make any sense. Why would the men find their attention inexplicably drawn to her, except for her hideousness, which wasn't the point at all? I found the original, identified the problem, and composed the essay, winning the prize.

Since "barber" is not a common English word and our liaison's English was about as good as my Russian, she could only hear a Russian approximate. False cognate. This was the only explanation. They work the other way too. When Russians, in the course of normal conversation, describe a lecture as "exciting and inspirational" the Russian word for which is "pathetichiske," I hear only "pathetic." At the kiosks late at night, young men ask for "preservativi" and I'm imagining cured pears when it's the Russian word for "condoms."

For a couple days, I tried to set the record straight. I spoke to Tanya about it. "Why do you think I was mussing my hair while I asked you? What do babas have to do with hair?" She clearly didn't believe me. I spoke to others in the cohort as well. "Like from my essay?" I said, "the one that won the prize? Imagine the irony!"

No one believed me.

So I was there with a group and by myself at the same time.

It turned out to be the best thing going for me. While the others dance a vodka-flavored merengue at a club called Havana Nights, I wash my socks in a bathroom designed so that you have to straddle the toilet to take a shower.

While the others are in classes, I check out the obscure museums, see Rasputin's actual penis and Peter the Great's collection of deformed babies which float in jars like smooth balls of fresh mozzarella. I live the real Russian life: isolated, wet feet, maligned.

And on weekends they check the city of fountains or the Tsar's Summer Palace or sun themselves bare- and flabby-assed on the rocky beach at the Peter and Paul Fortress. I take the bus to the provinces.

The Novgorod bus is late so I sit at the beer garden in the courtyard of my building and read the newspaper. Lena is sitting there with a friend, dark-skinned, maybe Tajek or Azerbajani. Lena hates me too. She hates me because I pee behind her office, a wooden shed with a keg inside it. My bladder is worthless and five minutes after a beer, I have to go. All the Russian guys go back there and so I do too.

Lena doesn't like this, but the only option is to take the eight flights of stairs to my apartment and stand in the shower to pee.

Lena, who doesn't think much of my Russian, says to her friend, "Take this goat, Choika. He doesn't speak a word of Russian, and he pees behind this box every day."

I buy a bottle of beer and some dried squid from her.

"You're very beautiful," I say in my admittedly heavily accented Russian. "Three words in Russian. Oh, look at that—seven, twelve." She spits over her shoulder.

Lena *is* very beautiful, but her friend even more so. I watch them over the top edge of the newspaper and when they look, drop my eyes to some paragraph: *Sergei V. Yastrzhembsky, Putin's senior advisor on Chechnya, suggests that Islamic extremists co-opt the black widows against their will to become suicide bombers. "Chechens are turning these young girls into zombies using psychotropic drugs," Mr. Yastrzhembsky said. "I have heard that they rape them and record the rapes on video. After that, such Chechen girls have no chance at all of resuming a normal life in Chechnya. They have only one option: to blow themselves up with a bomb full of nails and ball bearings."*

Choika stands up. She is wearing a half-shirt and there's a square Band-Aid displayed prominently on her hip. It looks like a nicotine patch, but the guide at the Erotica Museum who showed me Rasputin's penis said that they're the new fashion in birth control.

Choika and Lena hug each other and cry. Then Choika scurries across the street to where the bus has pulled into the station. I chug the rest of my beer and run after her.

The driver stands outside the bus smoking and collecting tickets. "Nice shoes," he says to me. He's in New Balance sneakers identical to mine. It's obvious mine are authentic and his are fake, the imitations you buy in the market. Already the threads along the tongue are pulled and loose. The sole rubber is separating. USA is embroidered on both our heels. "How much?" he says.

"They're my only shoes."

"It's okay. Not a problem."

Ahead of me in line, two babushkas lecture Choika on the length of her skirt. She tells them it's the fashion. They say something about she won't be welcome in Novgorod like that. She says in her opinion she'll be very welcome.

I watch her shoes, white strappy things with heels like icepicks, and wonder why it is I think the word *babushka* rather than *old lady*. It comes easier than other words. I wonder when I'll think *devushka* instead of *girl*. I want to think *devushka* instead of *girl*.

I grab the last seat across from Choika and the two babushkas, next to two passed-out soldiers. I smile at Choika. She clutches her bag and looks out the window.

The driver stands on the steps at the front of the bus and shouts, "Attention, attention. I am very sorry to report that the bathroom on this bus is out of order today. In light of this unfortunate development we will be stopping once or twice whenever the possibility for a bathroom opportunity presents itself."

The soldier to my left comes to. He reaches across the aisle and puts his hand on Choika's stockinged knee. "Oh Caucasian beauty," he says.

The babushkas bang their canes against the seats.

"Relax my friends," the soldier says. He removes his hand from her knee and puts it on mine. Choika never looks away from the window.

"Do you know the game submarine?" he asks me.

"I've heard," I say. The game is very popular among students. I had heard of those in my cohort playing. But no one was inviting me.

From what I gather a kind of gamemaster they call Captain locks a group of friends in a flat with several bottles of vodka and some pickles. They cannot bring watches, and all clocks are unplugged. The telephone and television are removed by the Captain and no cell phones are permitted. He locks them in the flat and goes about his life, taking the key. The players block the light from all the windows and drink, sleep, drink, sleep, eat pickles, drink, sleep, etc. They are not allowed to peek out the window or stop drinking while they are awake. Two days later the Captain returns and lets them out.

He smiles at me. "We have been operating submarine for ten days."

"It's a long time," I say.

"Our Captain—he forgot about us."

With his hand still on my knee, the soldier falls asleep again.

"You are giving away so much," the babushka whispers to Choika.

"Much or not much," Choika says.

Dear Motherfucking Travel Diary, all this business before the bus takes off.

I play out this fantasy: Choika is one of the Black Widows from the article.

And it makes a lot of sense. Her eyes never flinch, even when the bus slams into potholes, her gaze steady out the window. Her bag is not quite big enough for luggage yet larger than an ordinary purse, the perfect size to conceal a wad of nails and ball bearings. She is just old enough to have had a young husband who died recently in the war.

How would she know Lena then? That was the hole.... Unless Lena's family, hard up for money like most Russian families, had become Chechen sympathizers purely out of financial necessity, taking in Black Widows, housing them, feeding them, taking care of them while plotting out the best, most populated, most unexpected routes. That was how they managed to buy that box with the keg in it where they sold dried squid and preservativi. I look around the bus. It's packed.

I kind of get off on this idea. I can already imagine the cutline on the national news back home: Black Widow suicide bomber blows up bus outside of St. Petersburg, Russia. One American is among the dead. My one life reduced to that one line. I lean across the seat to Choika and whisper, "Your way is fraught with peril; your plight, an admirable one."
She does not turn her head.

"Devil," the babushka says, crunching on sunflower seeds. "Now you've got foreigners drooling."

I disturb the soldier's hand from my knee and he jumps to his feet, wobbling slowly into the aisle and teetering to the back of the bus.

The driver, looking up at us from his rearview mirror the size of an ironing board, yells at him. "Hey, jerk," he says. "The bathroom is out of order."

"I'll piss on the floor then," the solider says.

The driver swings the bus into the shoulder, knocking the soldier down. The brakes are still hissing and the driver is up, halfway down the aisle. The other soldier grabs his arm as he goes by.

"Reconsider any manly-man," the other solider says.

"No," the driver says, "nothing like that." The soldier in the aisle crawls to his feet again and lights a cigarette. "Friends," the driver says, "let me talk to you then, outside. Everybody, let's take a bathroom break."

"Where are we supposed to go?" a woman shouts from the back. "Under some death cap?"

"Find a nice tree," the driver says.

Choika stands up. I think, detonation.

"I believe someone asked you kindly, sir," she says. "Where exactly are women supposed to go?"

"I believe someone answered, miss. There's some congenial trees in the area," the driver says. "They're cleaner than most bathrooms. You have five minutes or we leave without you."

"And what about ticks?" one of the babushkas says.

"Make sure you get their heads," the driver says.

The babushkas break out some toilet paper and sell squares for four rubles each. Choika buys two. The passengers disperse into the forest.

I hold it and eavesdrop. The soldiers and driver stand around a boulder talking. There is a lot of nodding but I can't hear them. The soldiers deliberate between one another and say something back to the driver. Then they all shake hands and pee together on the boulder.

I go towards the tree I remember Choika going toward. Another woman I don't recognize steps out and yells at me for sneaking up on her. I use her tree after she's gone and when I'm done Choika and the soldiers are back on the bus and the driver is beeping.

I take the small portion of the seat the soldiers leave me. The soldier who'd kept his hand on my knee holds out his hand, this time to shake. "Andre Andrevich," he says. "Let me guess: Fritz?"

"American," I say.

"Even better," he says, scooting over to give me more room. "Share some beer with us." He takes a warm bottle from his duffle bag and hands it to me. "The danger in playing submarine is in the doors. Russian doors are the problem, but, well, let's say you don't have to worry about them when you have a responsible Captain. Our Captain was also interested in drinking. And one of the rules of submarine—

strictly enforced by players—is that you cannot look out the window and you cannot know the time, and as a consequence you never know how long you've been playing."

"You don't get light through the crevices?" I ask.

"You get, which is why you tape the curtains to the wall with electrical tape."

The other soldier knocks on the window to get Choika's attention. She is like a statue, a perfect flesh statue with a birth control patch on her hip. The other soldier hunkers down in his seat to try and see up her skirt.

"You should be in submarine for two days, but sometimes time goes slow and sometimes fast. We think it was the sixth day when we realized, perhaps time was going too slow."

"It seems impossible to me, to mistake six days for two," I say.

"Luckily, we had good amounts of vodka, and pickled garlic."

He replaces my beer and takes the empty. He puts the empties on the floor and says, "Watch this." He points at his watch. The babushkas set these newspaper hats full of sunflower seeds on the seat and pick up the empties. They drop them in plastic sacks and go back to eating their seeds. "Five seconds," he says, "a new record."

"You're throwing away money," one of the babushkas says. "You could use a manicure, but you are not accurate."

"You cannot hear through Russian doors," Andre says. "We were shouting. We thought we would die there. We were pounding on the doors, but this is like a mouse running on a pipe. We were on the top floor, Vadim screaming for help out the windows. Everyone thought we were just drunk."

"We were fucking drunk," Vadim, the other soldier, says.

"When the Captain finally arrived he tried to tell us that it had only been two days. I told him, 'Prepare to suffer' and he admitted that he had forgotten us, and he confessed—you will never believe this: he had been off playing submarine himself. He was a player in two other games of submarine before he remembered about us. Since he didn't shower, he didn't find the key in his pocket. He also lost our cell phones."

I tell Andre my story about "barber" and "baba," which he laughs at once I explain that in English a "barber" is someone who cuts hair. He elbows Vadim and tells him my story. He and Vadim crack up.

"Let me tell you," Andre says, "*all* women are whores."

"Watch your mouth," one of the babushkas says.

"I've written an essay about this phenomenon," I say to Andre. "It was awarded a very prestigious collegiate prize in the US."

Choika sits like a statue. Her bag in her lap, her legs crossed official-like. She hardly jostles. I am more and more disappointed that she has not blown us all up. I contemplate peeing into an empty beer bottle. Instead I set the bottle on the floor and one of the babushkas snatches it up.

The cops pull over our bus and the driver calls another bathroom break to deal with them. I am happy for the bathroom break, the first one on the ground, whizzing behind the wheel, and I'm climbing back aboard before everyone else is even off. The cops and the driver are talking near the front of the bus, and I see the driver hand them some money.

Choika steps off the bus and walks around the cops and the driver. I hurry back to my seat to watch her. She goes across the street and chooses a thin birch. She plants her feet in front of the tree, then squats, staring at her knees. I wonder if I'm becoming weird.

She stands again, tugging down the hem of her skirt. She doesn't even look when she steps onto the highway. She stands there in the middle of the asphalt. She lifts up one heel, wiping off the mud with toilet paper. Then she does the same to the other heel.

When she slides back into the seat, one of the babushkas holds out the paper hat of sunflower seeds to her and says, "Here, girl, you need to eat."

"There's no place to wash hands," Choika says.

The police come aboard, forcing their way to the back of the bus.

They crowbar the locked bathroom door open and a tower of shoeboxes collapses on them. The driver breaks for it, but Andre and Vadim trounce him in the aisle.

"You bitches," the driver says. "They were in on it," he says to the police as they bend him over the seatback and cuff him. "They wanted free pairs. Size forty-three and forty-five. Check them."

"A cunt to your mouth," someone in back yells. "You unscrupulous shit-ass," another.

Choika stands awkwardly, like she has to sneeze, and whips some kind of ball with wires out of her bag. She pushes something on it and hunches. She hunches again, like she's pushing in the top of a deflated volleyball with her thumbs.

"What is this?" one of the babushkas says.

I close my eyes.

When they're open the aisle is a knot of perfectly unharmed screaming bodies.

"Move," Andre says to me and I push out into the aisle.

The soldiers lunge across the seat, tackling Choika. A policeman pitches the bomb out the window. It lands in the street and rolls into the ditch.

As I'm swept off the bus, I'm thinking, Was she going to do that, did she have that bomb before I thought it? "Did I do that?" I say out loud and in English and no one can hear me.

Once off the bus the soldiers see their third chance to be heroes in three minutes. They yell furiously for us to get as far away from the bomb as possible. We are off the bus, dispersing into the woods, I more hesitantly than the group.

When the police stuff Choika into the back of the cop car I can see her knees are bleeding but she's not crying or shaking. She sits in the backseat staring out the window just like she'd stared out the bus window the whole ride, like nothing mattered.

The police and the soldiers crouch over the bomb. Andre tinkers with it and Vadim and the police back up.

"I never saw a Muslim dressed like that," one of the babushkas says.

"She was masquerading as one of our girls," the other says. "Sluts," she says and dumps a little purse full of coins on the ground.

"What are you doing?" one babushka says.

"She gave me eight rubles for the toilet paper."

A little boy runs up and starts collecting the money. His mother yells at him to put it down and come back to her. When he does she hugs his head and says, "I wish we'd be there" or something like that— I don't understand the exact phrasing.

I approach the solider and the police. Andre is still fiddling with the bomb.

"I know her name," I say.

The police turn around. Their faces twitch. They're really shaken up. "Who are you?" one of them asks.

"Foreigner," Vadim says.

"I know her name," I say. Then, "I heard her say it."

"It's crap," Andre says, "total crap." He leaves the bomb in the ditch. "What's her name?" Andre says.

"Choika," I say.

"Choika," one of the police says. He says it again louder and looking her way and she turns her head. I suddenly feel ashamed, like I gave her up.

"What is that?" Andre says. "Choika."

"Chukchi?" Vadim says.

"Never heard of it," Andre says.

"Friends," the driver says. He's still in the handcuffs. "Feel free to retake your seat, friend," the driver says to me.

I'm the first one back on the bus and one of Choika's gorgeous shoes is on the floor near my seat. There's a scrap of toilet paper stuck to the bottom of the heel.

The driver talks to the police and the soldiers as the other passengers reboard, absolutely silent. Even the chatty babushkas. They sit cramped together in the exact same spots they sat in before, leaving a wide space where Choika was. A policeman unlocks the driver's handcuffs and he comes aboard. He goes back to the bathroom and selects two boxes, restacking those that had fallen and shutting the bathroom door, which refuses to latch at first but eventually clicks. He hands the two boxes to the policemen. Then the soldiers and the driver reboard. I point to the shoe on the ground.

"Don't touch it," Andre says. "Forget about it." He kicks it under the seat.

The driver stands at the front of the bus. "Anymore crazy terrorists here?" he says. No one says anything. "I sure hope not. Next stop is Novgorod. Unfortunately, I'm sorry to say that the bathroom on the bus is still out of order."

The engine fires and everyone breathes deep. Andre hands me a beer. From the first sip, I feel the pressure build in my bladder. I am still waiting for something, anything, to blow.

S.A. Riley   8 September
Director of Air Defense Marketing
Raytheon Corp.
Hartwell Road
Bedford, MA 01730

Mr. Riley,

I am writing in regard to your fine Patriot missile defense system.
Of course, we all saw the Patriot's crackerjack performance in the
Middle East on TV, but certain developments recently have given
me--and some of my like-minded fellow citizens--pause to reflect on
the advantages of such a system for home use.

I'm sure you consider yourself a patriot, like I do, in the original
sense of the word, and if you've ever tuned your Marine Band to 3760
megacycles, just before sunrise, then you know what I'm talking
about. Being a patriot today means a little more than dry runs
through the national forest, if you catch my drift.

So, I don't need to tell you what's massing in Haiti or what they've
got parked off the Baja peninsula--the real source of what they call
"El Nino." You can understand the source of our concern. That is why
we have come to consider the service of your fine defense system.
We know your product is pricey, but try to put a tag on freedom.
Accordingly, I ask that you send me a color brochure on your latest
product line and perhaps answer a few questions:
        -Does the system work well in urban areas?
        -Could the system fit, say, in a panel van?
        -Will the system work by remote control, and if so, Mac or
        PC format?
        -Is it wired for 110 or 220?

In addition, please let us know when would be a good time to come
to the proving grounds for the demonstration.

I await your reply, sir, and will maintain a "holding pattern" on
our progress toward freedom until I hear from you. Enclosed is a
check for 3 dollars to cover the catalog postage. Is there any way
you could include a Patriot bumper sticker? I'd sure like that. Until
then, as the bible says, "before the final flash are true men
turned."

Your fellow citizen,

611 Sunshine Dt.
Tallahassee, FL 32301

Motherhood and Terrorism
by Amanda Eyre Ward

LOLA THOUGHT HER BABY SHOWER WOULD BE CANCELLED DUE TO THE beheading, but she was wrong. Karen McDaniels called early Friday morning to make sure Lola knew how to get to her house on Liberty Avenue.

"Oh," said Lola, "is the shower still on?"

"Well, why wouldn't it be?" said Karen, an argumentative edge to her voice.

"The attacks in al-Khobar," said Lola, "and...and the head." She swallowed, "I guess I thought..."

"Did you know him?" said Karen.

"What? No."

"Phew!" Karen breathed a sigh of relief. "Honey," she said, her voice slipping back into its buttery Texas twang, "it's all quiet now up there. You can't let these Muslim assholes run your life."

"Right," said Lola.

"And I'm making nachos," added Karen.

"Okay," said Lola, hanging up the phone.

Lola's husband, Emmett, looked up from the *Arab News*. "Who was that?" he asked.

"Karen," said Lola, "of Karen and Andy McDaniels."

"Great!" said Emmett, flashing a wide smile before looking back at the paper. His wispy curls were thinning a little. Lola remembered standing next to him at the altar three years before, looking at his black hair and thinking she owned every handful of it. Now she understood: she would lose it all eventually, and be left with a big, bald head.

"What's in the news?" said Lola.

"Oh," said Emmett, "same old."

Lola knew that the shooting spree on the Oasis Compound was not same old. Twenty-two people had been killed, and the terrorists

had promised to rid the Arabian peninsula of infidels. Infidels like
Lola. She had been dreaming of gunmen for weeks. In her dreams, a
man with a scratchy beard held her head against his chest. He smelled
like lemons.

From the moment she'd stepped off the plane from Texas—her back
sore from the nineteen-hour flight, her eyes blinded by desert sun—
she had felt a brewing dread. It was cool on the tarmac, and she found
out later that the whole zone was air-conditioned.

"They air-condition the *outside?*" she'd said to Emmett.

"They've got more money than you can imagine," said Emmett.
"They can do whatever they damn well please."

Day by day, fear had grown in Lola until she was the sort of person who others called paranoid. At the welcoming cocktail parties,
the compound softball games, Lola had approached the wives, asking
them *don't you feel afraid?* And: *do you ever wonder if we should go home?*
She found quickly that these were not the sorts of questions you asked
in Haven Compound. "You sweet little thing," Karen McDaniels had
said, putting a hand to Lola's cheek. "You need some hobbies and a little baby or two. And a drink. Somebody get this sweet girl a drink!"
Lola learned to talk about motherhood instead of terrorism.

"You're my wonderful Lola, that's who you are," explained Emmett
in bed one night, when Lola had drunk duty-free wine until she could-
n't keep from talking. Emmett scratched her back and said, "Maybe
take some tennis lessons."

"But I've never felt so *lost*," said Lola.

"Oh sweetie," said Emmett, "yes you have."

Now, he drained his coffee cup. "Off to the races," he said, glancing at
his beeper. The damn beeper woke them up some nights, paging
Emmett to discuss some drilling mishap. When it went off, Emmett
ran to the office as if he were a doctor, though what he worked on was
not hearts, but oil wells.

"What races?" said Lola.

"I don't know," said Emmett, looking embarrassed. "Just something to say."

"My mom wrote again," said Lola. "She says we're not safe here. She thinks I should come home."

Emmett put his thumb and forefinger to his eyes and pressed, a gesture that made him look old. "We're safe," he said. "I don't know how many times I have to say it. But if you want to go home, then just go."

"I have the baby shower today," said Lola.

"That will be fun," said Emmett, "won't it?"

"Sure," said Lola.

"Take care of Junior," he said, bending to kiss Lola's giant belly. The baby kicked Emmett, hard.

She stood in front of her bedroom mirror for some time. The master suite had thick carpeting and carved mahogany furniture. It was a bedroom fit for a sultan, with gold braiding and tassels around everything, even the Kleenex-box holder. When Lola lay on her bed, she tried to understand how she had ended up an oil wife underneath a garish chandelier.

"I don't know about this party," she said to Corazon, the maid scrubbing her Jacuzzi tub.

Corazon did not answer. Lola pulled on a black dress her sister had sent from Old Navy Maternity. It smelled of America: crisp, synthetic, clean.

"Are you afraid to be here?" Lola said. "On an American compound?"

Corazon stood up, her hand on her back, and pursed her lips. "What can I say?" she said. "You are a target, and I am in the way of the target."

The baby kicked. "Fabulous," said Lola.

Lola's mother had emailed four more times, begging her to come home from the Godforsaken desert with the baby. "They say we are protected," Lola typed back. "The attacks are in the north, and the compound is filled with guards. I will let you know what I decide. Anyway, I am off to a baby shower!!! (Can't wait for the loot.) LOVE, Lolabee."

Lola clicked Send, then held her head in her hands.

"Miss," said Mayala, the cook, tapping Lola on the shoulder. "Miss, your lunch is ready." Lola nodded and wiped her eyes. She turned to face Mayala, a thin woman with her hair pulled severely back from her face. "I made you the frozen pizza," she said, not hiding her disgust. "The Tombstone frozen pizza," she added.

"Thanks," said Lola.

As she chewed the slices, Lola looked around her gleaming kitchen. Just a year before, she had lived in a shabby apartment in Austin. Lola and Emmett had made pasta on a hot plate, drank beer from water glasses on the porch. Then Emmett finished his dissertation and took the job with British Petroleum.

"I don't want to be a professor in some crummy little town," he'd said. "In Saudi, I'll be working with the best scientists in the world, and the fact is we all use gas. Like it or not. Even professors use gas, Lolly. And BP will send us all over the world." His hands moved like birds as he described the years that lay before them. "We'll never worry about money again. You'll have maids—a cook, even!"

Lola was a bad cook, she'd never pretended to be otherwise. And it was true: she'd been bored by her job at the radio station. But now she missed flirting with Crazy Bob, the morning-show host. She missed the drive down Lamar in her Toyota Tercel, a hot cup of coffee between her thighs.

As Lola ate, she saw that Mayala, usually a frenzy of activity, was standing still in the kitchen. Mayala had seven children at home, but spent her days in Haven, cooking for Lola and Emmett. Often, Emmett worked late, and Lola sat alone at the long table with platters of food. She could hear her Filipino staff giggling and speaking rapid

Tagalog in the kitchen, but she did not dare to join them.

"Is something wrong?" Lola asked Mayala.

"No ma'am," said Mayala, but she did not meet Lola's eyes.

In two days, she would be gone, leaving behind a note saying, "I am sorry. I am scared. Cook pizza for ten minutes at 350 degrees."

After lunch, Lola went for a walk. Haven was surrounded by high walls, so she could walk outside without a head covering or long pants. The pool was filled with kids, and two blond teenage girls lay on either side of a boom box playing Aerosmith. As Lola walked by, one of them lifted an arm and pressed her fingers to her skin, checking her tan. Standing by the pool were two armed Saudi men dressed in guard uniforms, their sunglasses hiding their eyes.

Suzi and Fran waved as Lola passed the tennis courts. As doubles partners, they won every tournament. Suzi's husband, Carl, was Haven's best golfer. Emmett had encouraged Lola to join the Golf Circle, get out, make buddies, but Lola was uncoordinated and became dizzy in the heat. She preferred to read inside her cool bedroom, and had joined the Book Ladies only to shut Emmett up. The first book choice had been *Ten Stupid Things Women Do to Mess Up Their Lives*, by Dr. Laura Schlessinger. Lola was not allowed to drive outside of the compound, so Emmett arranged for a chauffer to take her into the city.

As soon as the limousine passed through the guard station, the landscape changed. Abruptly, green lawns and large houses were replaced by desert. The limousine, clean and black as they left the compound, became covered with a thin layer of sand as they moved toward the teeming city. They drove through narrow streets, and Lola saw groups of women in dark robes led by men who walked a few strides ahead of them. Some of the women held hands, and Lola felt a pang of jealousy. She had never had a sister, or a close female friend for that matter. She had always been the girl in the corner of the bar, staring at her napkin.

They passed fast-food restaurants—McDonald's, Kentucky Fried Chicken—and Lola saw the separate entrances for women and men.

The limousine stopped at a traffic light, and Lola saw three boys playing with a dog. The dog rolled over, exposing its stomach, and one of
the boys shrieked and knelt down, pressing his face to the dog's neck.
There were flies everywhere, flies that had somehow been exterminat-
ed from Haven.

Lola walked around the bookstore for an hour, hiding under her
abaya. From the eye opening, she watched the other women touching
each other, pressing fingers to the thick cloth. Lola could not bring
herself to buy the Book Ladies' pick, and bought Stephen King's *Carrie*
instead with her wad of riyals.

The baby shower was at four. Corazon made Lola sit down, then
rubbed blush into Lola's cheeks. At the radio station, Crazy Bob used
to sing to her whenever he passed her cubicle: *Her name was Lola. She
was a showgirl!* Life was simpler then, before Lola knew she should be
ashamed of her bare legs, her car, and her country. She couldn't help
it: Lola started to cry.

"I don't understand you, madame," said Corazon.

"My mom wants me to come home with the baby," said Lola. "I
don't know what to do."

"How about this nice headband?" said Corazon, taking the plastic
band from her own head.

"No, no," said Lola, but Corazon did not listen, sweeping Lola's
hair back, jamming the band in place.

"Maybe everyone should stay home," said Corazon. "Maybe every-
one should stay at their own home and never leave." Lola looked at
Corazon, whose home was the Philippines. "Wear the nice headband,"
Corazon said, staring coldly at Lola and hissing through gritted teeth.

The worst day had been when Emmett admitted he was glad she was
pregnant.

"But how could this have happened?" said Lola. She held the EPT
stick in her hand.

"This is perfect, don't you see?" said Emmett. "You're going to be so happy! The other women are happy, right?"

Lola could have flown home, of course. She could have had an abortion. But each day went by and she found herself still in Haven, watching her body change. *A mother*, she said to herself. It could have been laziness and it could have been a decision. Maybe it was both. Maybe a mother was what she was meant to be.

Lola knocked on the McDaniels' door, and Karen pulled it open forcefully. "Lola's here!" she screamed. Lola swallowed and followed Karen down her long front hallway. In the living room, twenty or so suntanned women sat on leather couches.

"Hooray!" said Beth Landings, holding her drink high.

"Do you want a gin and tonic?" asked Karen. Lola shook her head.

"Oh, come on," said Beth, "It's my bathtub special." Lola shrugged, and Beth ladled her an icy glass, saying, "It's not easy to make gin, you know."

"Yes," said Karen, "we do know."

"Carl once lit a cigarette while he was making booze. He almost blew up the house," said Suzi, who had changed from her tennis whites into a dress printed with fuchsia crabs. Suzi was one of the few women who was not from Texas, and she had decided to pretend Saudi was Nantucket.

"How are you feeling, honeybun?" said Karen, leading Lola to a La-Z-Boy. "Sit back now, make yourself at home."

"I'm tired," said Lola, "but otherwise I'm fine."

"Well, just relax," said Karen. Lola watched the hubbub, sipping her drink and eating whatever hors d'oeuvres Karen's maids brought by: deviled eggs, shrimp, nachos. She listened to the women talk about the stupidity of having to wear an *abaya* outside the compound. "For the Arabs," said Suzi, "your hair is like your boobs."

"At the mall yesterday, I saw someone with a few curls sticking out," noted Karen.

"That's like wearing a skimpy bikini," said Beth, seriously.

"That's like wearing a thong!" said Suzi.

"You went to the mall?" said Lola. As soon as she said it, she wished she had not.

"Sorry?" Karen looked at Lola, narrowing her eyes.

"I mean, isn't it dangerous? Should we be leaving the compound?"

Karen sighed. "Lola," she said, "you can either think about the nutters all day long or you can go about your business."

"That's true," said Suzi. She crossed one long leg over the other.

"Has it been this bad before?" said Lola. There was a silence.

Beth Landings ladled herself another cup of gin. "No," she said simply. "I've been here for ten years, and this is the worst. To be completely honest, I'm scared to death."

"We might go to Bahrain," admitted an older woman with very pink lipstick. "I'm sick of this...this fiasco," she said. "The Arabs don't want us here. The tide has turned."

"The terrorists just shot people," said Beth matter-of-factly. "They just stormed the fucking compound and shot people in the head."

No one spoke, and Lola felt her baby begin to move slowly, rolling back and forth in its warm home. It pushed against her side, tentatively, and then with force. It was trying to get out, but did not know how.

Karen McDaniels rose and clapped her hands. "Time for the games!" she cried, her face brilliant and brave.

The first game was the string game. Karen made Lola stand up, and each woman cut a length of string that estimated Lola's girth. Nervous hilarity ensued: every single person thought Lola was a good six inches wider than she was.

The I-Spy game was a silver tray filled with baby items. Karen let them look at the tray for a few minutes, and then she covered it with a sheet. Lola chewed her pencil eraser, trying to remember what was on the tray as the kitchen timer ticked. *Diaper*, wrote Lola, *Rattle*, *Teddy Bear, Bottle*. In truth, she didn't even know what half the items were. (She would find out later, for example, that the rubber bulb was a nasal aspirator, and not a rattle.) This made her nervous, and she resolved to read the books Karen had lent her: *What to Expect When You're Expecting* and *The Girlfriends' Guide to Pregnancy*. Beth won the I-Spy game, remembering seventeen items, including the rectal thermometer.

As Lola opened each present, the women made comments. "A Godsend," for example, when she opened the Diaper Genie, or "my Alice couldn't get enough of that damn toy," when she opened the Lazy-Bee Singing Mobile.

Lola looked up from opening her presents, and saw a guard through the window. He was looking straight at Lola, his hand on his gun. What if he was a terrorist? *Look at that pregnant American!* she imagined the man thinking. *Who does she think she is? She's as greedy as the rest of them with her fancy-ass presents. What does she believe in, I'd like to know?* When he saw her looking, the guard nodded and moved on.

Twice during the party, Lola caught herself running her hand along her neck, pressing at the tendons and the bones.

Karen drove her home and helped her unload the packages. Soon, Lola's living room was filled with bright toys. Corazon brought out a tray of lemonade and cookies, and Karen sank into one of Lola's sofas.

"Well, I hope you had fun," said Karen.

"I did," said Lola. "I really did."

"You know," said Karen, "a million years ago, I was in advertising."

"Sorry?" said Lola.

Karen patted her permanent. "You think I'm some dumb housewife," said Karen. "Don't look so shocked, miss. I know."

"I don't…" said Lola.

"You think you're smarter than everybody else," said Karen. "You think you know what's going on out there." She flung her hand, indicating the world outside the compound. "I'm here to tell you, sweetie, at some point you have to decide. And let me promise you, what's going on in there," she jabbed at Lola's stomach, "is a hell of a lot more interesting. You mark my words."

"You know," said Lola, "I'm feeling a little tired…"

"Let me finish my piece," said Karen. She leaned toward Lola. "You think you can waltz around here," she said. "You think you don't need all this…" she gestured to the living room, the sunken fireplace, the surround-sound stereo. "Well, darlin', you can't go home again."

"Actually," said Lola, "I think I might be going home. My mom doesn't want me to have the baby here. It's not safe."

Karen snorted, then took a breath and said, "In Texas, you're just some pregnant girl. Here, though, you're a queen. And that baby," she jabbed again, "will have it all. You think about that before you jump on Lufthansa." Lola was silent.

"Thanks for the lemonade, little chick," said Karen McDaniels.

When Emmett got home from work that night, Lola met him at the door. "Hey," she said, "let's go out to dinner."

"Out to dinner?" said Emmett. "What are you talking about?" He opened the side door of his car, took his briefcase out.

"I'm sick of this big fucking house," said Lola.

Emmett sighed. He had grown pudgy from eating too much and sitting at his workstation. Even with the leather shoes and the BMW, though, Lola could still see in Emmett the shy student who had once told her the story of a mountain range as they hiked, explaining with wonder its evolution over millions of years.

"OK, OK," he said, after a moment. "How about the Japanese place?"

"No," said Lola, "Out."

"The Mexican place?"

"You know what I mean, Emmett."

"Out of the compound," said Emmett wearily.

"Right."

"Look, Lolly," said Emmett, coming toward her. "It's nothing great out there. You've been out. You have to wear the…"

"The *abaya*. I know."

He set his face in a mask of calm. "OK," he said. "All right," he said, "fine."

Emmett changed into clean clothes and Lola put on the long-sleeved black robe and headscarf. As they drove the BMW down the busy streets, Lola watched the men drinking tea outside the dim cafés, the boys selling cigarettes. "We could have taken the bus," she said. Emmett snorted.

"They hate us here, don't they?" said Lola.

"Of course they don't," said Emmett. Then he added, "Well, some of them do. A few crazy ones."

"More than a few," said Lola.

"You know," said Emmett, "I work with people who are very happy we're here. What I do is important to a lot of people."

Lola turned back to her husband. The anger in her faded when she saw that he was biting back tears. "Emmett…" she said.

"Can't you be proud of me?" he said, staring at the unpaved road, where a cow was trying to cross the street. "Can't you just try?"

The restaurant Emmett chose was a steak house, lit up like a Christmas tree. When Lola noted this, Emmett told her to keep her voice down. They were seated at a table set elaborately for six. Next to them, a large Saudi family had already been served their dinner. The women scooped food underneath their headscarves gracefully. Lola watched them as she squeezed into a chair, but they took no notice of her.

"Skooch over here," said Emmett. "You're three seats away. And wearing that damn hood."

Lola moved closer, and Emmett put his hand on the fabric covering her knee. "Should we drink from all the glasses?" he said. "Should we eat off all the plates?"

He was trying to be charming, and Lola smiled tightly. Not that Emmett could see. For all he knew, she was baring her teeth.

They ordered filet mignon and Cokes. They talked about baby names, crib styles, how a well-done steak felt like the tip of your nose when pressed. Finally, Lola put down her knife and fork. "Em," she said, "we need to talk."

"Yeah," said Emmett. "I know. Just tell me. Are you leaving?" His eyes were large and blue, with bursts of white around the irises. He blinked in the dim light of the restaurant. There was something in his forehead, in the lines around his mouth: he was just as scared as she was. "And also," he said, "will you come back?"

"I have to go to the bathroom," said Lola.

In the ladies' room, two Saudi women stood at the mirror. They had taken off their headscarves, and above their dark bodies, their faces were bright, and topped with elaborate hairdos. Precious stones glittered in their ears and around their necks. One applied very pink lipstick to her lips.

There was a couch in the corner, and Lola sat down. She felt calm underneath the robe, with no skin exposed. She could walk out of the restaurant and into the street, joining the groups of people out for an evening stroll. She could take a cab to the airport, and fly home, or to Tahiti. Nobody would notice her: she was just a blank expanse of cloth in the shape of a woman.

Lola thought about going home. She could live with her mother, in Sugar Land. Her mother lived in the same small house that Lola had grown up in, but now it was surrounded by Houston's nasty sprawl. Lola thought about her baby, and her mother's cracked linoleum floor. Lola saw herself: a sweaty, pregnant girl on her mother's front porch, kicking at a rusty metal chair.

Without warning, the lights in the bathroom went out. Lola heard her own shallow breath. The women at the mirror fell silent. As Lola's eyes adjusted to the darkness, she saw them putting their headscarves back on. They walked past Lola quickly, and she smelled perfume.

She was alone. At prayer time, they cut the electricity, she knew it. But she imagined a man in the doorway of the bathroom. She imagined cold metal against her temple, a blade to her throat. The man would take pictures of her, afterward. He would post a video on the Internet.

The baby moved, and Lola put her hand to her stomach. She felt the baby throb against her skin, a second heartbeat. It kicked and kicked, blissfully unaware.

It occurred to Lola that she could tell the baby the Jacuzzi tub was an indoor pool. The baby would think that Corazon loved it whole-heartedly, and not just because she was being paid. And when they were forced to evacuate (which they surely would be, sooner or later) the baby would know only that they were together—a family—and safe.

Though she felt far from home or a hope of home, she cradled the baby and whispered, *I've got you.* When it was born, Lola would lie on her expensive sheets and hold the baby to her breast. To the baby, Lola would smell like a mother, and the ridiculous chandelier would look like stars.

Newholly

by Ryan Boudinot

MY WIFE AND I BOUGHT THE HOUSE THREE YEARS AGO IN A BOUT OF panic. After our portfolio did a nosedive, we thought we'd never afford a decent place within the Seattle city limits. We're in the Newholly neighborhood on Beacon Hill, an experimental development of subsidized public housing mingling with for-sale homes. Sometimes urban planners from out of town visit to walk around and wonder if such a concept would work in their own cities. Into this neighborhood have come first-generation immigrants from Somalia, Ethiopia, and Vietnam, gay couples priced out of Capitol Hill, African-American families. There is a three-year waiting list to get into the subsidized homes, while the for-sale homes linger on the market, prices sliding gradually south. Families who qualify to live here under the guidelines set by the Seattle Housing Authority raise their children in a place that is clean, friendly, and within walking distance of playgrounds, a library, and a community center that provides ESL classes. If you buy a house in Newholly, you're testing your liberal values as if against some formula, weighing fears of economically challenged neighbors with hope for the transcendent nature of community. This place has grown on Sylvia and me, with easy access to downtown, children who beg to pet our dog, halal barbecues in the park. Cultures of origin recede and individuals take their places. There is much gentleness here. I just can't stand it when the Somalian woman next door beats her children.

Seattle has the highest concentration of Somalian immigrants in the United States, and Beacon Hill the highest concentration in Seattle. We're just a mile or so from the Maka Market, a Somalian grocery that was raided by the FBI in the months after 9/11. The accusation went something like this—Maka's wire service, which local Somalis used to send money home to relatives, was allegedly a method to channel funds to the Taliban. During the raid, agents emptied the shelves of toilet paper and bread, diapers, canned food, candy, meat, etc., sending the entire inventory to a landfill. The incident caught the public's rattled attention for a couple days then disappeared into news archives, though I don't think the incident has ever strayed far from my neighbors' thoughts.

The boys next door, Mahaad and Musharif, play the same game all afternoon. One of them hides in their backyard storage shed while his brother pounds the door with a toilet plunger handle, shouting something in their native language that sounds like "Oaty-oat! Eye effey eye!" After a while the one hidden in the shed emerges and a great battle ensues, with gun noises and grenades made of dirt clods gathered from the yard's many molehills. They don't seem inclined to play anything else. The girl, about eight, named Luul, appears to narrate the game with a horrible splitting screech that makes it difficult for me to write. I rarely see the father of this family. I've heard he works three jobs, parking cars at a hotel, washing dishes at a seafood restaurant, laundering linen at the VA hospital. The mother, Deka, drives a purple minivan and dries the family's clothes by draping them over the back porch railings. Occasionally one of the boys makes the other cry, and Deka shoots out of the screen door as though she's been springloaded into the house, grabs the offending child, and drags him back into the home where she beats him with an implement that makes a nauseating smacking noise. I'm guessing it's a wooden spoon. I reflexively save whatever document I'm working on and stare numbly at the keyboard, debating again whether to call Child Protection Services. I never do.

My wife, who has a regular day job, is never around when the beatings occur, but I occasionally IM her to keep her informed.

thashznit: it's happening again. i think musharif this time.
smartiepants: Jesus, call CPS then.
thashznit: i don't know the number.

smartiepants: Aren't you on the Internet?

She never provides the response I hope for. I count on Sylvia to bolster my indefensible plea of ignorance and justify my inability to make
an adult decision. I escape into my Word doc and interrupt the flow
of the book review I'm working on to lay down the givens:

>   The woman next door beats her children.
>   They are refugees from Somalia, and are not American citizens.
>   They appear to be Muslim, based on superficial indicators like the
>   mother's clothing and their names.
>   Listening to the woman beat her children offends me.
>   I am resistant to calling Child Protection Services because:
>   I am lazy.
>   I don't entirely understand their language or culture.
>   I am hoping the beatings will just stop on their own.

The phone rings, the dog wants me to extract his chewie from behind
the couch, I need a snack. I leave my document open and, when I
return an hour later, nudge the screen saver into remission and add a
sixth given:

>   I am afraid the government will do something unpleasant to this
>   family if I report them.

One afternoon in late 1998 Sylvia and I were running around the lake,
both having recently acquired positions at startups that no longer
exist. About a mile into the run Sylvia pointed at a telephone pole.
    "What's that up there?" she exhaled.
    "Lost-cat poster?"
    "Nuh-uh. Revenue opportunity."
    By the time we'd finished the run, we had the basic business plan

in our heads. Concept: A Web-based lost-pet solution. How it worked: Pet-losers registered, posted pictures, descriptions, and reward amounts for their missing pets. The database was searchable by zip code, breed, fur color, etc. Users could pull up listings of lost pets in their area, then sort the results any way they wished, by reward amount, for instance. The higher the reward amount, the more prominently we'd feature your listing, and the bigger cut we'd get when your pet was found.

We went through a round of financing. We lasted a year, in which I expensed everything I ate. We purchased a television that we never took out of the box then sold it on eBay at a loss. Sylvia and I always remind ourselves that the one tangible benefit of losing three quarters of our net worth was bringing Mr. Sloppy into our lives. Mr. Sloppy was an insecure pug we found on one of our frequent late-night neighborhood recons. Never claimed by his owners, he became a permanent fixture of our couch. Slop has always appeared overly concerned about our well-being, spinning in tight, breathy, nervous circles whenever we argue.

> thashznit: mr. sloppy misses you.
> misssmartie: What's he doing?
> thashznit: curled up in his bed giving me the look.
> misssmartie: You should take him out on a walk.

I copy and paste the word "walk" into a voice emulation dictionary application, turn up the speakers, and click Play. "WALK," the slightly Latino-sounding female voice says, "WALK. WALK. WALK."

Mr. Sloppy leaps from his bed and places his paws on my leg.

"Hey Mr. Sloppy, wanna go for a—"

"WALK."

Mr. Sloppy whines, snorts. Outside he sniffs the beauty bark for evidence of other dogs' urine. He looks like a fire hydrant with legs. A former boss once told me that if she were reincarnated, she'd like to come back as the dog of a childless couple. Slop's got that kind of life. His leash cost a hundred bucks and is made of ostrich leather.

As we walk deeper into the neighborhood, the architecture remains a limited menu of four or five designs. We come to the perimeter, a street of twentieth-century brick houses through which generations of Asian immigrants have filtered. Jet fuel smells menace from the direction of Boeing field. Mr. Sloppy does his business next to a Stop sign. Judging from his level of fascination, it has been tagged by many dogs. Daniel, a kid I have gotten to know, rides up on his bike, initiating conversation, as is his habit, with questions he already knows the answers to. His Sonics jacket looks ten sizes too big.

"Are you taking your dog out to go to the bathroom?"

"Yep."

"Does he want his privacy?"

"He's done," I say, retrieving the turd with a blue *New York Times* bag.

"How much did your dog cost?"

"Five million dollars," I say, and from a certain point of view, this isn't a lie.

"Nuh-uh. Does he bite?"

"Only little kids."

Daniel looks puzzled. The last time he asked me this question I told him no. "Is this a different dog than you had before?"

"No, same dog. But that's the same question you asked before. You know him. He likes you."

Daniel drops to a crouch and Mr. Sloppy obediently rolls onto his back for a belly rub. "Good girl, good girl, Mr. Sloppy," Daniel says.

"Hey Daniel, do you ever play with Musharif and Mahaad?"

"Ooh, you like getting pet. That's a good girl."

I repeat the question.

"No, I don't like them. You can't trust them. They jacked my friend's shoes one time. They're from Somalia."

"Is that why you don't like them? Because of where they're from?"

Daniel shrugs. "Those guys get on my nerves."

"What about the dad? I haven't seen him in a while."

"He went back to his country."

"When? To visit?"

"Mr. Sloppy likes belly rubs, don't you Mr. Sloppy?"

An ice-cream man arrives, one of the down-market types, an operation consisting of a loudspeaker mounted to the roof of a blue minivan, a couple ice chests in back, stickers plastered to the side door advertising the inventory. I'm resigned that Daniel's attention can't be recaptured. He leans on the door of the vehicle, concentrating on his decision. The driver looks like no one I would ever choose to give my money to, unshaven, smoking a cigarette, ashes falling onto the convex surface of a plaid flannel shirt stained with Popsicle drips. Children stream from their houses, crawl over backyard fences, and approach the vehicle to purchase treats or beg for freebies. Luul, Musharif, and Mahaad emerge from behind a mailbox and stand on the sidewalk. One of the boys kicks the fuzzy border of an untrimmed parking strip. I can tell they have no money but want to be part of the neighborhood spectacle, as if this street doesn't get hit by an ice-cream man literally fifteen times a day. As the other kids thin out and walk away with their treats, I nod at Luul and say, "What would you kids like?"

They quickly check each others' eyes, communicating systems of desire and inhibition. A hypothetical dinner discussion among their family occurs in my head. *Don't take anything—money, treats, whatever—from a white person.*

Mahaad steps forward and points at a sticker depicting a Neapolitan sandwich. As I reach for my wallet, Luul pulls her brother by the arm and scolds him in Somali. Musharif steps forward and asks for a banana fudge bar. Luul, outnumbered, lets go of Mahaad's arm and tries to apprehend her other brother, but it's too late. He's already been handed his treat and runs away backward, taunting. The driver hands the little one his ice-cream sandwich and Luul turns to me, her lower lip trembling angrily.

"It's okay, it's my treat," I say, "Do you want one?"

The driver coughs. "Look, man, I got other neighborhoods."

Luul shakes her head and walks away. I pay the driver and remind Daniel not to litter. He picks up his wrapper and follows my dog and me to our street. Rounding the corner I notice that Musharif and Mahaad have dropped their wrappers in my yard. I pick them up and slowly walk into the alley. I hear Deka yelling inside their house. "That family sure fights a lot, don't they?" I say.

Daniel is concentrating on a worm that has dried on the sidewalk. "Yeah, one time Mahaad came to school with a black eye. Catch you on the flip side!" Daniel sprints in the direction of the community center.

Mahaad and Musharif are engaged in their game again, banging on the storage shed, yelling, "Oaty oat! Eye effy eye!" They seem not to notice me. As I get closer, I hear an argument from within the house. Musharif bangs on the door of the shed with a shovel handle. "Oaty oat!" Bang. The mom yells in Somali, a blurred sequence of syllables. Mr. Sloppy whines. Luul screams, begging, "No mommy no mommy no mommy!" I unlatch the gate. Bang. As I walk across the yard, the boys remain engaged in their play, unaware I'm behind them. When I reach the porch I finally understand what it is they keep taking turns yelling at each other. Bang. The door of the storage shed bursts open. I take the porch steps two at a time. Behind me, a torrent of verbalized ordinance. I beat on the door. This whole time the boys have been saying, *Open up. I'm FBI.*

Deka opens the door. The boys finally notice me and fall silent. Luul stands behind her mother, huffing tears.

"Okay, look. You can't just fucking beat your kids, all right? I'm sick of hearing you abuse your children. I can hear it every time. And I'm telling you to stop. Or else I'm going to have to call CPS and they'll drag you to court and then to immigration and then you'll be on your way back to Somalia. Ever hear of the Patriot Act? That's the

America you live in. I respect your religion, your culture, your god, whatever, but I can't allow this kind of abuse to happen next door. You have to stop."

From a distant block the warble of the ice-cream man's truck slowly seeps from the neighborhood. Deka never breaks eye contact. I can feel the boys behind me, hands on their weapons.

"She doesn't speak English," Luul says.

"What?" I say.

Mr. Sloppy whimpers. Deka shakes her head, responds with a long string of Somali punctuated by the words *United States* and *Patriot Act* and *deported*. She looks at her daughter and appears to ask a question. Have I put Luul in the position of telling her mother that I'm going have them deported?

The shovel handle catches me in the small of the back. I go down in a mess of fists and leash and a bag of shit. I'm on my back. My dog lunges, spraying slobber. I get a broom handle to the face. Another blow clips Mr. Sloppy's front left leg. He yelps, I shout, "You little fuck!" and kick hard, my foot finding Mahaad's chest, knocking him off the porch into the yard. Everything stops.

"I'm sorry I'm sorry I'm sorry," I say, running to the boy, "Come on, breathe breathe breathe."

The boy gulps air and turns it into a long, mournful wail. I pick him up and carry him to the house. Furious, Deka pulls him away from me and tends to him on the couch. Luul crouches sniffing in a corner, softly petting Mr. Sloppy. My left hand is sticky with dog shit. My eyesight is all fucked.

"I'm so sorry," I say feebly. Then Musharif screams and hits me in the back of the head with something hard.

I wake to a car alarm. The strange house is dark, lit by street light through the blinds. I'm on a couch and Mr. Sloppy is asleep between my legs. I don't know if I'll be able to get up. My back and head throb. A plastic bag of water that used to be ice slides off my shoulder as I rise.

"Luul?" I say, "Someone? Hello?"

I find the bathroom and turn on the light. Through my one good eye I see that my head has been bandaged with strips of an undershirt. A bandage has been applied to a cut that I didn't know I had on my right hand. I check my phone and see I have five new messages, no doubt from Sylvia wondering where the hell I am. With Mr. Sloppy under my arm, I return home.

It's a couple weeks later and I have not seen the family or their van. I'm convinced I will never see them again. A truck from Seattle Housing Authority shows up and a couple guys start hauling stuff from the house—furniture, bedding, toys. When I ask what happened to the family, they shrug. One of them says, "We're just here to clear out their shit." None of the family's neighbors seems to know their where-abouts, either, or if they do, they aren't telling me. I worry about those kids, but what can I do for them now? I walk my dog past their house and am preyed upon by a grotesque thought, a thought I will not even share with my wife, that wherever that woman is beating her children, I at least hope it's in the United States of America.

Richard B. Cheney   17 September
The Shadow Government
Washington, D.C.
United States of America

Dear Mr. Cheney,

I'm writing you today for a position in the shadow government. I hope
you'll find that my talents and accomplishments will make me a
perfect candidate. I haven't attached my resume or anything—that
would disqualify me, right? But let me assure you, Mr. Cheney: I'm
the man for the job, however shadowy that job might be.

I admit I've never shown much interest in government. At Covina High,
all the student council types were piss-pantsy for seconding motions
at mandatory rallies. My tenure at Covina, cut short by other
prospects, was one long homeroom announcement for public service,
self-sacrifice and representing the will of the student body. Come
now. But a *shadow* government—a shadow government, I'm convinced,
is right up my alley. I have a feeling that you, too, Mr. Cheney,
were the kind to share a few smokes in the Mormon Church parking lot
so you'd arrive late enough to miss that loudspeaker every morning.

As for my qualifications, an afternoon of legwork can confirm my
abilities. If you'll check the police logs for North Hollywood,
you'll see that a little something happened on the evening of August
11th, 1999 on Briarwood Avenue. I may have had a hand in that. And
there's a Greyhound locker—number 332—in the downtown terminal that
you may be interested in. I don't need to tell you guys the combo.
There's also an example of my handiwork—visible only from the air—
on top of the Smart & Final in Studio City. My references are
available upon request.

I want to thank you in advance for this opportunity, Mr. Cheney. I've
never worked belowground before, and I can only imagine the special
effects. One question—would I myself be in the shadow government,
or would I be someone else?

You strike me, sir, as a man with no regrets. Well you won't regret
this. And of course, you can count on me to deny this letter ever
took place. I believe it was Brutus who first said "Don't ask, don't
tell," though he said it in Latin.

Enclosed is a check for three dollars for forwarding me the necessary
security badges. You just tell me which elevator to step into, and
down we go!

Sincerely,

ADAM JOHNSON

P.S. — Matthew 3:14, if you know what I mean.

John Ashcroft: More Important Things Than Me
by Jim Shepard

• Creative Self Doubt

When people have honest questions about where I stand or what I'm doing—in politics, it happens all the time—I've learned not to take it as an insult. In fact, I often find that their concerns mirror reservations I might have had on my own. Their honesty helps me clarify the situation. Nobody wins when anyone holds grudges.

• Electability

Folks say, Here's a fellow who doesn't spook moderates, who's actually electable. That word pops up a lot: *electable*. Paul Weyrich had some people over one night and we were lounging around out on his porch and he suggested that I was more than just presentable; I was a guy who could go on Jay Leno and play a couple of tunes with the Oak Ridge Boys.

Pessimists claim my only base is the pro-family, religious vote. They say, "Where else can he go? The country club? The boardroom?" My answer is that those aren't the only places to look. My answer is that I'll take my chances with the American people. I served two terms as governor in a Democratic-leaning state, I had a national profile as a Senator, and, yes, I have support among what the media calls the Religious Right. In my gubernatorial reelection I carried 64 percent of the vote, the best showing of any Missouri governor since the Civil War.

• My Principles

My principles are out there for everyone to peruse, and always have been. Whenever I get more than four people in a room, I tell them: you examine the record, and let me know if you find anything that's contradictory or troublesome. And if you think you do, you come back to me, and we'll clear it up on the spot.

In the Senate, I fought against national testing standards, activist judges, and the nomination of a pro-abortionist Surgeon General.

I forced the first floor vote ever on term limits and had to fight my Majority Leader to do so. I wrote part of the welfare-reform law allowing states to deliver services through churches and private agencies.

I promoted the de-funding of the NEA. The average guy who wants to go down and see Garth Brooks, he doesn't get a federal subsidy, but the silk-stocking crowd that wants to see a geometric ballet in Urdu, they get a break on their tickets.

When it comes to bills, I don't trim and I don't pork things up, whether the doors are closed on the session or not.

And I keep reiterating, wherever I go: it's against my religion to impose my religion on others.

• Ethics

I tell people that I know about scandal. During my second term as governor, I had an overeager staffer who when he heard about my boy's need for some books on Queen Elizabeth for a homework assignment, called the state librarian at home and got her to open the library after hours. The press got ahold of the story, like they get ahold of everything, and I quickly took responsibility. Around the house we call it Homeworkgate and joke that we learned from our mistake. A columnist for the St. Louis Post-Dispatch wrote about the whole thing that "If a state ever had a less exciting governor than John Ashcroft, I never heard about it."

• Turning Heads

I hear that I first started turning heads after the charges became public that Monica Lewinsky had turned the President's. Most everyone in my party maintained a code of silence in the early going. I did not. I said publicly in an address to the Conservative Political Action Conference that January, "Mr. President, if these allegations are true, you have disgraced yourself and the Office of the Presidency, and you should resign now."

That's what I said. It bears repeating: "Mr. President, if these allegations are true, you have disgraced yourself and the Office of the Presidency, and you should resign now."

• Atlanta

If I've got one problem at this point in time, in perception terms, it's Atlanta. Atlanta was a nightmare. I dropped the ball there and I'm the first to admit it.

I was nervous. I started right in, once introduced, on principles, and what I stand for, and there was a point a paragraph or two into my notes when I realized that the silverware wasn't going to get any quieter, and flopsweat set in. I was fighting a losing battle with overdone filet mignon for everyone's attention.

It didn't help that Forbes was going on next and that he got about ten standing ovations for saying mostly the same things. *Steve Forbes.*

A nightmare. I get the shivers going back over it, I don't mind admitting.

"Shiver shiver shiver," Janet says, sometimes, late at night, lying next to me.

• Ethics

It's fashionable I guess for people to talk down Jimmy Carter, but let me say this: Jimmy Carter was an unimpeachable straight-shooter who restored people's trust in the Presidency. And don't think the American people couldn't use a little of that particular medicine right now.

• The Transports of Love

Hollywood likes to showcase the tyranny of romantic infatuation—how two people might abandon their friends, family, and beliefs all in the name of an overpowering emotion—but my father didn't raise me that way. He wasn't a stoic and didn't despise emotion. He believed that delayed gratification was an essential practice for success in life. He always said, *Don't jeopardize the future because of the past.*

A woman from a national magazine wrote that I had a Boy Scout's haircut and a choir boy's magnetic machismo. I wrote her a note explaining that I appreciated the joke, and that I didn't think magnetic machismo was what we needed in a President at that particular point.

• Helpmate
Janet says that after God she puts family first, everything else second, and nothing third. During the campaign for the Senate she was asked if she minded being a helpmate. "No," she said. "The same way I don't mind being a math professor or writing textbooks."

• Sex
Once in a diner a fry cook said to me—I guess in an attempt to destroy his customer base—"I'll tell you one thing: I'm not getting any tonight." What I should have answered was something I thought as I drove away: that our country was affluent in sex but bankrupt in love. Prostitutes have a sex life. Animals have a sex life. Human beings should have a *love* life.

The right results come first from working hard to make the right decision, and then working even harder to make the decision right.

• Thrift
Missouri remains one of the cheapest places to buy gas in America. My staffers tease me because I've been known on drives home to run the tank down to near-empty so I can save a few dollars by filling up on the other side of the Mississippi.

• Why I Supported the Death Penalty as Governor
I was the ultimate appeal to correct error, not reward regret, emotion,

or even religious conversion. Becoming a Christian removes us from *eternal* penalties.

• Public Civility

The original rules of debate for the Constitutional Convention in 1787 did not allow conversation when another member spoke. No reading of any kind was permitted during debate, and no one was allowed to speak twice unless everyone else had spoken once.

• Things to Work On

We're all works in progress. I know that I sometimes don't make a sufficiently forceful impression. I know that I can seem to people, as Janet likes to put it, too settled on my own road. There's a little motto painted onto the serape of a toy donkey on my desk: *"We're all here to learn from one another."* I look at that motto every day.

• Recurring Dreams

Janet notes that I'm thrifty even with my dreams. I tend to have the same one for weeks running. They stay in my head. My most recent one features Barney Thomas, one of my father's oldest friends, who's sick now. My father called him The Judge when I was growing up.

• R&R

I give visitors to my office copies of my ten-song tape, "The Gospel (Music) According to John," which I composed and produced myself.

• Friendship

Harry Truman said, "If you want a friend in Washington, buy a dog."

• Friendship

When I was state auditor of Missouri, I had seats on the fifty yard line for Tigers games. When I lost reelection, I couldn't get into the end zone.

• As the Seasons Change

Growing up I never imagined that I would one day need a man to work five days a week just to organize my schedule, let alone that I'd have an after-hours recording that goes like this: "Hello, I'm Andy Beach, scheduler for Attorney General of the United States John Ashcroft. If you'd like to request an appointment, please fax your request to the following number…"

• Ambition

The Presidency is like running the mile. You have to run the first few laps, and run them hard, before you know if you're really even in the race.

In 1998 Paul Gigot asked, in the *Wall Street Journal*, "Richard Nixon and Watergate helped make a president out of an obscure Democrat named Jimmy Carter. Can Bill Clinton and Monica Lewinsky do the same for an equally unknown Republican?"

• The Judge

Two months ago he sent a letter I still haven't answered. Usually I'm a bear on correspondence. I haven't even finished reading it.

In the dream he's as nice as can be. He quotes the first line of his letter: "So, John, the sawbones has come through with the bad news that apparently I've got the lung thing everyone's been worried about."

• Moderation

Do we think a four-time murderer is only 'moderately' dangerous?

Are drugs in a schoolyard only 'moderately' a problem?

In combat, do we want our fellow soldiers to be 'moderately' brave?

Are we so sure that 'moderation' is always a good thing?

• The Long View

Includes the understanding that the verdict of eternity stands above the verdict of history.

• False Pride

I'm constantly on the lookout for it.

• Losing to a Dead Man

My theory about elections is mirrored in what I hold about all of life. For every crucifixion, a resurrection is sure to follow—maybe not immediately, but the possibility is always there.

• Melancholia

I became governor ten years ago. Twelve, I guess. Time flies.

• The Hard Road

Like anyone else, there are weaknesses I've had to overcome to get to where I am today. A reporter once said that I speak like I'd rather be gigging fish on the Osage, and I dropped him a note telling him that that was because it was true: I would.

• Secret Discouragements

Distractions don't seem to want to leave me in peace when my faith in myself is shaky or my defenses low. Janet calls them The Secret Discouragements. I think:

—In a February 1998 poll of registered Republicans in New Hampshire, 0 percent named me as their first choice for the nomination.

—Even John Kasich got 2 percent.

—I'm not a natural self-promoter.

—I don't like the way I look when I eat.

• Unfinished Projects

The letter on my computer is entitled *Untitled*. So far it has the address and no date and two lines: *Dear Barney: It was terrible to hear about your terrible news.*

• Always on Offense

During my first term as governor, Missouri landed both the Royals and the Cardinals in the World Series. There was speculation as to who I'd be rooting for. I rooted for both. My wife and I made a special hat the night before, half and half, red and blue, with bills on both sides. I flipped it around between innings to the team that was batting. An editorial the day after accused me of indecisiveness or double-dealing or both. But a letter-writer from Hannibal hit the nail on the head: there was another way of looking at it, he said. Governor Ashcroft is just always on offense. And he was right.

• John Ashcroft in the Pocket of Big Tobacco

Who pays for years and years and years of government litigation? Who is it that foots the bill so the trial lawyers can pocket billions?

• On Being Part of a Persecuted Minority

Most of those who criticize me for my religion haven't even taken the time to discover just what my religion is. The Assemblies of God is a Pentecostal denomination, so I know what it's like to be a part of a minority and mocked for one's beliefs. When the mockers come after me, I refer them to two bumper stickers distributed by AG pastor Fulton Buntain: "It's Never Too Late to Start Over Again," and "It's Always Too Soon to Quit."

• On Pushing That Liberal Rock Up the Hill

I used to tell my son when he got frustrated about his math scores: You know, there are times that maybe God will call us to do something that doesn't have an apparent success about it at the moment.

• Learning About Values

My father was a pastor and a college president. I remember as a very young boy hearing his early morning prayers, and tiptoeing downstairs to sit beside his knees. So that I was shielded by his body as he pleaded for my soul.

• Learning About Values

The day before he died, in the presence of a small group of family and friends, he reminded me that the spirit of Washington is arrogance, and that the spirit of Christ, on the other hand, is humility.

• Learning About Values

He was on the sofa, and struggled to get up to help family and friends pray over me. I said, "Dad, you don't have to struggle to stand and pray over me with all these friends." He said, "John, I'm not struggling to stand; I'm struggling to kneel." And he left that couch and came and knelt with me.

• Why Should We Believe in the Resurrection?

After losing my first race for Congress, I was appointed State Auditor. After losing the election to maintain that post, I was elected State Attorney General. After losing the election as chairman of the Republican National Committee, I was offered the candidacy as US Senator. After losing the reelection campaign for US Senator, I was appointed Attorney General of the United States.

• Learning About Values

My role models are: Jesus Christ, Abraham Lincoln, J. Robert Ashcroft, Barney Thomas, and Janet Ashcroft. With no apologies, and in that order.

• Standards

No schoolteacher could have gotten away with the behavior that Bill

Clinton did. No principal, no college president, no corporate president. That he wasn't forced to resign tells me that our standards for
the presidency are lower than they are for virtually any other job in
America. And that, to me, is a disaster.

• **Deception**

How can we expect individuals to be faithful to us if they're not faithful to the people in their own families?

• **Government**

Revival isn't something that comes from government. Government is
not an agent of spirituality. But it can be a moral force. It's said you
can't legislate morality. Well, I've got news for those who say that: *all*
we should legislate is morality. And we certainly shouldn't legislate
*im*morality.

• **What's in My Heart**

Have I been the man I could be? No. What's in my heart? What do I
spend my time thinking about? Could I at any moment make a clean
breast of it to people; let them see, *so here's what I've been thinking?*

I get teased for starting every staff meeting with that phrase: "So
here's what I've been thinking."

• **Having Good Memories**

Is like having gold in your spiritual bank. Nothing can take the place
of them. Nothing can diminish them. Nights I can't sleep I remember
floating on my back with Dad down the little stream behind our farm,
the sun on our faces, the leaves spiraling overhead. When one of my
colleagues from across the aisle is going on about this or that victim-
ized minority, I remember my father and The Judge taking three
straight Saturdays to help me with my soapbox racer. Their faces come
back to me when I don't expect them, and when I do. Their faces are
a gift I have to be strong enough to carry.

• Mr. Perfect

Janet gets a kick out of it whenever a publication decides I'm Mr. Clean or Mr. Perfect or whatever they've decided to call me. She's happy for me but she always makes a wry little list of recent shortcomings to keep my head from swelling. "All well and good, Mr. Perfect," she said after the most recent article, in the *Southern Partisan*, "but you still haven't called Barney back."

• Unfinished Projects

Dear Barney:
- terrible to hear about your terrible news.
- don't want to lecture an old lawyer on the law.
- know full well that spirit of Christ is humility
- imagine how it felt to read you never thought you'd "find Bob Ashcroft's son in the pocket of Big Tobacco"
- full slate
- sleeplessness
- wanting to write forever, feels like. Took stock, made notes, as way of preparing self.
- Really took stock
- City on the Hill

• Dad's 21 Life Lessons

#4 Silence sometimes shouts.

#5 Creative self-doubt fertilizes the field of creativity.

#7 Never eat your seed corn.

#8 When you've considered all your options, work to expand your options.

#11 The lives of fathers and son are intertwined; when one dies, the other is diminished.

#12 A father should not only pass on his strengths, wisdom, and insight, but also how to handle weaknesses, failures, and insecurities.

#13 When you have something important to say, write it down.

#15 Little things mean a lot.

#21 Saying good-bye is a way of beginning to say hello.

• #22

When I was eight, my father took me to the sleepy Springfield airport, once a World War II training field. He was an amateur pilot. We walked up to a 1941 Piper Cub, climbed in, and took off. A few minutes later, he shouted over the engine noise: "John, fly the plane for a while."

"What do I do?" I shouted back.

"Grab the stick and push it," he said. I did. We went into a sickening dive. He pulled us out. He had a good chuckle, and I had a good lesson: actions had consequences. And when I put my hand to something, I could make a difference.

• The Melancholy Truth

Each of us is required to exercise leadership, even if it's limited to our personal relationships.

• Groundswells of Support

The Judge said when a politician claimed there was a public outcry for him to run for office that it meant that his mother and father thought it was a good idea. A groundswell of support meant that an aunt and uncle agreed.

My houses are filled with plaques and honorary pictures, keys to various cities: temporary acknowledgements of the offices I held, not indications of the man I am, or hope to be.

• Flattery

Think about it: virtually any positive remark you could make about Jesus would be true.

• The Long View
I try to adopt a forward-looking approach, focusing on what I might become, not on what others are saying about me today.

• Attitude of Gratitude
My father didn't allow us to use the phrase "I'm proud of…" "Say you're grateful for it," he always said. "Not proud."

God doesn't ask us to sacrifice our children to Him. He sacrificed His Son for us. Pride doesn't enter into it, here. Gratitude is the appropriate response.

• Inner Reserves
Six weeks after my brother's funeral, my father had a massive heart attack.

• What Family Is All About
My brother had lived in the same town, and used to drop in on him every other day. My father told him he didn't need to feel as if he had to come by all the time. My brother answered that a phone wouldn't work for what he wanted, because sometimes he just wanted to lay eyes on him.

• Good Fortune
The story of the Asian man who commissioned a work of art to represent good fortune, the artist free to choose any form or method of representing it. He chose three lines of calligraphy:

Grandfather Dies

Father Dies

Son Dies

The wealthy Asian said, "How can this represent good fortune? Everyone dies!"

The artist said, "The good fortune is in the sequence."

• Gullibility

When someone promised my father something, he assumed that that person was telling the truth. Every so often someone would say to me, "Your father sure was gullible." But who'd want to be raised by a cynic? Believing in the best and giving others the benefit of the doubt may not be the most astute financial advice, but it's the only spiritual advice.

• Despite Everything

Despite everything, I could hear sometimes in my father's voice the way a certain insecurity invaded his thoughts. A few times he said to me, "If I weren't a college president, I wonder if anyone would still care about my opinions."

• Carrying the Ball

When people say pictures don't lie, they fail to realize that our favorite pictures try to suggest that our best moments are persistent moments. They're not. We might have looked like that for a second, but then our hair moved, our clothes wrinkled, our expressions got tired, our faces sagged back to normal.

• Writing

There's something about being able to put writing down and pick it back up that makes it special. Maybe we have a struggle getting what we need to get out face to face, or on the telephone. Maybe the deliberate pace of writing allows us to express ourselves more clearly.

• The Reason for Discipline

The very nature of Judeo-Christian culture is choice-driven.

• Sunday School

When I was in Sunday school one of our songs went like this:

Be careful, little eyes, what you see;

Oh, be careful, little eyes, what you see.
For the Father up above is looking down in love;
So be careful, little eyes, what you see.

• Punctuality

My father was never on time: he was always *early*. On time was not an option. If you weren't early you were late. We were always the first to church, the first to school, the first to work.

• More Important Things Than Me

Because of his ministries, he was never home in the summer. At Little League I'd look up and see all the other dads. As I got older I realized that the most important thing my father ever taught me was that there were more important things than me.

• Road Trips

Once I was an appropriate age, I was regularly invited to go along on his ministry trips. Everyone talks today about getting involved in their children's worlds. My father invited me into *his*.

• Hindsight

For a while, I thought he was ignoring me. It turned out that he was *building* me.

• Respect

Once when I was twelve I had just heard him address a group of college students, and he turned to me and said, "What do *you* think, John?" He asked my opinion. You know what that said to an adolescent boy?

When I traveled with him, he quizzed me about tensions or contradictions in any of the concepts he'd been dealing with. I wanted to be able to respond correctly, so I listened as if nothing else mattered.

• Our Own Little Prisons

Do yourself a favor: the next time you're driving with someone and you see that faraway look in their eyes, and you wonder what's going on in their heads—*ask*.

• Courtesy

Even in his latter, potentially lonelier years, my father was passionate about taking the pressure off people. He was always adamant about one part of his dinner invitations: "Come when you can and leave when you want to."

• Discovery

I'm a fan of the discovery school of education. When education focuses exclusively on comprehension, a crucial spiritual element is lost. An educated person is someone who's become addicted to the thrill of discovery. If someone tells me they're feeling prematurely old, I tell them: buy a telescope, go visit a new culture, work through a college textbook.

• Open Your Eyes

There's a spot on a twisting farm road near our place in Greene County where, at the right time of year, in the right weather, tarantulas make their crossing. Most drivers don't even notice, but I like to stop and watch, and I've been known to pick up one or two and take them home to Janet. I'll set one on the kitchen counter when I know she's coming. She'll scream loud enough to make me think it's all been worthwhile, but she doesn't appreciate it. She tells people that it's a family joke that I enjoy and she endures.

"Why would you do that?" someone might ask. That's the wrong question. We saw something new. We enlarged our lives.

• Cookies

My father never let people leave without putting something in their hands. He developed a signature gift, a plaque he had produced for the sole purpose of giving away. The calligraphy read *As long as he sought the Lord, God made him to prosper*. I've never been sorry for anything I've given away (whereas the same is not true for anything I've kept or purchased).

Once I was back in Missouri I visited The Judge four days running. I said to him, "Is there anything I can do for you?" He said he could go for some chocolate chip cookies. I went back to the house and started assembling the ingredients.

"What are you doing?" Janet wanted to know.

I told her I was making cookies. It was something I wanted to do for myself. She watched for a while and then went about her business. The stirring, the mixing, the baking, started paying me back. I started to process my prayers and work through my anger at the cigarettes that had shortened his life. I underbaked the cookies so they'd be good and moist. I made them small to stack in a Pringles can. I delivered them when he was asleep.

• Generosity

Political liberals take the admonition to be generous in giving as an admonition directed toward the government. In actuality, it's the reverse. Real givers are people who enjoy giving away their *own* money. Beware the generosity of those who make a living giving away *other people's* money.

• Staying on Message

All the good groups in the world, and a few bad ones, bring their causes, purposes, and bills to my office virtually every day, and if I don't happen to speak out on their particular concern at least once a week, I get asked, "What happened to you? Why are you silent? Don't you care?"

What some of these groups don't understand is the necessity of staying on message. Try to do everything and you end up doing nothing. It's like physics: if you don't concentrate your force, you don't penetrate the wall. Some issues have other senators as their champion, and I may stand behind them as a strong supporter. What each of us has to do is determine the primary emphasis of our calling. A good colleague of mine understands this: he says he has 365 titles but only 2 speeches. My father repeated the same things his entire life. Because he stayed so focused, it was impossible to be around him for any length of time and not know what he believed in.

• Write It on Your Hand
Character is what you're made of when everything else that might hold you up evaporates on the spot.

• Memories With Staying Power
Everyone was standing when I noticed my father lunging, swinging his arms, trying to lift himself out of the couch, one of those all-enveloping pieces of furniture that tends to bury you once you sit in it.

• Goodbyes
Back in Washington in our little one-and-a-half room apartment, in an alley just off Second Street, Janet and I had just fallen asleep when we heard a rattling of the iron bars on the door. She thought it was someone trying to break in. I said, "No. It's my dad." The next morning we heard the news.

• Goodbyes
I was told that in the Emergency Room, he finally said to the doctors, "Boys, you better just quit. You're hurting more than helping."

Everyone who knew him joked about his goodbyes. He waved like a person stranded on an island. Fifty, a hundred yards down the road, you'd look back, and he'd still be waving, his arms going like he was helping to park a jet.

• Goodbyes

As a boy on days when there were no Little League games I'd get a bat and a dinged-up softball and go into a field by myself and play All-Time Home Run Derby. It was always the same six guys in a round-robin: Mel Ott, Ernie Banks, Eddie Matthews, Ted Williams, Jimmy Foxx, and Mickey Mantle. I'd bat for each and after each swat I'd have to troop after the ball and find it. "What're you doing?" Janet finally said, after having watched me from the kitchen window for about twenty minutes.

• Hellos

I stood there in the field, holding my softball like an apple. Somewhere I'd lost my bat. Janet was wiping her hands on a dish towel as she walked across the alfalfa stubble. There were apple trees and behind them a beautiful twilight, with our farm spreading out around us. A contrail made a quiet little line across the sky. I was Attorney General of the United States. My father was sitting on my bed. He was telling me that things don't *happen*; they're *made* to happen. He had his palm to my face. He had only my welfare in mind. This was the only world we knew. This was the world that was swept away.

The Politics of War

From the desk of...

JOHN WARNER
19052 E. BRIARWOOD DR.
AURORA, CO 80016

April 19, 2004

William Kristol, Richard Perle, et al
The Project for the New American Century
1150 17th St. NW
Washington, D.C. 20036

Dear Friends,

Why didn't you tell President Bush to invade Western Australia first?

I've been playing Risk: The Game of Global Domination since I was eight years old and never, never have I seen someone win the game by massing their forces in the Middle East at the beginning of the game. Too many borders! Impossible to reinforce! Enemies from all directions! Australia, on the other hand, is easily conquered. Start in Western Australia, make a straight-line march through eastern Australia, then on into New Zealand and New Guinea, and finally up to Siam, sealing the entire continent and guaranteeing an extra two armies per turn for the duration of game. (Ask Secretary Rumsfeld if those would come in handy.) Once in Siam, you can leave the remainder of your provinces virtually unguarded and mass your armies of the Far East to eventually move north into Siberia, Irkutsk and Kamchatka, ultimately overtaking the entire Asian continent (seven extra armies per turn), including, finally, the Middle East.

Starting in South America is okay, too, if your brat cousin Ronald refuses to play if he doesn't get to go first, and Africa will do in a pinch if you want to change things up, but you better roll some sixes, mutherfuckers, or you'll be knocked out of the game, which means you're available to do stuff like pick up the dog crap in the backyard, or wax your grandfather's back, "since you're just watching." (Thanks, Mom.)

I hear that, after watching President Bush's press conference, Mr. Kristol was "depressed." If he was depressed, think about the rest of us, who weren't part of the shadowy extra-governmental cabal that helped install him in the White House in the first place.

The history books will write your epitaphs and they won't be pretty: "Neoconservatives: A late-twentieth-, early-twenty-first-century American political movement that stressed the supremacy of the American empire, but was too stupid to invade Australia first."

Think it over,

John Warner
John Warner

CC: Paul Wolfowitz, John R. Bolton, "Scooter" Libby, James Woolsey, Tony Blair, Midge Decter

Tough Day for the Army
by John Warner

THE ARMY WAITS, NERVES JANGLED, FOR THE WORD.

Waiting, the army sits, awkward and uncomfortable on the molded orange plastic waiting-room chairs. The chairs offer little cover from ambush or sniper. In normal times (which these are not), the army would never willingly choose this location.

Forward scouts were dispatched long ago to the window by the counter (behind which the bun-haired woman sits) to retrieve the word, and they are much overdue.

The army thinks a little air support might be nice, just in case, a little softening up of a couple of thousand tons of high explosive, maybe a dash of incendiary, clear some clutter, strategic-like, surgical. Air support, despite the noise, the chaos, the debris, despite its origination with a rival branch of the service, has always been oddly comforting to the army. In times past, as the concussion from the air support bombs would wave over them, the army would think: *take that suckers. Bet you didn't bargain for that, suckers. You are dead dead and dead, suckers. Suckers.*

But their radios broadcast only static now. They know that it is possible (probable?) that headquarters has been compromised, but they soldier on because this is what soldiers do.

Perched on the tiny, scooped-out chairs, the army is clumsy in its bulging packs, dangling entrenching tools and various weapons. The army tries to be as silent as possible, but this is, in reality, not silent at all. Truth be told, the army makes a racket. Their boots are thick and hard at the soles—with the slightest twitch, the leather creaks disagreeably around the ankle—and it is a fact that because of an excess of design, ingenuity, and Yankee know-how, the average infantryman is well overloaded, poundage-wise, with "necessary" gear. (Note: in battle, when the actual deadly exchange of flying metal commences, it is well-known that pretty much only the rifle is deemed necessary. Maybe the helmet just a little, in case of a glancing shrapnel blow, but mostly just the rifle, and yes, the helmet if possible, but only if possible, let's call it an extra, a bonus.)

Other guests of the waiting room stare as the army accidentally knocks stacks of old magazines from end table to floor. Carefully, the army picks up the magazines, restacks them, then casually, very casually, so as not to attract attention, leafs through one and rips out colorful recipes that look suitable for cooking over sterno.

An old woman says: Those are old, the magazines. There's newer ones somewhere. The receptionist hides them. It's like a game to her.

The army thanks the woman kindly for that advice and asks her if she thinks the pictures accompanying the recipes look good. Don't they look good? the army says.

The woman shakes her head, smiles ruefully, says: Sure, of course the pictures look good, real good, good enough to eat, ha ha ha, but they don't look like that when you cook them. Don't look like that at all, no sir. If you ate the actual objects that were used in the composition and creation of that photograph, you'd be...well I sure wouldn't want to...what I'm trying to say is...pain...You'd experience some pain for sure, explosive pain even...we're talking toilet-hugging-for-sure kind of pain, maybe...who knows?...worse?...hospital pain, real gurney-clutching-tear-your-own-heart-out, tunnel-vision-blackout kind of pain. You see what I'm getting at?

The army nods in the affirmative. Armies know of these things, these things and worse.

The woman says: That picture there is what's known as professional food photography, wherein you substitute the food with something that looks more foodlike when photographed in two dimensions under controlled lighting conditions. The nibblet corn is really spray-painted rubber and that there asparagus is made out of retired fake Christmas trees dragged out of Dumpsters. The chicken is old eraser bits molded under precise heat and rubbed shiny and golden with dandelion extract, which is well-known for this kind of thing. I'm surprised you haven't heard of this.

We've been away, busy, the army says, casting shameful eyes downward.

I'd just hate to see such nice boys fooled is all. It's all a trick, you see. Sometimes now they use computers too. The idea is that one thing becomes another, then it's not lying.

The army nods, sees its hulking reflection in the office glass, and thinks that, tactically speaking, this all could be a mistake.

But what choice?

Near the receptionist's desk, the forward scouts softly clear their throats, and tap their fingers near the dried-up pen permanently chained to the counter, but the receptionist remains glassy-eyed and unmoved.

Among the army, Lumpkins clicks open the bolt on his carbine, removes the bolt, eyes down the barrel, clicks the bolt shut again, clicks open, removes, eyes down, shut again, says to Henderson: What do you think the word's gonna be?

Word's never good, Lump. Never.

Maybe today?

Nope. Never.

Let me tell you, I once had a sister she was so pretty that...

We all did, Lump. Get in line. Take a number. Get over it.

This is an army's life, hurry up and wait.

Lumpkins works his poem...

I once had a sister
she was so pretty that...

...but can't get any further. Words fail, frequently.

At least, in times past, I've done some pretty fine talking with my gun, Lumpkins thinks:

Ratta-tatta-tat
take that.

The army worries about the forms. They filled them in as best they could, smiled as they were handed to the receptionist, but it is always so hard to know what might be appropriate, what, precisely, they are looking for. Under the heading for "Competencies" they recorded the following:

I guess you could say that mostly, we're an ultra-efficient killing machine. We have our problems, our inevitable shortcomings, sure, but we're probably the greatest killing machine the world has ever known, although this is tough to say (meaning difficult to gauge) since we've been underutilized, occasionally misused, and, in recent times, when thrown into battle, have taken on mostly the backward and overmatched, because, really, what's a spear or a bunch of rocks against a smoothly bored chunk of lead and other metals fired from a precision, gun-type instrument wielded by a soldier trained to a razor-fine peak of physical and mental fitness? In any hands, untrained hands even, these gun-type instruments are deadly, very much so deadly; rocks and spears, especially those wielded by the nutritionally deficient with their spindly arms and depleted musculature, are not so much deadly, not these days anyway, so when you're talking the com-bination of deadly instruments and a force (again, physically and men-tally quite, quite primed; this cannot be stressed enough) that is ready/willing/able to use said instruments for their designed purpose (and let's not mince words, that purpose would be killing), well, and you must agree, you've got something pretty potent happening there. Meaning, we are not something you would like to mess with in that kind of situation. And sure, you have what is known as the historical/technology factor, say if you had a time machine and you sent us back to face, for example, the Huns, or better yet, the Mongol Horde, on their own terms, their turf if you will, well that might just be a tough bitch to crack (we sure as hell wouldn't go down without a fight, though, you can bet on that, last man standing, etc., etc., etc.), but you bring the Horde here, to our present-day reality, you bring them here, invite them inside our house of pain (don't bother taking your animal-hide covering off because you won't be staying long!), and by the time they finished rubbing the surprise from their eyes and said the shortest prayer possible to whatever it is those godless fucks hold dear, we would give them a serious stomping. We would wrap up those stinky, inbred, slant-eyed motherfuckers in a shit storm of truly biblical proportions, real Book-of-Revelations, Wrath-of-God shit rained down upon them, by us, because we are more than qualified (eager, even) to do so. So all that aside and everything taken into account, ergo, it is more than fair to say that as of this moment, we can't be touched in terms of killing.

The response went well past the five or so crowded lines provided on the form, lines that would be insufficient for any answer, let alone one as complete as the army's. This meant the army had to write in the margins and on the reverse side, and use arrows and write "over" and "cont." and all manner of things, and the army felt as though their warning sensors detected a scowl cross the face of the bun-haired sentinel when they slid the finished product through the slot, beneath the protective glass.

Eventually, the forward scouts return, heads hanging, sans word. They say the word will come when it is ready, in essence, when there is word, but as of now, no word. Who knows when? They don't, *so stop asking.*

This is the soldier's life, hurry up, then wait. Mostly wait...wait... wait...wait...

Do you remember? Lumpkins asks Henderson.

Yes, says Henderson.

Do you remember when we were on that mission in the faraway country where there were the skinny brown men with the stained teeth from the betel nuts who carried their antiquated and slow-loading rifles beneath unbuttoned cloth shirts that billowed behind them as they charged toward us, heedless of our ability to cut them down with well-placed volleys of withering fire delivered from strategically situated vantage points that maximized the shooting field, but at the same time minimized the danger of injury or death due to friendly fire?

Yes, I remember. We were fighting in the streets to establish order and subsequently to banish the feudal warlords and install the properly organized democratic government. Also, to provide food to the hungry, of which there were very, very many. Those men that charged at us held bullets in their teeth so they could reload as quickly as possible. The bullets looked like metal fangs. On the other hand, we could reload by changing ammo clips in approximately 1.6 seconds.

Do you remember how the men sometimes, as they charged toward us, shielded themselves with children, thinking that we would not shoot children? Lumpkins says.

Yes, Henderson says.

It's fortunate that we are such good shots that we were able to shoot the men but avoid harming the children, Lumpkins says.

What were we supposed to do? They were trying to kill us, after all, which despite the practice and training we'd endured was sort of surprising, how much they could want to kill us, Henderson says.

And do you remember the special rounds we used that were designed to go through armor, but had the unfortunate effect of passing *too* cleanly through their human bodies and thus failed to knock these charging men down upon impact as more traditional small-arms ordnance does, and how the men, clutching the small children would continue to advance even as they were shot again and again and again?

Yes. I remember the same way you do. I remember terribly and often.

Do you remember the liberation? The time we went to give them their rights as declared by God and the United States of America and they kept trying to blow us up?

Yes, they hated us too.

I didn't hate them.

It wasn't our fault, or theirs.

Do you remember how I carried that old Royal typewriter every-where, how I would bang out paragraphs of memories even as they happened, how once, as I crouched behind an overturned car, getting something down, that old Royal deflected a bullet destined to deliver a mortal wound and lost only the use of the nearly nonessential X key in the process?

Yes, yes, and I had the old transistor radio with the foil wrapped around the antenna that we would set up in barracks and dance to rhythm and blues music and get high and share good times as our smooth-muscled torsos flashed with sweat and...

In the waiting room, as the varying people wait for their varying rea-sons, wait for their varying orders to send them into the various recess-es of the building (or beyond), wait to be hurled to their varying fates, throats are cleared, sideways glances exchanged, legs crossed and uncrossed, foreign bits are surreptitiously picked from teeth while no one (in reality, though, everyone) is looking. A child grips an empty plastic cup in one hand, and with the other, rubs the corner of the cardboard cover of a worn-out picture book, peels the layers until the cardboard is frayed and soft as tissue. The child lifts the book to his face and sniffs between the paper layers, thinks: *No one has smelled this before. No one but me.*

The army wonders if they should amend their answer on the form and mention the looting prevention, the quelling of the garden-vari-ety civil unrest, or the dam building—sandbagging—how they deliv-er food and supplies to the poor and war-ravaged. These are the peace missions, but of course even the fighting missions are *in the interests of peace* meaning that they are there to establish peace where there is none, working as the handmaiden of peace, if you will, a peace forged out of their irresistible might. Does that seem contradictory?

A slash of light on the carpet disappears as the sun moves behind a more impressive building outside. Not darkness in the room, exactly, but somehow a room without light.

Henderson thinks: *Maybe a warning shot. Just to juice things up.* But does nothing, just like the rest.

Lumpkins tries his poem again:

I once had
a sister
SHE WAS
so pretty
that I could
have…

Tired of waiting, the child throws the book down and totters across the floor, banging its hand over its mouth, whooping like an Indian.

Finally, the receptionist looks up and it is clear, the word is here. The whole room sits at the edge of their seats. Breaths are held.

Something is coming, and it's heading this way.

Peaches

by Glori Simmons

ON THE MORNING AFTER ERNESTO DIAZ HAD BEEN STRUCK BY A TRAIN on the crossroads, Al Shepherd woke early and returned to the site. Outside it was predawn, crisp and quiet. He rolled down his window and breathed in the dusty air. It had been weeks since it had rained and everything smelled parched, even this early in the morning when most would say it was still night. As he drove, he remembered the memo he received last October that explained the timer's malfunction and the too few replacements the railroad had sent along with it. At the top was the railway logo's acorn-shaped shield and below, the type that said that they would not take responsibility. It would be up to Al.

He had spent two long weeks trying to decide which of his twenty-nine intersections were worthy of the upgrade, whether to base his decision on the number of cars that crossed or which had low visibility. Finally he chose the seven crossroads that the school buses used, leaving the remaining three timers in their boxes on the storeroom shelf for an emergency. One of these timers bounced on the seat next to him now as he turned off of the washboard road toward the intersection. This was the emergency he had planned for, and it gave him a sick feeling in his gut.

He'd made the wrong decision those months ago; now there were four children without a father. The Diaz accident was gory, worse than Al had seen in the war—no, not worse but surprisingly the same, only sadder somehow there at the lonely crossroads with its two sides of safety. On the other side of the tracks, Diaz's day would have been ordinary, just another fruit delivery in the busy picking season. It was as if Ernesto Diaz had been nearly home free, just ten yards to go to cross the tracks and eight miles after that to the warehouse where he would have unloaded the wooden crates of peaches, which were now, like his body, tossed and smashed along the rail.

It had happened before, and now Al wondered if it had been the timer that had taken Leo Taylor's son, hit by a train on prom night. That was on another track and before the memo. There had been talk that the boy had been drunk, so in the end, the family had declined an investigation, but Diaz had children and a wife who spoke little English. They would need money and Al was pretty sure some lawyer would read about the accident in the Spokane newspaper, drive up to offer to take on their case, and start asking questions.

The crossroads were still, the train not due for another forty-five minutes. Al pulled up to the side of the road just in front of where the arm and the electrics box attached to the thick metal pole. He turned off his truck, but left the key in the ignition so he could shine the headlights on his work. When he leaned over and felt around beneath the seat for his flashlight, it occurred to him that his old Remington wasn't there. He couldn't recall the last time he'd seen it. Maybe it had been missing for days, weeks even, stolen. Maybe his son, Clark, had taken it out to clean. Maybe Clark intended to act on his words. Al tried to remember if there was any ammo in the gun or in the kitchen drawer.

He stepped down from the truck and walked to the cross-arm, his open door chiming into the early morning darkness. A helium balloon with a teddy bear was tied to the pole and a bouquet of daisies leaned against the base. He sorted through his keys. The door creaked on its hinge as he opened it and shined his flashlight in at the maintenance record taped inside. The timer was three years old. Sure enough, it was the faulty BGF100. According to the log, Al had been the one to put it in. He considered writing in the new timer for nine months ago, when the memo and replacements had been issued, but decided against it. He'd play dumb. Better to say he'd changed the timer as a precaution following the accident, if discussion ever got that far.

He unwired the bad timer and held it in his hand. Here it was: the thing that had made all the difference, no bigger than a heart or one of the peaches tossed along the ground. No heavier than a grenade.

The matter of seconds: a hammer, a spring, an internal clock. It was this sort of timing that had placed Clark far enough from a grenade to allow him his life.

Just an hour ago, Al woke to find his son sitting in the living room, undressing his wounds and picking at the dark bruises in his legs. He looked up at Al and told him that they felt like worthless bags of shattered glass. "I wish I'd lost them. Better yet, I wish I'd lost the whole thing—my legs, my brain. I wish I were dead."

Al hadn't known what to say to that. The muted television was showing an advertisement for an Ab Reducer. On the table by the chair, there was an open beer can and the letter from Clark's girlfriend, Sylvia, that he'd received the day before. She was on vacation with her family, and since she'd been gone, Clark hadn't really moved from that chair, so that the living room was beginning to smell like a sickroom. Al would have liked to ask what the letter said, if Sylvia was having a nice time in California, but his son was picking anxiously at the blisters on his leg. Al hated thinking of the shrapnel that would continue to work its way to the surface for the rest of the boy's life.

Al had stood in the darkness of the hallway, afraid to touch his son, watching the actors in workout clothes roll their bodies along the ground with the help of a blue contraption. He'd been a coward. Now, standing at the crossroads, he tried to remember if the Remington had been somewhere in the shadows of that dimly lit room.

Most of what he remembered about his own difficulties after returning from the jungle was from stories his ex-wife, Dot, had told him—her waking to find him staring out the window as if he were on watch. She had learned to touch him slowly and then firmly so that he would not startle. He had suffered in Vietnam, but not so directly as Clark, who had returned from the Middle East three months ago. Just nineteen, the boy had no money, no plans, and enough metal in his legs to hold up a dozen magnets. All summer Clark and Sylvia sat in Al's shaded house, watching television, eating everything out of the fridge, and dirtying the dishes. Al hoped Sylvia would learn what

Clark needed; he hoped the letter had something in it that could comfort the boy. But he sensed that the relationship was coming to an end.

Clark left for the war optimistic and patriotic. He was a cross-country runner and had a head for history and the way things worked. He hoped to travel. When Al and Dot had divorced, it was Clark who had risen to the occasion, learning how to cook and clean and make Al's bachelor life more bearable. Al wished he could do the same for his son now, but Clark's pain made the boy edgy and morose, distant. Al wondered why Dot did not come to visit more often. Didn't she care about her Clark? Didn't she remember how it had been for Al? He wished Dot had been there this morning; she would have known how to reach out from the darkness and comfort their son. She wouldn't have been afraid.

After the divorce, she'd become a sort of floating presence, sometimes nodding with empathy and other times pinching her lips together and shaking her head in a disappointed way. Right now, he could see her scolding him about this timer. He knew it wasn't right. He looked out across the tracks. What about death, would that be easier for his son, he wondered, but stopped short of the answer. A father should never think in those terms.

Al had always thought life was about timing, that each day had its own series of crossings. Sometimes a man would have to wait at them: like the summer Dot said she was choosing between him and Marvin Hill, or the four months when Clark was away at the war. Then time seemed to slow, as if he'd pulled up to a track as the train crossed in its own sweet time, the boxcars empty and meaningless. Other times, there would be nothing to hold a person back. It was like getting to the crossroads just as the red light of the caboose was receding into the distance and the cross-arms lifted, inviting you through to the other side. Good timing. He thought of Clark on the cross-country course, his slim, muscular legs moving evenly as he broke from the pack of runners. But even good timing could yield something bad. It was never under our control.

It had been like that on the spring day Al waved to his friend Frederick for the last time at this very crossroads. When the arms lifted and the two passed by each other, Frederick held up an imaginary beer to his mouth to suggest they meet later at the old Quonset hut for a drink. He'd never gotten there, dead from a heart attack on the side of the road just a half mile up, and Al alive waiting over one then two beers. Al would like to tell his son this: it's never been up to us, not in everyday life, and not in love.

He took the new timer out of the box and plastic, tossing the wrapping on the ground. He was moving slowly, and he knew this was wrong, that he should be hurrying to get back to tell his son that it wasn't up to him to decide the timing of his life. He had survived for a reason. Al put the new timer into place. It was clean, almost shiny, next to the other rusty parts, but it wouldn't take many days for it to build up a patina from the dust. He attached the pair of red wires to one set of screws, the yellow to another, then the blue. He pushed the test button and backed away from the pole to watch as the cross-arms began to flash and slowly lower. He picked up the clump of daisies, sniffed, and then locked the box.

Yesterday, Marisela Diaz had arrived with her four children, calm and dignified. The deputies had tried to keep her from the tracks, but when she saw her husband's mangled truck, she broke away and ran up to look in its shattered window. Then she slid down onto the gravel and broken glass. No one knew enough Spanish to calm or comfort her. When the children saw their mother crying, they began to wail too, their faces turning red. The smallest sat down on his mother's lap and began to tug at her breast.

Except for the peaches, the intersection was cleared now, as if nothing had happened. That was how the railroad liked it. The coroner's office had taken away the body. The deputies had gathered what was left of the dead man's possessions and put them into an empty peach crate—a loose shoe, his shattered and bent sunglasses and watch, the felt cross that hung from the rearview mirror. Then, the cleanup crew had moved in to do the best they could with the metal and glass. This finality is what his son wanted. It made Al sad to think he understood.

Al walked toward the rail, stepping on a peach and then another one. Balancing on a tie, he tried to see what Ernesto had seen. The tracks were on a curve that headed into a patch of cattails. Ernesto had never seen the oncoming train, at least not until it was there, right there on him. Maybe Al should wait and make sure the train triggered the timer right; maybe he should be going, getting back to his son. "I'm just following orders," he said out loud to Dot one more time as he neared his truck. He could hear her clicking her tongue against the roof of her mouth. He couldn't understand how she, who had left him and Clark, could end up so judgmental. She didn't know, did she? She had no idea what it was like. "Don't judge me, woman," he yelled out.

The sky was just beginning to turn pink. Flies buzzed. Al reached into his pocket and pulled out his pocketknife to cut the string to the balloon, watching as it lifted over the pole and into the sky. Breathing in the sweet, ripe smell of the peaches, he moved slowly. He squatted down to pick one up, wiping it on his pants. It was perfect, unbruised and whole. He held it there in his hand, this perfection that had survived the crash, wishing it had been so good for Clark, and then he bit into the flesh, eating his way around the pit, taking one slow, deliberate bite after another as the sun rose and the day began, juice spilling down his chin.

War Chain

by Avital Gad-Cykman

Desert

THE DESERT WIND HAD TAKEN OVER SINCE EARLY MAY. IT WRAPPED ITSELF
around people and plants, leaving them dry and dusty. The sound of
the news rose from every house and workplace every day, every hour.
It wafted in the powdery air. The heat embraced the town into the
desert and barred the place so thoroughly, a stranger wouldn't have
known the desert from the town, the town from the desert. And in the
desert, the townspeople knew, some day soon there would be war.

Somewhere up north, a mountain stood under a snowy top and
above rivulets of water. For a while it balanced the domain of the
advancing desert. Then, the snow melted away.

They were waiting. The dispute would occur in the south, north,
and east. It could close like a handcuff, but the Mediterranean Sea
would keep it unlatched on the west.

The young people were fully awake. They stopped slipping
through time on the force of inertia alone. The air burned like hot
pepper in their nostrils, the grains provoking little explosions in their
bodies. Their chests were full with unsettling moments. Even in their
sleep, their nostrils quivered and their feet swung and kicked. Their
dreams left them convulsing with sneezes, and they couldn't remember what they dreamed.

The children collected branches and stones to build weapons.
They promised each other to protect their homes, and they longed for
the excitement of fighting. They wrapped one another with gauze and
moved about like mummies.

One by one, the men were recruited. The children clung to their
fathers and brothers, wishing the army had called them as well.
Sorrow hit them for the first time when they were left behind.

And they grew and grew up every day, an army of children sworn by their fathers to take care of the family. Ha! Just let their mothers try to ground them. They were finally noticed. They recognized their force. They had an enemy, and it defined them as an enemy too.

When young soldiers, tired even before the war broke out, came home for short vacations, they spread the scents of sandy shoes and oily weapons. Their mothers sniffed at their sleeping sons and imagined the whole desert smelled that way. The fragrance remained inside their noses and throats, stinging like thorns.

The war would start that summer. The young soldiers would be free to perform the clever maneuvers and efficient fighting they had been training for in the past months. They dreamed about returning to their girlfriends as heroes.

A poet had described them as the silver tray on which the country would be served to its people. They did not feel like the tray but like its holders, the hosts. They would exercise their new power even at the cost of their lives.

Children put in envelopes dried flowers and sent them to the soldiers with cakes their mothers baked.

While the soldiers would eat the cakes, the hot air would carry the wrapping papers and the flowers away until nothing colorful or sweet remained, only a desert.

Fingerprints

They squatted, blurry eyed, in the middle of a street, a neighborhood, a crumpled city of floury dust and shattered glass on blocks that had originally been houses.

"Aren't we just the kind of people who'd give their life for the sake of information?" she said, twisting her lips into a smile.

"You were that close to being a hero," said he, his thumb closing against his index finger.

That they had endured what others couldn't—a bombing— proved them no better or stronger than what they used to be. He, a photographer of autopsies, corpses, and damaged bodies (crushed bones were as common to him as broken mugs). She, a journalist or more, a professional blond, a practical Marilyn exchanging her goods, the promise of her round breasts, for news.

She'd stand so close to her source, a man mostly, he would see the small freckles rolling toward her scarcely hidden nipples.

Through her sources, they had learned there would be an attack. They didn't, wouldn't, prevent it. ("No way we should. We'll manufacture reality instead of documenting it.")

They hadn't known its rage would hit them too. A blast and its outcome are as predictable as a hurricane.

He blinked in shock when a piece of glass beside him cracked. Where were they? All-gray streets breaking into pieces looked as if they belonged to the same country. He and she had worked as a team in the Middle East, then in Europe, and back, and then again. And now Africa was on their map as well. His work had been good, but not sensational enough to overshadow hers.

He licked his lips and tasted ashes. "I know a good place to wash ourselves if it's still standing," he said in a hoarse voice.

"It was less scary than I'd imagined it to be," said she. "It simply happened."

"We'll look human again after a good wash and dinner. Boy, do I feel dirty."

"I twisted my ankle," said she, as she tried to rise, collapsing back.

"Look at me. No, turn your head. You have blood on your cheek."

"What? How bad does it look?" She pressed her fingers into the blood on her face.

"Not bad. It looks like a torn string. You skin was so perfect, it will make it interesting."

She touched the edge of her wound, the droopy flesh. Her eyes were bright again. "The rest of the crew?" she asked.

"I've got some pictures of them."

"You what? Wounded journalists are not an item," she said.

He spoke slowly, considering each word. "Depends how famous

they are. Martyrs are always welcome." He took his camera out of his bag, then, with a second thought, dug in once more for the knife. He held the knife decidedly, as if with a slash he could expose the future he had planned. "Don't you want to join the crew and be a hero?" he asked.

She wasn't listening. She turned her head brusquely, suddenly noticing small fingerprints on the glass beside him. A child had pushed his open palms against that window. The thought tore her heart. Something stirred within her womb.

She said, "Look at these fingerprints. He was not much older than a baby." She was not one to cry, but she did.

Dumbfounded, he observed the glass, but from where he was now standing, the prints were invisible, elusive like peace.

He would see the fingerprints if he put himself in her place, but that, he wouldn't do.

Scream

It's a scream inside you that saves you every day. You see skeletal people becoming ghosts, your parents. You know you are going to lose them. You won't lose yourself even if you wanted to, and you do, you do want to vanish, not exist, but you need to live. You hold no hopes. There is no point in going on living, but there's a scream, a rush of black air rising like a tornado inside you.

The dead people faze you as much as the armed ones. What if it were you? Soon, your father. The pneumonia sucks his breath. Under the ribs you can see clearly, his sagging lungs hang almost empty. He can whisper his scream until he's mute. Mother follows him every-where.

You want to kill your torturers, and you desire to be on their side. Joining them creeps into your mind, reminds you that you are not your own master but a shadow without a body, a shadow in search of a body to throw the shadow on the ground.

They loathe your race. They kill you one by one and in masses. In other places, people worry about paying bills and weight problems. Such things have been extricated from your days. You haven't thought about anything for weeks. The pole of your life goes right through you and curves and hooks you. You're meat at the butcher's, if you lose the scream.

You don't put peace or hope in words. Your body keeps taking one breath in, one breath out. You know you are living. You wish for nothing. Dreams are not real, and you need reality—only one different from yours.

You jump on the quid lying on the ground. It is all about quid for seconds, then, it will be about crumbs, a cigarette. When you win it, you're the monster. When you lose, you're a rag. How will you survive your own survival if the war ends? You'll detox it from your system. You'll find the exact spot from which you can extract despair. You'll move quickly forward as if you knew how.

Survey of Impact

by Laurenn McCubbin & Stephen Elliott

Here we go.

The air-raid sirens have been ringing for half an hour and it's become clear they aren't going to stop.

It's cold in Baghdad at night and we're both wearing blue fleeces, a coincidence of what we brought from home—

my home in San Francisco, a small studio with wooden floors and a moldy shower. Amy's in upstate New York on a communal farm.

She gives me that look she's been giving me since we got here, two human shields on the same bus from the Syrian border.

Two Americans squatting in an Iraqi power plant, an obvious target in the first wave of bombing. The Iraqis certainly consider it an important target, or they wouldn't waste two Americans on it.

Outside the air is crisp. All around the power plant is the faint smell of bleach.

All of the lights have been shut off and there are only the black shapes of the Baghdad skyline, buildings like obelisks. The stars are enormous.

I wish it could always be this peaceful, except for the sirens, which interrupt all of it with their constant screams. The sirens are loud enough to feel but I am steadily getting used to them.

I didn't leave much behind to come here except a good job with the University and a dead father who died three weeks before I arrived in Amman. I boycotted his funeral. I didn't want to hear the rabbi speak of his virtues. Everyone always speaks so well of the dead. "De mortuis nihil nisi bonum", as the Romans would say.

I have no illusions about the conflict, though I suppose everybody feels that way. Everybody feels like they live without illusions, that they have the most accurate read on the news. I remember the papers before I left.

The New York Times predicted up to ten thousand casualties on the first day of the bombing. The Village Voice placed the number at a hundred thousand. Z Magazine said it could be upward of half a million.

Harlan Ullman, the architect of the Shock and Awe strategy, compared it to the nuclear weapons at Hiroshima.

People believe what they want to believe, then they find the news source to back it up.

But I don't think I'm right to be here. This man Saddam Hussein, who our handlers refer to affectionately as Papa, is not a good man. Even the other human shields don't think he is good. Rather they are anti-America, or anti-war, or just anti-Bush. But for me, I'm not here for any of that. I'm trying to exist. The world is making a decision and I want to have a seat at the table.

Because for so long now I've been so sad.

The original human shields didn't come to Iraq voluntarily.

They were seized from airplanes with stopovers in Kuwait just before the first Gulf War. They were businessmen taken from buses.
Six thousand hostages were taken. Most were quickly released. But a few hundred, about the number of the volunteer human shields here now, were not released.

Hussein went on television patting the head of an English child. The shields were shuttled between military facilities. Some were driven out to the desert in the middle of the night, ordered to their knees, and then loaded back onto their buses.
A practical joke.
I read about it before coming out here, what happened to those original shields. The hostages. Many still have psychotic episodes, post-traumatic stress.

I read about them in the Financial Times. They said we were denigrating their name with what we were doing. As if, by coming here voluntarily to live in power plants and water supply facilities, we were making fun of them. It's a good argument, though irrelevant when looked at through the larger lens of history, and the still-larger lens of a single person's life.

There was talk among the shields when we first arrived, fear that we would be forced into places we didn't want to be.

Corralled into factories manufacturing poison gas, strapped to the hoods of tanks shuttling forward to meet the troops.

And that maybe the Iraqi people, from their own anger and frustration, would take it out on us, pulling us limb from limb, the way the Palestinians did in Ramallah, storming the police station to get the two Israeli soldiers being held there.

The picture in the newspaper:

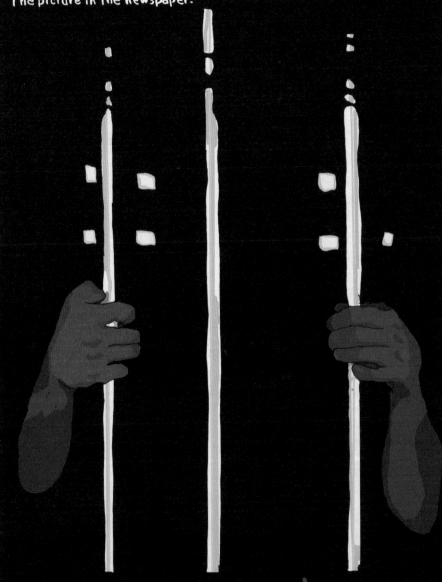

Mob rule.

The first desert whistle streaks through the black tapestry. We call them whistles, the missiles and low-flying planes breaking the sound barrier. The man who looks after the cafe nearby told us that word.

He is a kind man, with thick black hair, who always laughs and never charges us for our tea.

He jokes, when we are there watching the television, "Listen, the sky is whistling again."

Then he smiles broadly and does a little tap dance.

It's funny every time.

The fire bursts into explosions of bricks and rubble and dust and screaming.

There are more whistles, drowning the sirens, and then the sirens are completely gone and there are only whistles.

The obelisks fall to the ground as the sky streaks with white and the space between heaven and earth is lit orange and burning.

I'm knocked to the ground in a wild explosion from the wind. I crawl back toward the door and inside the plant, where Amy is huddled in the corner.

Pull!

by David Amsden

for Steven Amsden, Specialist, United States Army

I.

FIRST THING MY FATHER DOES WHEN HE FINDS OUT I JOINED THE ARMY is wedge himself behind the wheel of the Bronco and head to Gilbert's Guns. A storefront situated between Pev's Paintball and a discount crematorium called Simple Tribute, that's Gilbert's: like a decent joke everyone just ignores anyway. In theory, this little sojourn was us celebrating—but anyone who knows my father knows the man's a lifelong chaser of contact highs, and he went alone, not even a grunt in my direction, so I guess you could say the "us" part is relative. I'm fine with this.

"Dinner is served," my father announces, back from Gilbert's, and his voice crawls though the house like something feral. I'm down in the basement, slumped sideways into the corduroy couch and watching pro beach volleyball on ESPN 2, contemplating masturbation. A bite in the lower spine edges up into my mind—that's his voice reaching me—and I stand up, crack my neck, head upstairs. The basement has no windows, is always dark no matter what time it is, dark and fungal smelling, and it's not until I get upstairs that I remember it's still light out, still daytime. On the dining room table my father has proudly spread out his bounty: a Smith and Wesson S1911 .45, a Kel-Tec P-3AT, a Kimber Stainless Target II 10MM with skeletonized trigger, and a pair of Benelli Sport II hunting rifles that look ready to take out a pterodactyl. But of course I couldn't name them back then. I have no idea what I'm looking at.

"Benelli's yours," my father says.

"What?"

"One of them Benellis. Yours."

"Which one's a Benelli?"

"The one you see two of."

"This is mine?"

"Pick it up."

I pick it up. I can't say it has any effect other than implanting in my mind's core the weird notion that, if loaded and aimed properly and discharged, this object could kill someone. But everyone feels that when they first hold a gun—faces flicker across the backs of your eyes, hollow-cheeked, making your fingers twitch—like how the first time you hold a baby all you think about is what could happen if you accidentally dropped it, flashing on the mother's wrath and sorrow while her kid's still in your hands. And in my case I have to admit it isn't a wholly unfamiliar thought—just the vague notion of killing, I'm talking—when in the presence of my father.

"It loaded?" I ask.

"How's it *feel?*"

When he was my age, my father wanted to enlist, craved it, but it was Vietnam, late in the game, and the nightly news reports weren't the most effective ad campaign for the armed forces: body counts, massacres, protesters taken seriously. Not so enticing. He ended up an accountant for a tire store—hobbies include collecting Chuck Norris movies and visiting historic lighthouses—and has been waiting for a vicarious vessel into the military ever since.

"That's fourteen hundred dollars in your hands," he's now saying. "Took out a loan. Two loans."

"Jesus," I say.

My father's many things, but until three minutes ago gun connoisseur was not one of them. Just understand that much.

"What am I gonna do with this?"

He contemplates for a bit.

"You're in the *army*, boy," he finally says, voice booming an octave lower, like he's just made some kind of point, and then his mouth shapes into something strange, a smile I've never seen before: wide and gleaming and almost vulnerable. I don't feel like now's the time to say I'm relatively certain the army will supply us with weapons, should the need arise.

I'd filled out the application the night before, in the parking lot of the Patriot Center, though even now I'm not about to pretend I knew that piece of paper wobbling in my vision was an application of any sort, let alone one to the army. I'm there to catch a concert with friends, a show I'm going to save myself the indignity of naming—just know I blended right in having a smeared cannabis leaf shoddily tattooed to each forearm and a dime sack of dust tucked into my sock's padded-heel section. It's a warm night, humid, the parking lot littered with yellow-toothed kids leaning against dented bumpers, the cherries of their cigarettes fading in and out like fireflies. At the entrance of the arena I spot a chin-up bar, a molassesy black guy around fifty years old sitting next to it: chapped upper lip, scarred left eyebrow, high school basketball championship ring where a wedding band should be. The guy's clad in full-on soldier regalia, exudes raw humorlessness.

"Twenty chin-ups," he's saying, "and a free T-shirt's yours."

Says this over and over, like someone's pulling a string in his back. Everyone ignores him, these kids with lopsided struts and rage howling across their faces. Every third one cross-eyed to a degree, girls with belly piercings slithering wormlike from exposed stomach rolls. For me, I don't know. A nerve gets struck. Track down my gym teacher from seventh grade, and he'll tell you—about how I was something of a chin-up guru back in the day, a fourth-period legend, in large part because I was blessed with a salamander's height-to-weight ratio. "Just the weight of a bitch" is how Mr. Banzinni used to put it, watching me inch up past that rust-addled bar. And because here in the parking lot I'd just smoked a dust-laced blunt, and because dust-laced-blunt-smoking for some reason gets me nostalgic for the days before I knew what dust-laced-blunt-smoking was, which were the days of seventh grade, or at least the days making up the first half of seventh grade—

well, these factors knot up, and light a short fuse in my brainstem, and I tell my friends hold up a second.

Tell them I was something of a guru back in the day.

Up close and personal the guy reeks of ironed cotton and spray deodorant, the sort of disturbing inhuman smell that's pungent in a way you feel clawing at the roof of your mouth. He says I have to fill out a form before "going into battle with the chin-up bar," says it's protocol of some sort, insurance purposes, de facto policy, some string of words that chips to pieces before my mind has time to compute. I say whatever, in large part just to get him to stop making noise, worried one of my flash headaches might be coming on. The form is attached to a plastic clip-board. A crisp pad carrying a hundred of the same sheet of paper. I scribble down my name, my address, the date, fill in all the blanks.

Handing him the form, I decide to be a comedian and say, "The few, the proud—"

He cuts me off. "That's the marines," jaw tensing like for some reason he's trying to crush his own molars.

"What?"

"This is the army."

"Oh."

"An army of one," he says, and I feel stupid because now I remember the commercial.

In the end I manage only two and a half chin-ups, and the black guy looks me straight in the eye, pokes a finger in my sternum, says, "What I'm wondering now, son, is whether or not your pussy's tight?" Something my friends take to resurrecting the rest of the night with the sort of unhinged gusto that lets me know I'll now be Tight Pussy for the next few months, at minimum.

All the same, the next morning I get a call about my application to the army. A gnarled voice squeezing through the holes in the receiver congratulating me for my courage and bravery, for having what it takes, and then asking a series of questions, the gist of which are: *You in?* I'm sitting at the kitchen table, in boxers and a wifebeater, looking like Al Bundy's my personal idol. I'm eating a half-defrosted waffle with my hands, no syrup. I say sure, I'm in, having nothing better going on and feeling a rare smile pushing against the insides of my cheeks.

"What about them others?" I ask my father, still staring at the guns.

A triangle of sunlight is knifing through the kitchen window, turning dust motes into cells dividing in a microscope, and I wonder if I could go blind staring at all that polished metal, wish it were possible to an extent. I've always envied blind men. Especially those that could see for some of their life before going blind. I've heard that over time they forget what everything looks like—colors disappear, shapes lose shape—save the things they want to remember, the memories they need. Those ones are etched into their dead pupils like wood carvings.

"What about 'em?"

"That's a lot of guns."

"Beautiful machinery. Craftsmanship," he says.

"Planning a terrorist attack?"

"You're a *soldier* now," he says, ignoring what I thought was a decent joke, considering this is only summer of 2000, and there's a long silence as each of us processes his statement as actual fact. *A soldier now.* I almost want to laugh, search out the hidden cameras, and in these dense, drawn-out seconds I realize something. Or that's not quite true. First I get one of my flash headaches—a spike drilled down the center of my skull that screws with my left eye for a second, constructing a wall of scattered snowflakes where my peripheral vision should be—and *then* I realize that in my hands I'm still holding the Benelli. I cock it up to my shoulder as if I know how to use it, and pivot, so the barrel is now right up against my father's grinning face, an inch away from his waxy forehead: that study in ruptured blood vessels, creased flesh like fault lines.

"Hand*crafted*," is all he says.

* * *

This town we live in, this place: down at the base of the Chesapeake, where the bay opens up like it's trying to swallow the ocean but ended up choking it instead. Langston, a town so small people in Langston squint at you funny when you tell them you live in Langston. There's one of everything, but only one. You pick up your mail at the post office. People leave their keys in their cars, or at least they used to—now they tend to point at people like me and my friends and say things have changed, shake their heads, say they don't know what happened, reference Columbine. It's obvious my father's going something related to crazy without a woman around, but he's sworn off marriage after the catastrophe that is my mother—close your eyes and imagine a hair-sprayed medusa selling helium balloons at the mall, bracelets jangling up and down her arms like shackles put there on purpose. There she is. That's her. Four years after divorcing, they were still sleeping in the same bed, till one day my father comes home and there's the manager of a chain of leather goods stores sitting on the edge of the bed, shirt untucked and unbuttoned, using a shoehorn to get his loafer on. As my father told the story one night as I was trying to fall asleep on the couch, what happened next is the two just glance at each other, shrug a few times, and my father decides this may be a sign he's no longer welcome, that his home is no longer his home. And somehow here in Langston he's not getting the message that potbellied, half-demented, anti-marriage middle-aged men are not what middle-aged women are looking for. Those women, they're like mail-order brides: searching for someone who'll propose within a week, a body to feel for in the night that feels a lot like the last body they were feeling for. That way they can convince themselves that nothing's changed, that everything's the same, how it's supposed to be.

Can't really blame them, when you think about it.

I'm living down here because I spent my first year of high school being told from pinched mouths that my potential wasn't being ful-filled, that my attitude wasn't properly aligned, that they really wished my parents would return their calls, and the next two walking out the front door and then climbing up the side of my mother's house and crawling back into bed, which is not something even our haggard public school system gives grades for. An hour after I was kicked out of school, my mother kicks me out of the house, and I move to Langston because family's family, and my other options are what you'd call non-existent. Also, I won't deny it: I'm somewhat concerned for my father, see him as something pathetic, a decaying statue of a leader everyone deemed corrupt long ago, someone in need of some company. Even if I still grind my teeth whenever he comes within fifteen feet of me.

That's the past two years, summarized, fat trimmed, folded up origami-style. Been working at a Blockbuster for a year and a half. Just turned twenty. I used to rag on guys like me, throw eggs at their cars, moon their girlfriends.

You in?

As if there's any other response.

I get assigned to Kentucky for Basic, Fort Knox, and in the weeks leading up to my departure my father and I join a shooting range, where we make thrice-weekly appointments to go trapshooting with the Benellis. The lobby is cracked linoleum floors, deer heads jutting out of the walls, a cross between a hunting lodge and a juvenile detention center. Inhale too eagerly and you get that acrid gunpowder smell in your nose, making your eyes water. I've never been a gun person, never really part of a gun family, so far as I knew. Saw one once, a pistol, at a party when a kid pulled it on another kid and we all sprinted across that dead-grass lawn like it was hot coals, laughing as we piled into some numbskull's car. But that's it. I figure I'll loathe it. That I'm just humoring the guy, seeing how many times I can get that smile to flare up across his face. But within a week I'm body-taught to crave the Benelli's kick against the collarbone, how you go flash-deaf and your throat feels pried open, like you've been underwater and are now coming up for air, with each shot. Whereas my father tends to fire his one bullet and miss and then mutter something meaninglessly authorita-

tive like "Looks like my mechanism's off," my aim is spot on. I'm good.
I feel purposeful. I know what I'm doing before I know what I'm doing.
My headaches subside. I see the white disc and everything else goes
silent, calm, the edges just smooth out. Every needling thought, every
misaligned memory, every persistent flashback—there it is, plastered
on that white disc, turned to dust when I pull the trigger.

Like I'm the blind man, controlling what I need to forget.

Within a week I'm immune to missing—same way I am later on
during the nine weeks of Basic, the only one in my set to get a perfect
twenty hits from both the foxhole and prone position, probably
because an M16 has no kick whatsoever compared to the Benelli.
"You could press this up against your *balls*, men, fire off a whole clip
and not feel a thing," is how our sergeant put it when explaining the
M16's direct-gas system. At the range my father almost never gets a
hit, though he never complains. Instead he tells anyone within fifty
yards of us that his shooter—that's what he calls me now, Shooter—is
in the army, is a soldier, and then, as if the two are somehow linked,
he'll rattle off the names of his guns, discussing them like he's preparing for a test. It's embarrassing in a way I can feel carving out the hollows of my teeth, but the guy seems proud, so I go with it.

Something about the Benelli, my skills, I don't know: some part of
the equation bloats me reckless with a new sense of confidence, a
cockiness, which the night before I ship out to Kentucky manifests
itself in my first date ever since moving to Langston—my first date
ever since *ever* if we want to dwell on details, unless you count feeling
up nameless, passed-out, pale-skinned fifteen-year-olds while closing
your eyes and pretending their damp breasts really belong to Shannon
Kelly, your second grade obsession, though I'd rather not go there.
Chick's name's Becca. Reddish hair, a pink birthmark crawling up the
side of her neck, green eyes. We get to talking at Blockbuster, and I
won't lie: for the most part she's heinous, the type of girl my father
refers to as "the reason God invented paper bags," which is to say she
isn't heroically obese and could be decent if you shut one eye and

avoided direct eye contact with the other and drank too much, which, in the name of truth, is probably an accurate description of how she, and most everyone, thinks of me.

Anyway.

So we go to the movies. So we go to Izzy Crane's, Langston's one bar, where the buzzing neon beer signs make her severe acne invisible. She tells me she lives with her uncle, who sometimes hits her, but it didn't hurt that bad, especially compared to the last uncle she lived with, who used knuckles instead of palm. I say that sucks and tell her my mother sells helium balloons at the mall and just married a guy I've never met who works in leather goods and once made me eat a bar of soap using a fork and steak knife. She says touché and asks about my father. I say, "You ever go to, like, a park? And see some guy, potbellied, sort of demented looking? And he's kicking his dog in the ribs because his dog forgot how to sit? He's that guy, or was before our dog died. He means well, though." She laughs and when she laughs the heinousness recedes completely and I feel something fierce pulse through my bones and she tells me she thinks I might have a good heart—key word is *might*, she adds. I say thanks even though (and here I wink) she *might* be wrong. Out of nowhere she takes a maraschino cherry from behind the bar and sticks it on my tongue. I tell her I hate cherries, which is a lie, but now I'm feeling vulnerable and need to say something. Ten minutes later she lets me finger her in my Dodge Neon, emergency break pressing against my gut, making me flash on the time my ribs got cracked by a cop's nightstick because I threw a forty at his cruiser—a forty that missed—and it turns out she's Barbie-waxed, something up to now I've only experienced on the Internet. That's the point when I say let's go back to my house, and right now I'm thinking, okay, so this may not be what love feels like, or maybe it is, who cares. It's as good a send-off as they come.

Except all this is before we get to the house.

First thing that greets us on the other side of the front door is a wall of noise—grenades, gunshots, shrapnel, the wild vibrato of random shouts and screams—clearly coming from my father's hi-fi system, technology he's proud of like you can't imagine, unless you too are a subscriber to Modern Stereo, Hi-fi Today, Home Theater Monthly, and the Sonic Man. Becca and I walk through the house silently. Against the balls of our feet we can feel the uneven wood flooring vibrating the way bridges vibrate in heavy traffic. I take her hand, and again there's that bone-pulse feeling, and for a moment I think everything may work out. You never know. Maybe I'm not leaving tomorrow. Maybe there's more time. Maybe. When we head down into the living room, the sound is so loud we can't hear our footsteps and then we see him, my father, splayed out on the corduroy couch, the Benelli across his lap, the rest of the arsenal scattered on the coffee table. I feel the sour itch of a headache coming on. It's been a while. On the TV is the opening of Saving Private Ryan, Tom Hanks doing it up in Normandy—so you could call this my father's version of participatory viewing. The headaches start off as a little brain shiver, sometimes they end there, often they don't. Once I saw something on TV about panic attacks, pills you could take, but I couldn't relate to any of the dilemmas the people were stressed about—the price of tuition, job interviews, mort-gages—and figured my headaches must be something else, something personal. When my father sees Becca and me he stands up, turns, so the Benelli is now pointed right at us. I doubt this is on purpose. My father, in case it's not yet apparent, is something of a drinker.

"A soldier now," he says. "My son."

He's swaying a little, and his words collapse in on themselves. Deciphering each one is a small pop quiz.

"Forgot to mention," I tell Becca. "I'm in the army. I'm really sorry about this."

"Hear that surround sound?"

"It's okay," she says.

"He leaves tomorrow. Gone," my father says. "Dolby."

"I think I'm gonna go, though."

"Shooter," my father says as she turns around.

II.

So I tell that story—the whole deal, from my father's buying the guns to us becoming regulars at the range to his literally putting my one prospect of decent ass in the crosshairs the night before I leave for Basic, though I leave out the part about the headaches, because out here that part could get me in trouble—I tell this all to Grip one night when I'm on guard duty and he can't sleep because of the heat and comes out to smoke a cigarette. You're not supposed to smoke outside at night, but we hide the cherry in a Coke can and six months into this no one's said anything. Second I finish my story Grip cracks up, lips tight and pulled back toward his dangly earlobes, teeth like blue sparks. The kid cracks up so hard there's only sounds for half a second, then raw silence, taut sinews in his pink neck, his whole twiggy body quaking.

"Barbie-waxed!" he says when he gets his voice back. His voice sounds the way a hyena's would sound, if hyenas could talk. "I like that. That's good. With permission, I'm gonna use that."

Then, slowly, like he's learning Latin: "*Barbie-waxed.*"

Don't know what you'd call Grip and me. Not friends, exactly. More like a random collision that neither of us have complained about, excuses to talk out loud and say whatever nothings come to mind without joining the ranks of the certifiable. We met three months ago when both of us were on Shit Duty, something no platoon sergeant had prepped us for. Since our bombs destroyed the base's already-decrepit plumbing, a crew now has to dispose of our unit's fecal matter by dumping it into steel barrels, pouring in helicopter fuel, tossing in a match, stirring with a shovel till it's ash. A daily procedure. Takes hours. Odor's the sort of thing you'd remember in a coma. The whole scene is so miserably rank all you can do is look at the guy stirring across from you and laugh: all this about American technology, and going to war ends up meaning stirring human shit in the middle of the desert in a country you had no intentions of visiting when you filled in those blanks three years ago because your gym teacher used to call you a bitch. The other thing about Grip is the kid's only eighteen, and I like the idea of this little rat constantly looking up my way, gray eyes like vacuums, thinking because he's a private and I'm a specialist that I got answers tucked away in my mind like secrets that could do anyone any good.

"Benelli," he says. "That's a sweet gun, though."

"But I didn't know shit then," I say.

"Nice kick, I bet."

"You don't even know. Feel it behind the *knees*."

"You bruise up?"

"At first," I say, tapping the left side of my clavicle. "But then you find the right spot."

We're quiet for a bit, passing the Coke can back and forth, taking drags, staring out at the expansive pitch black, so dark you feel like you're swimming in an ink jar. Every now and then a camel spider skitters past our feet, a kind of hybrid between rat and caterpillar and armadillo. We have silent competitions to see who can kick them farther. I tend to win. For a while there was a rumor—later proved false—going around that camel spiders carry an anesthetic-like poison in their fangs, deadens your skin in one quick bite, so they can start nibbling away at your flesh and you've got no idea. One night I confessed to Grip that I have a reccuring nightmare where I wake up with only half an ear, even though I knew it was all bogus.

He said, "Yeah, I have that one too."

It's early November now, and every so often you'll get what passes for a cool breeze out here, but the thing is, it doesn't matter. Our bodies are too tweaked to really process anything correctly, our nerves and whatever internal gauges out of whack, dulled and supersensitive at the same time. I was on guard duty maybe a month ago, and out of nowhere started to freeze, teeth chattering, goose bumps, the whole deal, so I changed into my winter fatigues. For kicks I decided to check the temperature, figuring a cold front must've come in, knocked the mercury down to around fifty degrees. Turned out to be ninety-five. I laughed to myself and then flashed on the one homeless guy in Langston, sports a stained North Face even in mid-July. I've never seen him sweat.

"Hey," Grip says suddenly, sweeping his arm around like he's drawing a half circle on a blackboard, "you think anyone'll make a movie about *this?*"

Such a standard comment: one your hear every day out here, part distorted hope, part necessary cynicism, part something to say, but right now it hits me like it's pumped into my mind through electrodes glued to my temples. I'm reminded where I am, why I'm here, what's happening, that I'm on night duty, the only solider on. So I decide to pull up my NVGs and take a quick scan, though this must be my fiftieth night duty and the most exciting thing I've seen is a camel spider kicked thirty feet. Through the NVGs I see flat green desert, then green mountains in the distance like paper cutouts, then a graveyard of green MIGs that didn't even get off the ground before our bombs dropped. I yawn, then cock two more degrees to the left, and that's when it happens, when I see them, those two staggering green bodies, coming toward the base. Toward us.

I drop the Coke can, a soft thud against the sand.

"What the fuck?"

"What?" Grip says.

I hand him the NVGs.

"See that? Over there?"

"They coming this way?"

"Lemme get those back."

He hands me the NVGs.

"They armed?"

"How should I know?" I say, feeling a hot chemical sting wash over my face before clamping down on my neck, tight, speeding up my breathing.

"They're just *green.*"

* * *

Here's something funny: because of my aim, how precise it is, I got placed in an infantry unit even though I'm a mechanic by training, wasn't meant for combat. I never complained. Never said a word. Tell the truth, I was into the idea of seeing everything first, the earliest to know what's what, backlogging stories to tell, missiles I'd later deploy to impress chicks if the need arose. All the same, before reaching the base we didn't take hardly any resistance, just a whiff here and there, the worst of it being a guy getting shot in the calf; three weeks later he was fine. We'd driven through a small village during the day, nothing but a few dusty hut-looking things they call homes, and everyone came out with flowers, tears in their eyes, murmuring things we could-n't understand. We made sure not to flash thumbs-up because appar-ently out here that's like giving someone the finger—same with wav-ing your left hand. It was exactly what we were told would happen. Like these people got the same briefings as us, the same memos. But we ended up lost that night, going through the town four hours later, figuring we'd get treated like it was an encore performance, more flow-ers, more tears, but instead our only greeting was the pop of muzzle flashes, the sharp ding of bullets against the Humvee. We weren't expecting it. We weren't smart. That's when he took the bullet in the calf—Garcia, a guy I've never liked, tends to get with the girls you were gunning for, rubbing it in your face in the form of choppy cam-era phone videos of the girl stripping. His leg was hanging off the side, stretching out a cramp. I saw where the fire was coming from, and shot someone in the thigh, grazed another's neck—minor wounds to each, or so the medic later insisted. The firing stopped. I got a medal. It's strange: right before I pull the trigger, I flash on the range, to shooting traps, the edges smoothing out. I focus only on what matters, or doesn't matter. Calmness. Ease. Just a spinning white disc in the center of my head. Then I squeeze down.

And wait for my father to slap my back, say I did it again.

When we pulled into the base three months ago, it was a step away from completely demolished—bombs from this war, from the last war, you couldn't tell the difference. The runway was shards of concrete, fragmented and useless, looked like scattered pieces from a gigantic puzzle. Squat buildings without walls, a destroyed watchtower, cut in half like a tree. Broken glass everywhere. The scratching scurry of rats every time you took a step. Inside, we found bowls of boiled potatoes strewn on a fold-up card table, being eaten by flies. "They were eating *potatoes* when the bombs came," someone in the unit said, shrugging. "Potatoes. How weird is that?" We went to work, burning all the enemy uniforms, random papers that served no intelligence purposes, all their filthy dishes, trying to make the place as livable as possible. We unwound reams of concertina wire around the perimeter. Still no electricity, no plumbing, but eventually we got Porta Potties, workout equipment. Other units arrived. Within a few weeks random civilians started showing up, hanging around the edge of the base, always in robes, always smiling, selling everything you could imagine: DVDs, TVs, ACs, sodas, shish kebobs. Between missions we'd pile a few of us into a jeep, go shopping, typically get ripped off.

Not a bad scene, all things considered.

But a few weeks ago the marines came in and took control of the base—something about stepped-up combat, the details were vague by the time they reached the lower ranks—and first thing they did was kick these people out. Pointed guns, said get out of here. A week later we had our first mortar attack. It missed, did no substantial damage, the only one so far. But still. Every day we're now told that everyone's an enemy, everyone, everyone—but don't fire unless you're sure. It grates on you. Like say you're on night guard duty and you see two random green bodies approaching: your mind bleaches out, your stomach shudders, your tongue turns to burlap. You realize you don't have any idea what's happening, what you're supposed to do.

"Maybe they can't see the base," says Grip. He's talking faster than usual all of a sudden.

"Yeah, maybe."

"Maybe they're just walking. It's dark as shit out here. Maybe they're just walking. I don't know."

"Except they're coming this way."

"Right," says Grip. "But I don't know."

"We need to approach," I say.

"Maybe they're just walking."

I look over at Grip and see the leaden circles under his eyes twitching, like parasites digging under his skin, trying to get out, or burrow deeper, some kind of muscle spasm. His nose is freckled, more so out here, making it look bigger than any face deserves. All I know about him is that he's from Oklahoma and got caught stealing a car— *Grip* is what the cop called him because he wouldn't let go of the wheel, even after he ran out of gas—and tells good stories, most of them lies involving threesomes, low-grade crystal meth, and a Def Leppard impersonation band. Right now he's just in fatigues, no helmet, no weapon. Since I'm on duty, I'm in full battle rattle: M16, flak vest, helmet, LBE stocked with a flashlight, a canteen, extra ammo, fragmentation and smoke grenades, first aid. I weigh an extra sixty pounds, feel like the Stay-Puft Marshmallow Man. Duct taped to the inside flap of one pocket is a crumpled Blockbuster receipt, three years old and faded, its back reading *Becca 301-424-5670 XX*. Don't ask me why. Just because.

"In my LBE," I say. "I got grenades back there."

"Gren*ades?* What?"

"I don't know. Just hold it up. Point it at them. Come on."

"You sure?"

"No."

"Shit," says Grip, after taking a smoke grenade. "I don't have NVGs. Can't *see*, man."

"Just follow me."

Explosives taped to ribs, C-4 wrapped around thighs. RPGs buried in the sand. People paid fifty bucks to pull the trigger to feed their family—the stories have been reaching the base more and more. For a while we laughed, figured it was like the camel spiders: people starting rumors so they could feel they were actually at war. But then the marines came through, all business. And the other day someone said a reporter told them it was all true, swore to it, even had photos. That one was harder to write off, convert to a punch line.

"You have your book thingie?" I ask.

"What?"

We're heading toward them now, at a clipped pace, coming up on the concertina wire.

"With the language? Translations or whatever the fuck? We're about a hundred yards away."

Past the wire now.

"I left that thing in Ku*wait*."

"Damn. Me too."

I feel a sharp convulsion ricochet through my skull, and at first I worry it's a headache, something I hid from the doctors once I was signed up for infantry. Because what can I say? I was excited. I was thrilled. Didn't want to spend my time here changing tires, screwing bolts. Haven't had one yet, not even the shiver. A second passes and I realize what I'm feeling isn't a headache, thank God, but a twinge of recognition, a ripple of luck, because the one word in their language I remember is *kis*. Means stop. Staring at the book on the flight to Kuwait, that one shot off the page and stuck, made me grin and flash to back in the day, when I was still in school. How whenever I'd try to kiss girls all they'd say was stop, stop, stop.

"*Kis!*" I yell, sixty yards away now, picking up the pace and pulling up my M16, safety off, switched to semi and aimed right at their green bodies. I have fired my weapon plenty since that first hint of resistance, plenty of hits among them. But this is different. Just Grip and me. What if they're just civs? What then? They say they'll back you up no matter your decision, but everyone knows this isn't true. Guess wrong and you're on the front pages, an example, put in jail. My bones feel rubbery. My palms dipped in Vaseline. What if they're not civs? What then?

"*Kis!*"

I'm charging now, all instinct.

"*Kis!*"

I see their hands go up.

"They put their hands up!" I yell to Grip. "*Kis!*"

They drop to their knees.

"They're on their knees!"

We're close enough now that I figure it's time to remove the NVGs, that the goggles will come down and the two guys will be right there, glowing in the night, hands up and quivering, wanting nothing more than to stand up and turn around and sprint off to who cares where. It's been routine. No problems. Another day, another night. But when I remove the NVGs something happens, all I get is the pure expansive black, different now, ceaseless, thick and tormenting. It's the same tic in my left eye, except no snowflakes this time. Just black. Just nothing. I hear our footsteps, but they're louder than they were a moment ago, echoing almost. What's happening? It will pass. I hear Grip's clipped breaths, though they sound weirdly distant, muted, attached to a different moment in time. It will. I hear strange sputtering voices, quick and high-pitched, and it sounds like there's more of them suddenly, three, four, eleven. "*Kis!*" I yell again, and it's just then that I smell different bodies, that musty, cinnamon and dried-sweat odor, and I feel that I'm being touched—fingers on my knuckles, just grazing, then on my neck, my chin, my eyelashes, my palms, grabbing at my shoulders. *What's happening? What's happening?* Without thinking I jerk the butt of my gun hard and fast, up and to the left at an angle, and I hear a sharp cracking noise that I know right away is bone. Second I hear it my pupils dilate, my headache fades out, the echo dies down. My vision returns as if being poured like liquid through an opening in the center of my head. I see them now. Only two. Right in front of us. Right there. Shit. One's got blood seeping from a broken nose, sprayed across his cheek, on his torn robe, on the sand.

On the left sleeve of my fatigues.

Then Grip's voice comes back from wherever it went.

"Chill! Chill!" he's yelling. "What're you doing? I think that guy's speaking *English*!"

Another something funny: two weeks ago a sandstorm blew in, lasted twenty hours, a relentless twenty hours that trances out your mind, makes you numb and foggy. The sand's so fine it sticks to everything, coats walls, gets caked in the rims of your eyes and corners of your lips even with your cravat pulled tight around your face. You just sit them out. We played cards, Grip and me and some others, didn't even have to hide our hands because the sand kept coating the cards like paint. At one point my platoon sergeant came over, tapped my shoulder, told me the dates of my mid-tour leave. The wind was loud and livid, and I couldn't hear him, had trouble processing what he was saying. All I heard was muted sounds, like someone talking with a pillow pressed against his face.

"Wait. What?" I said.

Also sitting with us were twenty guys I don't know. Their unit had just arrived, the latest in a string of new arrivals.

"Mid. Tour. Leave," the sergeant repeated, shouting now, enunciating the words slowly, like he was teaching a special-ed class for the partially deaf. "Your ass. Is going. Home for. Thanksgiving."

"Oh!" I was yelling now, too. "Thanks! Yes, sir!"

He handed me a piece of paper, walked away.

"Two-week *tease*," one of the new guys then said. He had small blue eyes jammed into a doughy face like beads in clay. "Fucking weird, man. I just got back, right? Watched a cartoon movie about a *whale*—was alright, actually. Think my girlfriend might be pregnant again. Fuck."

They call it a two-week tease because that's exactly what mid-tour leave is. Anyone who's served six months out here gets put on a list, and when your name comes up you get to go home for two weeks, get a taste, before coming back to the base for another six months. In Vietnam they went to Thailand, slept with whores that smelled like patchouli, came back with gonorrhea they'd tell their wives and girlfriends was jungle rash. We have better technology, which means we get to see the same families we joined the army to get away from. It's supposed to boost morale—our little contact high with reality—but the cold underlying point to mid-tour leave is it means you're going to be out here longer than you were first told you'd be here, another six months minimum. Call it a sentence. An order cloaked in courtesy.

All the same, I'll say it: those dates seared into my mind, started teasing immediately. Ever since that afternoon all I do is try to picture it, home, being there. Warm water. Paved roads. Women who don't look like men. Thanksgiving. My father's letters to me are all handwritten catalogs describing the new guns he's purchased, six since I shipped out, bringing his total to fourteen, but he stopped writing regularly after my third month, which is pretty common. I get it. There's only so much you can say. For some reason my mother decided my being here was the perfect chance to get back in touch, to bond, make up for lost time. She writes me once a week, mundane dispatches describing the lives of people I've barely heard of as if I've known them forever: leather goods Phil, his four sons whom she refers to as *your brothers who miss you.* I get that too. But I never write her back. As for my father, I can't help it: I think of seeing him. I think of it and think of it and in a letter home I let him know when I'll be back, the approximate dates, flight times. The other day I got a letter from him saying he'll be at the airport, also mentioning that he's been at the range every day, and just bought another gun, an antique Colt 1851 .36 revolver. *Possibly Confederate,* he boasted, adding two sentences later that he also picked up a new chair for the basement. *Reclines in twelve different positions. I've only figured out nine. Anyway, I miss you, boy. Be safe, I've been seeing on the news that*—

I leave tomorrow morning.

This is what I'm thinking, that I leave tomorrow and here on my last night this is the practical joke I get, this is the punch line: two green bodies appearing from out of nowhere, forcing a headache. Maybe they know I'm leaving. They're going to keep me here. I can feel my heart beating in my chest and my eyes sting with sweat, but things are coming back into focus. Okay. I can feel the air rushing into my lungs. The two guys look about thirty, skinny in torn dirty robes, faces unshaven. Skin dark and burnt-looking. They look exactly like the sort of people you see in any city waiting for the bus, a little desperate but really just looking to sit down, relax, fall asleep. Except for the fact that one's bleeding from his face, looks like a poster boy for police brutality.

"What are you *doing?*" Grip's still saying. "What the hell? Why'd you *do* that?"

"What?" I say. "It's fine. What? We need to search them."

"We *did*," says Grip. He's shouting now. I don't look at him but I can feel his confused eyes all over me. "We just *did!* They're just *civs*, man. Nothing. What the hell? Why'd you bust his *nose?*"

"No, I *know* that," I explain. "Never mind."

Grip has no idea what to say to me, so he doesn't say anything.

Everything's coming back into focus. Tomorrow I leave. They don't know. Searching them I could feel the spaces between their ribs like finger grooves. Their skin was dry, like parchment, tissue paper. I was touching them but I was blind and thought they were touching me, so I hit him with the butt of the M16. Then I come back. Grip said he spoke English and he's talking now, still, his mouth moving, and it's true, it is a familiar word.

"Tackle."

His hands are still up, shaking, some combination of fear and muscle failure. The skin of his elbows is dark purple, flaky and caked in dirt. The blood continues to run out of his nose. I can't stand looking at it, and so I say to Grip, "Take this," handing him my M16.

"What?"

"Just take it."

"Tackle."

"But what about this grenade?"

"Give me the grenade."

"Why's he saying 'tackle'? He keeps saying that."

I put the grenade back in my LBE, then reach for the first aid. *Becca 301-424-5670 XX.* It's this pouch, I forgot. Ha. I find the gauze, a bandage, some Neosporin. Her thighs were smooth, between her thighs too, all of her, almost like she was a seal, something aquatic, jeans so tight I had tiny abrasions on my knuckles the next morning, from the denim's friction against the back of my hand. I take the guy's hands and slap them down like overgrown weeds, shake them casually so he knows he can relax. I look at the other one to let him know he can do the same thing. I don't know why I keep her number there, kept it through Basic, don't know what I'm thinking, don't really care. There could've been others, blurred faces, collisions with nameless flesh during weekends away from base. But I don't know. Somehow those encounters passed me by, lacked appeal. After giving him the gauze to clean up the blood, I put some Neosporin on a Q-tip and motion for him to shove it up there, into his nostrils, deep. "So it hurts," I say. Where were they walking from? What are they looking for? What happened to them? "Look, I'm sorry." Reluctantly, he obliges. She had on cheap cotton underwear, the elastic loose, spent, like hands had been there before, so many hands, but that didn't matter. Her lips were small and narrow. He hands me back the Q-tip and I motion for him just to chuck it in the sand. He's clean now. That's better. I give him a small bandage, and he places it under his nose, smoothing it out like he's fixing his moustache. At one point I kissed her neck, and for a split second, half a split second, less, right now, I can taste the perfume, feel my eyes buckle because she's wearing one spray too much. Lilac. Lavender. As if I know.

"Tackle," the guy says again.

"What?"

And now his friend talks too: "Tackle. Tackle."

"That's not English," I say to Grip.

"Jesus Christ. What's he saying?" Grip asks. He's talking quick again. "Why's he saying 'tackle'?"

"It's not English."

"Tackle."

"*Tackle?*" I ask. "Tackle what?"

"Tackle!" he screams, over and over now, and then his friend joins the chorus—"Tackle! Tackle!"—and Grip starts yelling too. "What the fuck's he *saying*, man? What are we supposed to do with this? What the hell is tackle? Tackle what?" And it only gets louder, more ruptured and convoluted, their voices merging and refracting to the point where they've become shattered noise. But this time I don't panic. Not again. I listen. And a cell buried deep in the back of my mind comes alive, splits, mutates, I don't know, and I remember being on that flight to Kuwait, studying my language book, picturing myself out here. We all thought it was hysterical that you fly commercial when going to war: Delta, American, it was one of those, rented by the army, our weapons stored below in the baggage compartment, same stewardesses as any flight. You have to put your seat back to its upright position when taking off and landing. Please watch this brief safety video. Pull the strap tight around your waist. Put the tray-table back in place. Please. Thank you. Store your carry-on under the seat in front of you. Three weeks later you're shooting someone in the neck, getting a medal for it. I left the book on the plane, I remember, yes: in the pouch behind the seat in front of me, tucked behind a catalog selling $300 nose-hair trimmers—

Tackle.

Tack.

Ackle.

Akle.

Akl.

Wait a second—

"He wants *food*," I say. "*Akl*. That's food."

"Food, yes!" the guy says, the bandaged one, his wet black eyes lighting up. He's just had an identical experience with the word *food* in his head, felt it travel from the massive, chaotic continent of random noise to the secluded island of precise meaning. For a moment it's like we're not strangers, like I'm not the guy who six minutes ago went psychically AWOL and shattered his nose. We are the same. I know you. But then that moment passes.

"Tackle."

"Food."

"Tackle," I say. "Food. Okay."

"Jesus Christ," says Grip.

III.

Ten days: that's how long it takes just to get to Kuwait. We get in one helicopter, and the moment it takes off, word comes in we may get shot down—increased mortar activity, insurgency strongholds to the south, I tune it out—so we land, wait a few hours, then get in a different helicopter so the same thing can happen. It's more nerve-wracking than missions. At Baghdad International I spend seven days in a single room, laying on a cot, surrounded by soldiers I don't know who are as antsy as I am. Everyone jokes that, knowing the army, these ten days probably count as part of the tease, that we're just getting a long weekend in the States. Eventually we hop a C-130 to Kuwait and the next morning I'm in a bright sterile airport, sitar pop music drifting out of invisible speakers, boarding a commercial airline, destination Dulles airport. The smell of the plane is so clean it's almost frightening, hurts. I overhear a stewardess with clear braces and big, hazel-flecked eyes talking to a solider, telling him, "Oh, we're so honored. You don't even know, honey. It's *hard* to get these jobs—we all put in for them. It's like a lottery."

Food. That's all he was trying to say.

Twelve hours later we're all walking down the gate at Dulles, a slow march, hearing the applause before seeing anything, like walking into the middle of a high school football game and having no idea what's going on, who's winning, who's losing, who's playing, what sport this is, what state you're in. The lighting is harsh and silvery. Under the high plaster-white ceiling people are hugging, crying, weeping, some stoic, others almost deranged with happiness. In the distance businessmen rush to make their flights, jogging for three steps, then walking for another three, then jogging again, cell phone cords dangling from their ears like a minute ago they were plugged into the wall and broke free when no one was looking. The guy I was sitting next to on the flight gets handed a jelly-faced baby, a teary chick with a pierced eyebrow next to him saying, "Look! This is your father! Daddy! Here he is!" Everything seems in slow motion. It takes me a moment to find my father, standing in the back, thumbs tucked into his pockets like fishing lures, rolling back and forth on the balls of his feet. There he is. When he sees me the skin on his cheeks tightens and his mouth becomes a thin straight line. That's him. He looks nervous, vaguely frightened, and just then something funny happens: I see myself through his eyes. My tanned skin, raw and sand-burned. Fifty pounds heavier than the last time he saw me, none of it fat. My chest is flat and wide, my shoulders broad, broader than his ever were. I almost feel guilty.

"So," he says. "Here you are."

"Here I am."

We nod for a little, both chewing our bottom lips, a habit I picked up from him. He reaches out to shake my hand.

"Whoa there. That's a good grip."

"Yeah. Been working out."

"Can tell."

"There's nothing to do over there," I say, "but lift."

"Right," he says, like he understands what I mean, and we make our way to the baggage claim. Everything in the airport sparkles. I want to eat the benches, chew on the carpet. We gave them food, MREs, two chicken and rice, a chicken patty, a jambalaya. I gave the one I hit my canteen, told him to keep it. But he'll run into people, and he'll say what happened to his face, what I did, what *we* did, and then what? What then? My bag is the second to last to come out, and once I've picked it up my father says, "Well..." and then he's quiet again. Just taps his foot, looks around, bends back his fingers but his knuckles are already cracked. What then?

"Well," he says. "I booked us time at the range."

I'm still dazed, not sure I hear him correctly.

"What?"

"Figured it's what?" He looks at his Timex, taps it with his finger. "Nine now. We could be there by noon, oneish. Get in a few hours."

There are few things I'd like to do less right now than sit in a car for three hours so I can stand on a slab on concrete and fire a weapon into the sky. But my father's face, it's contorted into this look I've never seen before: scared and well-meaning, a touch desperate, three qualities I didn't know that face was capable of pulling off. I imagine him at home, every day, killing time. I imagine him at the range, alone, making small talk. I imagine him under the sink, fixing a pipe that was working fine, just because. So I grin through my teeth, scratch my ear, and say that sounds like a fine plan. I even make a joke that he'd better be ready, that I've had some practice. Because of a jackknifed tractor trailer, there's heavy traffic and it takes longer than three hours to get to the range. Every other car has a ribbon sticker glued to its rear, some yellow, some red, white, and blue, some an awk-ward fusion of the two. Support our troops, they say. I imagine people at grocery stores, at Home Depots, seeing the stickers in line for the cash register, throwing them in with the rest of their stuff. Who man-ufactures them? Are there whole factories? How much are they mak-ing? Must be millions. Gotta be.

By the time we arrive at the range, the sun is setting and the sky is weird with purples and pinks, a few jet streams licking the clouds. It's a busy hour, and the line to shoot is five deep, everyone but me and an overweight guy in his fifties. When my father tells them where I've been, a few of them say, "Ah, so this is him," and a few of them just shake their heads. They all have questions, the same questions I'll be asked by everyone over the next two weeks. Is it hot? No, seriously, like *how* hot? Dry heat, right? Some will ask in whispers, some will look me right in the eye like they're in on it, know exactly what it's like. Everyone has a different technique, a different definition of tact. Did you fire your gun? Did you shoot anyone? Did you kill anyone? Know anyone who got killed? Wait. Seriously? How many? I'm sorry. I'm sorry. Two nights from now I will see my friends, we'll be playing Ping-Pong and drinking beers in one of their parents' garages, and one of them will miss the ball completely while asking, "Are you for real? Hold up. Just from that *chin-up bar?*"

And I'll say, "Yeah. Pretty funny, right?"

Each man walks to the line, yells "Pull!" and the voice-activated machine—a new addition—grunts and flings a trap into the sky. Most of these men haven't shot a bird, a deer, haven't shot anything living, just these white discs. The first two are good, get hits immediately. Everyone says nice work. Three days from now my mother will call, insisting on seeing me, and because I can't think of a clever way to say no, I'll say fine. She'll rejigger Thanksgiving as a welcome-home party, and she'll look exactly the same, amazingly, her hair a frozen monument to everything wrong with the mid-eighties. At one point her husband, Phil, will pull me aside and say he can get almost any stain out of almost any fabric, before going on to explain in detail the benefits of time shares. But when I tell him I've saved up $4,000 from being over there, this won't register, he'll just blink at me, excuse himself, and just then a part of me will crave getting back over there, back at the base. With each shot I feel something career up my spine, and my throat goes dry, feels like I've swallowed steel wool. I cough and spit. "Dry air on that plane," I say to my father, and he nods, then steps up to the spot because now it's his turn. He takes a while checking his gun, loading it. The sky is darkening, the shadows long and deep, and each second passes like a chisel thrust between the gaps in my vertebrae. When he finally shoots, my father misses, furrows his brow, and says, "Think the loading switch might be bent." The other men shrug and nod. There's no such thing as a loading switch. It's my turn. The Benelli feels foreign in my hands, so perfectly clean and rounded, heavier than I remember.

Handcrafted.

"*Pull!*"

Right when the machine grunts I feel it, the shiver, knowing it was coming from the time I was standing in the airport, from the moment he mentioned the range. The ground feels angled, shifting, and because of the snowflakes I can't see the trap. In my head I'm still hearing the other shots, the ones before me, one after the other after the other, every shot I've ever heard, igniting like echoes in my chest. Tackle. Food. That's it. That's all. At the last second I open my right eye and I find the trap just as it's arching down to the horizon, that white disc, looks like a comet, something planetary, orbiting, beautiful in a way, and right after I pull the trigger I feel something: a punch in the middle of my back, quick and sharp, like something is cutting into me, deep, through me, trying to pry me open, leave me exposed. Then the snowflakes again. Flaring up in both eyes now. Closing in until my vision's just a pinhole. I wait for the burn, for the metallic taste of blood to seep through my cheeks, under my tongue, against my gums, for my knees to give out. I wait for it. I wait for it. But then I realize it's just my father's hand, slapping me because he's proud.

The Translator

by Courtney Angela Brkic

WHEN MY SON WAS AN INFANT, I MEMORIZED EVERY DETAIL OF HIS BODY. I unfolded his softly curled hands and examined the fine lines of his palms. The creases were something a potter might leave in clay. His legs fit neatly into the hollows of his chest and his back curved like the spine of an aquatic animal, as if nostalgic for his pose before birth. At first, I did not know how his toenails would survive the air, how objects so small had the capacity to grow. His hair was soft, like the fuzz of a graying dandelion. It bore no resemblance to his father's coarse blackness or my dark brown color, and it occurred to me that even a newborn's hair is the product of residency in his mother's belly. As my son has grown, so has his hair toughened into this world, but I could not bear to throw those first downy cuttings away. Instead, I sealed them in an envelope and identified its contents with a black pen. I keep it in a desk drawer, where his milk-teeth are soon to join it. *Light of my eyes.* You are shedding your toddler's skin.

He still enjoys sitting on my lap when I am working. He watches the marks my pen makes with wide, solemn eyes. He is learning the alphabet and sometimes holds a pencil inexpertly in his hand to write out the characters of his name. He can also write the names of his parents. *Mommy* is a caterpillar that wanders across the piece of paper. *Daddy*, the unsteady footprints of a baby bird.

Last week he stopped and pointed to the English letters that bled from my pen. "What are you writing?" he wanted to know.

I was translating verses from a long-dead poet, and had just finished a line about warm bread in our children's hands. "I am putting our language into their language," I told him. "So that they can understand it."

He considered this. "Why don't they just learn our language?" he asked.

The suggestion was so undeniably logical that I laughed. "Our language is very difficult for them," I said and could see him considering my words. His father has the same expression on his face when he thinks very seriously about something. And his father does not understand why I spend the hours at my desk, either.

"They don't pay you for that," he tells me. "They don't care about our poetry."

"It's important to me, *habibi*," I tell him. "It makes me happy."

But he only grins, a little bitterly, and shakes his head. "You think that if they read our poetry, it will change things?"

I do not tell him, but that is precisely my hope. How could anyone read the words of those poets—the ones who lived on mountaintops but loved the world, those who spoke gently about love—and remain unmoved? It is my own response to those words, across a gap of centuries, which encourages me. So I sit at my desk until my neck aches and my eyes begin to blur, stalking words in English. Their movements have a ferocious beauty I can recognize and I occasionally stumble upon patterns so correct and beautiful, that tiny bumps appear on my arms.

Sometimes at night there is the sound of gunfire and I stuff cotton in my ears. I frequently write by candlelight—as the old masters must have done, I remind myself—because electricity is a force that seems to die on a daily basis. When I blow the candles out, I sit for a moment until my eyes become accustomed to the dark. But the strange gnawing follows me even there. *Will some young girl take a flashlight to bed,* I wonder, *and weep over these words, the way that I did with Sylvia Plath when I was fourteen?*

When I crawl into bed beside my husband, he draws the blankets over my shoulders. He presses his lips to my forehead, and tells me, tiredly, "You are dreaming, *habibti*."

* * *

I am an interpreter for Battalion One of the Liberation Forces.

In the beginning I traveled with them around the city, patrolling the Zones of Confrontation and helping communicate with civilians we met. On the first day, they gave me a Kevlar vest and showed me how to fasten the straps. It took me a long time to get used to wearing it. It was summer, and I sweat so profusely beneath the armor that I felt as though my body were shriveling like a raisin. I needed a hand up into their vehicles, mechanized monsters that looked like the bastard children of jeeps and tanks. My husband, who is a doctor, would massage my neck in the evenings so that I could even hold my head upright the next day.

We patrolled the city, the place where I was born and which I have known since childhood, but whose streets were suddenly alien. I was dismayed to realize that I was forgetting the way those streets looked before, as if my remembered city had been as steadily eroded as the real one had been bombed. Instinctively, my imagination added whitewash and repaired gardens but I was unsure whether the resulting picture was recollection or pure invention. It was like the face of a family member who has died, whose features you have sworn to commit to memory but which began to fade almost immediately.

During that first week, we passed an old woman standing by the side of the road. Black smoke poured from a shop behind her. I caught a quick glimpse of her face, through a tiny window in the vehicle's door. It was like a snapshot, a single moment of clarity in an otherwise blurred landscape. Tears had cut paths through the soot on her face and she was holding something in her hands. Before I could see the object more clearly, we had passed her. Since then, I have wondered what it was. A singed pillow? I ask myself, as I lie in bed at night. A half-burned ledger for her family's business? Sometimes I believe that I saw a tiny, charred hand with delicate white branches on its palm. It seemed to wave at us grotesquely, but had clearly been clenched in the moment of death.

"What was that?" I cried out to the sergeant, twisting around in my seat and forgetting that there were no windows in the rear of the vehicle. Somewhere behind me, down the slow unfurling of days, a woman stands on the street holding an unidentifiable bundle in her arms, weeping.

Sergeant Brandt has twin daughters at home, in Minnesota. He carries a picture of them wherever he goes, and showed it to me one day when our vehicle was crawling through the city. They are five years old and sprawl on an oddly shaped sled in the photograph.

"It's a Flying Saucer," he explained. "Plastic, so they don't hit their heads on anything sharp."

He was the first to ask about my family and, thereafter, always asked after Ali. Once, he even gave me chocolate to take home to him. Ali put it experimentally on his tongue, but then grimaced and spit it out into my hand. I ate the bar myself, though I didn't tell Brandt this, and remembered Boston, where I lived for several years as a little girl.

He had also seen the woman beside the road. I am certain of it. He didn't answer me but his voice was strange when he radioed our coordinates.

* * *

My mother takes care of Ali during the day. She has been living with us since the first days of the war, or, as she calls it the "benevolent occupation." She doesn't like that I am working for the Americans. "Is it for this you studied literature?" she asked me once, while I learned a vocabulary list in which words like "APC," "AWOL," and "Air-to-Ground" swam in front of my eyes.

It isn't that she dislikes the Americans. Quite the contrary, she has always remembered Boston fondly. She likes to reminisce about Filene's Basement and Newbury Street. Even the monstrous snow has become a thing of beauty to her.

"Do you remember, Sara?" she asks me. "How the banks would be piled so high on either side of us that we had to walk single file, and couldn't see anything but the sky above us?"

It isn't dislike but fear that makes her wary of my work. Threats have been made against "collaborators," and we do not tell our neighbors where I go every day. But we have all accepted the situation, even my husband, whose hospital wages are no longer enough to feed us. After the first few weeks, when medicines became more widely available, he became slightly less desolate. He has brought some supplies home—bandages, antibiotics, and several bags of plasma.

My mother dreads my work, but silently. She is afraid that I will be in the wrong place at the wrong time. I think she has fantasies of our moving to the countryside, where she was born, living off of fruit trees and goat milk. But we have heard that things are bad in the country, as well.

She loves her grandson, and so the two of them chatter to each other all day long. Sometimes around noon I look at my watch and know that she is cooking something on the stove, and that Ali's toys are spread on the dining room table.

"Clear that away!" she will tell him in mock severity, the way she did with me when I was his age. "There isn't enough food to share with your friends."

And he will shout to her, happily, "But, grandmother, they're hungry, too!"

And she will bring an empty pot to the table, and pretend to feed his toys with a wooden spoon. "Time for us to eat," she'll tell him when she has finished.

* * *

My husband and my mother are much happier since I have stopped accompanying the patrols. Now, I go to work each day in the "safe zone," a lengthy process and the most frightening part of my day. Although I have an identity card with my name and picture on it, I have to wait in line to cross into that enclave, which is cordoned off from the rest of the city. I keep my identity card firmly tucked in my blouse until I reach the soldiers at the gate. They have begun to recognize me but, still, we must go through the formalities. They swipe my card in a machine, look from my picture to my face and back again, and I am allowed to walk past the checkpoint. I once had a nightmare that the rest of the city fell away while I was in there. That I returned to the gate in the evening and the city was simply gone. The "safe zone" was an island surrounded on all sides by water and my family floated out there, somewhere beyond the guard shack.

Two weeks ago, a car bomb exploded near that checkpoint and several people were killed. One of them was an interpreter, just like me. We had spoken a handful of times. Her husband was also happy that her work was confined to the "safe zone." The minute I heard the news, I knew there would be reports on the radio and asked to telephone my mother to tell her I was unharmed. She had already heard the news and was beside herself. "Sara," she whispered hoarsely into the receiver but did not say anything more. We are lucky that the telephone wires were working that day. I never told my husband about the other interpreter.

* * *

My writing desk is my decontamination chamber. It is sufficient for me to pick up my translations where I last left off, and I am clean again. I dream of preparing a compilation of poems from my country, and write lists of whose work to include. It is a tricky business, as I have learned. Some of my favorite poems do not lend themselves to translation. Others about which I am ambivalent suddenly reveal themselves in unexpected ways in English. Each poem dies in its conversion from Arabic, and is reborn in slightly different form. In this way, I both murder and resuscitate.

My family has no idea about the nature of my other work. It is partly shame that prevents me from telling them that I work in a prison and interpret during interrogations, and partly concern for their own well-being.

Several nights ago I turned from my desk at home to find my husband watching me from the doorway. "When I am at the hospital," he told me, "I like to think of you sitting here."

But, of course, when he is at the hospital, I am sitting light years away.

I was told that some of the detained would be former members of government, others would be insurgents. A few might be civilians. My identity would be protected, I was assured. I am allowed to view the prisoners, first, through a one-way window, to make sure that I do not know them, to prevent any form of recognition. As of yet, I have recognized no one. And so, in the seemingly airtight rooms, I spend days repeating the interrogators' questions in Arabic, then the answers in English.

I no longer work with Brandt and his men, but with intelligence collectors. They are tougher men than Brandt's soldiers. They don't grumble to me about cancelled leaves or the heat. It is as if they do not notice these things.

At first, I thought naively that they, too, felt shame. That this was at the root of their hardness, but I have changed my mind. These men are consumed by the mission of their work. I cannot put my finger on it, but their eyes make me uneasy. Every day when we finish, I am absurdly relieved when they tell me, "You can go now." In the moments before they say these words, as they lean back in their chairs or straighten the papers in front of them, I expect them to pass judgment. I have the irrational fear that they will tell me I can't go home.

My husband thinks that I am translating documents and something in my stomach contracts painfully every time he comments on my sallow skin. "Don't they have windows in those American buildings?" he asks me. "You look like you need a day in the sunshine."

Last week we had a day off together for the first time in months.

We spent it in our tiny garden, drinking coffee, reading newspapers, and chasing Ali between potted plants.

At one point he caught my hand and held it against his cheek, the way he used to do when we were first married. There is a lot of silver in his hair, now. It appeared almost overnight, and I smoothed his hair with my hand. For the first time since this all began, I felt like crying.

* * *

The narrow windows in the interrogation rooms are too high for me to look through. They block out the light and the air in the rooms is stale. Once, a prisoner asked what the weather was like outside. "Is the sun shining, sister?" he asked. "Are the pomegranates growing on the trees?"

The man was a civilian, and quite young. He had violated a curfew, he said, by taking food to his mother. His eyes reminded me of my son's.

I translated his words. It is a requirement that I translate everything, but he looked at me reprovingly. "I'm not asking them," he told me. "I'm asking you."

* * *

A month after I left Brandt's unit, a pregnant woman in distress flagged them down. From the vehicle, they couldn't see that she had wrapped explosives around her belly, underneath her clothes. Two of the soldiers walked quickly towards her. The men who stayed with the vehicle said they knew the minute the two realized their mistake. In the split-second before the detonation, they stiffened as if a current of electricity had shot through their bodies, from their feet to their heads. Chunks of shrapnel, pavement and bone flew like horizontal rain at the others. One large piece partially severed Brandt's right arm, below the elbow. The doctors at the base had to amputate it, and Brandt went back to Minnesota and his twin daughters. Although I did not get to tell him good-bye, I often think of him. I picture how his left hand pulls the sleigh with the two shrieking girls through the snow behind him. The stump of his right arm carves the air in front of him.

* * *

Stars are flames in the bowl of night.
No, I think, and scratch it out violently.
At night, stars light up the sky like flame.
I draw horizontal black lines through this one. The ink makes the paper so moist that the tip of my pen tears it like damp tissue.
Stars, like flame, in the firmament.
I stare at the sheet of paper, then shred it with my shaking fingers. I blow out the candle.

* * *

The woman in the interrogation room is as old as my mother. She was a minor figure in the old government and I can vaguely remember seeing her on television. As she sits at the table, her face is a controlled mask. She refuses to answer any of their questions.

"What is your name?" she finally asks me.

I look at her dumbly, then translate her question.

"None of your fucking business what her name is!" the interrogator shouts in the woman's face.

"None of your business what her name is," I tell her.

She is silent for a moment, considering me. A cold feeling starts in my chest.

"You are their robot," she spits out finally. "You are their tool."

"I am your robot," I tell the chief interrogator. "I am your tool."

Yet another prisoner begs me to get word to his wife. "She must be beside herself," he says, then tells me her name. "At night they beat us," he adds, quietly. "But don't tell my wife this."

I have to be very careful. Sometimes other translators stand behind the observation windows to make sure that we are interpreting exactly. I choose my words for the interrogators very carefully. One of them slams his fist on the table. "Your wife thinks you are dead!" He does not seem to register the part about the beating.

"I will try," I tell the man quickly. Then, "Your wife thinks you are dead."

I open my eyes wide, and hold my breath. If he smiles, it is over. But his face betrays nothing.

But I cannot find her family name in any of the city's old phone-books and no one I ask has heard of her. I do not see her husband again.

* * *

There have been more suicide attacks and my husband comes home from work with tired eyes. "Almost all of them civilians," he tells me, but will not speak more about it, only tells me. "Dead civilians. Missing civilians. Civilians in their jails."

I lower my eyes.

Only our son seems unaffected. When there is water, he splashes happily while I bathe him before bedtime. But in the middle of the night he has started crawling into our bed again, and the three of us lie side by side, looking at the ceiling. There are sporadic mortar attacks at night. Shells fall randomly on houses and in gardens, with-out rhyme or reason. The first night that Ali fell asleep between us, I rose to carry him back to his own bed, but my husband's whisper stopped me.

"It's better this way," he told me. "This way, none of us would be left behind."

* * *

My memory is playing strange tricks on me. It is as if the words I knew are being supplanted by the new words I must learn. As if there is only so much room in my head for vocabulary, which is strange because I was a girl who loved words the way other children love dolls. I twirled them around my tongue in rhymes and wrote their names with pebbles in the dirt.

Brandt's men taught me American slang and I taught them basic Arabic phrases. The interrogators know an odd word in Arabic, but to a specific end. They are not unfriendly, but I can see a certain suspicion in their eyes when they regard me. There are rumors of "terrorist moles" who have infiltrated the "safe zone," and there have been any number of "troubling incidents."

"How come you don't cover your hair?" one of them asked me once while we took a break.

"I've never covered my hair," I told him with a small smile. "I spent part of my childhood in Boston." I regretted the words as soon as they were out, as if they could explain it.

But he broke into a sudden smile. "Hey, I'm from Boston."

I looked at him, smothering a smile. "Why don't you wear a Red Sox hat?" I asked.

He looked at me with a blank expression, then nodded slowly.

I think I have pinpointed what differentiates these men from Brandt's unit. On the city streets, those soldiers had depended on me as much as I depended on them. Without me, they were lost in a morass of language that made no sense to them. In these small rooms, however, I am incidental, and as much at their mercy as the prisoners.

Their commanding officer has the same quiet confidence that Brandt had, and the men listen to him without question. He even tells me about his young wife in Georgia and that she is pregnant with their first child. I tell him about my Ali, and he looks at the photograph I carry with me.

"A good-looking kid," he tells me.

But I often remember that prisoner's words: *At night they beat us.* I think about this when I sit in the interrogation rooms, when I eat my lunch in the mess hall. I look around at the very young faces, the faces of men not so much older than my son when you consider it, and the same age as many of the people they are questioning. *At night they beat us.*

The commanding officer is a good man. His young wife smiles out from the photograph he shows me, and her arms are wrapped around her enormous belly. But there is one fact that turns over and over in my mind, and I can barely concentrate in the interrogation room because of the noise it makes. *At night they beat us.* He had not even flinched at those words.

* * *

In the end, I have been reduced to my lowest common denominator and it is only my voice that they care about. I am a verbal alchemist. I turn our language into their language, and back again. Usually, they do not even look at me. They certainly would not care that I am withering in the interrogation rooms, that the sheaves of paper on my desk have gone untouched for days.

"Go work," my husband will tell me after dinner, giving me a gentle push.

But I shake my head each time. You were right, I want to tell him.

Conversely, I am often the prisoners' only focal point. There are days when I think I can't stand their eyes any more. On my way home, I decide a hundred times not to return. But we need the money. And I need to see my son's face as he sneaks a hand into my purse to find the piece of fruit I have taken for him from the mess hall every day.

I have several times dreamed that my husband is under interrogation. That he looks at me in horror.

"How could you, *habibti?*" He asks me, near tears.

But their rules are such that I am unable to respond.

Sometimes I am the one they interrogate. I am seated at the table opposite them, and my hands are folded so tightly in my lap that my fingernails draw blood from my palms. Sometimes I am holding poems, translated into English. *I will give you these pages*, I think, suddenly optimistic again. *And you will understand. You will understand!*

But when I look down I realize that my blood has disfigured the writing. It has added dots and dashes that make the script unintelligible even to me. Sometimes I realize that it is not poetry that I am holding, but my son's first attempts at penmanship, in a language they cannot understand. Mommy is a wandering caterpillar, I want to tell them. Daddy, the delicate trail left by a baby bird.

Contributors

Chris Abani is the author of the novels *GraceLand* and *Masters of the Board*. His poetry collections include *Dog Woman*, *Daphne's Lot*, and *Kalakuta Republic*. He is the recipient of numerous literary awards, including the 2001 PEN USA Freedom-to-Write Award, a 2003 Lannan Literary Fellowship, and the 2005 PEN Hemingway Book Prize.

Andrew Foster Altschul is a lecturer in Creative Writing at Stanford University. His work has appeared in *Fence*, *Swink*, *One Story*, *StoryQuarterly*, *Pleiades*, and the anthology *Best New American Voices 2006*. His first novel, *Lady Lazarus*, will be published next year by Harcourt.

David Amsden is the author of the novel *Important Things That Don't Matter*. His fiction and non-fiction have appeared in *Slate*, *Salon*, *Details*, *Nerve*, *The Wilson Quarterly*, and *New York* magazine, where he is a contributing editor. His story, "Pull!," was written as an homage to his cousin, Steven Amsden, who was in Iraq with the army for the first year of the war and who helped to make sure the author, who lives in Brooklyn and has never been in the armed forces, understood the details.

Aimee Bender is the author of *The Girl in the Flammable Skirt*, *An Invisible Sign of My Own*, and her latest collection of stories, *Willful Creatures*. Her short fiction has been published in *GQ*, *The Paris Review*, *Harper's*, *Tin House*, *McSweeney's*, and other publications. She wrote "Even Steven" for an anti-death penalty event in Los Angeles.

Ryan Boudinot lives in Seattle. His work has been nominated twice for the Pushcart Prize and has appeared in *The Future Dictionary of America*, *Black Book*, *McSweeney's*, and the 2003 and 2005 editions of *The Best American Nonrequired Reading*.

,tney **Angela Brkic** is the author of *Stillness: and Other Stories* and ,ıe *Stone Fields*. Her work has been published in *Zoetrope: All-Story*, *Harpers & Queen UK*, and the *New York Times Magazine*, and her translations have appeared in *Modern Poetry in Translation* and *The Kenyon Review*. She teaches at Kenyon College. "The Translator" is based on her own experiences as a translator in Croatia and Bosnia-Herzegovina and, more particularly, as a response to the shooting of interpreter Luma Hadi in Iraq by two US soldiers.

Ron Carlson's most recent book is his selected stories, *A Kind of Flying*. He is afraid of snakes. And elected officials.

Seattle resident **Sean Carman** is an environmental lawyer for the federal government. His work has appeared in *Created in Darkness by Troubled Americans: The Best of McSweeney's (Humor Category)*; in the magazines *Art Access*, *Bridge*, *Pindeldyboz*, *ReadyMade* and *Monkeybicycle*, among others; and on the *McSweeney's* and *Comedy Central* web sites.

Sandra Cisneros was born in Chicago in 1954. Internationally acclaimed for her poetry and fiction, she has been the recipient of numerous awards, including the Lannan Literary Award and the American Book Award, and of fellowships from the National Endowment for the Arts and the MacArthur Foundation. Cisneros is the author of the novels *The House on Mango Street* and *Caramelo*, a collection of short stories, *Woman Hollering Creek*, two books of poetry, *My Wicked Wicked Ways* and *Loose Woman*, and a children's book, *Hairs/Pelitos*. She is at work on a children's book, *The Cry Baby*, a book on writing, *Writing in My Pajamas,* and a book of short stories, *Infinito*. She lives in San Antonio, Texas.

Doug Dorst is a former Wallace Stegner Fellow at Stanford and a graduate of the Iowa Writers' Workshop. His work has appeared in *McSweeney's*, *Ploughshares*, *ZYZZYVA*, and other journals, as well as the first *Politically Inspired* and *The Future Dictionary of America*. His first novel, *Alive in Necropolis*, is forthcoming from Riverhead Books.

"'Level Orange' is adapted from a segment of *Monster in the Dark*, a play I'm developing in collaboration with foolsFURY Theater Company (San Francisco) and Shotgun Players (Berkeley). The play is an attempt to explore fears both societal and personal, as well as the narratives that accompany them. Those narratives, obviously, can be used in different ways: to explain, to delight, to unite, to shock, and – as we're reminded daily – to perpetuate those fears and to exploit them. In the current form of the play, the radio voice in 'Level Orange' recurs from time to time, sometimes sinister, sometimes malicious, sometimes patently absurd, and sometimes an uncomfortable mix of the three."

Dave Eggers is the editor of *McSweeney's* and the author of three books. He recently served as co-author of a fourth, called *Teachers Have It Easy: The Big Sacrifices and Small Salaries of America's Teachers*. It advocates higher teacher pay, everywhere and across the board.

Alicia Erian is the author of *Towelhead* and *The Brutal Language of Love*. Her work has appeared most recently in *Penthouse* and *The New York Times Magazine*.

"My inspiration for this story, as with every story I've ever written, is a rather unfortunate incident."

Avital Gad-Cykman was born and raised in Israel and now lives and writes on an island in Brazil. Her work has been published or is forthcoming in publications such as *Glimmer Train*, *McSweeney's*, *Prism International*, and *Other Voices* and online in *Salon*, *Zoetrope: All-Story Extra*, *Salt Hill Review*, *3AM*, *In Posse Review*, and elsewhere.

"I was born in Israel. At twelve, I sent packages to soldiers and painted car lights dark blue, between the sirens of the Yom Kippur War. I missed my father, who had died from cancer a year earlier. He had gone through a concentration camp, three wars, and an accident, to be finally hit by death when I loved him so much. But now I came to understand why he had died. My best friend told me that he had been chosen not to witness the Yom Kippur War and the death of other fathers, sons and friends. This is the spirit of the stories I write about wars."

Ben Greenman is the author of *Superbad, Superworse*, and the upcoming novel *Candidate*. His fiction has appeared in the *Paris Review, Zoetrope: All-Story*, and other publications. He lives in Brooklyn.

"During the whole flap over Terri Schiavo's care, I had an email exchange with one of my closest childhood friends. He's politically conservative but not in the unthinking, irritating way – or at least I don't think so. He's always happy to debate a point and to furnish supporting information and analysis. Talking to him about any political issue is refreshing, especially since there's such a sameness of opinion among the people that I know. At any rate, he was dismayed with the media coverage of the Schiavo case, and he sent me a long email explaining why. Reading it reminded me of the intractability of political opinion and of the fascinatingly personal aspect of it. Then for some reason I started thinking that it would be fun to be an international assassin. The result is this story, 'How Little We Know About Cast Polymers, and About Life.'"

Otis Haschemeyer is currently working on a novel, the first chapter of which is "The Soldier as a Boy." He is a former Stegner Fellow at Stanford University, where he now lectures, and a graduate of the MFA Writing Program at the University of Arkansas. His work has been published in numerous journals and magazines. He is very pleased to be included in this anthology.

Michelle Herman is the author of the short novel *Dog* and *The Middle of Everything: Memoirs of Motherhood* as well as the novel *Missing* and the collection of novellas *A New and Glorious Life*. Born and raised in

Brooklyn and educated at Brooklyn College and the University of Iowa Writers' Workshop, she now lives with her husband, still-life painter and born-again political cartoonist Glen Holland, and their twelve-year-old daughter, Grace Jane Herman Holland, in Columbus, Ohio. She has taught since 1988 at the Ohio State University.

"El Fin del Mundo" was born when Stephen Elliott asked her for a "politically inspired" story and she had to face the fact that she never wrote anything inspired by her fervent political feelings: she had always had the sense that her politics were white-hot, utterly unsubtle, and thus untranslatable into "art." Her writing, she had always believed, was subtle, nuanced, indirect. The only way she could imagine writing a story out of her outrage was to find a point of view that was unashamedly *un*subtle – frank, direct, passionate, unimpeded: a kind of howl. She thought immediately of her daughter's despair over both the 2000 and 2004 elections, and realized that if she could invent a child of roughly her daughter's age, she would be freed of her own delicacy and subtlety. Setting the story in a Spanish-immersion school was a kind of formal demand – the way a poet will decide to write a sestina or a villanelle – to make this as difficult as possible for her (for she herself speaks no Spanish). The trouble between the parents emerged between the lines from draft to draft – proving that no matter how a writer tries to do something "different," her same old writerly self – with her same old writerly preoccupations (her psychic fingerprint, as she is wont to call it in the classroom) – will sift its way up out of the smoke.

Adam Johnson is the author of *Emporium*, a story collection, and *Parasites Like Us*, a novel. He teaches creative writing at Stanford University and lives in San Francisco with his wife and two children.

Stefan Kiesbye is the author of the novel *Next Door Lived A Girl*. In West Berlin in the 1980s, he worked as an actor, coffeehouse reader, drag queen, and nude model. As a radio show host, he covered the '91

Gulf War. Stefan currently lives in Ann Arbor with his wife Sanaz and is working on a new novel. You can visit him at www.skiesbye.com.

Karan Mahajan is twenty-one years old, grew up in New Delhi, and is an associate editor for *Stumbling and Raging*. This is his first publication.

Laurenn McCubbin is the author and illustrator of the Xeric Award Winning *XXXLiveNudeGirls* (with Nikki Coffman) and the illustrator of *Rent Girl* (with Michelle Tea) and *Quit City* (with Warren Ellis). Her newest book, *Baby Girl Bollenger*, will come out in June 2006. www.laurennmccubbin.com

Audrey Niffenegger is a writer and visual artist who lives in Chicago, where almost everyone she knows has been quietly despondent ever since the last election and where the only words that bring any cheer are "Barack Obama."

Eric Orner is an illustrator, cartoonist, and animation artist. His work was recently featured in *Attitude 2—The New Subversive Alternative Cartoonists* (edited by Ted Rall). He lives in Los Angeles with his partner, Stephen Parks. A feature film based on Eric Orner's comic strip, "The Mostly Unfabulous Social Life of Ethan Green," (and titled the same) premiered at the 2005 TriBeCa Film Festival and will be released commercially in early 2006. www.ethangreen.com

Jeff Parker's stories recently appeared in *Hobart*, *Ploughshares*, *Tin House*, and *Life & Limb: Skateboarders Write from the Deep End*. For the past seven years he has co-directed Summer Literary Seminars in St. Petersburg, Russia, and he co-edited *Amerika: Russian Writers View the United States*. *The Drinking Game*, a short story collection in the form of instructions, will be published by Jovian Books in 2006.

Neal Pollack is the author of three books of satire, including the cult classic *The Neal Pollack Anthology Of American Literature* and the rock-n-roll novel *Never Mind The Pollacks*. He is a regular contributor to *Vanity Fair, Nerve.com,* and many other publications. Pantheon Books will publish his memoir of parenthood and bohemian dissolution, *Daddy Was A Sinner,* in fall 2006. He lives in Austin, Texas, with his family.

"I wrote this story because I've been poking around for a spiritual dimension to my life, something I always swore I'd never do. This was my attempt to explore some of the questions of Jewish identity that have been troubling me, while still not losing my preferred comic tone. Also, it's always fun to mock hipsters."

Ellen Rossiter is a published poet who has also exhibited her original photography. Her non-artistic jobs have included employment as a book binder and a short stint as a dancer. She never confused the two. She lives in New Jersey.

"The genesis of this story is as short as a chapter of Genesis. I was talking to a friend of mine, and he asked me if I had written any fiction lately. I told him that I didn't really write fiction. He looked confused, and then he reminded me that years before, I had shown him notes for a story about a woman who was secretly pleased that her soldier husband had been shipped out. I remembered almost nothing about the notes save what he told me, but I was intrigued enough that I tried to reconstruct the story from scratch. All of everything—car bombs, dead bodies in rivers, helicopters over cities—was in my mind while I was writing."

Jim Shepard is the author of six novels, most recently *Project X*, and two story collections, most recently *Love and Hydrogen*. He teaches at Williams College and in the Warren Wilson MFA program and lives in Williamstown with his wife, Karen, two sons, a tiny daughter, and some harried and unreliable dogs.

Glori Simmons was a fiction fellow in the Wallace Stegner Program at Stanford University from 2003-2005. Her book of poetry, *Graft*, was published in 2001. The story, "Peaches," was inspired by intersecting pieces of journalism: the 2004 *New York Times* investigative series "Death on the Tracks" by Walt Bogdanich and the wrenching stories of Iraq War vets returning home maimed and in extreme psychological and physical pain.

Amanda Eyre Ward is the author of the novels *Sleep Toward Heaven* and *How to Be Lost*. She is married to a geologist, but they do not live in Saudi Arabia.

John Warner is the co-author (with Kevin Guilfoile) of *My First Presidentiary: A Scrapbook by George W. Bush* and author of *Fondling Your Muse: Infallible Advice from a Published Author to the Writerly Aspirant, A Hands-On Guide to Writing Your Very Own New York Times Bestseller*. He is the editor of *McSweeney's Internet Tendency* and lives in Greenville, South Carolina.

"Tough Day for the Army" was originally started long before September 11 and was the beginning of what was supposed to be a novel exploring the misadventures of the army as it tried to find its way in a world that no longer had use for its might and talent. Boy, was that wishful thinking.

"The Open Letter to William Kristol, Richard Perle and President Bush's Other Neo-Conservative Puppetmasters" was originally much angrier, a missive of the "screw you" variety. After cooling down, I recognized that mockery was a more effective weapon.

F. S. Yu lives in San Francisco.

Associate Editors

Anthony Ha is studying urban studies at Stanford University. He is a winner of the Dell Magazine Award for Undergraduate Science Fiction and Fantasy Writing and believes in his heart of hearts that certain members of the current administration must be extraterrestrials.

Greg Larson is from Denver and is writing a thesis on Jack Kerouac. He believes that Ellen Rossiter's "Questions of War" is best paired with a snifter of cognac warmed over gentle flame. He will not seek re-election in 2008.

Ashni Devendra Mohnot graduated from Stanford in 2005 and is now pursuing a Master's at the Stanford School of Education. She is originally from Bombay, India, and is currently writing a novella about her city.

Marc Joseph

Editor

Stephen Elliott is the author of four novels, including *Happy Baby,* and the presidential campaign memoir, *Looking Forward To It.* His work has been featured in *The Best American Non-Required Reading, The Best American Erotica, Esquire, The New York Times,* and others. He lives in San Francisco, where he hosts the Progressive Reading Series. www.stephenelliott.com

Acknowledgments

This anthology came together as a result of the good will and collaboration of a large group of individuals. Special thanks go to Kate Nitze and Khristina Wenzinger, who were responsible for shepherding this book through to completion; and David Poindexter, who was willing to commit to publishing this book over a ten-dollar buy-in game of poker. Editors who got the word out about this project include Brendan Vaughn at *Esquire*, Joshua Kendall and Amber Qureshi at Picador, Coates Bateman at Nan A. Talese/Doubleday, Eli Horowitz at *McSweeney's*, Andrew Leland at *The Believer*, Andrew Snee at *The Sun*, Anika Streitfeld and Pat Walsh at MacAdam/Cage, and Tobin Levy at Nerve.com.

The most thanks must go to the associate editors: Greg Larson, Anthony Ha, Karan Mahajan, and Ashni Devendra Mohnot, without whose hard work and good taste this book could never have been created.